FLORIDA GIRLS

A Novel

The Queenpin Chronicles
Book 1

L.L. KIRCHNER

Published 2024
Printed in the United States of America

Print ISBN: 979-8-9858152-2-1
E-ISBN: 979-8-9858152-3-8

For information, address: LILA BOOKS, 30 E Huron #1404, Chicago, IL
60611

❀ Created with Vellum

"Most of us have compromised with life.
Those who fight for what they want will always thrill us."

—Vivien Leigh

Prologue

FLORIDA HAS LONG BEEN A TARGET OF PUBLIC OUTRAGE. As far back as 1922, the *New York Times* warned its readers:

```
FLORIDA PURITY LEAGUE MOVES "TO PROTECT
THE MARRIED MEN."
ST. PETERSBURG, FLA., Jan 25 — Mayor
Frank Pulver had a request today from
the St. Petersburg Purity League that he
appoint a bathing suit inspector, formal
communication from the organization
stating that "the league intends to
protect the married men from the wiles
of the sea vamp."
```

THE ENSUING "SWIMSUIT SHAKEDOWN" MADE NATIONAL news, launching an enduring interest in beach-going, specifically to St. Petersburg's beaches. It was one of the more successful publicity stunts in history, dreamt up by the city's promotional guru, John Harris Lodwick.

After a dazzling run, however, the Depression toppled the tourism industry. Still, the indefatigable Lodwick kept up his efforts, continuing to plant stories of a Floridian paradise in newspapers as far away as Chicago, Charleston, and Bloomington. By the time Roosevelt announced his New Deal, St. Petersburg was first in line for Works Progress Administration dollars.

Drawn to this promise of renewal, in 1932, Lloyd "Doc" Young moved his wife and two children to St. Petersburg to capitalize on what he perceived would be a ready market for his "Forever Young" elixir, a 29 cent potion he sold for $1.99. Young would go on to establish the Sun City Emporium, which he billed as "the world's most unusual drugstore." A three-story retail space, Sun City covered an entire city block and sold everything from chewing gum to mermaid shows to Doc's now-infamous medicinal cure. Lodwick and Doc met during these hurly-burly days, developing loss-leader programs such as selling dollar bills for 95 cents, and fresh hot breakfasts for two pennies. No scheme was too outlandish to pursue.

The onset of World War II, however, slowed the movement of goods and people. And though Lodwick and Young reconvened to discuss fresh ideas to reinvigorate development, Lodwick wouldn't live to see the rebound. In 1942, while traversing his beloved metropolis, the tireless promoter slumped forward in a streetcar, dead from a heart attack at 52.

Thus, it was up to Doc to realize the plan he and Lodwick had conceived, with a few key differences. Whereas Lodwick wanted to attract visitors by writing articles about beautiful women, Young wasn't one for writing press releases. Besides, he reckoned it would generate more ink to export the news. Doc's proposal? The Sun City Emporium Girls, a touring troupe of young women who could project a wholesome innocence while wearing two-piece bathing costumes, not to mention other assorted goods from Sun City's new line of women's wear. "We'll send the girls out on a War Bond tour in my old Crossley!"

But war rationing was still in effect, and items like gasoline and spare tires were hard to come by. Doc would have to take his plan to the town's movers and shakers.

"St. Pete's the perfect place for returning GIs to spend their entitlement dough," Doc Young enthused in his presentation to civic leaders. Mayor Williams jumped at the idea, except for the name. Showing his lack of imagination and decidedly provincial flair, the mayor felt that slapping a commercial name on the tour, even one that was a nickname for St. Petersburg itself, would discourage the financial and goodwill support they needed. Instead, they became known as the "Florida Girls." Though whenever possible, Doc insisted the store's name accompany the moniker, making for the clunky and never used addendum—*of Sun City Emporium.*

Eventually, the tour would reach as far as New York City and Los Angeles, ushering in a new era of prosperity for St. Petersburg and the Sun City Emporium alike. And so it was that Florida's postwar population explosion became part of history.

Like most stories, this is but one version. The public version. Lodwick may well have put the bathing beauties idea in the minds of the Mayor and Doc Young, but the war bond tour was the handiwork of his wife, one Mrs. Kathleen Young.

Even with the extreme changes in American life brought on by the war, no one could have guessed what she put in motion. In the end, the tour would involve US Air Force Intelligence, organized crime, and a power no one saw coming, the so-called *Girls*. Well aware that their looks were being used as a lure, they couldn't have cared less. The girls were running their own con.

This is their story.

ONE

MISS THELMA MILES

THELMA MILES SQUINTED THROUGH THE WINDOW AS THE Greyhound pulled to a stop in front of a massive store. Shading her eyes with a gloved hand, she took in the all-caps sign lining the flat roof of the three-story building—SUN CITY EMPORIUM—and spanned the entire block. Underneath, in cursive, it read World's Most Unusual Drugstore.

"All right, ladies and gents," announced the bus driver. "This is our St. Petersburg stop. We've reached Sun City right on time. Noon on the dot. This is your thirty-minute lunch break. Don't be late because we never are! We leave for Miami at twelve thirty sharp whether you're on board or not."

While the other passengers bolted off the bus, Thelma slid her delicate Bulova bracelet out from under her glove to check the time. One minute after noon.

Dammit, she thought, wiping her forefinger on her jacket's gray gabardine sleeve. *I stained these already?*

She slipped off the gloves, popped the clasp on her handbag, and dropped the pair in beside her dog-eared wallet, which held sixteen dollars and seventy-six cents, all the money she had. Plenty to see her through to Miami and a few days at a hotel, but she'd skip lunch and settle for the Mars bar in the bottom of her purse. Not that she was worried about finances, not yet. With the boys on the front lines, work was plentiful for women. But how long would that last? Ever since D-Day, the war's end felt near.

Without movement, the air inside the bus began to thicken. This wasn't one of the Greyhound's sleek new air-conditioned "Silversides" but part of its sweaty older fleet. Thelma dug back into her bag for her gloves to fan herself and reconsidered the candy. It was too hot to eat. Why not at least disembark in her new home state? Pulling her gloves back on, Thelma checked her watch. About a minute had passed, plenty of time to stretch her legs and return by 12:25 p.m.

As she stepped off the bus, Thelma lifted her hand to her brow. The midday sun was surprisingly strong. Wanting to portray herself as a modern woman—to say nothing of sparing expenses—Thelma had foregone the suit's matching hat, an old-fashioned relic of her mother's generation. In Florida, however, she might have to reconsider on sheer practicality. Even with the shade, the glare obscured Thelma's vision. A twinge in the air made her nostrils flare. Was that the sea she smelled?

"Million-dollar party! Read all about it!" she heard a newsboy sing. *Some things are the same everywhere*, she thought with a smile.

"Keep it moving," crowed a woman from behind, causing Thelma to wonder if her mother had reached out from beyond the grave. She turned to see a visibly pregnant woman from the bus. Mumbling, "Sorry," she stepped aside.

As her eyes adjusted, Thelma took in the crisscross of trolley lines overhead, a long trail of green benches lining the side-walks, and palm trees. *Palm trees! If Ma could see me now*, she thought. Vivian Miles had forever romanticized Florida. But she wasn't there to honor her mother's memory. Florida was simply as far away as she could get from her old life.

Sandwich boards lined the sidewalk: "Hosiery painting, three dollars!" "See the dancing chicken!" "*Best* lunch in town!!"

Dancing chickens? And *lunch?* Thelma hoped the two ideas were not related. Back in Keokuk, she'd spent enough time around farms to know the only way to get a chicken to dance was to electrify the floor.

She couldn't help but notice, too, the prices were excellent. A loaf of Dandy for fifteen cents? Onions at ten cents a pound? No wonder the other passengers had sprinted for the doors like they were passing out gold bars. Why not go inside? She could grab a Coca-Cola. How much damage could she do?

A distant crack of lightning sounded, and Thelma felt the air was closing in around her. Droplets of rain patterned the sidewalk. The sky remained bright, but the weather had changed in an instant.

TWO

MRS. KATHLEEN YOUNG

KATHLEEN YOUNG RACED FOR SUN CITY'S FRONT DOOR AS much as her pencil skirt allowed speed. *Damn fabric rations*, she thought, opening the door moments before the storm hit.

Though she'd gone to save her sandwich boards from being destroyed by the rain, she couldn't help but notice an extraordinary creature gawking beside the Greyhound. Despite the young woman's ill-advised wool travel suit and stupefied stare, there was an air of intelligence about her.

Clocking the newsboy, Kathleen stopped herself just under the overhang, hands to her mouth paired with a wide-eyed stare. She studied her chalked signs, about to be ruined by the rain.

"You stay right there, Mrs. Young," the newsboy said, dropping his papers inside the double doors before he set about collecting her boards.

"You are a love. Thank you, dear." She smiled, letting her hands rest on her ample chest. "Don't forget that one there. For the auditions. And would you mind? Be a love and put them back when the rain stops. Thank you, dear."

Casting a look back at the young woman, Kathleen noticed her clothes were oversized and surmised the purchase had been a misguided attempt to ensure the suit would last. Worse, she was heading farther south in it. Kathleen tsked and shook her head but covered quickly. "This war," she said, now looking in the newsboy's direction. "Kids have had to grow up so quickly."

Nodding, the girl looked toward Kathleen, who at once noticed two things. One, she appeared oddly pleased to have been addressed, as if this was somehow unusual. And two, her beauty was startling. Peering out from underneath a thick mantle of jet-black locks was a pair of amber-colored eyes, the kind you couldn't look away from. Everyone on the bus was, of course, on a journey. But a girl with those looks and that outfit on a Greyhound was running from something. That took Kathleen back to her own getaway. She must've been the same age as this girl when she ran off with Lloyd, though, surely, her clothes fit better.

Clearing her throat to recover, Kathleen tilted her head toward the door. "Why don't you come on in and grab a bite?"

A flush rose at the girl's throat. She was either embarrassed or developing a heat rash.

"Is there an automat?"

Embarrassed, Kathleen decided. She must've read about automats in a magazine. This wasn't New York City. "We'll get you back to your bus on time." Kathleen winked. "And our prices are pretty close."

Without waiting for a response, she dug into her bosom and produced a dime. *Stained those brand-new gloves, too,* she noticed.

"Give this to him, would you?" Kathleen motioned toward the newsboy, turned on her peep-toe pump, and went inside. Today was a big day, and she'd no more time for dilly-dallying over thoughts about the great unwashed. She had troubles enough.

THREE

THE TIP

Thelma looked at the dime in her hand, wondering if it was a test. Her eyes found the newsboy, stacking the store's placards. "That lady left this for you," she said, joining him under the eave and handing over his tip.

In one swift move, the newsboy pocketed the money and regathered his papers, offering one to Thelma.

"Here ya go, miss."

Had the pair of them sussed out that she was strapped? The woman, though petite and curvy, had exuded the authority of money. Thelma was going to have to improve her game; she'd spent six dollars on the handbag alone. "No, the tip was for you. I didn't do anything."

"Take it," he said, shaking the black-and-white newsprint at her. "When the sun ain't shinin', they're free."

"Oh," Thelma said, willing her eyebrows to stay low. Reading would be a good diversion for the rest of the ride. Maybe they had a good movie-star gossip column. Between her rush to make the bus and desire to leave everything behind, she'd forgotten to bring the old copies of *Scene-o-Rama* she had lying around. She wasn't about to throw money away on magazines now. "Thanks, then. Don't mind if I do."

As she accepted, Thelma felt a tingling in her palms, a sign a premonition was coming on. Glancing at the top story, she alternated her grip to shake out her hands. Thelma wasn't interested in these unpredictable portents, only wishing they'd go away.

**MILLION DOLLAR DEFENSE BOND PARTY —
AUDITIONS TODAY**
Local store promises one million in
dough for our doughboys!

ST. PETERSBURG, FLA., OCT. 20, 1944—Sun
City Emporium is hosting auditions today
to fill the talent roster for their
upcoming Million-Dollar Party on Sat.,
Dec. 9. Owner Lloyd "Doc" Young vows,
"We'll raise a million dollars to bring
our boys back home if I have to pay from
my own pocket!"

Gasping, she looked up at the kid. "This Young fella... Is he crazy, or what?"

"You tell me, miss. You think that lady'd marry a crazy man?" He winked.

Was the child flirting?

"Doc Young ain't crazy. He's rich!"

With a smirk, Thelma tucked the paper under her arm. As her mother would say, crazy and rich weren't mutually exclusive.

"You oughta try out, miss," he said.

The newsboy pointed at one of the signs: Sun City Girl talent auditions today! 3 p.m. sharp!!!

Thelma shook her head and strode toward the door; she was neither a singer nor a dancer. Nor did she play any instruments. "Thanks, kid," she called over her shoulder, "but I'll be long gone."

Inside, the Emporium delivered on its promise of "unusual." The left half of the bottom floor was a grocery, while the right side was divided into distinct sections, each selling its own specific merchandise. There was a row of barber's chairs, a shoeshine stop, and a large cigar display. Thelma wondered where the actual pharmacy was. As she began to make sense of what all she saw, she noticed a lunch counter at the center of the floor, flanking a set of mechanized stairs. The location meant it could be seen—and smelled—from every department. Suddenly, Thelma was very hungry. Maybe she'd skip supper.

As she headed toward the counter, Thelma felt a tug at her skirt and looked down to find a towheaded girl of maybe seven or eight years old, wearing polished Mary Janes, bright white ankle socks, and a perfectly pressed pink dress. Poor little rich girl, thought Thelma with a grimace, noticing the girl's resemblance to Shirley Temple. The child burst into tears.

"Hey, kid, I don't mean to have that effect on people," Thelma deadpanned, bringing forth more tears. *Ah. The girl must be lost.* Though she'd had an immediate reaction to the child's appearance, Thelma couldn't help but relate to her plight. Her heart softened. "Oh, I'm sorry."

Stretching to her full five-foot-nine-inch height, Thelma could scan in every direction, but she saw no one who appeared to be searching for a child. Dropping to her knees, she tried again. "Are you lost?"

The girl nodded.

"What's your name?"

Instead of speaking, the girl clamped her mouth shut. Her eyes bulged, and fat tears reappeared.

"Oh, there, pumpkin." Thelma patted her head awkwardly. She'd never spent any time around children, but she could recognize a lost girl. "It's all right. We'll find your mother. She must be worried sick." *There's nothing worse for a mother than to lose a child*, she could hear Vivian Miles saying, even if, in her case, it was a threat that translated to *You can't leave me*.

Once the girl had calmed somewhat, Thelma asked, "Do you remember where you last saw her?"

The girl looked miserably toward the grocery store then at the dining area then back at Thelma. She was clearly afraid. Where could her mother be?

As if sensing her distress, the girl began to cry again.

Thelma wondered if she might be a mute, like that Helen Keller. "Hush now, sweetie pie. She can't have gone far," Thelma reassured the child as much as herself. "We'll find your mommy. Take my hand."

The girl's crying subsided once they linked hands, even though, once they stood, Thelma's certainty faded. The grocery area was bustling, with patrons roaming amongst boxes of detergents and baskets of onions piled high. At the foot of the escalator, she noticed a sign with an arrow pointing up: Beauty Parlor, 3rd Floor. She wondered what was on floor two. The girl's mother could be anywhere. Thelma looked at her watch; it was edging past a quarter after.

"Pardon me," Thelma began saying to anyone in earshot, just to get them to look in her direction. Even if the child's mother wasn't yet searching for her daughter, she'd react upon seeing the girl. But Thelma stopped short of calling attention to a lost girl. In the line of work—*previous* line of work, she reminded herself—she knew what happened to young girls left to fend for themselves. *What if her mother* wasn't *looking for her.* But she mustn't consider that.

She wandered farther, and the maze only deepened. The store covered an entire city block and had been built specifically to create opportunities to lose oneself.

"Were you here with your mother?"

The girl shrugged her shoulders. She still hadn't spoken.

Thelma looked at her watch—12:22. She couldn't abandon the girl and didn't trust leaving her with anyone besides her mother. Her hopes sank, but then she lit upon an idea—Mrs. Young! She could be trusted, she was sure. But where to find her?

The first store clerk she saw was ringing up a customer. Still loath to alert any more people than strictly necessary—especially since the child wasn't speaking for herself—Thelma moved into the adjoining space, a liquor store. That was when she saw her, a woman in a matching pink polka-dot dress with polished Mary Jane pumps, standing at a merchandise table, looking as if she hadn't a care in the world. The man behind the display refilled her wine glass while she dragged on a cigarette and leaned on a stool. So deeply engrossed was she in drinking, the woman hadn't noticed her child was missing. The girl didn't make a move toward her mother, either, and Thelma recognized in her the fear that somehow, she was about to get in trouble.

The woman still hadn't bothered to look their way. She just needed to get this over with and hotfoot it out the door.

"Ma'am," Thelma interrupted. Still nothing.

Had she forgotten she'd brought her offspring to the store? She'd seen this in her own mother, coming to in the middle of a sentence, oblivious to whatever had just happened.

When Thelma made it at last, the woman glanced in their direction, and her puffed cheeks fell as she pursed her lips. This was a look Thelma had seen before, one her mother had taught her to respond to with deference. "Those golden eyes and jet-black hair will make a certain kind of woman hate you," she could hear her mother saying.

When will that *voice die?* Thelma wondered.

"Ma'am?" she said, more sharply than even she intended. So what if the pair of them were far better off than Thelma and her mother ever had been? That little girl was in for a lifetime of torment. "I believe this is your child." So much for subservience.

"Hello, my darling!" the woman crowed, now ignoring Thelma completely to reach for her daughter. Instead of offering an embrace, however, she rubbed a spot of dirt off the girl's face. The girl didn't try to hug her either.

Of course she had her bus to make, but hadn't she always wished someone had talked some sense into her mother? Wouldn't a proper lady address this obvious transgression?

"Look, lady," Thelma began.

As the woman straightened and looked squarely at Thelma, the salesman began hastily gathering his goods.

"That's Mrs. Harper to the likes of you."

"The likes of me? Oh, that's rich. Mrs. Harper. You are clearly a drunk, and you have no business raising a child. But since you are—"

"Mr. Drucker?" The woman interrupted, looking around the store.

Thelma snapped her fingers in Mrs. Harper's face. "Since you are, you should know that you cannot leave young girls unattended. Bad things happen. Suppose someone else found her?"

Now, Mrs. Harper gave Thelma a more thorough appraisal, crossing her arms as she scanned her up and down. Thelma was glad she'd shelled out for the worsted gray travel suit.

"Listen, missy. Everybody knows me," Mrs. Harper said, suddenly sounding more sober than Thelma had imagined she could be. "And my family." Pulling her daughter close, she forced the girl into the folds of her skirt. "You're the only one that's lost here."

The woman's icy stare made Thelma wonder if she'd misread the situation.

Had she let her own problems cloud her judgment? She was trying to shake off her past, to be seen as something she'd never been, a decent young woman. But she wasn't fooling anybody.

Then Mrs. Harper spoke a language Thelma was sure she understood, waving at her just so her diamond ring flashed in one of the store's spotlights.

"You won't get any money from me."

This, Thelma wouldn't stand for. At least she knew exactly how to respond.

With dead eyes and a broad smile, Thelma slowed her words. "Listen, sweetheart, I'm not for sale to you or anyone else. But it takes a special kind of fathead to lose track of your daughter and then insult her rescuer. Why, do you know? There's a Greyhound stops right out in front of this place. It's bringing change." Thelma looked Mrs. Harper up and down for drama now. "You, ma'am, aren't ready."

Before the woman could speak, Thelma turned heel and hoofed it toward the exit, her only goal to get on that Greyhound. Long before putting her mother in the ground four days ago, she'd been dreaming of Miami's high-rises and sunny anonymity. At the door, she looked at her watch—12:33?

Watching the back of the bus pulling away, Thelma forgot all about Mrs. Harper.

FOUR

SUN CITY EMPORIUM

Ah, ya shoulda heard me last night
singing outside the Metropolitan.

Kathleen reached over her sandwich and across her slim writing bureau to the corner of her husband's massive oak desk —which he'd shipped in at great expense from Portugal during the store's expansion two years back—where the Motorola portable sat. She turned up the volume.

Why didn't you sing on the inside?
That's where I started.

No matter that she'd heard this routine a dozen times; Abbott and Costello always made her laugh. The sandwich, however, she wasn't sure about. She poked at the egg salad the cafeteria was testing out, using a new spread from Kraft—their Miracle Whip combined with relish and paprika. From the looks of it, Kathleen would've considered *unappetizing* to be a generous description. She took a bite. *Delicious, but an orange and green spread'll never sell.*

Before she could swallow, the office's private line rang. Slurping some coffee to clear her throat, she leaned over Lloyd's desk to snap off the wireless and grab the telephone's receiver.

"This is Mrs. Young. How may I—"

Mr. Drucker in Fine Liquors didn't wait for her to finish before launching into the unfolding kerfuffle. Despite the audition, they'd gone ahead with the Friday wine tasting. Mrs. Harper would've pitched a fit if they'd canceled. Her tantrum came anyway.

"I'll be right down." Kathleen grabbed a sandwich half and headed for the stairwell. She should've known better than to try to sit and eat.

Dismissing Drucker with a nod, Kathleen set on her target. *When there's trouble afoot,* she heard her mother's urging, *launch a charm offensive.*

"Good afternoon, Gertrude. How lovely you and your daughter look. I—"

"Kathleen, were you aware there is a *bus stop* in front of your establishment?"

The question gave Kathleen the perfect entrée. "Oh, how rude of me! We've been so busy with the war bond party we haven't thanked you properly for hosting that lovely fundraiser that made it possible. It wouldn't be there without your support."

After grabbing a bottle of Dom Perignon from behind the case, Kathleen threw one arm around Gertrude and held her offering out with the other. "It's a meager substitute, but please accept this as my apology. I'll check the calendar and be in touch about having you and Henry to Sunday supper. We're really getting people thinking about St. Petersburg as a post-war destination, all thanks to the Harpers."

Gertrude blinked even as she hungrily accepted the bottle. "That was a marvelous party." She nodded, causing her hat to drift toward her left ear. "But... all these changes... Are they for the better?"

She had to calm this woman. They'd secured support for the tour from the city and state, but Mrs. Harper's support was key to meeting the Million-Dollar Party goal. Why had Lloyd made such a fuss about calling it a Million-Dollar Party?

Kathleen looked into Mrs. Harper's eyes, which showed a genuine fear. "Gertrude, of *course* they are." She pried the woman's hand away and gave it a squeeze. "Why, they'll make this city a better place for little Bessie here."

Smiling, she tousled the girl's blond curls as a way of acknowledging the child and further extricating herself. "And you're the social glue."

Mrs. Harper was nodding now, her shoulders softening.

This was the moment to strike. "Which reminds me. I've put down the Ladies' Club for three tables at the Million-Dollar Party. *C'est bon ça, non?*" The fact she'd come from Richmond enabled Kathleen to get away with linguistic murder. She loved dropping French phrases, knowing most would sooner agree than ask what she meant. And when a conversation didn't suit her, she often pretended not to understand direct questions as if she were indeed French. They could refuse to accept her, and she could pretend to be unaware.

Squeezing Mrs. Harper's hand, Kathleen looked at her gold Longines. "Look at the time! The Sun City Girl auditions are about to start, and I really must run. *Au revoir!* Enjoy the champagne!"

* * *

THELMA CRUMPLED THE TIMETABLE. IT WAS FRIDAY. There was not another service to Miami until Tuesday the following week. Weekend travel was reserved for servicemen. *Goddamn war*, she thought.

"Your burger," the waitress said, placing the plate before her. "With relish."

"Thanks," Thelma said, looking up and realizing she'd been so lost in thought she'd not noticed her server earlier. Her platinum bangs just grazed her moon-shaped eyebrows, which would've given most a perpetual look of surprise. But there was a hint of sadness touching this woman's deep brown eyes. She looked to be in her mid-twenties—young enough and without a ring. *Could be a good source of information.* "Say, you wouldn't happen to know if there's a women's hotel nearby, would you?"

"You looking for a place to stay?" She pursed her lips. "You okay?"

The question nearly undid Thelma, but now was not the time to break down. "Oh, yes. It's simply... I've missed my bus to Miami. With the travel restrictions, I can't get back on until next Tuesday. Obviously, I need a place to stay in the meantime. A reasonable place."

"You got family out that way?"

Again, the frankness stopped Thelma. She'd no family anywhere, and now she wasn't sure she had enough money to make it to her final destination. How could she have been so stupid?

"Never mind," the waitress said. "I'm sorry. My dad always said I ask way too many questions. He's dead now."

"Oh, I'm sorry to hear that," Thelma began, torn by her twin desires to hide and to commiserate. "My ma just died. She was all the family I had. Always talked about living on a beach..." But then she shook herself, ever so slightly, to snap out of this reminiscing. She'd never leave her past behind talking about it like this. "I won't make it there if I'm not careful."

"We have beaches here." The waitress tilted her head back and guffawed. "That look on your face! For the life of me, though, I don't get why anyone would choose Miami over St. Pete when everything you need's here." She paused before holding out a chapped red hand. "Name's Peggy. Well, Margaret, actually, Margaret Holmes. But everyone calls me Peggy. I just don't like the name Margaret."

"Thelma Miles," she said, reaching for Peggy's outstretched palm.

"Well, Thelma, if you really want to start over, you should come to the Sun City Girl tryouts today. You're sure pretty enough." Peggy pointed at the paper Thelma had folded on the counter. "If we win, we get to be in a movie."

"Win? I thought it was for some party."

"You have to read the whole thing, chickadee. See?" She tapped the paper. "The party kicks off a tour that ends in a beauty contest out in Hollywood. Winning team gets to be in a movie."

Thelma looked up and saw that Peggy was now grinning madly, revealing a fetching gap in her front teeth.

"Anyways, if you can wait ten more minutes, I'm off the clock. I'll point you in the right direction. The Soreno will be perfect for you. Cheap and cheerful."

By the time Peggy returned, Thelma had made up her mind to try out. She'd resolved before leaving Iowa she'd never be so broke she'd turn to men for money. If she made this team, she reckoned, she'd never need to ask for help.

* * *

"Pepper?"

23

Kathleen heard from the hallway. If Lloyd was using her pet name, he must need a favor. No matter what Lloyd brought his wife, he knew she'd fix it, the real "doc" of the two. And she always did. She'd been in love with Lloyd since she was seventeen. "Yes, dear?"

"The reporter's down at the cashier's desk. Imogene something, a *lady* scribe!" he said, wiggling his eyebrows.

Smiling, Kathleen sat back and regarded her husband. She noticed he was sweating and paler than normal.

"What's wrong?" He grinned. "I thought you'd like that."

Though Lloyd's hair had gone silver, it was still thick under his straw bowler. Ill or not, he was dashing. They stood eye to eye in stockinged feet and in outlook. This mutual understanding was what had compelled her to leave a comfortable life for a man decidedly outside her social strata, a man nearly twice her age. Even now, some nineteen years later, though her mother hadn't spoken to her or met her grandchildren, Kathleen had never regretted choosing Lloyd. He'd always recognized exactly who she was.

Before Kathleen could respond, the phone rang. Lloyd picked up the receiver then turned to his wife. "Matteo Giancarlo's here."

"We need to occupy that reporter so he can slip in unnoticed," Kathleen said.

Lloyd lifted and lowered his hat like a vaudevillian, modulating his voice. "I'll give her the grand tour, take her around—"

"No way, mister," Kathleen interrupted. "Not with how you look already."

Lloyd stiffened. He hated being reminded of his illness. "Pepper, I'm *fine*." He tapped his jacket. "I've got my Forever Young right here."

They wouldn't have their store if it weren't for the tonic—a twenty-nine-cent cure-all he sold for one ninety-nine, generating income even on a half-off sale—but they both knew how much good the potion did. Between the humidity and the day's stresses, she feared Lloyd would be coughing up blood in the middle of his speech.

"Button," she began, using his nickname to set the tone, "you do give the best tours. But why don't we let Bertie handle this one? We both know he needs to take on more responsibility." She saw him considering her words. Time to move in.

Rising from her seat, she pressed her body suggestively against his. "We have too much to lose to let some fresh-faced reporter louse up the works now." Whispering in his ear, she reached for his cock—flaccid as usual. "If I can sacrifice this..."

She hated playing this trump card, but there wasn't time for a discussion. For all the puffery around his medical background, female anatomy was one area where Lloyd "Doc" Young had real knowledge. He'd taught Kathleen pleasures she'd never dreamt possible. But all that was in the past. The Pifco Electric Vibrator he'd given her on her last birthday was meant to be used alone, their sex life another casualty of his emphysema. The least he could do for her was rest.

"We're only doing this tour so we can leave the store to Bertie and Archie. Our sights need to be on Carlsbad, with its temperate climate and healing springs. We're saving your life."

At Lloyd's nod, Kathleen moved back and gave her husband a peck on the cheek. "I'll go get Matteo. You, sit. Call security and get Bertie to that front desk."

He grabbed her elbow.

"You think Salvatore sending his kid is a bad sign?"

"How could that be?" Kathleen lied. "The boy is his only son, and he shouldn't feel slighted that *I'm* meeting him instead of you."

Kathleen didn't like deceiving her husband, but when it came to Lloyd, she was fiercely protective. But she'd wondered the same thing. Since expanding Sun City two years back, they'd desperately been trying to dig out of debt, rid the store of the Giancarlos's little numbers game, Bolita, and leave their sons a clean, profitable business. Meanwhile, the Florida air was making Lloyd's emphysema worse by the day. Even if Sal had sensed their escape plans, he couldn't stop the tour now. Too many politicians were involved.

"All Sal Giancarlo has done was make the fuel and tire rations possible."

A grin played at Lloyd's lips. "Is that all?"

"Oh, behave," Kathleen gave him a playful push. "Why don't you finish my sandwich?"

Lloyd looked at the orange-tinged sandwich triangle. "I thought you were trying to *save* my life."

Kathleen narrowed her eyes. "You of all people should know appearances can be deceiving."

FIVE

MATTEO GIANCARLO

MATTEO GIANCARLO ROLLED UP TO SUN CITY IN HIS Hudson Commodore just as his favorite song was ending. "My sweet embraceable you," he sang along with Bing Cosby as he checked his reflection in the rearview. Noticing the black curl he liked to dangle down the center of his forehead had drooped, he revved the engine and, with the deftness of long experience, twisted the lock between his fingers. Satisfied with the result, he cut the motor. Where was Doc?

According to his Vacheron, it was 2:45 p.m. *No sign of the old man.* Pleased as he was someone else was running late, he was annoyed there was no one there to greet him. He sure as hell didn't want to run into any ink slingers. This competition would've been a swell diversion if it weren't for the damn press they'd invited.

On the plus side, maybe he'd spot some girls heading to the audition. They had to be desperate. No nice girl would do this, he was sure. He'd never let his daughter anywhere near the stage—soon as he had one. Still and all, he'd take one of the girls for himself. The usual crowd over in Tampa bored him lately.

Donning his hat, Matteo got out of his car, lit a cigarette, and leaned against the fender. He hated waiting, but as much as he loved his car, after the competition, he didn't want to drive back to Tampa just to turn around and come back later for the Bolita drop. But what would he do in the meantime?

Down the street, he spotted the theater marquee; a double feature would do the job. He shaded his eyes to read the sign and felt the sun warm his forearms. *Heaven Can Wait*—an idea he agreed with, even if he didn't have a clue what the movie was about. But why were they showing it with *Laura*, which had the world's dumbest plot? He'd been around enough corpses to know ya didn't fall for 'em.

That was when he spotted the sandwich board in front of Sun City's doors. Auditions Closed, he read. "Those fuckers," he hissed. "They don't call us?"

He was turning to get back in his car when he heard a young woman behind him.

"There you are!"

Looking over his shoulder, Matteo saw only Archie, the youngest of the Youngs.

"Right this way, sir."

"What happened with the auditions?"

The kid smiled, pushing his glasses up his nose. "That's where I'm taking you. This isn't the door."

"Huh?"

Archie's eyes widened, but he kept his dopey grin plastered and waved Matteo forward. "C'mon this way."

Matteo dropped his cigarette on the ground and followed Archie to a side entrance, irked he'd waited at the wrong place. "Who sends a bunch of gorgeous women to the side door?"

Archie shrugged.

Soon enough, they reached the loading dock where Matteo collected the nightly earnings. Mrs. Young was waiting there.

"Matteo, what a delight to see you," she said.

This was more like it. "Ma'am," Matteo said, appreciating how—despite two kids and the mannish jacket that was supposed to be the fashion—the lady had kept her curves. For an older broad, she was gorgeous.

"We're thrilled you could join us," Mrs. Young said with an inviting smile. Matteo wondered if she might be hot for him. Wouldn't be the first lady with an older husband who'd made advances. Ol' Doc Young had to be at least twenty years her senior. "We have a special viewing room just for you."

He followed her down the hall opposite his usual path. He was so busy thinking about the lines painted up her legs he didn't notice they'd walked into an office where a dented metal desk inside faced the wall.

"Security," he said, reading aloud the word painted in the gilt letters on the door's textured glass panel. "Am I in trouble?"

"Oh, Matteo." Mrs. Young smiled and squeezed his arm. "You're so funny."

She was definitely hot for him.

"These," she said, gesturing toward two neatly wrapped boxes that shared the desk blotter with a phone, an address book, and a newspaper, "are for your father: a silk tie from our new collection and a silver cigar cutter, in appreciation for what he did for Bertie."

Matteo didn't have a clue what she was talking about, but people were always giving his father gifts. He might keep the guillotine for himself.

"And this," she said, pointing at a thermos and mug, "is for you. Hot cocoa."

Hot cocoa? What did she think he was, a child? Maybe she wasn't flirting. Putting on his most charming grin, a lopsided affair that worked plenty well enough, he asked, "Ya got anything to spike that with?" He slid a heavy glass ashtray at the far end of the desk to within arm's reach. "And where's the real attraction? Where's the girls?"

Patting Matteo on the arm, Mrs. Young produced a flask from her hip pocket and dropped a generous pour into his mug. "Just in case the newspaper isn't enough, this oughta keep you company while you wait for the show to start."

She pointed at the wall in front of the desk. "This wall faces the stockroom so security can keep watch when we receive shipments," Kathleen said, looking more pleased than seemed reasonable. "It's actually a two-way mirror. See-through. Except there's a curtain over it now, of course."

"Hate to rain on your parade, Mrs. Young. But what good's a see-through window if the side you wanna see is covered up?" People were always misunderestimating him, but he was no dummy.

Mrs. Young blinked.

"Smart man," she said, smiling.

Matteo puffed his chest.

"I've only just installed the curtain. Once the girls are presentable, I'll pull it back so you can watch the proceedings. Now I must run, but please make yourself at home. Mr. Young and I may be in and out, but no one else should stop by."

Without waiting for a reply, Mrs. Young turned on her shapely leg and marched out the door. Leaving the thermos untouched, Matteo gulped down the whiskey she'd poured and looked around the room—nothing but a wall of filing cabinets. He might've snooped inside, but they were locked. Besides, he wasn't much for reading and was even less the sort to keep himself occupied. Presently, he began burning sections of the newspaper in the waste bin, imagining what it would look like to see this whole store go up in flames.

* * *

WHEN THE HEAD OF SECURITY CALLED KATHLEEN TO report the fire, she chided herself for leaving the kid with a newspaper—and in a closed room, no less.

"Ya hadn't oughta leave a boy like that alone," their security man had said. "He kept the mess to the bin, but that kind of stink? That's the kind don't come out."

Later still, long after the ashen smell dissipated, she'd wonder what Hank had known about the Giancarlos and why he hadn't told her. Or had he been lulled by Matteo's rugged good looks too?

SIX

IMOGENE FUCHS

THEY'D NOT YET CLIMBED THE FIRST SET OF ROLLING stairs before Albert Young began flirting. "How does a pretty girl like you end up with ink-stained fingers?"

"Why, a lot of us went off to work when our husbands went to war, Mr. Young."

"Albert," he said. "Mr. Young's my dad."

But she wanted him to address her as Mrs. Fuchs. "How many floors are there, Albert?" She didn't need a tour but felt it was impolitic to refuse. She'd shown up at the appointed time, but the auditions hadn't started.

"He still away?"

Imogene looked at Albert, not comprehending. Where was the boy's jacket?

"Your husband."

This boy. She was a representative of the *St. Petersburg Times*, for heaven's sake!

"He's home," said Imogene, staring straight ahead as the stairs climbed. "With a Purple Heart."

"What do you do for fun?"

At last, they were spat out on five—toys.

33

"Oh, look at this!" Feigning delight, Imogene Fuchs reached for the first thing she saw, a cardboard box that read Slinky. "My daughter has been asking for one of these. I'll come back when it's her birthday." If there was a benefit to motherhood, it was this—invoking her child was an efficient way to tell a fresh punk to back off. Not that she'd any intention of purchasing such a gadget for her daughter. She'd already gotten her Sally a Raggedy Ann doll, much more practical. The last thing she needed was a spoiled child on her hands.

"Wouldya look at that? Getting late," Bertie said, checking his watch in afterthought. "C'mere. We'll take the back stairs. We'll come out at the audition. Plus, it's like another special tour. Nobody except the people who work here get to see it."

"How... delightful," she said, certain he failed to notice her faint praise. Not that she minded the stairwell—of course she'd worn sensible shoes—but the boy didn't even ask.

"There you are, Bertie! Good job," a woman said.

Fuchs wondered if the two were related. This tiny person barely reached the reporter's shoulder. Not that Albert was a giant. He and Fuchs were about the same height, and no one had ever accused her of being tall. Compared to Bertie's black hair, large nose, and full lips, the lady had fine features, with dark-blond hair falling in perfect waves to her shoulders. The boy looked ready to roughhouse in the alley whereas she was coiffed to perfection. Even the lines painted on the back of her legs were dead straight. And their demeanor could not have been more different—the woman was commanding.

"I'll take it from here, son. You go and bring your pop from the office."

Mother, thought Imogene, hoping neither caught her eyes widen.

"Mrs. Kathleen Young, delighted to meet you," the woman said, reaching her hand toward Imogene in introduction. She drew Fuchs close. "Working girl to working girl, I'll make sure you're out in time to file your story and still be home to put on supper."

Gratitude fluttered in Imogene's chest. No one ever considered her needs as a wife and mother, not even since she'd broken out of Classifieds and onto the City Desk. Having her husband home 'round the clock didn't change that it was still up to her to get dinner on the table.

"I'll pull you a meat loaf and all the fixings from our diner."

A thud of disappointment hit Fuchs, and she scolded herself. She was there to report, not fawn, no matter what her editor said. "Just stick to the grip and grin, Fuchsy," Briggs had advised as she headed out the door. "This ain't no Pulitzer. It's a puff piece." But she had her own goals.

"Thanks, Mrs. Young. I can't accept a free meat loaf, but I'll happily buy one."

"Who said anything about free?" said Mrs. Young without missing a beat.

Had Imogene misread the situation?

"Have a look," said Mrs. Young, moving toward the stockroom's porthole window. "Know any of the girls?"

Fuchs peered through the glass at a study in Revlon red and victory rolls. Folding chairs were sandwiched between cases of detergent and stacks of dry goods, it was standing room only and three deep all around. A stage was fashioned from a large wooden pallet and topped with a piano.

"Is that Doris Juergen?" asked Imogene, surprising herself.

"It is! Do you two know each other?"

Imogene didn't care for it when interviewees asked her questions. "I wouldn't say that. I covered their house for the June Garden Spectacular issue."

"Yes! I remember that. Aren't the grounds at their Gulfport estate lovely? Who else?"

Imogene wanted to turn these tables. "What can you tell me about them?"

"That girl," Mrs. Young tapped the window. "In the peach dress with the keyhole neck? She's Mayor Williams's daughter, Millicent. Quite the musician."

"Really?" Imogene was surprised. Weren't most society girls this age preening for husbands instead of jobs? Had the war changed the status quo that much?

"*Mais, bien sûr!* And oh, see her? Strawberry blonde with her nose in a book?"

Imogene squinted.

"She's the girl next to the Viceroys display. Helen Fuller. Her father's head of city council. Divine singer."

Mayor? City council? Bring in the police chief, and we're set, eh? Imogene changed tack. "But they're all so lovely! However will you decide the winners?"

"Why, dear, it's a talent show. While our selections will take into account their beauty, charm, poise, and glamor, today's winners will be picked for their special talents." She stopped and looked at Imogene. "You can write that down."

Imogene wrote—in the shorthand she was once more grateful her mother had insisted she learn—"Fundraiser and out-of-town tour. What's in it for a local store owner? What's with all the rich girls?" Then she hit her notepad with the tip of her pen to let Mrs. Young know she could proceed.

"After we kick off with the Million-Dollar Party, we'll perform in New York and Chicago and Vegas. We have a packet for you with the full itinerary, singing and dancing—"

"So it'll be kind of like a USO tour?"

"Yes, exactly right. Only, the tour culminates in a competition in Los Angeles. The winners of that contest will get a movie contract."

"You don't say," Imogene said. "How did you manage to arrange all that?"

Tilting back her head, Mrs. Young let out a practiced laugh. "My dear, as you'll soon learn, Doc Young has pulled out all the stops for the Sun City Girls."

Nodding, Fuchs was scribbling on her pad when she stopped abruptly. "Wait. Did you say 'Sun City Girls'?"

"Why yes, after our store."

"Hmm. Editor's got me covering the Florida Girls," Imogene said slowly. "I'll get that straightened up. I'm sure you know what they're called."

Fuchs, pen poised to capture a reaction, was disappointed when an older man interrupted.

"See anything you like?" he asked.

Was that Mrs. Young's father? Of a similar height and build, though Mrs. Young was maybe a tad taller, he did share Bertie's ruddier complexion. But his eyes shone bright blue beneath his silver hair and old-fashioned bowler.

"Mr. Young, meet Mrs. Imogene Fuchs," Mrs. Young said.

"Imogene," he boomed. "Lloyd Young. Call me Doc. Pleased to meet you." He pumped her hand vigorously three times then turned and gave Kathleen Young a peck on the cheek.

Interesting.

"Dear, why don't you give Imogene here some quotes while I give your intro?" said Mrs. Young just before pressing through the doors.

Doc talked about his beginnings in West Virginia, the family's move to Florida during the 1920s boom, and something about his Forever Young elixir at a single counter. Did he expect her to put this claptrap in her story? Did Briggs?

"Doc, why are you doing this now? With a war to win, our readers might wonder if this tour is the best use of American resources."

Smiling in a way that felt almost grandfatherly, Doc clasped her hand. "Excellent question, Imogene. Follow me for the answer. And don't forget your Brownie!"

The room burst into thunderous applause as they entered. Sun City's stockroom was heavy with the scent of women—perfume, stale smoke, and striving. Imogene snapped a photograph then watched in awe as Doc Young transfixed the room with that same story about opening the Emporium during the Depression.

But how are they getting the gas rations? These girls are prominent enough here, but they aren't famous. To Imogene's surprise, Doc Young made good on his promise.

"Since the Battle of Normandy, the end has been in our sights. Now—thanks to the G.I. Bill—returning vets will be looking for a place to call home." Here, he paused for dramatic effect. "We want those young men to come to St. Petersburg."

Clever Gus, thought Imogene, admiring his appeal to the man-hungry crowd as she joined the now genuine applause.

Doc continued. "What better way to get our boys' attention than with Sun City's new line of ladies' bathing costumes? Introducing Playtime Swimwear!"

With that, he pulled the cover off the rack, revealing a row of brilliant, if skimpy, swimming suits.

Doc leaned forward to take Imogene's hand. "Let's let these girls disrobe in private."

Disrobe? Imogene tried to look back through the glass, but it had been covered. She had to keep her reaction out of the story, but she surely could get one of the girls to talk about this astounding turn of events.

SEVEN

THE AUDITION

For a moment, Thelma was reminded of the "receiving room" where customers appraised the merchandise, but the comparison fell flat as soon as Doc made his announcement and the exodus began.

Murmurs of "I never" and "We're leaving" could be heard around the room.

She looked at Peggy, the girl from the diner, who'd walked her to her hotel. "The Soreno." She grinned. "Cheap and cheerful."

"I'd say our chances just shot up," said Peggy, her voice low. Neither could suppress a smile—almost half the room, gone.

Thelma chose a two-piece bathing costume—yellow, with fuchsia flamingoes—she'd never tried one on, let alone owned such an outfit. No need in Keokuk.

She changed quickly, leaving her clothes on the rack, and returned to her seat. With nothing else to do, she reached into her bag for her lipstick and noticed that, somehow, her gloves were dirtier still. Not that it mattered. She wouldn't be covering her hands in this climate. She used them to hide her wallet and put out of her mind what she'd have to do if she ran out of money.

Peggy interrupted her thoughts. "That color looks great on you."

"Thanks. It's Off-Duty Red." Thelma smiled as if she'd had a choice. The paper bag doubling as her suitcase had ridden away with the bus. Without a toothbrush to her name, there was no point even visiting the water closet down the hall. The Emporium's low-price lure was irresistible. The necessaries were so inexpensive she'd splurged on the Bésamé. Since then, she'd been wandering the aisles. A live mermaid show? Shrunken heads carved into coconuts? Forever Young elixir? She wondered about the kind of people who called St. Petersburg home.

"That"—Thelma waved at the white, figure-flattering one-piece Peggy had nabbed—"looks gorgeous on you."

"Those are the Youngs' kids," Peggy whispered into Thelma's ear when the boys were called back.

It was such a rarity seeing boys their age Thelma couldn't help but stare. Not that she felt any pull. Her experiences with intimacy had been limited to activities that funded her mother's drug habit. She'd shut the door on all that and would never owe anything of herself again.

On closer inspection, she was sure the shorter one, with glasses, was too young for service. But the older one looked at least her age, and she'd turned eighteen in August. What kept him from the draft?

"No pressure, ladies," Mrs. Young said from the back of the room, where she'd just pulled back a large curtain to reveal an enormous mirror. "But it's time to start."

Thelma marveled at Mrs. Young's authority. A tiny, curvy Jane Russell type but with lighter hair, Mrs. Young managed to be businesslike and alluring at the same time. Doc liked to talk, but Mrs. Young was the one in charge. Had Thelma stumbled into a possibility far better than the simple life in Miami she'd been dreaming of for years? What if she could not only escape her past but create a brighter future? For once, Thelma realized, her desire wasn't to get away from something but to get—even some of—what this woman had.

"Whatcha gonna sing?"

Peggy's interest took Thelma off guard. Had she made a friend too? "I'm thinking 'Minnie the Moocher.' You?"

"'Stormy Weather.'"

Thelma's jaw dropped. Her choice was a crowd pleaser meant to conceal a mediocre singing voice. Peggy's was the opposite.

"I'm more than just a pretty face," said Peggy, pushing her palms upward to meet the bottom edge of her bob.

Thelma coughed to cover her laugh but still earned a glare from Mrs. Young.

"During the auditions, try and be as quiet as possible," she said as she walked to the front of the room. "When we call your name, you'll sing a few bars of 'Boogie Woogie Bugle Boy' in your range, and we'll move on. We must finish by three thirty, which—you may as well learn now—will get the photo in tomorrow's paper. Lucille Alcott?"

Thelma and Peggy looked at one another. That meant each girl would only get about a minute. Peggy was probably disappointed, but Thelma wondered how she'd hide her voice. As the auditions got underway, however, she relaxed. There was a strawberry blonde with a lovely high voice and another woman who sang low. But otherwise, they all sounded a bit like Thelma. She'd almost convinced herself she'd sneak by in the middle range when they called her name. "Thelma Miles?"

She felt a blush rise at her throat.

"Hello, Thelma," Mrs. Young began. "Did I see you earlier today? Where're you from?"

No one else had been questioned, and it hadn't occurred to her to craft a story. She never wanted to talk about the life she'd left behind, but her past wouldn't stop rearing its head. "Good luck with that, Blabbermouth." *Blabbermouth.* Vivian Miles's most-used nickname for her daughter.

"Chicago," rolled right off Thelma's tongue. She had been born there.

"Shee-CAW-go?" Lloyd whistled. "Just like the Bugle Boy himself. What brings you all the way here?"

Whispers went around the room, and Thelma's neck went from light pink to crimson. "My mother passed away a short while ago, and she loved Florida."

There was truth to this—her mother had rhapsodized often about some trip to Miami—but she expanded. "It was her dream we'd move here. This is as close as I could get to realizing her dream."

To her gratification, Doc Young put his hand to his chest and nodded.

Mrs. Young smiled. "Lovely answer. Please, go on and sing."

Clearing her throat, Thelma asked Archie to take it from the top like she'd heard the others do, jumping in at the refrain.

He was the boogie-woogie bugle boy of Company B
And when he plays boogie-woogie—

"THANK YOU!" MRS. YOUNG CALLED OUT THEN MOVED ON to the next name.

Nothing to do now but wait.

* * *

Lloyd and Kathleen Young huddled in Receiving to finalize the winners. The swimsuit reveal had winnowed out fewer girls than Kathleen thought it might, but the winners were obvious.

Their own Peggy Holmes—a known entity—was a classic mezzo-soprano. Then there was Helen Fuller. Even if her father wasn't the head of city council, she was the only true soprano in the group. Doris Juergen came from the oldest money in town and had a decent contralto. Her dark hair and eyes made for an appealing physical contrast to the platinum blond Peggy and redheaded Helen too. Lloyd agreed, between the photographs and the radio play, the crowds would line up.

"We can't ignore Millicent Williams," Kathleen said. "She's the mayor's daughter, and he was key to getting those tire rations. And Hattie May Harper's mother has already bought tables for the Women's League. Of course, Lillian Wright's obvious."

Lloyd rubbed his brow with the palm of his hand. "Matteo's going to want *some* say."

"He's a *child*. And who would we cut? Hattie May?"

"To me, Lillian Wright's the low-hanging fruit."

Kathleen's jaw dropped. The Wrights were one of the wealthiest families in Florida, if not the country. Their name wielded power far beyond the backwaters where they were currently moored. "You know the Wrights are an asset far beyond the Million-Dollar Party, and we need to think past St. Pete. It's the tour that's putting money into our California fund."

"Oh, come now. She's not a *Tampa* Wright." Lloyd frowned. "You only want her because her father owns the competition."

Sighing, Kathleen tapped her foot. Then remembered

herself. Stroppy was not the way to move her beloved. Tugging on his bow tie, she offered a flirty grin. "If we must sacrifice, let it be Hattie May. It's not like her mother can return the League's tickets, and the girl will be a challenge."

Instead of smiling back, Lloyd looked away.

Kathleen narrowed her eyes. "This isn't about Matteo at all. You already promised Gertrude, that old sot. You're managing *me*."

"She came to me personally this afternoon, carrying the bottle of champagne *you* gave her."

"Well, then, we're agreed," Kathleen said. "You get Hattie May. I get Lillian. We just convince Matteo someone on the team was his idea."

Lloyd swooped in to kiss his wife just as Archie burst through the door.

"Ew, cut it out, you geezers!" he cried. "Company!"

"Matteo!" Lloyd jumped away from his wife, just shy of a shove. "Please, pass our sincere thanks along to your father for speaking to Congressman Wiles about Albert. Boy doesn't have the constitution for war."

"Aw, an exception. That's what you was talking about," Matteo shrugged, palms facing up. Between his pin-striped zoot suit and the cigarette dangling from his lips, he looked so much like the *idea* of a gangster that an involuntary smile formed on Kathleen's face. "We sure appreciated that sugar and bacon you sent over."

"Our pleasure." Kathleen smiled, motioning to their younger son. "Archie, go find Bertie and make sure he keeps that reporter occupied while we make the final decisions."

"I know who I want," said Matteo, not waiting for the door to close. "That girl with the dark hair and those eyes."

They knew who he meant, but both Youngs flashed looks of bewilderment.

"You know the one, Doc," he said, bumping his elbow into Lloyd's arm. "In the getup with the flamingos."

"Thelma, was it?" Lloyd looked at his wife.

Kathleen squinted and cocked her head.

Matteo rolled on. "Yeah. Sure. Put her on the list."

Smiling evenly, Kathleen reached for common ground. "I see the appeal. But our overall strategy rests on radio coverage. We simply must have singers—"

"My dad can get you on the radio."

Kathleen and Lloyd exchanged a brief look. Salvatore Giancarlo might've been a big deal in Tampa, but both doubted his influence extended to New York or Los Angeles. Wasn't his main expertise staying out of the media?

"Did I stutter? I *said* the girl with the eyes."

"But..." Kathleen looked past Matteo to the stockroom door, wishing the reporter would emerge. "Why, we don't know anything about her."

Now, Matteo looked amused. Eyeing Kathleen, he drawled, "About *her*? You think she might be running away from her family to get married? Ain't they supposed to be single?"

Without betraying her thoughts—namely, how dare this numbskull reproach Kathleen's past—she moved on. "So the team will be"—she caught Lloyd's eye—"Hattie May, Millie, Peggy, Helen, Doris. And Thelma."

"Great. And one more thing," said Matteo. "My father wanted me to pass along a request."

EIGHT

GEORGE WRIGHT

George Wright saw the platinum bob first and ducked behind one of the columns separating the drugstore's soda counter from the toys and games. What was Peggy Holmes doing at his uncle's shop? Ever since Lloyd Young had opened that monstrosity down the street—thanks only to the fame and money he'd made selling his snake oil in his family's very store—neither set of employees patronized the competition. Not that she would've expected him to be there; he was on leave, and his uncle wouldn't have known who she was. Hanging back to watch, George saw her.

Behind Peggy, a raven-haired beauty sidled up to the counter. George wasn't the only one to notice. The pimply-faced new kid—instead of greeting the customers and offering the water they kept poured and ready to go in glasses—stood staring.

"Formica!" he heard Peggy say as she tapped the edge of a quarter against the countertop. "I don't like it much, but it's more modern than our painted wood."

"We don't have a soda fountain," the other girl said, looking around. "But if you keep talking like this, we're going to get caught for sure."

Sassy and gorgeous, thought George. I like that.

"Hey, Toots. Yoo-hoo!" Peggy called to the kid, tamping a pack of cigarettes on the back of her hand. "Two root beer floats, please."

"Make mine a vanilla cream," Thelma interrupted. "I've got to watch my waist."

George thought the weight consciousness a mark against her, having no clue that Thelma had never had thought such a thought in her life. Her sole concern was the potential cost of alterations, which Kathleen had made clear would be the girls' responsibility should they change dress sizes during the tour. All George knew was he liked a girl who could eat.

"Have one of these," Peggy said, offering a Pall Mall. "They'll keep you slim."

It was all too much for the new kid, whose root beer pour overflowed immediately. Sliding behind the counter, George grabbed the soda jerk's paper cap, mashed it on his head, and muttered, "I got this, munchkin. How about you refill the creamers and the napkin holders?" He wondered how his uncle ran the place without him.

Whipping the cleaning towel he'd used over his shoulder, George turned to face the women and serve their drinks. "Two sodas."

"George!" Peggy said.

"The one and only."

"What're you doing here?"

Leaning on the counter behind him, George ran a hand through his dark-blond hair then crossed his arms. "I was about to ask you the same thing."

Peggy mashed her cigarette into a Wright Pharmacy ashtray. "You first."

"Well," the dark-haired girl said, took a long drag, and stubbed out her smoke before she spoke. "This seems friendly."

"Aw, Thelms, we're just joshing. Aren't we, Georgie?"

Peggy turned on her stool to face Thelma. "Me and Blue Eyes over there were in the same class. We kid, but he's pure gold." She looked back at George. "You gonna propose to ol' McFatty or what?"

George's smile faded. His mother had asked about his intentions regarding Hattie May that very morning, driving him out of the house, across the bridge, and into his uncle's store. He loved the simplicity of the pharmacy—stocking goods people needed and selling them at fair prices. Not that his parents' wishes were complex. They wanted him to follow in his father's footsteps—go to Harvard, get a law degree, and then join the family business with a wife who'd keep him local. But he couldn't imagine that future, not since joining the air force.

"Well—" he began.

"Sheesh, Peggy, you're making me dizzy. Give the guy a minute."

George thrust his hand toward her. "George Wright. Pleased to meet you."

"Wright? As in Wright Pharmacy?" she asked, staring at his hand without returning the shake. Pursing her lips, she stared at Peggy. "I haven't been in town for twenty-four hours, and you're getting me in trouble already?"

Peggy's eyes widened. "Oh, it isn't like that. We're not really forbidden from—"

"I'm just teasing," Thelma said, turning to grab George's hand. "Thelma Miles. It's a pleasure."

A jolt shivered through George, and for a moment, there was only Thelma, her amber eyes, and something he hadn't noticed before—a faint half-moon scar on the edge of her cheekbone. He had to resist the urge to reach for it. Instead, he leaned in, close enough to catch the scent of Coty talcum powder. "George Wright. How do you do?"

Peggy laughed. "We covered that."

A dampness broke out on George's upper lip, and he quickly wiped his face with the towel.

"See? I told you. Nothing to worry about. At this rate, he'll forget we were here before he ships out."

"I didn't think that paper hat matched your outfit." Thelma took a sip of her cream soda, nodding. "Delicious—thank you."

"I'm on leave. How about you? What brings you in here?"

Though he'd been addressing Thelma, Peggy answered. "Aw, Georgie, you know we don't have a soda counter." She winked. "Besides, I wanted to take her someplace new to celebrate. You're looking at two brand-new Sun City Girls!"

George nodded, his eyes oddly blank, as if he was trying to retrieve the name from his memory.

Thelma laughed, a sound George could live in. "Well, this doesn't bode well," she said.

"Thelms, he's a war hero. He's got lots on his mind. But you remember? The big war bond party Doc is throwing? Will you be here for it? It's in a few weeks, on the anniversary of the Pearl Harbor attack—"

"Peggy, I'm going to have to cut you off," Thelma said, motioning to her drink.

They all laughed, and then George congratulated them.

"Your cousin was there. She tried out?" Here, Peggy leaned toward George and stage-whispered. "She made alternate, but you didn't hear that from me. Paper will be out tomorrow."

"My lips are sealed." George made a motion as if locking his mouth shut and tossing the key. "Shouldn't be too hard, since I ship out in a couple days."

"Well now, that is too bad," Peggy smiled. "One less man at the Million-Dollar Party."

"Your drinks are on the house."

"Thanks," Peggy said, just as Thelma was saying, "Oh no, we couldn't possibly accept."

"Speak for yourself," Peggy grinned and then swallowed a spoonful of ice cream. "If she wants to pay for hers, so be it. But I say thank you very much."

Thelma gave the slightest smile, and the floor nearly gave way beneath George. "Really," he said. "I wouldn't dream of charging you."

"Okay, then." Thelma dropped a dollar onto the counter. "This is for you. Thanks for your sacrifice." She turned to her friend. "Come on, Peggy. It's almost time for the *Music in Manhattan* matinee."

Slipping off her stool, Thelma marched for the door. Peggy looked despondently at the counter. She hadn't come close to finishing her float. "See ya, Georgie. Take care of yourself. You make us all proud."

OUT ON THE SIDEWALK, PEGGY WHACKED THELMA ON THE shoulder. "Why'd you go and do that?"

"Well, I do know a thing or two about men. Always leave 'em wondering how to please you."

Peggy squinted at Thelma. "Listen, pal, don't take this the wrong way, but... you don't have a shot with George Wright. His family would never allow it. They expect he'll be president someday."

"Me?" Thelma was taken aback. Objectively handsome as George was with his crest of hair, square jaw, and dimpled chin, she never thought about men that way. She tried not to think of them at all. She knew well enough how they thought. "Silly goose. I've no designs on that boy. That was for your benefit."

Peggy wrinkled her nose. "Ah. I have less of a shot than you.

I was old for my grade, and Georgie's a year or two younger. Smart kid. But anyways, I prefer older men."

At this, Thelma couldn't help but laugh. "Let me know if you find any. As in any men at all."

Peggy joined her laughter. "You're all right," she said. "Also, just so ya know, ya don't tip the owner."

For a moment, Thelma felt a prick of shame. She hadn't known not to tip. Would she ever learn how to conduct herself? He'd be gone soon enough, and there was no telling if he'd return. Then she remembered. "Isn't this his uncle's place?"

"True, but, well, Georgie's loaded."

Vivian Miles's voice rang in Thelma's head. "Rich folks will always take your money with glee whether you owe it or not. How do you think they stay rich?"

Though she had less than ten dollars left to last her till their first payday, she decided it had been the right move. "But Pegs, doesn't it feel scrumptious to throw money at a man?"

"I guess I never thought about it, but"—she linked arms with Thelma—"when ya put it like that, it does."

Giggling, they headed toward the theater as a wind kicked up. Pulling her jacket closer, Thelma felt conflicted. Peggy's suggestion had lodged wormlike in her brain. Was she attracted to George? The so-called intimacy she'd experienced had been forced upon her, and she was not keen to revisit that ordeal. Whether Peggy was right, it was best not to think about George Wright. He seemed the type to affect a devil-may-care attitude while in fact caring very much.

NINE

THE TALENT

Rehearsals were held on Sun City's fourth floor, opposite the Youngs' office in a utility room dotted with buckets, mops, and cleaning powders. There was just space enough for the troupe to stand abreast and kick at the air. Excited as she'd ever been, Thelma was the first to arrive. Soon Millie and Doris arrived, then Helen. After brief hellos, they stood to the side, deep in a conversation Thelma wasn't invited to, till Peggy's breezy entrance broke things up.

"Morning, chickadees," she said, overturning a bucket to make a stool. "Where's our Beloved Brat?"

Thelma smirked at the old film reference, but before she could say anything, the door swung open, and in strode Mrs. Young, exemplifying Maeve's advice about the transformative power of clothing. Looking every bit the dance instructor despite her petite, curvy frame, Mrs. Young's hair was tied back, and she had on flats, a short-sleeved black turtleneck, and the dungarees she'd instructed the girls to wear. *Another expense.* Luckily, Thelma's black T-strap pumps were acceptable footwear, and Peggy had given her a white button-down from a bin of castoffs at Sun City.

When Thelma learned their first paycheck would come after the Million-Dollar Party—they were to be paid monthly "like real salaried gals," as Mrs. Young had put it—she'd rationed herself to pennies a day. If it weren't for all the publicity landing her credit at The Soreno Hotel and free food at the Emporium, Thelma would have to choose between eating and sleeping inside.

"Ladies!" Mrs. Young clapped. "This is a tight space. But I'll have you know Mr. Bob Hope has been known to perform on a plank laid out between two trucks. And, in addition to staged performances like the Million-Dollar Party, we'll be running shows on the road, in all kinds of conditions."

Passing out a list of tunes they were to know—all big hits, but evidently, there were things called melodies and movements to learn—Mrs. Young kept up a steady patter. "On the road, Bertie will be in charge and act as emcee on the road, but Peggy will oversee the logistics."

Thelma regarded Peggy anew. Was she going to have to mind herself around her only friend?

Good job you figured that out now, Vivian Miles piped in. Thelma shook her head, wondering if she'd ever have a chance to miss her mother.

"My singers?" Mrs. Young pointed next toward where she stood. "Helen, Doris, Peggy. You'll practice here.

"And Millie, I've brought you a surprise!" Mrs. Young pulled back a sheet to reveal a box emblazoned with the word Solovox. "It's a portable organ! Has its own speaker!"

The other girls rushed forward to see the strange device while Mrs. Young described how it worked. "The range is B6 to F1, with four registers: bass, tenor, contralto—"

But Thelma held back. The only thing she'd ever learned about music was that she couldn't sing. She glanced over the set list. The mix of tunes, upbeat and dramatic, ended on Dinah

Shore's "I'll Never Walk Alone," a slow song that recognized the sacrifices war had demanded. *Brilliant.*

"Hattie May and Thelma?" she heard, snapping back to the moment. "You'll work the crowd, bringing up servicemen to teach them jigs. For now, you practice on each other."

Thelma looked around the room in a panic. Millie was setting up by the trio. Hattie May and Mrs. Young stood in the center, waiting.

"But," Thelma stammered, "I don't know any jigs."

Her new boss didn't blink. "Perfect. During rehearsals, you'll stand in for the servicemen till you know the dances."

"Mrs. Young?" Hattie May piped up. "I've brought my tap shoes."

After slipping into her tappers, Hattie May jumped up and started dancing, incongruously agile for someone with a generally languid air. Her rhythm got all the girls on their feet.

For a moment, even Thelma forgot her worries. Hooting, she cried, "Look at her go! That girl can slap the rails with the best of 'em. Go, man, go!"

Hattie May scored an instant solo, while Thelma eased into Bertie's role as master of ceremonies. Bertie would take over on tour, but for now, Thelma had found a place.

While Peg, Helen, and Doris sang, accompanied by Millie playing tunes, Mrs. Young called out dances for Hattie May to teach Thelma. The girl knew every dance imaginable. "Forward, re-placing your weight on your back leg, and stepping together. One, two, three, four. It's just a one-two quick step there. Slow, quick-quick, slow. Yes!"

Every now and again, Mrs. Young would bark. "More pep, please! You're there to make these men want to come back home."

Eventually, they settled on teaching the mambo and the Lindy Hop, the most popular dances of the day.

As the day wore on, the girls grew tired, except Thelma. Besides the fact that a day of song and dance was less wearing than fifteen minutes in her previous employ, she'd never known the pleasure of creative teamwork. Then Archie arrived with their first outfits—a simple navy short paired with a striped tie-front shirt—shrieks sounded, and everyone jumped from their seats.

"Girls! Please! We're still a place of business," Mrs. Young said though she looked giddy herself.

Mrs. Young went on to list the tour's forthcoming highlights, kicking off the season at the Tampa Downs, with stops at various bases up the East Coast all the way to New York City and the Tricorner Baseball Game. But all Thelma could think of was their final stop, the Memphis Belle competition in California. Now was the time to ask.

"Excuse me," Thelma said, speaking as she shot up her hand.

All heads turned to face her, and a slight wave of nausea tickled at her solar plexus. Mrs. Young crossed her arms and tilted her head as if to say, I'm waiting.

Thelma dropped her hand. "The tour finale... in California? With the movie contract? What do we have to do to win?"

Mrs. Young's face fell ever so slightly, and Thelma knew then that her question was unwelcome. Almost immediately, however, the mask reappeared. "Why, the same way you earned your spot on the team. Poise, grace, and talent. Let's work on all that, shall we?"

The store owner moved on. "Now, as you know, you'll be making your formal debut at the Million-Dollar Party. But your first event is this Friday, in Tampa, for a new fleet of trucks. The mayor will be there to thank his sponsor, who's also our sponsor, Salvatore Giancarlo."

Thelma noticed, with some surprise, that Millie Williams furrowed her brows. Wasn't she the mayor's daughter?

"Mrs. Young, do you mean Tampa's new sanitation trucks?" Helen asked.

"Why, yes. Very good, Helen. You know your civics though I'm not surprised, given your father's position on the city council."

"What?" Hattie May stood, spilling her new clothes onto the floor.

"I'd pick those up if I were you," Mrs. Young said. "You have to pay for any damaged costumes."

Hattie May yanked her clothes off the floor before returning to her defiant stance, arms akimbo, waiting for a reply, but Mrs. Young's description—"just a couple of hours" and "no performance, just photos"—failed to appease. The strike of tap shoes sounded. Hattie May was walking out? There was no way Thelma was going to let her dream slip away before it started. Without thinking, she signaled to Mrs. Young and followed Hattie May.

Given the clacking, her teammate wasn't hard to track to the employee bathroom, where she was bent over a sink, tube of lipstick in hand, poised to finish the sentence on the mirror: *Mrs. Young is a—*

"Don't be a nincompoop," Thelma said, grabbing toilet tissues from the dispenser and wiping away the lipstick. "You think she won't know who wrote that?"

Hattie May scowled into the mirror. "What's it to you?"

By Thelma's estimation, Mrs. Young had every right to be annoyed by Hattie May. "Don't be a sourpuss. Kathleen is hard on us all."

Turning to face Thelma, Hattie May crossed her arms. "You don't understand. My mother will be furious."

Thelma took a step back. "Mothers can always find ways to

be furious," she said. "You just have to beat her at her own game. Remind her that she wanted this for you."

Hattie May lifted her already upturned nose. "She never said that."

"Isn't the Women's Auxiliary supporting the tour? How bad would you dropping out make her look?" Thelma could see Hattie May considering this new information and felt a spike of jealousy that this girl had never needed to figure out how to manipulate her mother. Was that what it was like to have a father, someone always in your corner? She had no way of knowing that fathers could come with problems too.

Turning heel, Thelma strode toward the door. No longer angry, Thelma was calculating. She'd met the girl's mother. "Or fine, suit yourself," she called over her shoulder. "Leave the tour and go back to your life at home."

The sound of tap shoes soon followed her.

TEN

MAEVE O'REILLY

APPLAUSE GREETED MAEVE O'REILLY UPON HER ENTERING the Youngs' well-appointed penthouse suite at the Flor-de-Leon. "I appreciate the enthusiasm." The seamstress laughed. "But I haven't done anything yet."

Maeve took in a new baby grand that had appeared since her last visit. Somehow, the Youngs had found a piano in an ivory lacquer that matched the tables and upholstery. How on earth did anyone raise two boys in that environment? Maeve tried not to cluck as she fanned herself with her shirt. Her standard uniform, white balloon-sleeved blouse and Navy dirndl skirt, had failed to keep her cool on the sticky cab ride from the airport. She looked out the south-facing balcony, a study in green laden with vines, palms, and even a rubber tree. If she lived here, that's where she'd spend all her time. The window in her Lower East Side tenement looked directly into the building's so-called air shaft.

Before Maeve could return her gaze to the room, her long-time client Kathy Young swooped in. "Ladies, this is Mrs. Maeve O'Reilly. Maeve has been my personal couturier since designing my debutante gown." She beamed at Maeve.

"Maria?" Kathy called into the kitchen. "Would you show Mrs. O'Reilly to the guest room so you can freshen up."

"I'll take a spot of tea too, please, Maria. If Kathy doesn't mind." She knew the nickname would needle her, but really, introducing her as Maeve to the girls and Mrs. O'Reilly to her housekeeper. "Come close, girls. Here're the looks I've put together."

As they leaned in, there was a knock at the door. "Maria? Would you?" asked Kathy.

Before Maeve could extract the designs from her slim leather portfolio, Maria returned with the day's paper. Kathy snatched it and tore the pages open. "We're here!" she said, holding up a center spread with delight before reading aloud. "In a stunning display of talent and beauty, nearly a hundred girls tried out, but only six were named... Florida Girls?"

Kathy stopped speaking, thrust her jaw forward, and read ahead, her lips silently mouthing the words. That couldn't be good.

"Well, you can read the rest yourselves. Congratulations! And don't you look beautiful in those swimsuits?" Kathleen looked toward Maeve then pointed at one of the girls. "Thelma, why don't you go first? I'm going to call Lloyd. With the good news."

So much for freshening up, thought Maeve as Kathy left the room. Her luggage was still with the doorman anyway. She peeked over Thelma's shoulder. Not that she could read the fine print—decades of sewing had taken its toll on her vision—but the accompanying photographs were clear enough: Sun City's stockroom, filled to the brim, and a second showing the Youngs flanked by seven girls.

"There on the end," Maeve asked. "Who's she?"

"Lillian Wright?" Hattie May answered. "Just an alternate. We don't need her here."

Maeve wondered two things: first, if the young Miss Harper was aware of her supercilious tone; and second, how long before she could call her real boss? She touched Thelma's shoulder. "Come along, dearie. Let's start this train rolling. Maria, just bring the tea back when you have it. Ta."

When Thelma looked up, however, Maeve was caught off guard. She'd worked with enough beautiful people she regained herself quickly, but between the girl's amber eyes and dark hair, Maeve understood Matteo's insistence.

Once in the guest room, Maeve opened her notions bag and directed Thelma to the folding footstool. "Stand here, please."

The girl nodded but stood frozen, a faraway look on her face.

"Dear heart, what's the trouble?"

Thelma shook her head and blinked. "I was going to ask you."

"Me?" Fading into the background was Maeve's specialty, not answering questions. "No trouble here."

Thelma sat, arms crossed but still talking. "That was a funny reaction Mrs. Young had. Like it was the first time she heard we were Florida Girls, not Sun City."

"I wouldn't make too much of that, love," Maeve clucked her tongue. "I expect it doesn't much matter to you either way."

Thelma stiffened.

"What is it, dearie?"

"Nothing. It's just..." She climbed onto the footstool. "Is it that obvious I'm not from around here? Chicago's different, but..."

Maeve waited, but the girl had trailed off. "Pfft. I don't expect it matters to any of you. Far as being different, lassie, use that to your advantage."

"But these girls all know each other already. They've known one another their whole lives."

"Doesn't that sound exciting," Maeve deadpanned.

They laughed together.

"There she is," Maeve said, unspooling her measuring tape. "Come on, now."

The seamstress could've worked more quickly, but she needed to take each girl's measure as well as their sizes, so she chatted as she worked. "Fine figure. Perfect for some of the dresses I've included. You'll turn some heads. Careful your sweetheart doesn't get jealous."

"I don't have a sweetheart. I thought we weren't supposed to."

My goodness, this girl wanted to be good. "Well, it's hard for any young woman nowadays. Great War's why I didn't meet Mr. O'Reilly till I moved to New York. Raise your arms, please."

"The war," Thelma said as if it had just occurred to her.

She was unusual, compelling even. That much was certain. But she was no threat. If anything, Thelma Miles struck Maeve as someone who would be loyal, even to her own detriment. Before sending her off to fetch the next girl, Maeve felt compelled to counsel her. "Always remember, a true friend is like a four-leaf clover. Rare as hen's teeth."

WHEN THE LAST OF THE NEW RECRUITS HAD GONE, KATHY rejoined Maeve in the guest room. In stark contrast to the front room, this space was a study in florals.

"So, Maeve." Kathy sat atop the bed, absentmindedly tracing the outline of a cabbage rose. "What do you think? Can we trust these girls?"

"You did well, Kathy. But what about that seventh girl? Won't I need her measurements too?"

"Lillian Wright." A smile played at Kathleen's lips. "Her father runs Wright Pharmacy. Remember? That fellow who claimed he owned Lloyd's Forever Young formula? Let's just say that naming her an alternate came with an added bonus."

Maeve reached for her tea but promptly spat it back into her cup. "Christ on a cross, that's gone cold."

"I'll fetch Maria."

But Maeve was standing before Kathleen finished her sentence. "Nonsense, I've been sitting all morning. I'll make it meself."

In one deft move, Maeve put her notions basket on the floor and was on the other side of the door. She passed the living room, where Maria was brushing pastry crumbs into a napkin. "Be a love and make me a fresh tea?" She set her cup and saucer on the end table and kept moving toward the master bedroom. "Ta."

Hoping she had a few minutes before any of the Youngs turned up, Maeve dialed slowly to keep the noise down. "It's me," she whispered into the receiver. "I can't really talk, but that Wright girl you asked about? Not even here. She's an alternate they've no intention of putting on stage. And that Thelma Miles? Absolute stunner, but—" She listened. "Chicago? Very eager to please, that one."

The door handle rattled.

"Call you later."

Maeve had barely stood up when Maria popped in with her tea.

"Miss, you went the wrong way."

"Oh! Silly me. I'm all turned around. My tea already? You are a miracle worker."

She was still thanking Maria as she slipped by and returned to the guest room, holding her cup aloft. "Maria is a wonder. Now, where were we?"

"Kettle's always on the stove," Kathy said as Maeve settled.

"We were talking about the girls. I'm hoping that between Peggy and Albert, things will run smoothly."

"You're not going?"

Kathy shrugged.

"Kathleen DeVane Young. Have you gone mad? Sending Bertie on the tour is putting a cock in a henhouse."

"Boys will be boys." She smiled. "Though honestly, what chance does he have with any of them? Helen is far too bookish. Hattie May's too snooty. And Doris is such a goodie two-shoes."

"And Millie has a beau. But—"

"What? They're supposed to be single."

"He's away on duty, Kathy."

"Mmm. Well, I can hardly wish them poorly. She'll be back from the tour before he comes home. If he comes home."

"When did you decide not to travel with the girls?"

"I can't leave Lloyd on his own, not in his condition. And it'll be good training for Bertie. Unless..."

"Unless what?"

"What about Thelma? Can we trust her? What kind of girl is she?"

Maeve looked into her teacup, suppressing a grin. *What kind of girl, indeed?* Hadn't Kathy DeVane been thrust from her beloved Richmond society for taking up with the much older snake oil salesman, Lloyd "Doc" Young, who also happened to be a divorcé. She didn't mind, but she knew Kathleen did.

"No need to worry about her, either."

"Oh? But she is a complete unknown."

"Dearie, all young women are unknowns."

* * *

Kathleen regarded the seamstress. Had she been wrong to trust her to gather information? Maeve knew how to make a world-class dress, but that wasn't the same as knowing who should wear one. Between her brogue and those coppery locks, Maeve O'Reilly certainly wasn't a candidate.

"Say, what was that in the paper? Florida Girls? I thought you were calling 'em Sun City Girls."

Rising, Katheen moved to the chair, irked by the subject change, though she longed to complain about it—apparently Lloyd had "forgotten" Salvatore Giancarlo's mandate. But Maeve wasn't the right sounding board, and why make a bad feeling worse? "Oh no. Florida Girls makes the most sense for our funding partners. We changed that name."

"I see," Maeve said. "Clever."

And so, even Kathleen began to believe the retelling was true.

"Oh, and dear, you know I say this for your own good." She paused to pick up her coffee mug. "Your t-h sounds like a d-h when you speak too quickly."

ELEVEN

FIELD REPORT 1

INFORMATION REPORT***EYES ONLY
SUBJECT: Tampa Port Recruitment
DATE: Dec. 1, 1944
AUTHORED BY: T. Nelson, Special
Services, ONA
TOPLINE: Develop surveillance contact.

IN DETAIL: SOURCES HAVE UNCOVERED A NEW PLOT BY THE
Nazis to enter the US by sea. Their target is
Tampa Bay, an area controlled by Salvatore
Giancarlo, a 64-year-old Italian and petty
criminal who uses the port to import goods for
his cigar business. Though notoriously antiu-
nion (and his primary accountant, Artemis
Klaus, a Kraut, is naturalized), Giancarlo has
made public statements and used his business
in support of the war.

. . .

RECOMMENDATION: IT IS IMPERATIVE THAT OUR PORTS ARE secure, and as such, I will conduct an exploratory meeting with our contact, withholding sensitive information as appropriate.

TWELVE

THE CHRISTENING

Doc Young's infamous Crossley—an aging twelve-passenger bus emblazoned with the Emporium's Sun City logo, to which the words "Florida Girls" had been added in cursive—ferried the girls to Tampa. The middle seats had been ripped out to make room for two long, thin tables with sideways-facing benches. Thelma was glad when Peggy slid into the space beside her, even if she fell asleep almost as soon as the bus began to move. As the only two Florida Girls who needed their paychecks, neither of them quite fit in.

For the life of her, Thelma couldn't figure out how she'd made the team. She knew why she would've picked her teammates. Peggy had that air of competence and already worked for the Youngs. Millie—a square-jawed straight shooter—was a capable enough musician and, perhaps more importantly, the mayor's daughter. Doris came from what she'd heard Mrs. Young call "old money," which seemed to mean rich. Other than the odd little parasol Doris often carried—"the sun's a demon on your complexion"—she was something like the group mascot with her peppy nature. Hattie May, so-called *new* money, looked and acted like a spoiled Shirley Temple, but she could really dance. And Helen, whose nose was always in a book, had the voice of an angel. Thelma couldn't sing or dance well, and she had no money or prestige.

"Welcome to Tampa," Peggy murmured into Thelma's ear.

She must've dozed off. Rubbing the sleep from her eyes, she saw they were in a dusty parking lot next to a small fleet of dump trucks and a raised platform. A cluster of men in dark suits stood about. They wore slim ties and pricey wristwatches, their hair greased back. She'd seen their type, always around the house in Chicago.

Like a jigsaw puzzle, the Sun City operation fell into place —the dollar-bill buybacks, the low prices, this tour. How had she not recognized the schemes? They were cleaning dirty money for made men, the very people she'd fought to escape, and here she'd stepped right back into it.

"Ladies!" Archie, the Young's younger child, addressed the girls from the front of the bus. He'd joined a couple of their rehearsals after school, alternately accompanying them and teaching Millie how to play the Solovox. Like the men near the stage, his ginger hair was slicked back, but between the curls he could not tamp down, his black horn-rimmed glasses and jug ears, the kid was a world apart from them. "We want you all on stage holding the ribbon. Except Thelma."

This day was going from bad to worse.

"You'll be cutting the ribbon with Mr. Giancarlo, so you'll wait behind the bus. Now, everyone, follow me."

There was nowhere to run, not yet. So Thelma stepped off the bus, ready to play the part. Reporters had begun arriving, and the phalanx of young toughs had disappeared. The lady reporter, Fuchs-something or other, was there, as well as a few more notepads and photographers. No audience—this was less of an event than a staged photo, making the new job feel even more like her old one.

Once Tampa's mayor alit from a Cadillac, the proceedings got underway. Distracted as she was, Thelma missed the speeches. What she could not escape was the quickening in her palms—a premonition beyond her willingness to explore—or the jolt of cigar smoke and musky citrus notes that slammed into her nostrils, alerting her to Salvatore Giancarlo's presence before she heard him whistle.

"Matteo said you was a looker, but wow." Sal elbowed the man standing beside him, a man whose hair grew alarmingly close to his eyebrows. Patting his shoulder, Salvatore whispered something into the man's ear—his bodyguard, Thelma presumed.

"Miss Miles."

Thelma jumped at her name. Salvatore Giancarlo was behind her. An enormous man—the top of her head wouldn't graze his second chin if his belly would've allowed her to get that close—he required space.

"Pleased to meet you, ma'am," thrusting his tennis racket of a hand toward her, she noticed he wore a pinky ring.

Thelma allowed a seductive smile to play at her lips, remembering this was one game she knew how to play.

Putting just her bent fingers into his oversized mitt, she cooed, "Well, I wouldn't miss it. But I'm afraid you're at the advantage, sir."

He smiled, practically on cue. The man had to be in his sixties, but he was as susceptible as any to shameless flirtation.

"Allow me," he said with the slightest hint of a bow. "Salvatore Giancarlo, at your service. Call me Sal."

Behind the animated charm front, however, Thelma sensed a hair-trigger rage that would not be so easily rendered harmless.

"Well, sir, call me Thelma. I think we're here to turn this ceremony into a press-worthy event, so let's give them a good show."

71

As if planned, the Florida Girls were introduced just then and marched across the stage holding the ribbon. Sal waved at the small assembly.

"At SG Cigars, we care about all of Tampa Bay. These trucks will—"

Was the old man trying to pass as a concerned citizen? His type didn't usually court the press. What else could he be importing from Cuba besides cigars? Guns? Drugs? Women?

"What do you say, dolly?" Sal proffered one side of a giant pair of scissors. "You gonna help me cut this ribbon?"

Without missing a beat, Thelma grabbed a handle. "I thought you'd never ask."

Keeping the apples in her cheeks high as the cameras flared, Thelma realized, *I can do this.* She didn't need to know this man's business, just as none of them—no one at all—ever needed to know hers.

SG CIGARS COMMIT TO PAPER DRIVE
The Drive to 'Save Paper' Is On!

By Imogene Fuchs

ST. PETERSBURG, FLA., NOV 19, 1944—With a generous donation of four new sanitation trucks courtesy of S.G. Cigars, Mrs. Rose Williams, the mayor's wife, and Mrs. Henry Harper, of The Women's Auxiliary, signed Uncle Sam's four-point pledge to collect paper cartons from households throughout Pinellas County.

In his speech, Mr. Giancarlo called his
donation "easy as duck soup."

"WHERE THE HELL ARE WE IN THIS STORY, PEPPER?" LLOYD
Young crushed the paper onto his lap in frustration.

"The picture's above the fold, Button."

Kathleen watched from her bed as Lloyd dramatically
pulled tight the page then licked a fingertip and continued on,
mouthing the words as his finger flew past them. He'd taken a
correspondence course that promised this technique would help
him retain more of what he read, but near as she could tell, it
only made him a slower reader at the same speed of forgetting.
She cut to the chase.

"All that matters is that photo, darling. Thanks to that, the
Million-Dollar Party will be well attended, and that's all there is
to it."

Satisfied she'd won the volley, Kathleen returned to filing
her nails and made a mental note to call Mr. Briggs, the editor of
the St. Petersburg Times, first thing Monday morning. How dare
that Mrs. Fuchs try to bury her Button.

THIRTEEN

THE LOTUS CLUB

THELMA WAS COUNTING WHAT LITTLE CHANGE SHE STILL had when The Soreno's stiff day manager knocked.

"Mind you, delivery service ain't included in your six seventy-five a week."

Thelma plucked the cream-colored envelope from the woman's clawlike hand. "You'll be taken care of, Mrs. Collins. Promise."

"You're already a week behind. I'm only extending credit because of the Youngs."

The lack of funds was why Thelma hadn't left already, but disgruntled proprietor was an instrument she knew how to play. Clutching the envelope to her chest, she turned her gaze on the manager. "You are an angel, and your charity won't be forgotten."

With that, she pushed the door shut and waited till she heard the steps groan under Mrs. Collins. Her fingertips brushed the thick, cream-colored envelope, which bore a gold-embossed G.

Salvatore? she wondered.

"Matteo Giancarlo requests the pleasure of your company at the Blue Note tonight. His car will pick you up at 9:30 p.m."

This must be the Matteo Sal had mentioned. How was he related to Salvatore? And how had he come by her address?

Thelma slipped down the hall to ring Peggy but stopped her arm in midair. She didn't fully understand Peggy's connection to the Youngs. Cradling the receiver between her shoulder and ear, Thelma asked the operator for the only other girl who seemed a bit of an outsider, chewing at her fingernails while she waited for someone to answer.

"I'm so glad it's you, Helen. What are you doing tonight? Besides reading?"

"Is my dud of a social life that obvious?"

Thelma laughed and explained the mysterious invitation to the Lotus Club.

"How do you know Matteo Giancarlo?"

"I don't," Thelma said a bit too quickly. Aiming for casual, she asked, "Who is he?"

"Matteo Giancarlo is the son of Salvatore Giancarlo and heir to the SG Cigar empire. That includes the Lotus Club and, rumor has it, a vast criminal network."

Sheesh. Thelma knew Helen was book smart, but the girl was a treasure trove. She'd need to be extra careful around her too. "Golly. Well, he's asked me to this Lotus Club tonight. I don't believe I can refuse. But I was wondering..."

"If I'd join you? You want the strength of numbers."

"You read my mind."

There was a long pause. "I'll agree on one condition."

"Name it," Thelma said, hoping it wasn't money.

"That we invite Doris."

"Doris? But..." Thelma stopped midprotest. *Of course.* She'd attributed the easy intimacy between them to the fact they'd known each other since they were children. And really, what better way for two women to get acquainted than at a racy club across the Bay where no one knew either of them? She'd met women like that in Keokuk, women who didn't care at all for men. For them, the job had seemed easier, or rather, they had better control over their clients than her mother.

But what if Doris liked men? Or had the two already established something? Matteo's invitation was only to her. She wasn't even sure about inviting one person. This was a bad idea.

"I understand. I do. But—"

Midsentence, her mother's voice interrupted her train of thought: *"Girlie, forget about a man falling for you. You get what you want while they're getting it up for you. That's when they'll give you anything."*

"Can you both be here at nine thirty?"

"Nonsense. Have his driver pick us up. I'll ask Doris to come here—"

So they did have some established relationship.

"That way, you can arrive fashionably late."

With a sigh, Thelma agreed. She'd take this as a win.

Heading back to her room, fresh possibility occurred to Thelma. Could she hide among these elites? Perhaps that was what the Youngs were doing, insulating themselves with socialites. Could it work for her too? Or had she soured her new life already?

Her palms tingled, and for once, she was curious.

The first time she'd felt the sensation was just before she and her mother fled Chicago. Vivian went under the radar in Keokuk, a small Iowa town best known for kicking out the Mormons. Insiders, however, traveled there for the low-rent flophouses that serviced farmhands in the surrounding countryside. Had that feeling ever been a good sign?

Plenty of terrible things had happened without the accompanying sensitivity. It hadn't come when Vivian sank into her

Nembutal addiction. Or when her mother, her world, could no longer do the work that supported them. Thelma shuddered, remembering Mr. Jim, who'd paid extra to be the first to pin her beneath his sweaty, heaving mass. It took days to be rid of his particular rotting-cabbage smell though he wasn't the last to bring a farm stench into the room.

But she wasn't trapped now, not permanently. Soon, they'd be off to California with a chance to win a spot in the movies. Or if the Florida Girls didn't win, she could stay and keep trying. She only had to evade these Giancarlos until then.

She'd just hung up with Helen before realizing something else—she had nothing to wear. Buying a new dress was impossible for the same reason she couldn't leave town. She was already down to one square meal a day at Sun City—the free lunch they got with rehearsals—supplemented with pulled sodas and diner leftovers that Peg gave her at the end of the day. Helen was far too petite and Doris much fuller figured. Peggy was the only girl that came close to Thelma's height. She was going to have to call her after all.

Peggy didn't hesitate. "Of course I'll bring a dress. Then we can head over together."

"But Peg, I can't possibly invite you too. Matteo's invitation was only to me."

"Don't start sounding like the cornhuskers who usually make their way here. Since when do men like the Giancarlos object to having showgirls around? But if you want to avoid Matteo over the long haul, you're going to need another man."

Thelma hated this turn of events. The only thing she wanted less than exposing a third person to her past was entangling herself with a man in the present, not even George Wright. The thought stopped Thelma. Where had his name come from? She'd never spent time around young moony-eyed women and didn't plan on becoming one.

"No, Peggy. I don't need a man's help, thank you."

"Aw, kid." Peggy tsked over the phone line. "See you at eight."

"But—" Thelma heard the phone line go dead.

THE HALF REFLECTION IN THE MIRROR ATOP THE CHEST OF drawers was startling. A young Vivian Miles appeared to be staring back. Running her hand along the sheer red sleeve of the gown Peggy had loaned her, Thelma wished like hell her friend would lend her the more demure black dress she had on.

Peggy was busy pawing in the dresser drawers. "Quit staring," she said without looking up. "We gotta fix your bustline. Where's that handkerchief from earlier?"

"Oh no," Thelma said, crossing her arms high on her chest. "We are not stuffing my bra for—"

A honk interrupted them. Glancing out her third-story window, Thelma saw that a Hudson Commodore had arrived. She looked at her watch: eight thirty. "That must be Matteo's driver."

"Rude," Peggy said.

"Prompt," Thelma said, shrugging. Glad she'd bought a Coca-Cola for dinner, she slammed it down to keep herself awake. Just like old times. Too much like old times. "C'mon. Let's go."

"But," Peggy protested, "you're not filling out that dress."

In response, Thelma grabbed her handbag and hurried out of the room.

"What's the rush, Thelms?"

"The sooner we get there," Thelma said, turning from the stairwell, "the sooner we can leave."

"Speak for yourself, Toots. I'm looking forward to this."

The relief of the cool night air was replaced by the stink of cigars inside the car. Before Peggy shut the door, Thelma informed the driver of the change in plans. "The house is in Roser Park."

The driver turned, his thick glasses announcing his 4F status for him. She hoped he could see well enough to drive, especially at night. "I don't got instructions for that, miss."

"You do now," Thelma said, mimicking Vivian's confidence, a necessity she thought she'd left behind. "Also, no cigars during this ride."

Before he could say anything, Thelma asked his name. "Thank you, Sam. That will be all. Or shall we call Mr. Giancarlo?"

Sam touched his cap and turned south, Thelma knew, because Tampa Bay was on her left. Otherwise, she wouldn't have had a clue if they were heading north, south, or back to Keokuk. She sank back in her seat, hoping to quell the nervous sensation in her stomach. She dared not look at Peggy. Using Matteo's name to get what she wanted already? Was this the first move in her inexorable slide in the wrong direction?

When they pulled up to a mansion, Thelma understood she'd been wrong about Helen. That girl's family was loaded too. So much for thinking she might be a fellow outlier. If this team was all about money, that did less to explain her presence.

"There's room, Doris," Peggy said, urging Helen to squeeze closer on the back seat to make room for their teammate. Thelma hadn't mentioned Doris was coming at Helen's request, but she didn't seem surprised. Had Peggy been aware they were together?

But Doris sat up front. "Car sickness," she offered as she slid beside the driver. Turning to face the rear, she draped her arm on the bench seat. "And I don't want to miss a minute. It'll be a hot time in the old town tonight, but you?" She waved her hand across Thelma's face like a magic wand. "You need more everything."

Peering around Peggy, Thelma's eyes caught Helen. She blinked as if to ask for help. But Helen, already frowning, nodded.

"Peggy's right. We're Florida Girls." She grabbed Thelma's bag and inhaled sharply. "No!"

"What?" asked Doris, craning her neck to see what was happening.

"There's no lipstick in here!"

"Peggy, give her yours," Doris said. "Your skin tone is closest."

"I've got brow pencil too," Helen said.

Helen went to work as the car roared into the night. Thelma was just as glad to retreat from the chatter.

"Duke Ellington has played The Lotus Club!"

"It's the weekend. There are sure to be some boys in blue. At least the Mosquito Fleet."

"I hear the lobster is divine!"

She wanted to share their enthusiasm but was too distracted. What did Peggy mean about cornhuskers? Had Matteo been at the Tampa event? He didn't seem like the type to read the newspaper. Were the Youngs in cahoots with gangsters, or victims themselves? If she couldn't be rid of her past, did she have any chance of saving her future?

The car slowed, pulling into a grand drive lined with royal palms. Red carpet fronted massive glass doors, set off by velvet rope strung across brass stanchions. A red carpet should've sent Thelma to the moon, but it was almost ten o'clock, and she was worried about getting home. Speaking to the passenger window she asked, "How will we find you when it's time to leave?"

"Mr. Giancarlo will say when it's time."

Peachy, thought Thelma though she said nothing as she watched him speed off.

Inside, Peggy took charge. She knew just what to do and where to go; she must've been before. First stop was the hatcheck girl, where Matteo must've had a lookout, because before they finished with her, a young man escorted them to a red leather booth at the edge of the dance floor. It wasn't the best seat in the house for seeing the band or being seen, which might've meant it was the best seat in the house. Thelma couldn't be sure. She had no experience with fancy supper clubs.

"Let's order champagne!" Peggy cried, waving to catch a waiter's attention.

Thelma grabbed for her arm. "Champagne? Peggy, I'm bust."

"Sweetheart, are you joking?" Peggy said, shrugging out of reach. "We're *guests*." With that, she flagged an older gentleman in a white coat, and proceeded to order not one but two bottles.

There was no more time to protest as, just then, a man tapped Thelma on the shoulder. Rounded and disheveled, she found him intimidating despite his jacket and tie. No amount of suit would stop him from beating the living daylights out of whatever got in his way. "Come wit' me," he said, leaving no room for questions.

Looking back over her shoulder, Thelma saw the waiter jotting down orders from all three of her companions. They weren't at all concerned. Maybe Peggy was right—everything would be fine.

THEY DIDN'T HAVE FAR TO WALK TO REACH A SET OF PLAIN-looking stairs. To Thelma's surprise, they went down. She didn't think Florida had any basements. *Is this actual hell?* she thought with a smirk, despite her worry.

The corridor was plain, but at the end was an ornately carved wooden door. *"The epitome of tacky,"* her mother would've said. But it was nothing compared to the area beyond.

The door opened into a kind of sitting room, where an enormous glass chandelier hung over a coffee table, decorated with what looked like gold leaf. The seating consisted of three overstuffed velvet couches with burgundy-and-gold scrollwork. Cigar stench hung heavy, and Thelma noticed two freestanding humidors. Beyond this area was a large oak desk, oil rubbed to a perfect shine. Photos of Sal and Matteo hobnobbing with various celebrities lined its surface, facing outward. She was disappointed to admit, between his thick dark hair piled high in a pompadour and the divot in his chin, Matteo was a hunk. The acknowledgement repulsed her.

Under any other circumstance, Thelma would've asked about the pictures, genuinely curious. What was it like to meet Orson Wells and Rita Hayworth? And was that Joe DiMaggio? But just then, she had to concentrate, to think her way out of this meeting.

"Have a seat," said the beefy man who'd led her down. Stubble sprouted around his attempt at a pencil mustache. "Can I getcha somethin'?"

She shook her head. She didn't want to owe more than she feared she already did.

He didn't wait for her to sit, so Thelma turned to inspect the paintings on the walls, portraits of saints in Rococo frames, not the kind of thing that interested her though she did wonder how they'd come to be in Matteo's office.

She peered into one of the humidors at the edge of a sofa. From the front, it almost looked like a lectern, but when she peered into the glass top, she found two rows of neatly arranged cigars. She wondered what made them special, pulling at the ribbon sticking out from the lid to open the door.

"You open it, you gotta smoke it," called a young man from the doorway.

She let go of the ribbon, and the lid dropped with a thud. "Mr. Giancarlo?"

"Please. Call me Matteo."

"Of course." She paused. *Too soon for negotiation.* She'd have to give in to this familiarity. "Matteo."

"Here," he gestured. "Have a seat, dollface."

But not that freshness. "Please," she said with a wink, "call me Thelma."

Dropping into one of the overstuffed club chairs, Thelma sat back and crossed her legs in slow motion.

If he was upset she'd brought three friends, he didn't let on. He got busy pouring them drinks.

"Now, that's better," he said, flicking droplets of water into the glasses before walking toward her, proffering a short, cut-crystal glass. "A good girl appreciates a good whiskey."

Ever mindful of her mother's fate, Thelma had, thus far, avoided alcohol. But for a moment to think, and to appease Matteo, she took a sip.

"Ah, I see you're a pro already," Matteo said then took a seat on the arm of her chair to face her. He brushed a hair from her face, letting his thumb linger on her cheekbone, near the scar her mother's lover had left her. "Are you a pro?"

Thelma had to restrain herself so as not to throw her drink in his face. Instead, she downed it and stood, surprised to find that ire and a little whiskey were good for her thinking.

"I'm sure you'd like to add me to your collection, like these paintings," Thelma said. "So let me tell you. I'm pro enough to know this isn't how these things work."

"Relax, sweetheart. I like 'em feisty, but you gotta settle

down," Matteo said. "All's I meant was maybe you already know your liquor. Beautiful girl like you... I could do so much for you."

So now they were negotiating. Had he turned those photos around to impress her? Any girl on the team would've loved to make the acquaintance of a Hollywood director—even Matteo could've guessed as much. She herself had bedded older, uglier, and more criminal men for less. Would it be so bad?

Matteo moved toward her and grabbed her hipbone, burying his face in her pudendum and jolting Thelma from her disturbing fancy. It took Thelma's every effort not to flinch but instead, extend slightly. Ruffling his hair—his most handsome feature—Thelma dropped her voice into a conspiratorial whisper. "Sweetie, I've got the curse just now."

Matteo's head snapped back in the most satisfying way. Before he could reply, two men in pinstripe suits barged in.

"Hey!" Matteo barked. "We're talking here."

"Sorry, boss," said the shorter one. "This is urgent."

"Jerry!" Matteo yelled. The man who'd escorted her down appeared in the doorway. "Please see the lady back to her table."

"Stay put, beautiful," Matteo said. "We got a big show tonight. Frances Langford is coming in. I'll find you soon enough."

But Thelma, after finding the corridors empty, raced back up the stairs and found the table. To her panic, the girls were toasting with champagne. How would they pay?

"Ladies and gentlemen!" cried the emcee, a woman dressed to look like a man. "Tonight, for your listening pleasure, back in the Bay for one night only, our hometown legend, Mr. Tampa Red!"

The announcement was another jolt. Tampa Red? He'd played with Tommy Dorsey in Chicago. His song "Don't You Lie to Me" was one Vivian Miles had played repeatedly on her

Victrola until the wax wore out. Was it an omen or a coincidence?

"Dance with me," Peggy said, tugging on her sleeve. "You need the practice."

Mechanically, Thelma rose.

"Plus, it'll be easier for Helen to coax Doris to the floor," Peggy whispered as she whisked them toward the floor.

Thelma wasn't sure why Peggy had said that. With the war on, girls dancing together was a common sight at places like this. Or perhaps it was her way of signaling she was savvy to the sitch. No matter—Thelma needed the break from the table chatter. But Peggy wasn't having it.

"Where'd you go?"

Thelma looked into Peggy's broad face and deep-brown eyes and felt her resistance melt. Or maybe it was the song. But she started talking. "Matteo propositioned me in his office."

Peggy raised her half-moon brows and stopped dancing midstep. "Come on, we gotta go powder our noses."

Taking Thelma by the arm, Peggy led her toward the ladies. Mirrors and stuffed chairs lined the walls between two sets of doors, offering a place to sit and talk in quiet.

"Spill it."

"Nothing happened. These two goons came in, said there was some kind of emergency, and he left."

"There's always an emergency with guys like that."

"And how. You see, Peg, I know guys like this. My mother was a made man's woman in Chicago."

The door swung open, and two women entered, heading straight for the couch opposite Thelma and Peggy.

"Hey, privacy?" Peggy barked.

But the girls just stared back. Thelma took charge. A full five-feet-eleven in heels, she stood and took a few steps toward the interlopers. "You heard what my friend said? We were here first. So scram. Unless you want me to get Jerry!"

"Nice trick." Peggy smirked when the girls were gone.

"I've learned a few," said Thelma. "Our life in Chicago was pretty good till, well... Vivian wasn't s'posed to have me—"

"You call your mom Vivian?"

"Sometimes. She preferred it."

Peggy's eyes went wide, and Thelma questioned her choice of confessor. If she was shocked that she'd addressed her mother by name, what would she think if she knew everything? But the story burned inside her.

"Ma made me hide in the kitchen when she had company. I was good at keeping myself occupied with books and drawing. But one night, I heard breaking glass in the living room." Thelma remembered running into the parlor but only flashes after that. Her mother on her knees, pushed against the end table with the iron legs and marble top. Shattered glass on the hardwood floor. The flash of a man's pinky ring. "Ma was right there in the living room with someone. I didn't understand what I was looking at, of course—I was ten. The real fight started when I showed up."

Thelma brushed fingertips to her cheek. "It's how I got this scar." Thelma looked at Peggy before continuing. She was nodding, and that's when Thelma knew what she'd seen in her. Every girl's story was different, but abuse left similar scars, especially in the eyes. "Who got to you?"

"Pops like to hit. Mom said he was different after he came back from the war, but me and my brothers were all born after he came back, and I'm the baby. All's I knew was to stay out of his way when he was in one of his moods. I started working for the Youngs when I was fourteen."

"Younger than me. I was fifteen when I started working."

"In Chicago?"

"No. Vivian took us to Keokuk, this farm town in Iowa. 'They won't think to look in this dump,' she'd say. And she was right. For a long while, things were okay. Then she got this toothache."

"The doctors gave her Nembutal. It took a while, but it got to the point she couldn't work. But she needed the Nembutal. So I... I took over. Till she overdosed, and I got on a bus for Florida."

Peggy was silent. Thelma looked down to find a stain on her skirt. She hadn't eaten. Closer inspection revealed the smudge was grease, Matteo's hair gel.

Why had she just admitted all this? And to Mrs. Young's confidante. Was she sabotaging herself or needier than she let herself admit? Blinking back the tears, she studied the floor's pink and black tiles instead.

"Hey, Thelms." Peggy cupped her chin and lifted her jaw. "It is *not* your fault."

Forced to look into her eyes, Thelma saw only acceptance. Tenderness pressed at her chest, and a tear fell. "But—"

"But nothing. My Pops was a miserable drunk. We tell everyone it was the Great War that killed him, but of course he didn't die until ten years after it ended. He drank our food money. We all had to do things to get by in the Depression." She smiled brightly. "I was a natural born thief."

Thelma took a deep breath. "I know you have to tell Mrs. Young. But can you wait till after our first paycheck? I'm bust."

Peggy's jaw dropped. "Tell her what?"

Thelma didn't know how, or if, to answer. "Aren't you her, I don't know, second-in-command?"

"That is rich. Sweetie, I don't think that woman considers Doc her second-in-command."

With the mirth of the shipwrecked, they both laughed. At

last, Peggy stood and smoothed her black pencil dress, extending her hand. "You ready to go back out there?"

"Go back? I'm hoping to avoid Matteo completely until we leave for the tour."

"That's it! That's how you're going to be rid of Matteo!"

"What do you mean?"

"By the time we're back from the tour, he'll have moved on to another girl."

Thelma wasn't so sure about that. Vivian's callers had viewed her as their property, and they were overbearing landlords. But the truth-telling spell had broken.

BACK AT THE TABLE, THEY FOUND HELEN FANNING DORIS.

"I don't know what happened," Doris said. "But I'm not feeling well. I can get a cab."

"Must be the crab," Helen said. "I'll take you."

Thelma looked at Doris. Her skin had turned gray, and sweat dotted her brow.

"Nonsense. I'll take her home," Thelma volunteered, seizing on the opportunity.

"That would be divine, Thelms. Look, Helen, there's still a whole bottle of champagne. And Frances Langford is *just* about to go on!"

Thanking Peggy with her eyes, Thelma agreed. "Oh yes, you both must stay and enjoy this night out! I'll hail a cab."

Had she really escaped this easily?

FOURTEEN

MERCY HOSPITAL

THEY WERE ON THE BRIDGE WHEN DORIS STARTED
panting.

"What's wrong?" Thelma asked.

"Can you..." Doris began but was too out of breath to finish.

"Pull over!" Thelma commanded the driver.

"Lady, it ain't safe here. We're on the bridge."

For a moment, Thelma regretted rejecting Matteo's driver.
He would've stopped. "Roll down your window!" she said to the
driver as she did the same across Doris's lap.

Doris thrust her head out just in time though Thelma was
pleased to see that much of the vomit stuck to the side of the car.
She flopped back inside.

"Doris, are you pregnant?"

"Pregnant! Have you met my mother?" She smiled weakly.
"I'll be fine. I just ate something that—oh, owww!"

"Doris, you are not fine."

"I am."

"Mister, take us to a hospital."

"Oh, Thelma, that's not—" Doris fainted.

. . .

THE HARSH LIGHTS IN THE EMERGENCY ROOM MADE Thelma wonder if she was hearing correctly.

"What do you mean St. Andrews won't treat her?"

The nurse in her pristine cap and thick-soled shoes pursed her lips. "We don't treat coloreds," she said, her doughy face turning a shade pinker though her resolve didn't waver one bit.

From the reception desk, Thelma looked back toward Doris, sitting motionless, her head resting against the wall, eyes closed. Her skin had turned ashen. *"You'll catch more flies with honey,"* she heard her mother saying.

"She's ill. She must've made some mistake when she was filling out her form—"

"No mistake. Matter of fact, she tried to say otherwise. But look at her."

Once more, Thelma turned to face her friend. Was her hair a bit kinky? What nonsense. What good were flies? "What difference does that make?"

The nurse dropped her jaw into her chin and lifted her eyebrows.

"Her mother, I'll have you know, is one of the richest women in this town."

"Listen, sugarplum, rules exist for a reason. Think about it. The girl has black blood. She needs to be seen at the colored hospital by people who will know how to treat her."

"Well, there's no arguing with that kind of logic." Thelma grimaced as she watched her sarcasm sail overhead. There was no time to fight, and besides, she wouldn't win. She needed a new plan.

She returned to Doris, hoping she might have improved. Instead, she was swaying back and forth, mumbling. She needed help—immediately. Did she even realize what was happening?

Turning toward the exit, Thelma hoped to find a cab dropping someone off. What she saw was George Wright, looking even more dashing in his leather bomber jacket and minus the paper cap.

"What are you doing here?" he asked.

She crossed her arms. "I could ask you the same thing—"

"I'd tell you, but you have to promise to keep it a secret," George winked.

She lifted her hand. "Doris is in trouble."

A crease appeared in George's forehead. "What's wrong?"

"First, you need to promise you'll keep a secret."

"Anything," he said.

She didn't trust him, but she was desperate. Swallowing, she spat it out in one go. "We need to get to the colored hospital."

"Come on with me," he said, grabbing her arm without hesitation.

THELMA HADN'T BEEN AWARE HOW SICK DORIS REALLY WAS until they got to Mercy Hospital, just south of town.

"It's a good thing you mentioned that shellfish," the doctor told her. "You got her here just in time. The new histamine treatment is a miracle. Two years ago, anaphylactic shock would have killed. Now, she'll be back on her feet in no time. She'll be here overnight, but there's nothing more you can do now. We've notified her family. God bless you."

Then he turned and walked away.

"I think he wants us to leave," George said.

"Leave her alone? When she almost died?"

"We aren't family."

"You mean we're not Negroes?" Thelma asked, annoyed. The scuffed floors and dimly lit waiting room was a far cry from St. Andrews. Was it too much for the boy with the silver spoon? And just when she'd hoped this George fellow was, if not completely trustworthy, at least reliable.

"No. I mean we're not her family. Please. You must be exhausted. Let me take you home."

Thelma took a deep breath. He made sense, she knew, but her friend had almost died on her watch. "I'm not tired."

"Thelma," George interrupted her thoughts, "I can't tell you what to do, but I don't think her family wants to see us, either. This is a secret. A big one."

Another reason, besides needing the paycheck, that Thelma should stick around. How else could she make sure this George would keep his mouth shut? She looked into his eyes to offer a witty rebuke but found she couldn't speak. The man was disturbingly captivating.

"Or we could get ice cream." George pulled a set of keys from his pocket and dangled the set between them. "These get us into the store."

The day kept getting stranger, but she had to admit ice cream sounded like just the right idea.

As they drove toward Wright's, Thelma was struck by what a difference a few blocks could make. The area around Mercy was overgrown with sawgrass palms, cypress, and Australian pine obscuring the moon. Once they reached Fourth Street, saltbox flats and rundown cottages stood close, separated by thin strips of sandy dirt. A few blocks north, the roadsides widened, planted with tall palms and promenades with benches.

"Damn benches," George said as they drove past. "I hope they get rid of those things."

"Really? How come?"

"Bad for business."

"But they're always packed with people."

"Haven't you noticed? It's only old folks, reading and gossiping. Makes the city look like a rest home, and they don't shop. Plus, coloreds aren't allowed to sit on 'em."

"What do you mean?"

"I mean, it's a city ordinance. Whole thing makes us look backwards."

Thelma was dumbfounded. In the world she'd come from, there was a market for every skin color. She'd not seen the dividing line of race so much as the equally false distinction of so-called class. Here, the hospital was just the start. She never would've expected to meet an open-minded rich kid. Was something off about this guy?

Thelma was still lost in thought when George appeared outside her window.

"You let me get the door," he said as he was opening her side.

Now she was on the defensive. "Are you trying to impress me?"

"I'd like to think I don't have to try." He winked and escorted her to the door at Wright's. "But that would take all the fun out of it."

Then he turned serious. "You should try trusting people."

Thelma's defenses flared. No way could she leave Doris's secret with him.

George flipped on some lights, and Wright's Drug appeared before her—bright and shining. Such a different environment from Sun City—a posher part of town, wider aisles, and far fewer signs. Given the prices, she'd shop at the Emporium whether she worked for Doc or not.

"Cream soda?"

"You remembered," Thelma said, finding it impossible to suppress her grin. Her experience with men aside, this was the closest thing she'd ever had to a normal date. "But actually, I'd like a sundae."

"Strawberry?" George smiled, revealing his dimples.

Thelma shivered, instantly and involuntarily drawn toward this man.

"But I should warn you, the hot fudge won't be hot."

"Perfect." Thelma blushed. *What is this feeling?*

George rolled up his sleeves and got to work, dropping strawberry sauce and lukewarm fudge over three generous dollops of vanilla ice cream in sundae glasses. She admired the muscles in his forearms, the fine hair as he finished off his creations with whipped cream, nuts, and candied cherries.

"Come on," he said, leading her toward a booth. "Now, we're just a couple of people having some ice cream."

"Just when I was getting used to being waited on."

"Play your cards right..."

"This is delicious," Thelma said, which was true, but she wanted to change the subject. Whatever the feeling, she refused to need or want it.

"My grandma's recipe. For the ice cream. She doesn't make it, of course. She's gone."

"Oh, I'm sorry."

"I never met her," he said, still cheery. "But apparently, it runs in the family. My mom passed young too."

"Mine too," said Thelma.

"When?"

"Let's see," Thelma counted back in her mind. "Almost five weeks now."

"Five weeks? My God, Thelma," George said.

But Thelma wasn't missing her mother just then. She felt held by George's cobalt eyes. "She was sick a long while."

He nodded. "Same with my mom. Died when I was eight."

"You were so young."

George nodded. "It was rough at the beginning. It doesn't go away exactly, but it gets better."

For the second time that night, Thelma felt her heart softening. She needed him sweet, which meant no more rounds of confession. She coughed, trying to dispel the sensation.

"Let me get you some water," George said, jumping up.

"You know, George, that's all right. I should be getting home. We've an early start in the morning."

He offered to drive, but Thelma declined. "I can walk from here. I need to make weigh-in tomorrow."

"Sorry, but not on your life. I can't let you walk the streets this late at night."

If only he knew. But George must've mistaken her look for apprehension about his intentions.

"I'll be a perfect gentleman," he said, staring deep into her eyes. His were, she noticed, the same shade of blue as Vivian's, and she wished she could change everything.

FIFTEEN

MILLION-DOLLAR PARTY

THE WEEK HAD FLOWN BY SO QUICKLY THELMA SCARCELY had time to think about the promise she'd made George. He'd walked her to The Soreno—a compromise—and told her he was shipping out the next day. Would she be his pen pal?

She couldn't turn down a man in uniform, especially one about to be deployed. How else would she make sure he kept his trap shut about Doris? Or that's what she reminded herself when she wasn't wanting to show off her new outfits and dance skills. Like now, in the dark-maroon rayon crepe with black grosgrain accents and a black lace peplum that teased her hips.

"Lookathere." Peggy joined her at the curtain separating their makeshift green room from the stage.

The Vinoy's Grand Ballroom boasted an orchestra section fronting a dance floor, with seating at an elevated platform flanking the room. To make their million dollars—a sum Thelma could not conceive—the Youngs needed to fill the room and sell lots of dances with the Florida Girls besides. So they'd put tables right on the dance floor, cramming an additional two hundred seats into the space, doubling capacity. Though she was not aware, Thelma would not have been surprised to learn that the chief of police needed a little extra convincing to over-look fire safety rules. After all, her mother's profession (and, briefly, her own) had relied on such favors.

"The décor is marvelous," Doris enthused, cooing at the red and blue streamers lining the walls, gathered into scallops held with bunches of white carnations. Each table had its own red, white, and blue floral arrangement, nested on a candelabra.

"I can't picture how they'd struck the tables after dinner," Thelma said. "It seems like the room should always be this way."

"Ech, you're both mad." Hattie May had sauntered up. "It's absolutely bombastic in here."

"Sourpuss," said Peggy.

Ever the peacemaker, Doris changed the subject. "Look! There's my mom. She brought Women's Rotary chapters from Gulfport, Clearwater, and Tampa."

Thelma followed Doris's finger out to a petite middle-aged, white-haired woman sitting at the center of the three ten-tops nearest the stage. She was dressed in a white satin gown bedecked with enough rhinestones to read by at night, and she seemed to be talking to all three tables at once. She wondered how the Juergens had kept this secret but knew better than to ask.

As she continued scanning the room, however, her mouth puckered. *Too many women.* The main attractions of the evening were candy girls, cigar girls, and Florida Girls. Who was going to buy?

"It's for the cause," Doris added, as if reading Thelma's mind. "These people will pony up for the boys."

There was a smattering of young men in olive drabs, men who must've been on leave. Dances would be bought on their behalf. The only other men in attendance were with their wives and well into their fifties or beyond. No sign of Matteo Giancarlo.

"There's my beau," chimed in Millicent, nodding toward the room's center table. Seated beside the mayor and Mrs. Williams was a slender young man in a dress uniform.

"An officer?" Peggy whistled. "Nice work."

Hattie May opened her mouth, but Mrs. Young had started tapping the microphone. Thelma had a hunch she was going to complain about the fact that the girls were supposed to be single.

"Ladies and gentlemen," Mrs. Young said.

Peggy dropped the curtain, and they all stepped back.

"Please take your seats so we can start the show. Thank you." Mrs. Young slipped through the curtain. "You quiet down back here, and no more opening that curtain. Your looks must surprise our guests. And I dare say, you've all got some touching up to do. We've got to raise another half million with these fine people if we want to keep our jobs, so break legs, everybody!" And with that, she was gone.

They moved back toward the makeup mirrors. It was a nuisance that Doc, being male, had neglected to install anything full-length. They had to rely on one another.

"What do you think of this?" Millie asked Hattie May, adjusting the veil on her pillbox hat.

"Very nice."

Thelma couldn't help but interrupt. "You want the hat to sit just so, pointing at your left eye." She reached up and pushed the hat askance.

Doris nodded approvingly, adjusting her own contrasting-color hat. "Leave it to the city girl to know."

Thelma felt a pang, but there was no telling them now that she was actually from Keokuk. No matter. Anything Thelma knew about fashion came from *Scene-o-Rama* magazine or the movies she and her mother attended religiously on Sundays, all of which Maeve had left in the dust. Thelma tugged at her elbow-length gloves, not too glamorous—not with all the wartime fabric restrictions—but none too ordinary either. "It's the latest trend. Day to night." Maeve had said. "Change the fabric, subtract a few bits and bobs, and poof! Sun City can sell these looks off the rack." Thelma had never worn such a fine outfit.

Her mother's voice crept in. *"Yeah, well, this Outfit isn't in it for the clothes."*

But Thelma was sure this wasn't *the* Outfit, though they had to be connected somehow. She'd discovered the Emporium's third-floor window ran a numbers operation for the Giancarlos, a curious game they called Bolita that involved drawing a number from a bag. How was it those two had no clue who the Giancarlos really were?

Then Thelma heard Mrs. Young introducing Doc. After the briefest Emporium ad she'd heard yet, Doc began whipping up enthusiasm for the war effort. "Many of our boys have been called to serve already. Now, it's our turn to do our duty. The girls you're about to meet have been working hard to help. I want you to think about what you can do..."

Thelma had to give it to Doc. He could flap his lips with the best of them. She closed her eyes and shut out the world around her, a withdrawal she'd taught herself when faced with a sweaty, grunting mass overhead. But instead of floating into darkness, she pictured herself gliding through their routines with ease. She couldn't wait to hear Peggy and Helen sing Vera Lynn's "A Nightingale Sang in Berkeley Square" or Doris's rendition of "I'll Be Seeing You." Relatively speaking, her dance solo was short.

The introductions began. She listened as Doc called each girl—all of whom were well known by some group or other in the audience. What if her name was met by a confused silence? At last, her name was called.

"And, in the latest summer fashion, the day-to-night dress, hailing all the way from Shee-Ca-*Go*, Miiiiiisssss Thelma Miiiilesss!"

Blood filled Thelma's ears as she made her way to the stage, where thunderous applause stopped her. Doc urged her forward.

"Aren't they lovely?" he asked.

Again, the crowd went wild. No wonder she'd come last. Thelma wasn't the tallest or last in the alphabet, but with the roll call complete, the other girls could signal for applause. It never occurred that the cheers could be for her alone.

"Remember, bidding for dances starts at one hundred dollars. But first, enjoy your dessert, apple pie and ice cream, of course! From Mrs. Young's very own recipe."

THE GREEN ROOM WAS AWASH IN ACTIVITY AS THE GIRLS changed into formal wear—floor-length pencil skirts with ruched bodices and buttons at the wrists. Each girl had her own signature color; Thelma's was a deep burgundy.

"Can you get this?" Helen asked as she fiddled with the zipper between her shoulder blades.

"I've got you," Peggy said, slinking over to give Helen's left breast a tug. "There. Much better."

Hattie May and Millicent, presumably more accustomed to such outfits, were already touching up their seamlines.

"Now who's going to see your legs?" Peggy snorted.

Hattie May tilted her head. "A lady isn't ready to be seen until she's fully dressed."

Peggy smacked her lips. "What about you, Millie? You holding out hope? We saw your man."

"A beau?" Hattie May asked in mock horror. "Why, Millicent Williams!"

Millie blushed.

"I'd rather not take the risk of smearing," Doris said. "I didn't put any on."

"Agreed," Helen said, smiling.

"Well, that's a different kind of hope," Thelma said, earning a snort from Peggy while Doris and Helen looked confused. She changed the subject. "I'm glad they have leg painters at Sun City."

"They won't be coming on tour with us," Millie said.

That was a point Thelma hadn't considered. She was going to have to practice applying hers in quick-change situations without marking up her dresses, but now was not the time. Once again, Doc was whipping up the crowd.

"...they hardly even had to practice, and you all know this number, so without anything further from me, I bring you... Sun City's Florida Girls!"

Archie sounded the first notes of "Boogie Woogie Bugle Boy" on his trumpet. He'd joined a few of their rehearsals and proven himself helpful and a skilled musician. Thelma wished he'd be joining them on tour instead of his brother, Bertie.

As the song got underway, Thelma discovered something. Being on stage was fine, but she couldn't have cared less about it. She could sing and dance passably, but what she truly loved was being part of this group of women. If she'd learned anything from her mother, it was that other women could be the fiercest competition but the best allies.

The audience joined the final chorus, and Doc wasted no time. "How about these beauties?" he asked, beaming as he walked in front of the line. "Now, each girl will walk across the stage, and the bidding will begin. Usually, the highest bid gets the dance. But we only have six girls, and we have a long way to go to reach our million-dollar goal, so tonight, every bid gets a dance!"

Instead of competing, Doc turned the bidding into an ante. It was going to be a very long night.

"Bids start at one hundred dollars. Doris?"

Before Doris made her way to the stage, her mother jumped up. "I'd like to donate a dance to two gentlemen here tonight! One thousand dollars each!"

Thelma's jaw dropped. The pot swelled as Doc called the girls in the same order they'd been introduced. When it was her turn, Thelma stepped on her hem as she moved forward, forcing her face not to reveal her worry she'd ruined her dress. She floated toward the darkness until she realized Doc was talking to her.

"What do you say to that, Thelma?" Doc moved away from the microphone and whispered to her, "Say 'Thank you' and get behind the curtain."

"Thank you!"

Was she in trouble?

* * *

WITH EQUAL PARTS HORROR AND RELIEF, KATHLEEN placed the final mark on the chart. The one-hundred-thousand-dollar bid had pushed them over the top. She was glad Lloyd had the good sense to accept immediately, since he'd pledged to use their personal funds to make the goal. Added to what the party and the tour were costing, closing that gap would've been the end of the Emporium and a swifter end to her husband.

Out of the corner of her eye, she watched the bidder—a stocky young man with a crooked hairline mustache—slip through the door. That could only mean one thing. No one in this town would make such a grand gesture without waiting for the applause. He had to be one of Giancarlo's men. She wondered what they'd owe for this.

The band began to play, and the waitstaff was just starting to clear the tables and chairs when Lloyd made a beeline for her. "Mrs. Young, we did it!"

"See, my love?"

"Well, if it wasn't for Matteo's bid—"

"Matteo?"

"Yes. Thank heavens. Now would you get Thelma a car, please?"

Kathleen looked quizzically at her husband.

"He wants those dances... for himself."

Kathleen understood, but Thelma, when she found her behind the stage, wasn't nearly so understanding.

"*That's* what just happened?" she demanded, too angry for words. "I... I..."

Kathleen didn't wait for more but whisked Thelma toward the exit behind the kitchen. Unfortunately, as they passed the enormous mechanical dishwashers, the girl regained her language.

"Are you saying he bought me? Nobody buys me. I didn't agree to take on that debt."

"Not another word," Kathleen warned, "till we get outside."

They passed steaming grills, potagers stirring vats of soup, and line cooks plating orders for the Vinoy's other restaurants. The smell of roasted meats hung thick. Finally, they came to a set of stairs. Once they were outside, the humid December night fell over them like a warm blanket.

The hotel's rooms were kept temperate with refrigerated air, and Kathleen had forgotten her own off-white gown. She could only hope her makeup wouldn't melt into its plunging neckline. It would show every mark.

"But my clothes," said Thelma. "They're in the dressing room."

"We'll have your things at the Emporium tomorrow."

"Tomorrow?" Thelma thrust her jaw and looked around.

If she'd known where she was, the girl would've run off already, or so Kathleen suspected. This wasn't how she'd planned things, but if Matteo wanted Thelma, the girl needed to fall in line.

"Thelma, sweetheart. You wouldn't even be on this team if it weren't for Matteo." Kathleen caught herself. She'd no intention of revealing the whole contest was a fix. "There wouldn't be a team at all. Everybody owes somebody."

"There's owing," Thelma shot back, "then there's owning. I won't be bought and sold. Not to a man."

Kathleen couldn't imagine the life that had brought this young woman into her orbit but knew she was alone in the world. Though she'd no wish to harm her further, her own family came first. "Now, you listen to me."

Thelma reared back.

"Do not make this a problem. Mr. Giancarlo likes you. That's probably the best thing that could happen to a girl like you, with no family."

When Kathleen said "family," a shadow passed over the fire in Thelma's eyes. She saw her advantage. Reaching into her bosom, Kathleen extracted a ten-dollar bill.

"Take this, and check in to the Princess Martha. Don't give them your real name. I'll have our driver take you. It's... Let's just say Matteo will never find you there."

"You can't pay me off either."

"Sweetheart, I'm just trying to buy you some time."

"When do we get paid?"

Now Kathleen had the girl right where she wanted her. "You'll get your first month's check after the Flamingo Derby.

Next day, we ship out. Then it's smooth sailing all the way to California."

Thelma's shoulders fell. Had Kathleen convinced her? She'd have to bring Lillian on board otherwise, and she had no intention of doing that.

Out front, Kathleen deposited the girl in the valet's care, who turned and smiled at the bill she offered. "My driver will be here shortly. See she gets into my car safely."

"I will," the attendant said, touching her fingers to the brim of her cap.

SIXTEEN

FLAMINGO DERBY

THE MORNING SUN BLANKETED THE SKIES IN TANGERINE, but in the shade of the loading dock, the air was remarkably chilly. The girls shuffled on their feet, still in their curlers, smoking and quiet. Kathleen exhaled when she counted Thelma among them, promptly forgetting to be annoyed that she and Peggy were smoking.

"Where's Bertie?"

Her husband's question jarred her. Alighting from the Cadillac, Kathleen looked around. If the bus was there, their boy had to be there somewhere.

"Mom! Dad?" Bertie yelled as he charged from the store. Mystery solved. "What're you doing here?"

"That's a fine good morning, son." Lloyd shook his head and moved to help the girls board.

Kathleen, at once dismayed and charmed by her eldest child, didn't stop to wonder why he'd been in the store or why he'd been surprised to see his parents. She did, however, have opinions about how he should comport himself.

"Bertie, this is opening day at the Tampa Downs. Everyone who's anyone will be at the Flamingo Derby today. Couldn't you have worn your sport coat instead of this varsity jacket?" Without waiting for an answer, she waved him away from the bus. "Help your father get the girls on board."

"Mo-o-om. How'm I ever gonna be in charge if you never let me run anything?"

How to explain that leadership could not be conferred, only earned? But Kathleen couldn't force the realization either. "Your time will come, sweetie."

As the Crossley chugged to life on Gandy Boulevard, Kathleen tuned out Lloyd's pep talk. The only person she cared about seeing that day was Salvatore Giancarlo. It was time to find out what that stunt at the Million-Dollar Party was going to cost the Youngs.

"May I have this seat?" Lloyd asked, breaking her spell. This was the first thing he'd ever said to her, and they replayed the conversation often.

"I don't mind if you do," she replied. "But my boss is gonna expect an order. And a tip."

He reached for her hand. "You look spectacular. We didn't need all these girls to sell our new line. You're knocking it out of the park."

He knew how to soothe her. Everything was going to be fine. They just had to get to Carlsbad.

ONCE THE GIRLS WERE SET UP IN THE DRESSING ROOM, Kathleen headed for the weighing room. Normally, there was power in letting your target come to you, but she wanted Salvatore off guard. She dipped into her bag for her compact, checked her hair and lipstick, then applied a daub of Bandit behind her ears. Her emerald dress highlighted the gold flecks in her eyes, while the salmon-colored neckline made the outfit appear revealing from a distance. Now, she was battle ready. Or so she thought till she reached the gate.

"I ain't got no broads on this list," said the guard.

"But..." Kathleen blinked slowly and tilted her face toward the floor, lifting only her eyes. "Mr. Giancarlo asked me to meet him here today." This was mostly true, though the invite had been to his box and not this sacred prerace area, the final stop before the race for horses and jockeys and owners alike.

Luck intervened.

The crowd parted just so, and there stood Sal, staring almost directly at her. She waved then tossed her hair, bringing Sal right to her.

He waved the guard away. "Come in, come in."

All smiles. "You know how to make a girl feel welcome." Kathleen had to take a moment, assaulted as she was by sawdust and horse scent. She'd been a fool to waste the perfume. Still, she counted on her disingenuity to sail right over his head. "I am so sorry to bother you here, but I'll be with the girls all day."

"It's no problem." Sal took Kathleen by the elbow and escorted her behind a column, out of view from the action. "I don't see Little Caesar taking the purse today. But ya never can tell, right?"

Leaning against the pillar, Kathleen jutted her hip just so, accentuating her curvy frame and hoping to appear agreeable, though for the life of her, she could not comprehend the appeal of gambling or horses. Her grandparents had kept a mule that bit, and that was as close to horses as she wanted to come. As for gambling, she worked too hard to throw her dollars away.

"Lemme cut to the chase," Sal said.

Close as they stood, Kathleen noted not a single stray hair in Sal's nose or brow. When in doubt, she relied on a version of the truth. "I like your style."

"I asked you to see me because of the new girl. Whatcha call her? Thelma something?"

Her again. "Miss Miles?"

"Yeah, that was it. I want her reserved. For me."

Kathleen made every effort to keep her face blank while swallowing the revulsion she felt. Lloyd may've had fifteen years on her, but Sal had at least twice that on Thelma. And was he aware Matteo had already staked his claim? She opened her mouth, intending to agree, but the words would not form. Again, the silence served.

Sal raised his chubby, squat-fingered hand. "I heard Matteo likes her. But that's what I want. In return for bailing you out at that party."

Kathleen clamped her mouth shut. Hadn't Matteo made the show-stopping contribution? Did it matter? She'd feared he wanted a bigger footprint for his beloved Bolita game. Hadn't she already sacrificed Thelma? At last, her mouth formed around the words "Of course."

Sal patted her on the chest, just shy of fresh. "Atta girl."

"You do realize we leave tomorrow, yes?"

"Yeah, sure. Send her over to the Lotus Club tonight," he said, now patting his midsection with relish. "And one more thing."

Kathleen's stomach dropped. *Let them perform first, at least.*

But that wasn't what he had in mind.

"Las Vegas?" Kathleen was dumbfounded. What was there but a few dusty casinos? "What would they do there?"

"We're building a place out there," he said. "A good photo will get attention, like what you did with the Florida Girls. That photo was everywhere."

It was no use explaining there was no news value in such an image. Besides, it would be the last stop of the tour. "Can do, Sal. We aim to please."

Less than an hour later, the Florida Girls had raised another forty thousand dollars and some change for the war effort, and Kathleen set about Sal's mission.

* * *

ON THE HEELS OF THE FLORIDA GIRLS'S SECOND SUCCESS, chatter in the women's room reached a near-deafening level. Then Mrs. Young appeared at the door, pay envelopes in hand. A hush fell.

"Congratulations, girls, you knocked it out of the park! It's all over the radio waves."

She began passing out the envelopes.

"Some of you have been docked for missing weight goals. Hattie May, you went over. Helen, you've lost weight. Thelma, your pay has been reduced because we've had to remove stains from some of your clothes. We're done for the day, but remember, tomorrow is an early departure. I expect to see you at the Emporium, packed and ready at six."

Thelma was bent over her envelope, counting, when she felt a hand on her shoulder.

"My dear."

She looked up at Mrs. Young. *Dear?* This couldn't be good.

"Come with me."

Mrs. Young shuffled Thelma into a deserted gift shop and got right to business. "Did I hear you went to the Lotus Club the other night?"

Thelma froze. "Wasn't that at your request?"

"Don't be smart with me. Yes or no will do."

"Yes."

"Was it a *date*?"

"Whatever are you asking, Mrs. Young?"

"Let's not be crass. You understand my meaning."

"You want updates on my love life?"

"It's in your contract. Read the fine print."

Thelma fluttered her lips. Bad old habit. "Matteo Giancarlo invited me, but I only spent a few minutes with him. Something came up."

"Good. Drop him."

Thelma grinned. "Delighted to." Before her boss could change her mind, she added, "Now, if you'll excuse me, we have to clear the ladies."

"We're not done."

What more could she want?

"Salvatore Giancarlo, you met at the sanitation fleet christening?"

"The Tampa dump?"

"Mmm. Well, he wants to see you tonight at the Lotus Club. He wants..." Mrs. Young paused. "An *exclusive* arrangement with you."

Before she could reply, Mrs. Young patted Thelma on the shoulder. "Good girl." She hastened to the door. "Hurry. You mustn't keep people waiting!"

Rage burned inside Thelma, but she refused to show her boss this time. Much as Mrs. Young had going for her, she was oblivious to goings-on under her nose. The Giancarlos. Bertie. Obvious as their shady dealings were to Thelma, she doubted her boss had the faintest clue.

A voice sounded over a tinny loudspeaker. "May I present, in his first race, Milk Shake!"

The crowd moved toward the track, and so did Thelma. She'd seen plenty of equines around Keokuk but nothing like these sleek and powerful creatures. She moved closer to the sound of their hooves on the track then, with a panic, saw that nearly fifteen minutes had elapsed.

Racing back to the dressing room, she found herself amidst a knot of men jostling for position around a small ring where the bookies inspected the merchandise prerace and made side bets. That was when she knocked headlong into Bertie.

"Hey, watch—"

"Bertie?" He was gambling?

"Thelma?" Bertie's face went crimson. "What're you doing here?"

"Save it," Thelma said. "We should both be somewhere else." But Thelma doubted Bertie was truly needed anywhere.

Recalling their rendezvous now, she looked toward the dusty, peeling rafters. Vivian spoke loud and clear. "Why are you taking orders from the likes of these?"

Her mother was right.

She'd do Salvatore one better. Instead of meeting at his convenience, she'd head to the club straightaway.

SEVENTEEN

BAG MAN BERTIE

Wiggle wiggle
Ooh, wee!
What's that I see?
Got to be jelly
What you say?
Must be jelly
No way!
Don't you see?
Got to be jelly 'cause jam don't shake
    like that

Listeners, those were the dulcet sounds of our very own
Florida Girls, singing their rendition of Glenn Miller's
"Jam Don't Shake like That." Readying for their cross-
country tour, raising dough for our doughboys, soon
they'll be cutting rugs from Jacksonville to New York
City, Chicago, and all the way to Cal-i-FOR-NIGH-A.
Here's to hoping our girls take home the Hollywood prize
and score big on the big screen.

Remember, folks, you heard it here at WTSP, thanks to friends like the fine folks at Sun City Emporium, where—have you heard?—Doc Young has just the thing for listeners worried about tummy rolls—Forever Young! Glow with health while you reset your waistline and stay... Forever Young!

Now to explain America's favorite pastime, two of America's favorite funnymen, Abbott and—

LLOYD REACHED ACROSS THE SOFA TO SHUT OFF THE Radiola, the look on his face filling Kathleen with joy.

"Now, that's what I'm talking about," he said. Grabbing his highball, Doc held it out for a toast. "Brilliant idea to record the girls."

They clinked as the door clattered. "That better be Albert."

"Now, Pepper. Remember what we talked about. We ask questions first. He is eighteen."

"Exactly. A donkey has better sense. He can't just disappear like that. Especially on a *tour.*"

"Hey, Mom. Dad." It was Archie, struggling with his trombone case.

"Darling." Kathleen took in her youngest, the copper-haired son so thoughtful and sweet. He was more like the grandfather he'd never met, whereas Bertie was more like his callous uncle. "What brings you home at this hour?"

"It's almost five, Mom. Band rehearsal is over."

Another ruckus sounded at the door. She'd been hoping to speak to Bertie alone. "Archie, I'm sure you have homework. Your father and I—"

Bertie rushed into the room. "Didja hear?"

"Archie, be a love and go to your room, please?"

"What did I do?" Archie asked.

"Do as your mother says and save the bellyaching."

As his brother turned to go, Bertie asked again, "So, didja?"

Kathleen was not sure she wanted to learn news that had Albert as its source. "Darling, please try to enunciate. You'll never make a mark if you can't be clear."

"Did. You. Hear?"

"Enough with this nonsense, son. We're not interested in gossip. Where did you disappear to this afternoon? Your mother and I had to do your job."

"You cannot simply abandon the bus, to say nothing of the Girls, while we're on tour."

"I'm not going on the tour."

Husband and wife shared a look before Kathleen looked up at her son, but now was not the time for questions. "Sit."

He complied.

"Of course you're going on the tour. We've been working toward this—"

"You guys, you're not listening. This is business. It's about Matteo Giancarlo. I saw him at the track. His number came up. He ships out next Tuesday."

Now, that was news. Bertie had no idea his II-A deferment had been helped along by Salvatore Giancarlo, but everyone assumed Matteo would never serve. How had this happened?

"I want to run the Bolita games."

"Albert DeVane Young!" The idea of Bertie running the games filled Kathleen with dread. "Don't be ridiculous. Mr. Giancarlo will appoint someone. And it won't be you."

"Don't s'pose you've noticed, Mom, but there's kind of a shortage of men with the war on. Besides, we've already talked about it."

"We who?" she asked but then realized with a sickening lurch what he meant. Since when was Salvatore Giancarlo *we*?

Kathleen looked at her husband. He was nodding. "Lloyd?"

"Son, why don't you let your mother and I talk?"

Kathleen could not believe what she was hearing, or seeing, as her son trod dutifully to his room.

"More whiskey, Pepper?"

She put her hand over her glass. "Button, you can't seriously be considering this."

Placing his drink on the coffee table beside his wife's, Lloyd reached for Kathleen's hands. "Albert has to start somewhere if he's going to take the reins for the whole operation."

Her husband was right, of course. But Bertie and his brother were a scant two years apart. She'd always envisioned them jointly at the helm, with Archie running the show like she did, while Bertie was out front, like his father.

"He'll run Sun City eventually, but isn't the whole goal of this tour to pay off the Giancarlo loan and rid the store of those games? I don't want the boys involved with the Giancarlos."

"Is it? Sure, we don't want to be forever in debt, but those games make real money. And we agree they're harmless. It's pulling numbers out of a *bag*."

"But they are not the future. We're doing everything we can to build this city and modernize. Those games cater to a different type of client than the ones we're trying to attract."

Lloyd nodded, slowly enough that Kathleen could tell he disagreed. "Pepper, my love. Until our spa is up and running in California, the only business we have is a discount emporium. Besides, the boy's already talked to Sal."

Kathleen withdrew her hands and crossed her arms. She wasn't as angry as she was frustrated. If Lloyd didn't have damn smoker's lung, she'd insist he sub for the bag man. Even if that scenario could work, Button was right about Bertie. It made sense for him to stay behind and take more responsibilities around the store but not to ratchet up his involvement with speculation games. She wasn't ready to concede.

Rising, Kathleen turned toward her husband. His skin had a slight pink to it. If she didn't know better, she might think fighting was good for his health. She kissed his forehead.

"I'm going to draw a bath and then go to bed. I'll pack in the morning. Maria's left ham salad in the fridge." She stopped in the hallway leading back to the bedrooms. "Oh, I almost forgot. Sal's added another command performance."

"What? You leave tomorrow."

"Right. It's in Las Vegas. After the Memphis Belle."

"The divorce capital of the world? Why the heck...?"

"I believe he's investing in another nightclub. More gambling."

Lloyd sat up straighter.

"Button, no. We are not investing in more gaming ventures. We are committing to grow the business that serves us best, health and leisure."

Lloyd relaxed back into the sofa. "Goodnight, Pepper. Enjoy your bath."

Everybody knew the women went to resorts to take the waters, and the men went to gamble. Everybody except Kathleen.

Like many women of means, Kathleen Young had grown up in a world where nefarious characters hobnobbed among the elite, moving in political circles and supporting charities like their Million-Dollar Party. Though she'd been the one to convince Lloyd to work with the Giancarlos, he'd no trouble taking to their ways to grease the wheels of industry.

EIGHTEEN

VICTORY RED

A car to the Lotus Club would've been cheaper from the racetrack than the Emporium, and after Bertie pulled his disappearing act, Thelma really didn't want to get back on the bus. But Thelma didn't want to arouse more suspicion among the troupe.

Clad in the gray worsted-wool travel suit she'd first worn to St. Petersburg, Thelma felt ready to take on Giancarlo. Years of pawing through *Modern Screen* and *Hollywood Stars Parade* had taught her how to dress for a role, and this was the perfect businesswoman foil. Where did these men get the idea she was theirs for the taking? Thelma was keen to disabuse the old man of that notion in person, though she chain-smoked three cigarettes on the way.

When they pulled up to the palm-lined drive, however, Thelma noticed the Lotus Club sign wasn't lit. There were no people about. The place wasn't open. What if Giancarlo wasn't there? What if he was home with his family on a Sunday evening?

Then she laughed out loud—nerves. Even if he wasn't there

yet, she knew he would be. Mafia business was always brisk on a Sunday night.

Thelma paid her fare and faced the club in the afternoon sun, this time taking in the details. The building—styled like a Southern mansion, complete with a wraparound porch—took up an entire city block. Enormous potted ficus trees guarded the entrance like sentries, and the fan-shaped detailing in the iron railing matched the door handles. There was even a red carpet. But the door was locked.

She stopped to listen for any signs of activity, but traffic on Franklin Street drowned out all other noises. A walk surrounded the building like a moat, so traversing the perimeter seemed the next logical step. Her impetuousness niggled. Surely, there was some special knock. What had she been thinking?

Thelma had made it all the way to the rear exit when she spied another lit sign, albeit far less grand than the one out front. It read simply, Service. And the door was wide open. Maybe she was going to pull this off.

The flash of a navy-checked jacket caught her eye.

"Step aside, miss," called a man carrying an enormous leather case.

The evening's entertainment was arriving. *What luck*, thought Thelma as she slipped right in. But her elation lasted only a moment. To her left, a checkerboard floor headed toward a kitchen. Straight ahead, the hallway led into the ballroom. She knew that Matteo's lair was accessed through a staircase at the back of that room, but where was Sal's office? The basement office hadn't appeared to be a shared space.

Then to her right, she noticed a narrow, unassuming staircase that led to a second floor. A door must've opened, for down the steps wafted the sickly sweet smell of cigars mixed with something like a fruity cream soda, Sal's cologne. Grabbing for the narrow railing, Thelma began to climb.

The hall at the top of the steps was dark as well, but Thelma could make out a set of double doors upholstered in red leather, with portholes ringed in brass that matched the half-circle push plate on each. The glass was etched with the words Club Room.

Thelma pushed one open, only to be stopped by two young toughs just inside an anteroom—doors upon doors upon doors.

"Hey, who're you?" asked the shorter, heavyset kid, the one Thelma imagined had something to prove.

She waved him off, figuring arrogance was the way forward. "Sal asked for me."

"Yeah," said his lanky other half, stepping between Thelma and the second door. "I bet he did."

They jeered.

"It's business."

"Sure it is," Arrested Development cooed. "But ya can't wait here."

"That's fine. I've no intention of waiting. Tell him Miss Thelma Miles is here. From Sun City Emporium."

"Everybody waits," the tall punk said, jutting his acne-spotted chin at her.

Thelma crossed her arms. "Fine."

Now, the fireplug stepped up and pushed his belly at her. "Downstairs."

Before he could touch her, she swiveled on her heel. "I said fine." And she marched back down the stairs.

THE GAL BEHIND THE BAR OFFERED THELMA A RUM AND Coke, but she wasn't about to start drinking now. Her mother really went downhill when she started drinking on top of the Nembutal. Or was it later, when sometimes alcohol was the only anesthetic Thelma could find? Regardless, she should keep her wits. "Just the Coke, please."

A few sips in, she realized she needed the powder room.

"Ladies' is just off the lobby." The bartender pointed.

"If they come looking for me—" Thelma cut herself off. *"Don't be easy to define. Let them wonder,"* her mother would've said. "Tell 'em they can wait."

Thelma wasn't sure, but she thought she read approval in the barkeep's smile.

At the mirror, Thelma took a good look. Even plain-faced, she appeared more mature than her eighteen years, but it never hurt to apply lipstick. She uncapped her favorite tube of Bésamé, only to drop it in the sink a moment later when a glamorous woman appeared beside her.

"Ya dropped something," she said.

Thelma scrambled for the broken tube. "I'm sorry. I—"

Thelma knew she was gushing but couldn't help herself. Between the woman's flaming red hair, half-moon eyebrows, and chunky gold bracelet with the necklace to match, she made an impression. What on earth was this starlet doing in Tampa? "I've seen your picture. You're in the movies!"

"Flattery like that'll get you everywhere," she smirked, pulling a small ivory comb from her black accordion-style handbag.

"*Manpower!* From 1941. That's it!"

"I gotta hand it to you, kid. That's pretty good."

Well, she had fed Thelma a line from the movie. "I knew it!"

The woman pulled out her own tube of lipstick and offered it to Thelma. "Looks better on you."

Thelma looked down and saw the same Victory Red. "Oh, I couldn't possibly—"

"Kid, you gotta learn when to say yes," she said, planting the lipstick on the counter between them. "Most people won't offer twice."

Before turning away from the mirror, the woman pulled another tube out of her bag, a more muted red that Thelma had to agree was a more flattering shade.

"But..." Thelma began, speaking to her companion's reflection in the mirror, "thank you, uh... I can't quite recall your name."

"Virginia. Virginia Hill."

Of course. How had Thelma not made the connection? *Manpower* was the only film she'd ever been in, and it was a bit part. Hill was recognizable from the celebrity rags she appeared in on the regular, always on the arm of one man or another—all made men, as Thelma recalled.

"Thank you, Miss Hill. Golly, you are more beautiful in person than in those magazines," Thelma began, feeling more courageous addressing the image in the mirror. Besides, it wasn't a complete falsehood. Only it wasn't beauty Hill exuded so much as raw sexual energy. "I wonder: do you have any tips for dealing with a man like Salvatore Giancarlo?"

Hill smirked. "What are ya, deef?"

Thelma knitted her brows.

"Know when to say yes."

To Thelma's surprise, a surge of grief spiked in her chest, making her eyes water. Up till now, she'd been propelled by a sense of righteousness, the idea that being right would matter. She hadn't come this far to end up in the same place she'd started, a service girl catering to the whims of men around her. But who was she fooling?

Hill had been in the movies and mattered enough to have her picture taken. Yet here they both were.

"Geez, kid, I'd make the world spin another way if I could, but..." She lifted her shoulders and frowned.

Thelma turned to face Hill, pinching the skin on her forearm to compose herself. She'd worked so hard to break free from the criminal world. "I cannot go back to that life."

At this, Hill nodded and shifted her weight to her back foot. Placing one hand on her hip and stroking the fox stole at her shoulders with the other, she asked, "Who said anything about yer old life? You think I grew up with furs? I came up in a one-room shack with a dirt floor."

Thelma opened her mouth, but no words came.

"Careful, you'll catch flies that way."

Thelma snapped her jaw shut.

Hill pulled her fur tighter. "Anybody can escape their past. Smart girls use it." She turned but stopped in the doorway and looked back. "All they see is your gams, kid. They never see you coming."

Then she was gone.

SAL'S OFFICE WAS SMALLER THAN THELMA EXPECTED, smaller than Matteo's. Or maybe the furniture took up too much room. Every item came with a flourish, from the brass tacks on the club chairs flanking the Oxblood leather couch, to the dark-green velvet draperies with scalloped valances, sheers, and blinds, to the faux Tiffany lampshades appointed with palm leaves. Even the air hung heavily with something that smelled like cream soda. She must've pulled a face.

"You like that? It's Florida Water. Doc orders it special for me," Sal said, his manner almost beseeching. Given that her only experience with men had come through her mother's clientele, supplication was not what she was expecting. What if Virginia Hill was right?

Sal stood and motioned toward the club chair. "Thelma, I'm so glad you could make it." He was smiling like some kind of moron. "Please. Have a seat."

Or maybe this was how it went with men who had real money, unlike the clients of her mother's whom she'd had the misfortune of knowing more intimately. Those lampshades were custom.

"I'd rather stand."

Sal whistled. "Not very cordial."

"Mr. Giancarlo, I have every intention of fulfilling my professional duties for Sun City Emporium, but I will not be tossed from father to son in a game I never agreed to play in the first place."

"Whoa there, girlie! This is no game. You cannot date my son."

"I'll date whomever I please!"

"I'll sit down, then," Sal said, plopping into his chair.

Now she'd done it. She'd gone and left the impression she wanted to date Matteo when, in fact, she never wanted to have to be in a room with either of them. But if she could get out of dating the old man, losing his son would be no problem. She leaned forward and put her fist on the desk. "Now, see here. Who I date's none of your business. Got it?"

"You're tough." He smiled. "I like that."

"Well, I don't mind if you do or don't. I—"

"Don't get the wrong idea. A little less talking suits you."

"Of all the nerve!"

"Can I get you a drink?" Sal asked, rolling sideways on his wingback chair toward a bar cart beside his desk.

"No. I don't drink, thank you."

Sal stopped midroll. "So you do have some manners."

"If you're trying to get on my good side—"

"I'm trying to figure if you got a good side besides that beautiful mug."

Thelma straightened, smoothing the front of her skirt. Shucking him off was easier than she could've dreamt. "Well, then." She turned to leave, but Sal—moving with astonishing speed for his size—inserted himself between her and the door. He could crush her easily. She reeled back.

"A drink might do you some good."

She crossed her arms and frowned. "I'm quite sure there's nothing I can help you with."

"Aww, c'mon. Don't be sour."

"I'm sure I don't know what you're on about, Mr. Giancarlo."

"Call me... Well, we'll get to that."

How was it possible to be so accustomed to getting your own way you dictated even the terms of endearment? She looked down at her peek-a-boo Oxfords. Were they too flirty?

"Thelma, I... I was real sorry to hear about your mother."

Her head shot up. "My mother?" What did he know about her mother?

"Vivian was..." He trailed off.

Vivian? He knew her mother's name? "I don't know what you think you know, mister. But I will not listen to you—"

"Thelma, I'm your father."

"Sir, I insist—"

"When I seen you at the collection services event, I had my guys do some digging. Your mom hid good. But I knew you looked familiar. Those eyes..."

Thelma looked down at his right hand and for a second time was struck by the chunky gold pinky ring with the bloodred emerald-cut stone he wore. The same ring had torn a chunk of flesh from her face before sending her reeling across the living room.

Touching her cheek, she looked back into his face. "I hate you!" she screamed.

Now it was Sal's turn to reel. Thelma took the opportunity to reach for the door handle... and run.

NINETEEN

THE TOUR BEGINS

December 11, 1944
Dearest George,

THELMA LOOKED OUT THE CROSSLEY'S DUSTY WINDOW TO watch rows of orderly citrus groves roll past. She'd no idea Florida was this green. Vivian only ever spoke of the sand, the sun, and the ocean.

She thought about filing her nails, but she'd just tucked her nail file back in her bag. Though she wouldn't have known what to call it, Thelma had writer's block.

At Keokuk High, they'd written letters to soldiers on the front, and those letters went out to strangers. *The weather's been dry; the Chiefs won again; we'll be here when you're back...* None of that applied, not even the weather. What could she say? Certainly not what she was thinking.

Apparently, my father is the head of the Tampa Mafia, and now that he's found me, he wants to bring me into the fold. But I won't be his prisoner like my mom was. Even after we escaped, we were never free.

Even the tour felt taboo to write about.

The road show is going gangbusters. After stops in Ocala and at Camp Blanding, we've cut out all the fluff from the Million-Dollar Party routine. Now it's all medleys of bawdy tunes like 'Boys in the Backroom' alongside sentimental songs like 'We'll Meet Again.' Even Hattie May's tap solo is more suggestive. My work as a call girl comes in handy here. I know just how to flirt behind the mic—I've become the master of ceremonies!

But already, she'd gotten a letter from George. He'd sent it before leaving town. Mrs. Collins, the old sourpuss at The Soreno, handed it over after she paid her rent. She'd obviously read it too. But all he'd written, "Still wiping the ice cream from my chin, and I miss you already. Shipping out tomorrow."

The note wasn't much of a guide. She did not miss him, she was sure. But she couldn't stop thinking about him. Because of Doris. He'd been so gallant in coming to her rescue, even if Doris hadn't given any indication she remembered anything about that night. Still, she'd made a promise to herself, and keeping her own word meant keeping George sweet. Just in case.

The road show is going gangbusters! They've already added more stops.

Thelma tried to recall which town was next, but beyond the contours the itinerary details blurred. They'd hug the coast and head north, stopping at various military bases and making additional "special appearances" Mrs. Young could book along the way. Near as Thelma could tell, what was "special" about those appearances was that they weren't connected to the military fundraising, more like straight-up, money-making vaudeville shows.

Peggy shifted, and Thelma crushed her writing paper into her handbag.

"War?" her friend asked, producing a deck of cards.

"Why not?"

She and Peggy moved to the table, joining Helen and Doris.

Turning cards over as quickly as possible, they collected hands till a match appeared, and Thelma cried, "War!"

Counting together as they placed the cards—"one, two, three, flip!"—they repeated the process until Thelma ran out of cards. Then did it again. And again.

"Ach! You win again. You have a real knack for this game, Pegs. I'm out."

Peggy cracked her gum and shuffled the deck. "Anyone else?"

Millie looked up from filing her nails. "No, thanks."

Helen was reading a magazine. "Lemme finish this."

"Hey." Thelma grabbed the magazine out of her hands. "That's the latest issue of *Screen Sirens*. Where'd you get that?" It was one of her favorites, and she hadn't seen it anywhere in St. Pete.

Doris's eyebrows shot up. "Ooh! They have the best horoscopes!"

Thelma looked at the rag in her hands. "They do?"

"Read mine!" Doris said.

Helen snatched back her periodical. "Everybody knows that." She thumbed to the back. "Mine first!" Instead of reading aloud, she frowned. "Make me a liar."

"What's it say?" Doris asked.

Exhaling audibly, Helen fluttered her lips. "Pisces. 'You prize honesty and justice and make an obedient and complying wife, but enemies beware. This month, you make an even more formidable opponent. If traveling, go south of your birthplace. Keep on high, dry ground.'"

"Eww. That is a dud," Doris grabbed the magazine. "Let's see. Cancer. 'This month, your stars favor honest endeavor.'" Doris grimaced as she read on in an exaggerated fashion. "'Manufacture of needed commodities, farming, dealing in livestock, and machinery are for you. Spending needlessly, or gambling are taboo. Don't abuse digestive system.'"

Peggy grabbed the magazine. "I'm a Taurus."

"No surprise there." Helen laughed.

Thelma felt like she was watching a film in a foreign language.

"'Don't harness yourself to one line of thinking or action. Be open to improved methods as change is necessitated by emergency. Embrace new ventures, and you will find new opportunities in work and in love.'" Peggy looked up. "That's a real humdinger. I'm ready for some new opportunities in love. What do you say, Thelma?"

Thelma's cheeks flushed. Was she supposed to answer that? She found this exercise uncomfortably revealing, even if no one else seemed to.

"What's your sign?" Peggy asked, mercifully off the subject of men.

That, Thelma could answer truthfully. "You know, I don't know."

Helen lifted her elbow to the table to rest her chin on her knuckles. "When's your birthday?"

"September thirtieth," she said reflexively, unaware what the information had to do with horoscopes.

"That makes you a Libra," Helen said.

"It's... Oh, you'll be a convert now," Peggy harrumphed before launching into a pitch-perfect imitation of private eye Richard Diamond. "'It's tops for you in all aspects although recklessness should not be mistaken for courage. Avoid the dangerous distractions of money, pleasure-seeking, and rash excess, and the big prize is just around the corner!' Ha! If plea-sure-seeking and rash excess isn't the big prize, I'll take the little prize."

Millie appeared, grabbed the copy of *Screen Sirens*, and sat opposite. "My turn," she squealed. "Virgo, okay. 'Several'—oh God, I regret this already." She laughed. "'*Unfavorably* situated planets suggest great care to avoid needless losses... mistakes... bungling situations. Familiar matters favored?'" She was whis-pering by the time she got to the last line. "'Untried ventures require more care.'"

"Excuse me." Millie dropped the magazine and scooted around the bench.

Thelma slid into the aisle so Millie could leave the table, nearly bumping into Hattie May in the process.

"Watch it," Hattie May said, breaking the spell as she dropped into the seat Millie had just vacated. "What's with her?"

Peggy moved on to a game of solitaire, Helen pulled out a book, *Paris Underground*, and Doris returned to her nails.

When no one responded, Thelma reached for the magazine, thrilled this game was over and eager to devour the latest cellu-loid news.

* * *

KATHLEEN WAS BESIDE THE TRUCK'S FLATBED, WATCHING the crowd when it happened. She missed the incident but was unsurprised when Hattie May ran past her in tears. Thus far, their shows had been a roaring success, helped along by radio stations that played their hit, "Jam Don't Shake Like That." Hattie May's increasing petulance made it obvious she felt excluded.

"So like I was saying," she heard Thelma cajoling the crowd

at Camp LeJeune, "if you want to be a real showstopper on the dance floor, if all else fails, practice your high scream."

By the time she was asking what they'd miss most from home, the boys' wallops suggested the interruption was either forgotten or assumed to be part of the show.

Forcing herself to move toward the bus, Kathleen considered her approach. Of course she'd dock her pay for abandoning a performance, but the girl wasn't motivated by money. Hattie May was curled into herself on a seat, her back facing Kathleen. She put her hand on her shoulder. "Leaving a show like that makes it hard to give you more stage time. You know that, right?"

Hattie May turned her tearstained face in Kathleen's direction. "He reached into my shirt!" she yowled, yanking away from her boss.

What was this girl on about? "Who?"

"The boy I was teaching the Lindy Hop."

"Are you sure? Could it have been an accident? Were you doing your high kick off a twirl? I bet he was confused."

"He squeezed my bare... You *know*."

But hesitation had lodged in Hattie May's cornflower eyes. Kathleen would take that as a success. She couldn't have the girl leaving the tour over something so trivial. Her role as a chaperone would be called into question. As far as she was concerned, this was a valuable life lesson for the girl.

"Darling, boys will be boys. You must learn to comport yourself when you're dancing with them, or this won't be the last time something like this happens."

Hattie May crossed her arms and looked out the window as Kathleen heard a distinctive stomp. This situation had to be rescued forthwith. "What do you say we switch to the Charleston stroll? No touching. And you can keep dancing on stage."

"Hattie May!" Thelma came clomping down the aisle. "Are you okay?"

Kathleen looked at Hattie May and raised her eyebrows. Hattie May looked away but slumped against the window.

"She's fine," Kathleen called out. "Just a spider in her dress."

"Oh, thank heavens," Thelma said. "I thought that soldier got handsy."

That girl's mouth, thought Kathleen. "Let me do the thinking, dear."

TWENTY

FIELD REPORT 2

MEMORANDUM OF INTENT/EYES ONLY
SUBJECT: New contact Tampa Port
Recruitment
DATE: Dec. 18, 1944
AUTHORED BY: T. Nelson, Special
Services, ONA
TOPLINE: Initiate Operation Torch Light

IN DETAIL: WITH THE BATTLE OF THE BULGE UNDERWAY IN earnest, reports are that German spies will soon infiltrate U.S. borders by U-boat. We must activate our plan to monitor Tampa's strategic port as soon as possible. After clashing with Salvatore Giancarlo in Tampa, now known to us as the head of a crew of local gangsters, we identified another target in Albert Young, who handles the money for one of Giancarlo's lottery games run through his family's drugstore. The 18-year-old is II-A and has accrued significant debt to the Giancarlos.

RECOMMENDATION: REQUEST $50,000 HAZARD PAY TO motivate Young's participation in the port surveillance operation near the Giancarlo headquarters.

TWENTY-ONE

NEW YORK CITY

"Course ol' Miz Young would find economy lodging in New York City," Hattie May said, squinting into her own reflection.

Thank heavens Hattie May isn't our roommate, thought Thelma, narrowly avoiding rolling her eyes, which all the girls would've seen, the way they were lined up at the mirror. Though there was a bit of desilverizing on the mirror, the room was otherwise far larger and better appointed than anywhere she'd lived in since the house on Chicago's Grand Avenue. Their rooms had private baths, for crying out loud. Mrs. Young divvied them up between two rooms—Thelma, Peggy, and Helen in one and Millie, Doris, and Hattie May in another— and welcomed zero preferences. Clever pairings, Thelma had come to realize.

The only girls who could effectively shut Hattie May down were Doris and Millie. Besides, if the Youngs were scrimping, who could blame them? The tour had to be costing a fortune.

"It's the nicest place I've ever stayed," Thelma said.

"Oh yeah?" Hattie May said. "How many hotels have you stayed in?"

Thelma widened her eyes. "Matter of fact, plenty. Not that it's your business." She didn't think now was the time to mention she and her mother had lived in one; it wasn't the sort little Miss Harper would approve of anyway.

"Just shut it, McFatty, will ya? Even my fold-out cot is better than the bus," Peggy said.

Thelma looked at Pegs in the mirror. "Hey, I offered to take that."

"Hattie May, we both loved that place in Cincinnati, the Pont-whatchamacallit." Doris bounced in her seat.

"Sit still if you expect me to put waves in your hair without charring your face!" But Peggy's amused tone belied her harsh words.

"Mmm. I forgot about that one," Hattie May replied in a monotone. "The flatbed truck we played out of erased it from my mind."

Thelma was glad for every stinking, exhausting, exhilarating minute of the tour. It left her without time to think about Sal. She'd evaded him before the tour began, but that luck wouldn't last forever. For the time being, if people believed she was with him—she shuddered at the thought—they'd leave her alone. Other than her hair color, she looked nothing like her father. Growing up, she'd imagined recognizing her father on sight, whether gazing into a matching set of amber-colored eyes or feeling a soul connection. But no. All she'd felt was that burning in her palms, a foreboding sensation she'd been trying to ignore for years.

"They sure as heck didn't have the Andrews Sisters playing downstairs!" Doris chimed in, drumming her fingers on the dressing table.

Thelma looked at them all in the mirror, primping. For once, it wasn't for a show but a rare night out—or in, as it were.

To Thelma, the idea of taking an elevator to a club to see one of her favorite acts—a real rarity in those days, since they were often in Europe, performing for the troops—well, this was the height of elegance. She looked at the ceiling and smiled. *Don't worry, Vivian. I'll tell you everything.*

Then she looked back at the girls. Where was Millie? Usually, she was the first to escape her roommates and join them.

"I'm going to go check on Millicent," she told the girls.

"Take your purse," Peggy said, twirling her pointer finger. "I'm locking up when we leave the room."

With a mock salute, Thelma looped her pleated ruche handbag around her elbow then hurried down the hall. The show started at ten o'clock, and she didn't want to miss a minute. "Millie," she called out while knocking. There was no reply. "Millie!" Thinking shaking the door might rouse her friend, Thelma tried the handle. To her surprise, the door swung wide. *Rich girls.*

She heard a noise in the bath. That door was locked. "Millie? If you don't open the door this minute—"

A groan emanated from behind the locked portal. Panic seized at Thelma's gut. "Sweetie?" Thelma took a futile yank at the door handle. "Can you open the door?"

She heard a thud.

Thelma rushed to the phone between the twin beds. "I'm going to call downstairs," she called out over her shoulder, only to be greeted by another moan, one that sounded like protest. Was Millie trying to argue with this?

Once housekeeping was on its way, Thelma knelt by the bathroom door. "It'll just be a minute now." Thelma tried to sound comforting but was making a hash of things. Millie had begun crying. In an effort to hear better, Thelma cupped her hands around her ear, but that did nothing to improve the sound. Finally, there was a knock at the door.

"Oh, thank heaven you're—" Thelma almost slammed the door shut. "But you're... You're a man."

"Last time I checked," he said then wheezed at his own joke.

Now was not the time to stand on ceremony. When had she turned squeamish? Thelma moved to let him in. "Right this way."

From his pocket, the man pulled an enormous ring of keys. Thelma said a silent prayer that the old gent would find the correct one. He got it on the first try then stepped aside to let the girl open the door. This wasn't the first time he'd been called to these rooms.

Thelma shoved past the janitor to reach for the door, only to shriek for him a moment later. Millie's torso fell back into the room as blood seeped across the tile floor, her toes pointed upward.

After the briefest moment to register the situation, the old man sprang into action. "Ma'am? I'll get the doctor," he said, now moving with an agility Thelma would not have guessed he possessed.

Millie was caught between the toilet and sink, where she must've fallen. She caught Thelma's eye and held her with a beseeching glare then puckered her lips and put her finger to them. Before Millie shut her eyes, Thelma understood. She yelled out the door, "Hurry!" She'd seen this go wrong before.

Should I have told the girls more about myself? It wouldn't have been the first miscarriage Thelma had helped along. She scrabbled around the tile floor till she found the knitting needle she needed to dispose of, which had rolled under the clawfoot tub. She wrapped the offending object in tissue before shoving it into her bag. Turning back to Millie, Thelma took her head in her lap. "You're going to be fine—don't worry," she repeated, swaying back and forth. But as the minutes ticked by, she wasn't so sure.

TWENTY-TWO

THE FRENCH HOSPITAL

As soon as she saw the gurney being wheeled through the lobby, Kathleen knew the girls were in trouble.

"Bertie, darling, just stay sharp. It's only been a couple of weeks. These things take time." She lifted her jaw as her eyes followed the nurse's white stockings across the lobby. "We'll speak tomorrow."

Before the operator could ask for another nickel, Kathleen placed the heavy black earpiece back in its hook and pushed open the bifold panels of glass. But the elevator slid shut before she reached it, obscuring any view of which number the nurse had pushed. She crossed her arms and waited for the ding that would indicate its destination. *Third floor*, not *the girls*, she thought, exhaling a breath she didn't realize she'd been holding in.

Ding!

Son of a gun, the thing's still moving. Who's going out at this hour?

Then she noticed the knots of people gathering in the lobby and remembered the Andrews Sisters were playing Club Rouge. Everyone would be out. Looking back at the numbers overhead, she saw that five stayed lit. It was the girls. She ran to the stairs.

It's not necessarily the girls, she told herself. *There are plenty of other rooms on the fifth floor.*

But she knew better. The tour had been going too well. Sure, there'd been some tense moments: the business with Sal, Bertie taking over Matteo's job as bag man, and then that dreadful base in North Carolina. But the bus hadn't broken down, and they hadn't been stranded anywhere and missed a show. And as the Florida Girls' songs played on radio stations up the coast, the increase in their commercial bookings only made the enterprise more profitable.

So lost was she in her thoughts, she almost bumped straight into Thelma Miles, who stood in front of an open door.

"What are you doing standing there? You look like some kind of criminal."

Thelma jumped and whipped around. "Oh! Thank God you're here."

Without waiting for Thelma to explain, Kathleen squeezed past her and into the cramped room where, in addition to two twin beds and a folding cot, the two nurses she'd seen downstairs were strapping Millie Williams into their wheeled cart. The girl was pale as milk. "What the dickens?"

The stout one with short curly hair and a white safari-style helmet looked her up and down. "You in charge here?"

Kathleen nodded, unable to speak as the gravity of the situation became clear. Without bothering to introduce herself, the nurse spoke in quick, clipped tones. Kathleen heard the words "possible miscarriage" and "bleeding to death" and numbly backed out of the room to let them pass.

"The French Hospital is closest. It's walking distance," said the nurse as they rolled by. "Ask the concierge."

And they were gone.

Kathleen's mind reeled. Millie had introduced her to a young sergeant at the Million-Dollar Party; she'd refrained from reminding her they weren't supposed to have boyfriends. And anyway, considering what she'd done for love, she was in no position to judge. The rest of St. Petersburg, however, would not feel the same. The war had changed things, but the Williams political dynasty still insisted on the appearance of purity. She wondered why they hadn't just gone ahead and gotten married, then she remembered how Lloyd insisted the tour be comprised of only *single* girls.

Or maybe it wasn't the young sergeant's baby.

Scolding herself for thinking the worst, Kathleen got back to the task at hand. There was too much at stake. She would *not* allow this incident to derail the tour, especially now that they were in the home stretch. Now was the time to be methodical, contact the girl's mother, and—with as little fanfare as possible—reach out to Lillian Wright, which also meant calling Maeve. She needed her coat—

Thelma touched her arm.

Taking a half step back, Kathleen cocked her head and regarded Thelma as if seeing her for the first time. The slim, fitted silhouettes they'd had to adopt because of wartime fabric rationing really suited the girl.

"What?"

"Shall we walk over now? To the hospital?"

"We? No, dear. *We* are not going anywhere. Go on to the show. I'll take it from here."

Thelma frowned.

"Now, now. Your face will freeze that way. Millie just needs to recuperate in private. She's going to be fine. Come on. Off you go."

Thelma looked toward the elevator then back to Kathleen. "I'll be worried sick."

"Oh, but I wasn't asking, dear. But since I can't be at the show," she began, having spotted in Thelma a person who responded well to requests for help, "would you keep an eye on the girls? Make sure Peggy doesn't get too wild. And keep Hattie May out of trouble, please."

Thelma's hand flew to her chest. "Of course, Kathleen. I'd love to help you. The girls will understand—"

"Say nothing." Kathleen pointed her index finger as her tone changed from persuasion to force. "There's nothing to say right now anyway."

Thelma nodded then reached around Kathleen to grab her purse and tuck it protectively under her arm. Turning at the door, she said, "I won't say anything to Sal either."

The little trollop thought she was going to leverage her *relationship* with Sal? Rich. Kathleen would have to deal with her later.

As KATHLEEN MADE HER WAY WEST TOWARD THE HOSPITAL, she was glad for the Persian lambswool coat she never got to wear back home in Florida. The January evening was icy. She turned up the collar and hugged the fur close to her neck. She'd lost weight since Lloyd bought this for her as an anniversary present.

She thought back to Thelma's remark. On the one hand, she admired the gutsy play. She'd been forced into an unenviable position as Sal's paramour, so she was going to get something out of it. Good for her. Then again, the last thing they needed on this tour was an upstart. Hattie May was bad enough.

Damn that Millicent. What fresh hell had she brung?

They were set to meet with Maeve that weekend to freshen up their wardrobes, and now she was wondering how many shows she might have to cancel. This wouldn't be the end of the tour—that would bring far too much shame to the family. Better to simply say the girl had taken ill, then she could go on and marry her beau, and this would all be in the past. But she wished they would cancel Las Vegas. Kathleen shuddered to think of it and wrapped her mink collar tight.

"Hey, watch it," an angry young man barked as he clipped Kathleen's shoulder.

Stopping, arms akimbo, Kathleen was aghast. But the man kept up his pace. To her befuddlement, fine clothes were no match for this city's indifference. Then she realized her error—walking against traffic, a city sidewalk quirk she'd learned on her first visit when her mother had asked her to go and fetch her a sandwich, and Maeve had taken her to a nearby White Tower. "If ya don't walk wid traffic," Kathleen could still hear her saying, "yer liable to get hit." There was only one paved road in Richmond at the time, but at the earliest opportunity, she'd introduced this sidewalk etiquette rule to her friends back home.

Kathleen put her head down and pushed into the correct lane, the chill wind increasing as she headed toward Ninth Avenue. Kathleen hated hospitals, but of course she had to go.

Inside, the first thing to hit her was the smell, a putrid combination of urine and Lysol that reminded her of her grandfather's last days. The French Hospital was a dark, cramped space, heavy with furnishings, Oriental carpet, and wood-paneled walls—clearly, the Bavarian side of France, more Germanic than baroque. But she tucked her observation away to tell Lloyd later and approached the woman behind the desk in all seriousness.

"I'm looking for a Millicent Williams. She'd have just been admitted by ambulance."

The woman directed her to the emergency area, but the girl wasn't there either. Had she gone to the wrong address? Kathleen looked out a glass-paned door and spotted an ambulance van. The woman behind the wheel wore a dark suit with a tie with a pith helmet emblazoned with a red cross. She couldn't imagine it was the same ambulance, but maybe she would have some information.

"Oh, yeah. Check the morgue. Heard about her. From the hotel. That girl died," she said, rapid-fire, a beat before realizing she'd been callous. "I'm sorry."

Judas Priest, this'll make a hash of things, Kathleen thought. Also, a beat passed before she grasped how heartless her response was, but now was not the time for mulling. There were arrangements to be made. This business could bring them all to their knees.

TWENTY-THREE

THE OBIT

MILLICENT WILLIAMS DIES IN NEW YORK CITY HOSPITAL

The Sunshine City's Brightest Starlet has Dimmed

ST. PETERSBURG, FLA., Jan 4, 1945 — Little Millicent "Millie" Williams, the 18-year-old daughter of Mayor and Mrs. Herbert R. Williams and beloved fiancée of John McKaye and elder sister to Raymond, Berenice, and Tommy Williams, died suddenly after an aneurysm caused massive internal bleeding.
The news of her tragic death yesterday rippled through hearts across the country as she'd performed with the Florida Girls, a dance troupe raising funds for the war effort. Miss Williams, a beautiful singer, dancer, and musi-

cian, can still be heard on the Girls'
hit single, "Jam Don't Shake Like That."
She had not shown any previous signs of
illness and was preparing to continue on
the tour to California.

The shock was so severe for the Williams
and McKaye families that arrangements
have not been decided at press time. Mr.
Young sent a message of sympathy, stat-
ing: "Your daughter died serving our
country, and for that we all owe a debt
of gratitude. Mrs. Young and I grieve
with you in this loss."

He said also that the tour would resume
shortly.

THE GIRLS HAD GATHERED IN MILLIE'S ROOM, SILENT.
Smoking. Waiting for Mrs. Young.

The furnishings were identical to those in the other room,
but everything about this space felt different. Tainted.

Peggy stood, leaning against the bureau. Thelma and Helen
huddled with Doris on her cot, perpendicular to the room's twin
beds. Hattie May, linens a-jumble, reclined against her bed's
polished wooden headboard. The bed parallel was Millie's, its
white chenille bedspread still crisp, untouched by the horrors
mere steps away.

Despite being the only one who hadn't bothered to dress, in
her cream silk pajamas with navy piping and matching dressing
gown, gold ringlets framing her face, Hattie May could've been
in a magazine spread.

Fat tears rolled down Doris's cheeks. Helen looped an arm
around her shoulders but made no move to dry her eyes.
Thelma clicked her nails.

Sad as she was for Millie and the life she'd never have, Thelma couldn't mourn the girl. They'd worked well together these past weeks, but they weren't exactly close. She wouldn't admit it, but as soon as the Andrews Sisters took the stage, Thelma had successfully pushed Millicent to the back of her mind. Her more pressing concern was whether this would mean the end of the tour. Were the other girls thinking about it? She couldn't be the one to bring it up. But maybe she could broach it. *Honey, just keep a lid on it,* she heard Vivian Miles scold, a warning Thelma had heard plenty but often had trouble heeding.

Hattie May broke the silence. "I can't believe she got a write-up in the *New York Times!*" she said, slapping at the paper on her bedside table.

Thelma looked around the room, but no one objected. *"Rich people are weird,"* her mother always said. *"They can afford to be."*

"We should've called Mrs. Young when we couldn't find Millie," Doris said.

Before she could stop herself, Thelma let out a snort. She'd seen how Kathleen Young handled tragedy.

Hattie May straightened up on her bed and looked at Thelma. "What's that?"

Pressing an oxford into the carpet, Thelma kept her eyes on the floor. "I just... Mrs. Young told me to go to the show." She looked back up. "I didn't see anything."

"But when did the paramedics arrive?" Hattie May asked, sinking her teeth in. "Didn't you notice something was seriously wrong? Why did you not tell us? You acted as if nothing was amiss."

"Knock it off, Hattie McFatty." Peggy stubbed her cigarette into the ashtray then fixed her steely gaze on Hattie May. "What do you know about men?"

"What's that supposed to mean?" asked Doris.

"Dorry," Helen said, squeezing Doris's shoulder, "we all know what *embolism* means."

Doris took in a sharp inhalation, and her eyes widened. Thelma realized that, except for Doris, they all knew. And even she got it now, which meant this kind of thing happened outside the world she'd grown up in. In Keokuk, she'd seen plenty of women—women without the means for a hospital—survive the ordeal. It truly had not occurred to her that a rich girl could die the same way a poor one did. Now, she wondered how Millicent had even known what to do. Her view of the world beyond the flophouse had been shaped by the movies.

Thelma got up off the cot, put out her own cigarette, and turned to face the girls. "I thought she'd be fine. I'm sorry I didn't..."

But they'd stopped paying attention. Silence fell again like a pall.

"Kathleen must've fixed it," Hattie May finally said and took taking a languid drag off her unfiltered Camel.

Thelma looked around the room. "Fixed? Fixed what? What do you mean?" Did Millie's family know what really happened?

"You are a puzzle," Hattie May said. "So worldly and so... daft."

"Hattie May." Doris threw her a sharp look.

"Where were you when the bottle blonde over there was calling me McFatty?"

As the girls bickered, Thelma grasped what had unfolded. She'd never considered the newspaper covering the death of someone she knew. The women she'd known just... *disappeared*. But performing an abortion, even on oneself, would've made Millie a criminal. It was why she'd tried to hide the needle, though, apparently, it did no good. But this was also why this tour would not end. That kind of scandal would do more damage to the Williamses than the Youngs.

The door burst open behind Thelma. "Ladies," Mrs. Young's boomed in her unmistakable trill. "I see you've read the paper. I'm so terribly sorry." She stopped herself and squinted at Hattie May. "Whatever are you wearing?"

"It's my *sleep*wear," Hattie May protested, pulling her robe shut.

Taking in her boss's smart navy-fleck suit with off-white piping, the perfect victory rolls framing her expertly made-up face, it struck Thelma that Mrs. Young and Hattie May were like reverse mirror images.

Mrs. Young took in a breath, closed her eyes, and drew up her shoulders then shook her head. "Right. Well. You all know we've a job to do. Millie was a darling girl with a bright future. She had the world at her feet but joined us to support the war effort. And this is just how we show those Nazis. The last thing she said to me was that we must persevere."

She couldn't speak when I saw her last, Thelma thought. But what could she say now? At this stage, she was complicit.

"Now. The arrangements. I will fly home with Millicent tomorrow."

The image threw Thelma into a tailspin as Mrs. Young, with her typical cheery efficiency, laid out their itinerary for the coming days. *When did she organize it all?*

"But we'll have to cancel a few upcoming shows. I'm sorry to say, Thelma, that includes our Christmas show in your hometown, Chicago."

Thelma could not have been more delighted. As much as she'd dreaded what might've been waiting for her there courtesy of Sal, she'd since realized these girls would've sniffed out her lie. These girls probably had more experience with the city than she did; she was twelve the last time she'd seen the place. She tried to look downcast, but attempting to appear crestfallen on top of mournful, she suspected, only made her appear as if in gastric distress.

"Those of you attending the service will fly with me, of course. But you two"—Mrs. Young looked pointedly between Thelma and Peggy—"will accompany Mr. Smith in the Crossley to Indiana, where we'll resume our tour. Peggy, I'm holding you accountable for ensuring there are no further mishaps."

Their boss paused, looking sternly about the room.

"If no one has any questions, I'll see you after lunch for the walk to Maeve's dress shop. Mind you're ready at one forty sharp. I've too many arrangements for any nonsense."

Mrs. Young looked at her watch.

Thelma, whose head buzzed with questions, wondered at the lack of response. Maybe dressmakers and planes and funerals were normal for rich people.

Doris broke the silence. "After our fitting, would anyone like to go to church?"

Hattie May shrugged. "Mummy insists I visit Aunt Dodo and Uncle Reg," she said then reclined fully and buried herself under her covers.

Doris looked up at Peggy.

"Church?" she asked. "On my one trip to New York City? Are you nuts? Light her a candle for me, will ya?"

Helen squeezed Doris's shoulders. "Of course I will."

That left only Thelma, who'd never been inside a church and wasn't keen to start the habit. Her mother had no truck with such sentimentality, eschewing it even in death. In her final days, in one of her few lucid moments, she'd argued against any kind of funeral. "There's no money for a burial, but you can earn a little by selling this ol' bag of bones to Doc Ames at Culver Stockton. They'll see to everything." It may've been a fevered dream, but Thelma had followed her mother's request. They'd done the same for other women who never made it out of the call house.

Thelma shuddered then attempted to morph her gesture into a shrug. "I was hoping to see Times Square."

Hattie May pulled her blankets down. "Ooh, pick me up a box of cream candies from Schrafft's!"

Before Thelma could ask how she might accomplish such a feat, Peggy intervened. "Tch-tch. Remember weigh-in, Hattie May."

"Oh, bother. We're walking everywhere in this city. I tell you, if I lived here, I'd never have to worry about my waistline."

"Well, you could always try Forever Young!" Thelma cracked before she could stop herself.

The joke was like a dam breaking, and the girls all started speaking at once.

"Thelma, I didn't think you had it in you!"

"Speak for yourself!"

"I won't ever be old enough to drink that!"

In their relief from the oppressive morning, they'd forgotten Mrs. Young was still in the room.

"Girls!"

Thelma was mortified.

"Meet me in the lobby on time. Mind that you've had your lunch and are presentable."

Before their boss had even crossed the threshold, the girls' snickering grew into loud, nervous laughter. Had the tour escaped collapse again, or was it waiting around the corner?

HATTIE MAY DRAGGED DORIS OFF TO SOME STEAKHOUSE because she was just *dying* for their mutton chops, but Helen got out of it by saying she didn't eat meat; Thelma would never understand the upper crust.

Along with Peggy, they grabbed sandwiches and coffee at an automat in Herald Square. Thelma was glad for less company but couldn't stop thinking how money hadn't kept Millie safe. Their prisons looked different, but these girls were trapped all the same.

"Cat got your tongue?" Peggy interrupted her thoughts. "You're pretty quiet, but this?" She waved her hand. "Is a real bore."

"Knock it off," Helen said, looking up from behind her magazine. Thelma thought she looked smart in the wide-legged pants and jackets with epaulets, part of Sun City's spring line. "We can't be social butterflies all the time. Now. Who's got a pen? I'm gonna analyze us. According to this quiz, your menu technique reveals your personality."

"You can use my pen if you get me a coffee." Peggy grinned, producing a nickel from the slit pocket in her suit jacket.

"Lazybones!" Helen said, sticking out her tongue as she grabbed the coin and slid off her chair.

Peggy turned and narrowed her eyes at Thelma, leaning in close. "I've made an appointment at the birth control bureau," she whispered. "After Maeve's, I'm going to get fitted for a French pessary."

Thelma's mouth opened, but she didn't know what to say.

Peggy sat back. "After what just happened, I think you should come," she said in her regular voice.

Her concern touched Thelma. She might not know about Sal, but she'd seen what happened with Matteo. She went with the truth. "I have one."

Then Helen was back, placing a cup and saucer on the counter in front of Peggy. "Pen, please," she said, holding out her palm.

Clever as she was, reading the room was not her forte. She began to go through the quiz. "Mmm. Black coffee, Peggy? According to this, that means you've been kicked out of a diner before!"

"Helen," Thelma stopped her. "Would you just—"

Peggy held up a hand. "It's fine. Helen, I called the Sanger clinic. I'm going after the fitting."

"Oh, that's a good idea," Helen said. "Do you want me to come with you?"

Thelma was astonished. Did wealth and family make no difference in a woman's life? And what did Helen need with a diaphragm? "You want one too?" she asked.

"No, silly, you have to make an appointment." She turned to look at Peggy. "But I'd come along as moral support."

"Nah, you go to church," Peggy said. "I'll be fine."

Helen looked at Thelma. "Why don't you go with her?"

Thelma's eyes widened. She wasn't sure how to respond.

"She says she already has one."

Helen tilted her head. "You have a *boyfriend*?"

"What's so surprising about Thelms having a boyfriend?" Peggy grimaced.

"I don't," Thelma said quickly, "but—"

"So you need another one." Helen wrinkled her nose. "Get another one."

"What?" Peggy said.

"Well, for heaven's sakes, silly, a diaphragm isn't *yours*. The man keeps it."

"This is news to me," Peggy said.

Thelma cast her eyes on the remnants of egg salad on her plate. It was news to her too. In her line of work, birth control was the woman's responsibility. Thelma looked up at Peggy. "I only have one," she said, certain her meaning would not be clear.

"Of course, you don't have to worry about anyone in your family finding it." Helen looked away.

"No, I don't have to worry about that."

"Oh, dear." Helen's eyes went wide, and she reached for Thelma. "I'm so sorry. I didn't mean anything—"

Peggy slammed her palm on the counter. "I always planned to go alone. Just figured I'd ask, all things considered."

Fortunately, the matter was closed.

At one forty-five, Mrs. Young led the girls out of the hotel lobby like a procession of ducklings headed for Maeve Reilly's showroom. What should have been an exciting moment in Thelma's life was, however, fraught.

Beyond the tragedy of Millie's death, Thelma was caught by the realization she'd spent much of her life judging her mother's choices. Now, she recognized that Vivian Miles just might have made the best of a bad lot. Her own father had died shortly before the armistice, not in battle but because of the Spanish flu. When Vivian's mother had remarried a man she'd only ever heard referred to as "the pervert," she'd fled as soon as she could, at fourteen. Even if Thelma escaped the Giancarlo family, she'd never circumvent the fate of being female.

"I would *die* if I lived here," said Hattie May, drawing her fur collar up to her ears.

"Did you really just say that?" Peggy glared accusingly.

That girl was just *looking* for a fight. For once, Thelma noted, Hattie May let it slide.

"We are a sight," said Doris, ever the peacemaker.

"Ooh! 'The Florida Girls in Winter' could be a magazine spread," Helen enthused, her blue eyes shining as she grabbed Doris's arm and leaned in. "Us in our bathing suits with fur hats and gloves against a snowy mountain backdrop."

Thelma knew she wasn't imagining the spark between those two now.

"Fake snow, though, right?" Hattie May said, looking up at the concrete skyline. "Cold air is bad enough."

"Honestly, you'd think we were crossing the tundra." Thelma shook her head, smiling. Whereas Thelma had only a beige wool silhouette coat, the others were bundled up in fur coats and hats. Even Peggy had borrowed one for the trip. Yet they all—besides Thelma in her Oxfords—wore slingback shoes. "It's no wonder you're freezing. Your feet forgot to dress for the occasion."

"Easy for you to say. Chicago *is* the tundra," Peggy said.

"And proud of it." *Feels like the Sahara compared to Keokuk in winter,* thought Thelma. "You girls need to toughen up."

TWENTY-FOUR

THE GARMENT DISTRICT

Maeve's shop was on the top floor of a four-story walk-up off Eighth Avenue, tucked into the back. Saving the cramped space were the three floor-to-ceiling warehouse windows on the back corner walls, large enough to illuminate the room despite the gray winter light. But it was the interior walls that blazed, lined with tantalizing bolts of fabric. At last, excitement rippled through the girls.

Mrs. Young greeted Maeve. They made quite the pair. Her boss—in her fitted worsted wool suit, sandy hair pulled tight into victory rolls—was the opposite of the taller and plumper Maeve, who wore a loose-fitting white shirt and long gathered skirt, her mop of bronzed curls piled into a loose bun held by a knitting needle on top of her head.

"Ladies," Mrs. Young began, "I'm thrilled to have you back with Maeve. She's going to be fitting the looks from our spring line on you today. I know it's a tight space—"

Thelma looked into the long narrow space. A heavy drape cordoned off the back corner, the dressing area, outside which four stuffed chairs were squeezed. She noticed the forms flanking Maeve's sewing machine were dressed in heavy velvet finery—exquisite but for what? Or whom?

"You're free to go when you finish, but mind, curfew tonight is eight, including Peggy and Thelma. We have a team meeting tomorrow morning at six sharp before the rest of us must leave to make our flight. I'll hand it over to Maeve."

"Girls, I'm terribly sorry for your loss." Maeve pursed her lips and looked down a moment. When she raised her head, her eyes were bright. "To make up for it, here's a surprise."

Smiling, she reached for the hatbox sitting atop her notions stand. As she bent to remove the lid, a perfectly coiled spring of hair escaped her topknot. Blowing the defector out of the way with a sharp upward exhalation, she extracted several slim packages. "For you!"

Helen clapped her hands to her open mouth.

"Stockings?" Hattie May said.

"How on earth..." Peggy said.

"They're *rayon*, not silk," Mrs. Young answered. "Perfect for our customers. Helen, you're first up." She raised her hand to quell the sounds of disappointment. "It's alphabetical."

Ignoring the signal to start, Maeve reached back into the box. "This is a nice color for you. Honeyglo?" She reached in and pulled out two more. "Oh, this one is nice for Peggy. Sundash."

Surrounding Maeve, they pawed through the selections, holding up the packages to color match their faces and offering opinions on the shades.

Once the hosiery hullabaloo subsided a bit, the fitting got underway. While Helen changed, Maeve showed Mrs. Young drawings. Doris was reading the novel Thelma had seen Helen reading on the bus, while Peggy flipped through a magazine Maeve had lying around. A soft snore escaped Hattie May's lips. Yes, death was everywhere then. Beyond the cancer, babies dying from croup, and everywhere influenza, people were damaged. Industrial accidents, wars, and polio left behind visible infirmities. Still, Thelma was struck by the girls' impassivity. Or maybe they weren't as soft as Thelma believed. She grabbed for an old *Life* magazine.

"Jerry Lewis got married?" Peggy asked, looking up from her rag.

"That was months ago!" Thelma said.

"Nat wa munnz ago!" Peggy repeated. "Don't be such a know-it-all! This is just from..." Peggy flipped her magazine around and looked at the cover. "October 15."

Doris slid her eyes over her book. "Well, that *was* two months ago."

"Oh, you didn't know either."

They laughed and went back to their various pages, occasionally sharing items, until Helen returned. "Hattie May," she said softly then gently shook her shoulder. The girl had passed out. Finally, she crooned into her ear, "Yoo-hoo!"

Hattie May started, nearly falling on the floor. "Crimanet-telies! Sneak up on a girl, why doncha?"

"I *said* your turn," Helen called after her retreating back, her cornflower eyes flashing with mischief. She took the seat next to Doris. "I'll wait for you."

Hattie May's fitting was taking much longer. Peggy looked at her watch. "Dammit, I'm gonna be late."

"Late for what?" asked Doris.

Peggy leaned over and whispered into Doris's ear. From the look on her face, Thelma knew she was blabbing about her pessary appointment.

"Later, slugs!" Hattie May called out as she bounced toward the door.

Peggy saluted. "Give my regards to Dodo."

"Doris?" Maeve called a second time.

"I'll switch with you, Peggy," Thelma said, glad it would eliminate any question of her accompanying her roommate to the Sanger clinic.

THELMA WAS DEEPLY INTO A REVIEW OF THE PREVIOUS summer's blockbuster, *Bathing Beauties*, when she heard raised voices near the door. Turning to see what the commotion was, she spotted an older woman decked out in a feather-topped turban, pearls, and a very fine full-length mink coat. At the moment, her access to the room was blocked by Mrs. Young's outstretched arm, bare almost to the elbows thanks to her three-quarter-length sleeves. *These women do not know how to dress for the weather.*

"Your missus is not here," she heard her boss insisting.

It was clear to Thelma, however, the woman at the door was no errand girl. Hopping out of her chair, she bounded toward the pair.

The woman in the doorway had to be at least a decade older than Mrs. Young and a good five inches taller. Her boss's disrespect, Thelma surmised, was a response to the rich red-brown ochre color of her skin.

"Tell Miss Maeve that Madame St. Clair is here. For her appointment." With that, the madame lifted her chin and looked past her human barricade, stomping her umbrella tip against the wide-plank wood floor.

"*Mrs.* O'Reilly is with *us*, in case you hadn't noticed." Mrs. Young harrumphed, nose high, and moved her arm toward Madame.

That was when the umbrella came down. On Mrs. Young.

Midstride, Thelma pivoted and ran toward the back of the room. "Sorry, Peggy. Maeve! Get out here quick."

* * *

In disbelief, Kathleen reached for the shoulder that had just been—however gently—undeniably struck. She'd fallen a long way since her coming-out party in '25, but this affront was too much. Behind her, she heard Maeve's voice.

"Queenie!"

In the eternity of the following moment, Kathleen turned and saw Maeve racing toward her, not stopping to pick up the measuring tape that fluttered from her shoulders to the floor. At last, someone was coming to her aid. But who was this Queenie?

"Maeve, I'm sorry. I tried to bar this—"

But Maeve brushed right past, her curled tendrils bouncing like springs all about her head.

"Madame St. Clair!" she said and then proceeded to embrace the frumpish creature in much the same fashion as she'd been welcomed just two hours ago. The woman must have been Maeve's housemaid.

"Maeve. Your colored woman just struck me!"

Cheeks ablaze, Maeve turned and widened her eyes, signaling silence. "Kathleen, Madame St. Clair is my client. I'm sure it was an accident."

"It was no accident," Kathleen and Madame said at once.

"Well, that's something we agree on," Kathleen muttered.

"There was no striking. I was merely trying to *faire place* so as not to fall back down those stairs of yours, Maeve. You really do need to find a new location."

Faire une place à ma fesse, thought Kathleen.

"Oh, my manners!" Maeve rolled right along. "Kathleen, may I present to you my dear friend, Madame Stephanie St. Clair, also a successful businesswoman."

St. Clair extended a gloved hand. "*Enchantée*, I'm sure."

She couldn't be French, though it might explain her atrocious behavior. She did have some sort of accent.

"And Madame?" Maeve kept going, pushing past any resistance before it could present itself. "This is Mrs. Kathleen Young. She and her husband sell a clothing line. Her models had a fitting today."

This introduction was bizarre. The order was all wrong, and to describe the Emporium as a clothing line? As Maeve could've predicted, Kathleen was far too flummoxed to do anything but rely on her upbringing. Taking St. Clair's gloved fingertips in her own, she purred, "Charmed."

And then her upbringing truly did rear its head. "Where did you say you were from?"

"I'm French," St. Clair said. "And you?"

"My people are from one of the very best families in Virginia, but we've come today from Florida."

Maeve interrupted. "Ooh! Look at the time! Already three. Madame, I'm so terribly sorry. I—"

Madame squinted at her wristwatch, puckering her lips. "Timeliness, Mrs. Reilly. *Mon dieu!*"

And then that Thelma inserted herself into the conversation. "Take my spot. It's no bother. I wouldn't mind stretching my legs around Macy's."

Maeve pounced. "You sure you won't mind? Oh, you're a gem."

"Maeve." Kathleen was astonished at the impertinence. "I cannot wait. There are arrangements to be made, I—"

By now, Peggy had joined the group, wearing a floral dress from the spring collection, her hemming pins still in place. She cut the storeowner off. "Oh, pshaw, Mrs. Young. You weren't too busy sending Doris off to oversee my huddle. You don't need to wait for Thelma. The person who needs the info is standing right here."

Maeve produced Kathleen's handbag and urged her toward the stairs. She realized her brow was furrowed and softened her face. No need to add a new wrinkle over this malarkey. Truth was, Kathleen had been about to leave. It was the principle. But now was not the time to kick up a fuss. "Yes, of course, if it will help you out, Maeve."

"Swell. Queenie, why don't you have a look at your new dresses back by my machine?" But Maeve continued coaxing Kathleen along. "I'll be right with you girls," she said.

Wriggling into her coat in the vestibule, Kathleen asked, "Maeve, what's gotten into you?"

"I'll have you know that Madame St. Clair," Maeve said, gesturing back toward her shop, "is one of the most richest women in the city."

Kathleen thrust her hat on her head. "*Most* richest?"

"And what business do you think that means she's in, eh?"

The first thought that came to Kathleen's mind, after noting how the dressmaker had failed to spot her sarcasm, was prostitution. She tugged at her coat. "I've no idea what you're on about."

"Really? You've the same *business* at Sun City Emporium."

Kathleen looked up from her fur-covered buttons. That damn Bolita game. "But aren't those people... Well, they're all Italians, not colored."

"Trust me, they are emphatically not all Italian."

As she walked east on Thirty-Eighth Street toward the hotel, a whisper of doubt entered Kathleen's mind. She felt vaguely duped by Maeve, though she couldn't think of a time her friend had ever lied to her. Her wedding dress had been Maeve's first solo project, and she'd since assumed it had been her business that helped the dressmaker open her own shop.

Hadn't they been friends?

Maeve was one of a select few who knew why the waistline of Kathleen's gown needed to be let out before the nuptials, but she hadn't been invited to the festivities. She was a step above the Youngs' other employees, but in the end, she provided a service.

That St. Clair woman could not have been Maeve's client when they'd first met. Then a connection struck her—Sal. When had they first talked about him? The advent of the Bolita games?

"If Mr. Giancarlo is willing to make sure your permits get approved, why wouldn't you sell his tickets?" Maeve had said. "It's a big draw. It'll bring loads of customers in."

Kathleen knew nothing of the infamous Bolita Wars, the month-long siege of nightly open-air shoot-outs that had ended the year before the Youngs moved to Florida's gulf coast. By the time she and her husband arrived, the Giancarlos had wrested the game—and its enormous profits—from the original Cuban operators.

By the time they'd struck their deal to expand the store and start running numbers for Sal in exchange for help with permits, the dearth of men created by the war had hatched a kind of détente. This had allowed the Youngs to remain blissfully unaware of the game's more unsavory aspects.

Had Sal introduced St. Clair to Maeve? Or had it been the other way around? When was the first time they'd talked about Sal?

As she stepped into the Hotel Pennsylvania's enormous revolving door, Kathleen remembered. What was it they'd talked about? It had been long before the remodeling, back when they first needed a permit but couldn't get an audience with the city.

"Ya been greasin' the coppers' palms a while to beef up patrols around the store, haven't you?" she'd asked. "Now, you're moving up to the big leagues, the politicians. Works the same way, only they call it campaign contributions." She could still hear Maeve's bright laugh over the scratchy long-distance line.

But she'd been the one to bring up Salvatore, hadn't she?

"I did just read about this Giancarlo fella," Kathleen had said.

In her recollection, Maeve had agreed only that Sal sounded like the right man for the job.

Or had Maeve suggested the article?

Crossing into the lobby, Kathleen looked at her watch. It wasn't yet 3:30 p.m. Despite her earlier bluster, there was nothing for her to do. *Hell's flames,* she thought. *I'm getting a bourbon.*

TWENTY-FIVE

THE FUNERAL

*Today at McQueen's Funeral Home, family, friends, and
fans gather today to mourn the loss of our mayor's
beloved daughter, Millicent "Millie" Williams. Her
short life was marked by—*

"Button, darling"—Kathleen put her gloved hand on
the seat between her and her husband, lifting her index finger
toward the car's radio—"would you mind?"

Lloyd reached for the wireless and twisted the dial off
before raising an eyebrow. "Music?"

"I think a little quiet would be lovely right now," Kathleen
said, reaching up to extract the pin from her black pillbox hat so
she could sink back into the Cadillac's bench seat. She needed
to strategize through the coming hours, but her eyes would not
cooperate.

"Pepper dear, we're here."

Through the slits of her eyelids, Kathleen saw swarms of
people in the parking lot. A valet headed toward Lloyd's side of
the car. She sat up and yanked the rearview, smoothed her hair

in the rectangular reflection, replaced her hat, and reapplied her lipstick—all before Lloyd came around for her door.

Showtime.

"Mrs. Young?" Lloyd grinned, extending his hand to help her alight from the car.

"Keep smiling, darling," Kathleen said through her own bared teeth.

The Youngs were yet in a precarious position. Had Millicent been discovered under the same circumstances in St. Petersburg, the Williamses would've kept the cause of death a secret. She and Lloyd would've had the upper hand. Since she'd been traveling with the Youngs as an *entertainer*, rumors about a lapse in the chaperone could swirl but only if blame was going around. But Kathleen had listed the cause of death precisely because everyone understood the code. So long as the delicate social maneuvering was handled properly, it would be best not to speak of the tragedy at all.

"Oh, yoo-hoo!" Gertrude Harper was waving her lace handkerchief in the air. "There you are. Poor Mrs. Young!"

Kathleen wasn't fooled. Those bulging eyes and flushed cheeks belied the concern in her voice. She'd already hit the sauce.

They were knotted in the church's large vestibule, like a wedding, except that this receiving line came before the service. Only family would be attending the graveside burial directly afterward. They just had to make it through this service. She pulled at Lloyd's elbow.

"There're the Williamses, Herbert and Rose. Let's get in line to pay our respects right away," she whispered in her husband's ear, steering him toward the Williamses.

"You smell terrific," he whispered back.

"Focus!" Kathleen admonished but only out of habit. She loved how he could turn any moment into romance.

"Oh, Kathleen," Elsa Juergen said, joining the line with her daughter Doris just behind her and Lloyd. "How awful that must've been. Thank you for organizing the girls' flights. Lloyd, your wife is a real dynamo."

Kathleen's shoulders slid down, and her jaw, which she hadn't realized was tight, unclenched. She'd spent *years* licking these people's boots for this type of approval. And none of it mattered now that they would be leaving after Archie's graduation the following year. Still, given the task at hand, this was an excellent start.

"You know whose fine qualities I've had the privilege of becoming acquainted with these last few months?" Lloyd asked, reaching out to pinch Doris's cheek. "Your daughter's."

Kathleen stood back, fiddling with her earring while her husband did the charming. The man could sell sawdust to a lumber mill.

At last, they reached Dr. and Mrs. McKaye. The doctor wore an outlandishly formal morning suit, but Mrs. McKaye— under a sheer black veil that stretched from head to knee—had on a fitted wool crepe dress covered with appliqué dahlias. The nerve! Of course the materials were all black, but wearing the flower of betrayal and dishonesty to the girl's funeral? Right next to Millie's poor mother? Tongues would wag.

"Doctor, Mrs. McKaye," Lloyd said, extending his hand. "We're so very sorry this happened. Millicent would surely have been a magnificent daughter-in-law."

Of course, Lloyd didn't see the significance of Mrs. McKaye's choice. Perhaps the tall, slender Mrs. McKaye was equally unaware. Perhaps no one in this Podunk town would think of it. Did she think Millie had been untrue? Kathleen thought there must be a special place in hell for women who couldn't imagine their male children's faults. She would remind her.

"It must pain your son he was unable to get leave again," Kathleen said. "It was, what, just two months ago he was here and we learned of their engagement? Poor soul."

Mrs. McKaye tilted her head ever so slightly and smiled—no teeth, and her eyes didn't crease. "But we're here."

Or perhaps she was angry with her son. Regardless, as a prominent family, the McKayes would be motivated to sweep this story under the carpet too. Kathleen nodded then found herself enveloped by two fleshy arms pulling her close—Rose Williams, Millie's mother.

When Rose released her grasp, she was almost pleading. "Who are all these people? I don't know why they're here."

Kathleen regarded the mayor's wife, pear-shaped under a high-necked crepe de chine dress with smocking through the neck and shoulders. Her thick ankles looked painfully cut off by her stiff brogues. She wanted to kiss her. *How could I have been worried?* The woman was far too wrecked to care about the Florida Girls.

As she and Lloyd were carried along by the line, Kathleen felt herself being watched. Scanning the crowd, she saw an unusual-looking man in a cheap beige overcoat and hat, staring straight at her.

She turned to face Lloyd. "Darling, will you go and find us some seats? I'll be right along."

"Sure thing," he said.

But when she looked back to where the man had been standing, he was gone.

"Mrs. Young," Gertrude Harper assailed at last. "How dreadful that must have been to find that poor girl. What happened?"

Smiling, Kathleen clasped Gertrude's hands. *"Le pauvre!"* She was ready for Mrs. Harper.

. . .

AFTER THE SERVICE, KATHLEEN INSISTED LLOYD GO HOME and rest while she handled the business of the day's end. Poring over the Emporium's books, she realized how much she missed seeing which inventory was moving, how the Sunday supplement had performed, and which items needed to be culled. The ability to quantify her efforts was endlessly gratifying, and engrossed as she was in the ledger, she missed the overcoat till he was in her office, rapping on the doorframe with his knuckle.

"Mrs. Young!" the man said with just a hint of Southern. "I didn't mean to startle you. Pardon. I was looking for Mr. Young."

Kathleen looked the man up and down, not an entirely unpleasant task. Between his thick dark hair and protruding jaw, he could be a Brylcreem model, though too tall and thin for her taste. He was undoubtedly the right age for service. What was wrong with him that he wasn't enlisted? Was he looking for work?

Slipping on her shoes, Kathleen stood and attempted to face him, but he was at least six feet tall. "How did you get in here?"

Overcoat lifted his cheeks—not quite a smile—but he didn't advance. "Of course. I'm afraid we've gotten off on the wrong foot." He dug into his pocket.

Kathleen reached for the phone on Lloyd's desk.

"Let me introduce myself," he said as he produced his business card.

Reminding herself not to squint, Kathleen read: Theodore Nelson. Office of Naval Intelligence.

"I can come back another time, ma'am."

"Mr. Nelson, I can't imagine what could be so important you'd arrive unannounced like this and on a Saturday, no less, but I'm glad it's me you found because my husband is very ill. Whatever it is you think he needs to hear, let me assure you. He does not.

"Anything merits talking about, you can discuss with me." Kathleen resumed her seat behind Lloyd's wide oak desk and gestured to the chair across. "Have a seat," she said, folding her arms.

"Ma'am, I really don't think—" He didn't finish his sentence. "Fine. This is... Well... It's in regards to your son..."

Dread clenched at Kathleen's heart. Had they discovered her son didn't qualify for his deferment? Mere months ago, dozens of men had gone to federal prison for three years over draft evasion. Bertie wouldn't survive it.

Kathleen kept her face impenetrable, a skill she'd mastered over many years in Florida's so-called high society circles. "And?"

"And Salvatore Giancarlo."

Had Bertie gotten caught with the damn bag? How would that kid ever run the store? Kathleen uncrossed her arms and leaned on her elbow. "And?"

"We've asked your son to keep an eye on the tunnels near the Giancarlos' club."

A knock at the door gave outlet to Kathleen's fear. "Maintenance!"

"Not now, Mr. Peters!"

"No, please." The G-man was already telling her what to do. "Business as usual. Don't want to arouse any suspicion."

How to explain that interrupting a meeting was not the way she did business? But dealing with Peters would give her time to think. After moving swiftly around the desk, she dispatched the head of maintenance into the hallway and took her moment.

While she signed the purchase orders Peters had brought, she fumed over the fact that her son had failed to mention this Nelson fellow. But she reckoned, whatever it was this man needed, if she didn't have the upper hand already, he wouldn't be in her office.

Smoothing her already helmetlike hair, she returned to Lloyd's desk, perched on its edge and crossed her curvy legs. "Mr. Nelson, I'm sure we're happy to assist you in any way we can. We're doing everything we can to assist the war effort. Now—"

"It's Agent Nelson," he said. "And that's good to hear. Because these tunnels are so well hidden, the only way to access them is to get past Giancarlo's men."

"Then why aren't you in Mr. Giancarlo's office?"

"At this time," Nelson went on in his low, deliberate tone, "we're in a bit of a, well, deficit when it comes to dealing with the Giancarlos."

Kathleen regarded Theodore Nelson—a handsome man, to be sure, but lacking in any magnetism. Wooden, almost— entirely impervious to flirtation. "I'm afraid I don't understand what you're getting at, Mister... Agent Nelson."

"After Charles Luciano helped us at the port of New York, we weren't expecting any difficulty. But Salvatore Giancarlo refused to work with us. So we gave Matteo Giancarlo's induction number a little boost to clear a path." He shrugged.

This was, Kathleen decided, the right moment for incredulity. "You're telling me you got information out of the infamous Lucky Luciano from prison, but you're unable to move in on a small-time hoodlum like Salvatore Giancarlo? So you sent his son to war?"

Nelson's pained smile creased the corners of his eyes as he looked down into his lap. "As I'm sure you're aware, we don't formally recognize the existence of any organized criminal activity within the United States. They're all, as you say, small-time. But Luciano is who led us to Giancarlo."

"So, what, you think as Albert's parents, we'll force our son to spy on the Giancarlos for you? Have I understood you?"

"Mrs. Young, we have reason to believe your son Albert is deeply indebted to the Giancarlos."

This was a shock. Of relief. The idea was ludicrous—

"Gambling. Horses. Bolita."

Or entirely possible. Bertie had been so eager to be the bag man. Why had he been inside the store the morning before they'd left for the Derby? And why had he disappeared afterward?

"We're also aware your family has no way to, uhh..." He paused again. "Cover the debt thanks to significant remodeling costs recently incurred. Essentially, you're all indebted to the Giancarlos."

Kathleen's chest seized as the realization flooded in. Whenever they'd needed a permit or help with construction issues, Salvatore had taken care of it. If he was getting kickbacks from everyone involved—from the unions to the concrete manufacturers—then Salvatore Giancarlo had not only been dangling the carrot of debt relief. He'd been holding the stick. She and Lloyd had been had by that scoundrel.

Agent Nelson coughed. "Mrs. Young, it's become clear that your son is running funds between your store and Tampa. With spies trying to infiltrate the port, we wanted to speak to Mr. Young about developing Albert as an asset."

"An asset?" She knew what he meant, of course, but was desperate to derail the conversation. More than she wanted to murder Salvatore Giancarlo, she would protect her son. Bertie thought of himself as a young tough, but that boy had the grit of a poached egg. Until now, she believed Bertie knew this about himself. His debt told her otherwise.

Agent Nelson set his chin. "Albert would continue his work and, in the course of his duties in Tampa, monitor the tunnels for suspicious activities."

"Suspicious activities? Like what?"

"People speaking German, for starters."

"You expect us to set up camp behind Salvatore Giancarlo's club?" Kathleen looked Theodore up and down. "How—"

"You're right. Now is not the time for humor. It's just that this Florida resistance is mind-boggling." Agent Nelson shook his head. "Anyhow, just think for a second—"

Kathleen was tempted to kick back, hoist her feet onto the desk, and cross her ankles. She raised her eyebrows instead.

"The Bay is too shallow for U-boats. The Germans will have to stop well before Sarasota and row ashore. They'll travel under cover of the night. Even though that journey will take hours, you're unlikely to see them. But they're going to have to leave their craft behind. We ran a similar operation with success despite miles of shoreline and scrub to hide their vessel. There's no place to hide near the tunnels. You'll see their boat."

"I don't know..." Kathleen shook her head.

"Mrs. Young, may I remind you: this is your patriotic duty."

Was he implying he knew about Bertie? He had so much *other* information. She checked his card again. "Special Security" was his only title. What did that even mean? "Agent Nelson, you keep talking about these *tunnels*. There aren't any tunnels in Florida."

Nelson smiled, not unkindly.

But still...

"Why don't you let us worry about that?"

It was the perfect opportunity to end the conversation. "Thank you, Mr. Nelson. I'm sure we will do everything we can. Now—"

But Agent Nelson wasn't finished. "In return, the government will pay his debt piecemeal to buy time and allay suspicion while the operation is running."

"I'm not—" Kathleen objected.

"And I'm authorized to pay you fifty thousand dollars in cash."

The offer stopped her short. "Just how much does Bertie owe?"

"A little more," Nelson said matter-of-factly. "About sixty-five."

Kathleen kept her gaze level. That very afternoon, she'd calculated that, assuming the Florida Girls bookings kept apace, they'd be able to leave the store in the black by the end of the fiscal year, a year earlier than planned. Bertie's debt would set them back significantly.

"We have a deal?" He extended his hand.

But Kathleen only looked at the G-man's outstretched arm then back at him. "You need to understand, young Theodore, if we agree to help, you will communicate on these matters through me. I will provide you with the requested information as we have it available. Is that clear?"

"Well, now, Mrs. Young—"

"There's no discussion here. *C'est fini.* Are we agreed?"

Nelson locked his steel-colored eyes on her. Not her type, but something stirred under his stare.

"Sure. Okay."

Now, it was Kathleen's turn to extend her hand. "Excellent."

They shook. "You seem disappointed."

He let go of her hand. "Isn't it enough we have to fight the enemy?"

"Mr. Nelson, you're the one who came to bargain. You're asking us to do something you cannot because you perceive our family to be down on its luck." She slid off the desk, indicating the interview was over. "And I haven't agreed to anything yet. I need to make some enquiries, then I'll be in touch."

"I'm not sure you understand the danger your son is in if he doesn't start paying his creditors."

"We're honored at the chance to serve." That was how she'd sell the scheme to Lloyd, she thought as a new plan unfurled in her mind. Bertie could not be trusted.

BACK IN '34, WHEN WORD REACHED NORTH THAT SAL HAD commandeered control of Bolita from the Diaz crew, who'd brought it from Cuba, Luciano had demanded a piece. Sal refused his "help," launching the Bolita Wars in earnest. Sal's brother was shot on his own porch. Had Luciano not gone to prison, the Giancarlos might've lost all of Tampa. Sal hated that man with every fiber of his being, possibly even more than the union-busting Homer Wright.

TWENTY-SIX

STEPHANIE ST. CLAIR

THELMA RUBBED THE CALLING CARD MADAME ST. CLAIR had sent to her hotel, a thick creamy piece of paper. It was pleasant to the touch and—she inhaled—scented with rosewater. Madame St. Clair was loaded, obviously. But why on earth had she invited Thelma to tea? And why had she accepted? She couldn't even blame Peggy for egging her on.

The moment Mrs. Young left town with the others, Peggy had met some man on leave and disappeared. After walking around the city aimlessly, Thelma found herself at the Rivoli movie palace, where she'd watched *The Princess and the Pirate* twice. Then she discovered Broadway's resellers.

One of the many plays Thelma couldn't resist, especially after her encounter with Virginia Hill, was the tantalizingly titled *A Lady Says Yes*. From the moment the lights went down through the standing ovation, she was rapt. So the reviews were a real shock.

"Get this," she said to Peggy on the rare morning her room-mate made an appearance. "The critic says it's 'lowbrow at best' and 'would drive a saint to drink.' Pegs, the play was hilarious. Men will do anything to appear virile."

"That critic probably called his own doctor from the lobby, asking if he could get a nose job for his cock."

Thinking about their conversation now, Thelma smiled and looked out the window just as the car pulled to a stop. The house on West 150th looked more like a castle than a brownstone, but that was what the hotel's valet had called the place. Walking up the steps to a set of heavy wooden doors, Thelma got that feeling in her palms again. She clapped her hands.

A young girl in pigtails answered, admirably ignoring the odd sight. "Madame will be along shortly," she said, stepping aside to let Thelma enter. "I'll take your coat."

While the girl hung her coat in the closet, Thelma peered down the long hallway. Paintings and photographs were stacked all along, from floor to ceiling.

"Right this way."

Walking behind her, Thelma gaped at the frames in the passageway. She'd never seen anything like these paintings, the bold colors and geometric forms. She wasn't sure if she liked it or not, but she would've liked to keep looking.

The sitting room was no less crowded. At one end was a fireplace—at the other, an upright piano. A crystal chandelier hung overhead. More photos and paintings lined the walls around the furniture and doorway. There was not a square inch of unadorned space.

"It's wonderful you could join us," Madame St. Clair said as she entered the room, now in a cloche hat and drapey cotton dress with sleeves tight to the elbow. It occurred to Thelma that, though the Madame's gowns might be new, she hadn't changed her style since the early thirties. "My apologies for the delay. Please sit, dear."

"I see you're enjoying my friends," Queenie said, gesturing at the walls. "They won't stop making things for me to buy." She widened her eyes in mock horror.

They made a bit of small talk: "lovely home" and "hope it wasn't too much trouble to find" and so on until the girl returned with a silver tea service.

"I can pour, Alma. Thank you. But before you go, would you play something for us? Make it something we can sing to. Miss Thelma here's a professional *chanteuse*."

With no hesitation, Alma sat at the piano bench and out rolled the opening notes of "Don't Fence Me In."

To say Thelma was astonished would be putting it mildly. The Youngs' home had been the first personal residence she'd ever seen with a piano, and here she was about to get an in-home concert. Alma's style was lively; Thelma couldn't help but tap her feet. Madame St. Clair began singing.

"Join in, now!" she cried, motioning Thelma to stand. Rising, the three finished the song together.

I WANT TO RIDE TO THE RIDGE WHERE THE WEST commences
And gaze at the moon 'til I lose my senses.
I can't look at hobbles, and I can't stand fences.
Don't fence me in.
No, Papa, don't you fence me in.

BY THE SONG'S END, THE APPLAUSE WAS MUTUAL.

"Okay now, skedaddle," Madame said to Alma. "You have school in the morning."

Thelma wondered who this girl was to St. Clair but thought the better of asking while her host poured. "Thank you, Madame St. Clair."

Madame St. Clair sat back with her teacup and let out a deep laugh. "Call me Queenie. Everyone does."

"Of course, Queenie," Thelma said. "How did you get here from France?"

Queenie laughed again. "Never been to France. My mother's French. I was born in Martinique."

Thelma didn't have a clue where that was, but it sounded French.

"My parents brought me here. Same American dream as everybody else," Queenie said with a smile, but she looked deeply into Thelma's eyes. There was a penetrating quality about her, conveying she'd no need to spill her secrets because Madame St. Clair could read them.

The doorbell rang.

"That'll be him."

Thelma knitted her brow.

"Listen now, Thelma, there's not much time.

"I understand you're trying to give Salvatore Giancarlo the runaround. You should know that man saved my numbers business. But here's something else you need to know—he did it to get back at Lucky Luciano for trying to take over his racket in Florida." Queenie paused, looking toward the hallway, where Alma was collecting the new visitor. "But that same man sent his own son off to war when he could've spared him."

Thelma sat, stupefied.

Queenie held her with a soul-piercing, kohl-eyed gaze. "You know exactly what this has to do with you. Remember, everyone wants something. Find out what it is before you dismiss it without consideration. That's how you gain the upper hand."

She rose and offered a slight bow, which Thelma found odd. "*Au revoir, ma cherie,*" Queenie said before exiting through french doors.

"Thelma?" Salvatore Giancarlo entered from the hallway, his massive frame blocking any hope of exit. "You're a real sight for sore eyes."

TWENTY-SEVEN

A LADY SAYS YES

"Hello, gorgeous." Sal, still blocking Thelma's exit, smiled approvingly, arms wide open.

Had she been anywhere else, Thelma would've lit a cigarette. But for all the gewgaws in Madame St. Clair's house, there was a noticeable lack of ashtrays. She crossed her legs and reclined, staying silent.

"Okay, Diego," Sal said to his meaty companion with the low forehead. "How about you wait in the car?"

Ducking through the doorway, Sal took Queenie's armchair.

Thelma heard the warning her mother had so often issued: "Don't ever take up with a made man. But if you do, don't marry him." As if Thelma was, like her mother, unable to resist male charms.

"Look, Sal, before you say anything..." She sat up. "I don't know who you think you're fooling here, but you had to know your Matteo was being shipped out before you said anything about being my... *father*. Just what do you want from me?"

Sal placed his impeccably manicured hand on his chest, still grinning like an idiot. "I don't even know what you're talking about, but you're cynical as hell. Real chip off the ol' block."

Thelma resisted the urge to run. This had to be resolved now. "Listen, Sal. I'm not interested in coming into the fold and marrying one of your capos. Those women only exist to suit their men. I—"

"Marrying? One of *my* men?" The light drained from Sal's eyes. "Who said anything about getting married? Thelma, I want you to run my casino in Vegas."

Run a casino? In Las *Vegas?*

"Listen, sweetheart. One day, gambling is gonna be legal in every state. By that time, our operations are gonna be one hundred percent legit. Capiche?"

She did not *capiche* but kept her face open, a trick she'd learned turning her mother's tricks.

"I need someone I can trust who don't got a record. I been pressuring Doc Young. He's clean, plus he knows how to run a business. But that kid of his has become a liability." Sal shook his head. "Then you came along. You're smart. Gorgeous. And you're blood. Santa Maria, it was a miracle."

She wanted to protest, to avow her desire to steer clear of anything to do with the Mafia or their dirty money. But the prospect of running a legitimate business? When would she ever have such an opportunity again? His words ignited a fire for something she'd never dared dream of, her own business. But, considering Queenie's warning, could Sal be trusted?

"Sal, I'm afraid I don't know anything about casinos."

"It's like any business," he said. "You got the gaming operation on one side and a luxury hotel on the other. Showgirls, fancy restaurants, deluxe accommodations, the works."

"But Sal, I don't know anything about *any* business."

"You think I knew how to run a business before I got here?" Sal sat back, pulling at his french cuffs to expose gold cufflinks. "I seen you. You got a good head on your shoulders, know how to think on your feet. Besides, you'll have our help."

Thelma leaned forward and gave him a cool grin. "I'll have to think about it."

Sal's face darkened. He was a man used to getting his way.

She put up her hand before he could speak. "I wouldn't be the person you want running your business if I just said yes, and you know it. Before we have a deal, I have to meet with your people in Vegas. I'm assuming you had the stop added to our tour, like the sanitation fleet?"

Sal's grin now was less toothy, less cretinous. A look of genuine appreciation. "This is gonna be the start of our legitimate empire. My legacy."

LATER, AS THELMA BRUSHED HER TEETH, SHE THOUGHT back to St. Clair's art collection. She hadn't amassed her fortune or her influence alone. The thing about power, she reckoned, was that it had to flow in both directions. Unless it could be conferred, such clout was mere prestige, easily revoked. To have the kind of protection St. Clair enjoyed, there had to be a stable of people on whom she could call, people for whom she'd offered protection.

Shutting off the tap, she heard Peggy at the door, humming. "When you don't have anything to work with," Thelma heard Vivian Miles saying, "work with what ya got." *Peggy.*

TWENTY-EIGHT

THE NEW GIRL

It was early February in Indiana, dreary as Thelma would've expected, except that she and Peggy were buzzing with excitement at the prospect of the team reunion. As soon as they saw the aircraft door open, they hopped off the bus to stand at the base of rolling stairs that had been wheeled out. Photographers started snapping photos. *Leave it to the Youngs to get this moment into the papers,* she thought.

Thelma was hugging Doris when she felt an elbow in her side. Peggy motioned toward the stairwell with her chin. Bertie was deplaning?

Doris saw her look and shrugged. "He's back on the tour now."

For a moment, Thelma panicked. If Bertie was around, what would her role be reduced to? Then she remembered—this tour wasn't her endgame anymore. Since meeting with Sal, her fantasies of a Hollywood escape had faded as her mind cleaved to the idea of running her own business. Thelma had never felt more grateful to have nabbed a spot on the Florida Girls tour. It had been a crash course in worldliness.

Ever since Sal had asked her about running his casino, she'd easily imagined dealing with unruly patrons. Her previous work history had taught her that skill. But seeing how the Youngs put together this tour had shown her another side of commerce. She'd need to think which acts would bring in the right publicity. How to advertise. The overall look and feel of things.

Watching her teammates in action had been an education as well. They came from money, but they had none of their own—no power. Madame St. Clair would have insisted the staff at St. Andrews treat her. Virginia Hill would have secured a proper abortion. They hadn't snaked their way into their lives through their prior work history but through audacity. Thelma would simply insist she weigh in on rooms and décor, staff uniforms, and new hires. The worst Sal could do would be to say no. Then she'd have another decision to make.

A flash of long blond hair on the tarmac caught Thelma's eye. A woman had stepped off the plane behind Hattie May, pretty as Veronica Lake and almost as tall as Thelma. Even the woman's clothes made a statement, a black drawstring skirt paired with a white blouse imprinted with musical notes. Thelma had never seen anyone quite like her in person.

"Who's that?" she asked Helen.

"Lillian Wright, Wright Pharmacy," Helen said.

"George has a sister?" Thelma asked, sounding more eager than she would've liked.

"Cousin," Helen said. "It was her father who gave George's dad the money to buy an orange grove. Now, the Wrights own half the real estate in Florida. Citrus groves to the west. Cattle farms up north. Plus half the railroads."

Once back aboard the bus, their boss—looking imperious as ever, sporting a black wool jersey dress with her hair pulled into a tight bun—handed Thelma her mail. One glance at the top envelope, and Thelma thrust the papers into her pocketbook, but not before her heart caught a beat. Letters from George—

she'd been writing him breezy updates every week without fail but hadn't heard from him since Mrs. Young had been gone. It took seeing his handwriting to realize how worried she'd been.

"George wrote all those letters?" Peggy whispered. "I've never been happier to be wrong about a guy."

"Nobody likes a snoop," Thelma said but then surprised herself by giggling like a schoolgirl.

Mrs. Young shushed them. Why was she always on her bad side? "Ladies, tonight we resume our regularly scheduled tour. There are only three weeks of shows till California. We're going to have to work nonstop to be ready.

"Now, you all know Lillian Wright."

"Not Thelma," Hattie May piped up.

Thelma had not missed the Harper girl.

"Quiet, please," Mrs. Young warned. "Anyway, we're stopping at a hotel before tonight's show so we can rehearse together. Margaret, thank you for overseeing things in my absence."

The girls exchanged a look; Peggy loathed her full name. "Oh, it was my absolute pleasure, Mrs. Young."

LATER AT THE HOTEL, THELMA CROUCHED IN THE bathroom with her letters—eight of them. They were supposed to meet up for rehearsal, so after sorting the envelopes in date order, she opened the first one. She'd heard of letters getting waylaid and was thrilled to see that he'd written immediately after the Grand Opening.

December 9, 1944

Dear Thelma,

I'm not much of a writer, but I miss you so.
I'll try to write as often as I can though there's
not much to say about this place. The food is terrible, and still there's not enough of it!

Okay, that's a Bob Hope joke I stole. He
visited our airfield with Rita Hayworth!

Other than that, we've been on the go near
constantly. In retrospect, this might not seem like
such a very long time to be apart, but right now, it
feels like forever, and gosh, I miss you. Your
letters mean the world to me. I read them over and
over again. I love picturing you on stage, joking
with the recruits just like Miss Hayworth. But
you're prettier.

Yours,
George

She wanted to tear through the remaining envelopes, but
she was already late. By the time she made it to rehearsal, the
rest of the girls were already gathered in the dusty ballroom.

"Not many balls in Indiana, I gather," Hattie May was
saying.

"Oh, look!" Doris hotfooted across the floor to a piano
covered in canvas, released the instrument from its shroud, and
plucked a few chords.

"You play?" Thelma asked.

"We all do," Helen said as the girls surrounded the
instrument.

Peggy looked at Thelma. "I don't." She had her ukulele and began to strum. Looking at Doris, Peggy hummed until her teammate picked up the tune. Then she began to sing in earnest.

"'All the day, long whether rain or shine, she's a part of the assembly line. She's making history, working for victory."

The rest joined in for the chorus, "Rosie—*brrrrrr*—the Riveter!"

The girls sang all nine choruses, and when they finished, applause sounded out from the door. They'd been so rapt in their own entertainments, they hadn't noticed the arrival of Mrs. Young and Lillian Wright.

"Brava, girls. That was stupendous!" Lillian said.

Thelma liked her instantly.

Lillian made a point, then, of going around and shaking everyone's hand. "Thelma Miles, so nice to meet you. I've heard great things," she said with a raising of her eyebrow before greeting Doris.

Once she'd finished, Mrs. Young asked the girls to settle down so work could begin, but Lillian stopped her.

"First, and I'm sure you'll agree," Lillian said, "I want you all to know how dreadful I feel about Millie. Who has memories they'd like to share?"

Thelma was astonished, not only that Lillian charmed everyone but by how decisively she'd shut down Kathleen Young.

After a memorial of sorts, the girls spent the rest of the afternoon rehearsing the simple song-and-dance numbers they'd devised for the War Bond Tour, but Thelma kept an eye on Lillian. She sang well enough but laughed at her own stage patter and often messed up her parts. The thing was she never apologized for any of it. More incredibly, no one seemed to mind.

"It's the fuck-off money she's got," Thelma heard her mother saying.

At first, she agreed that Vivian had a point, but as the day wore on, she was not so certain. Sure, the Wrights had the kind of money where it didn't matter what anyone else thought. But so did Doris and Helen. And even Hattie May. All of them combined still lacked something Lillian had, and Thelma sensed if she could figure out what that was, it would change her life forever. She had no idea such magnetism was a quality she already possessed.

BEGGING OFF THE GROUP DINNER, THELMA SPED BACK TO her room to write George immediately.

> Dear George,
>
> My heart skipped a beat when I saw your handwriting. It's not that I expected you to write, but I thought you'd at least write back. When you didn't, I was worried.
>
> Your note raised my spirits so, I've decided to ration—I'll read one each week, just as they'd been sent. Unless I get a letter from you in the meantime, not that I mean to pressure you! Heavens, there's pressure enough on you boys. It's just that waiting to read a more current note seems a silly waste of your letter-writing efforts.
>
> I've missed you too.
>
> Yours,
> Thelma

. . .

IT WAS A GRAY FEBRUARY MORNING, CLOUDY AND CHILLY AS they gathered in the motel lot just outside New Mexico's Kirtland Air Force Base, ready to board the bus. Likewise, the excitement propelling Thelma since the team regrouped had dimmed considerably.

On first meeting Lillian, she'd had high hopes for their prospects, but Bertie as emcee was a disaster, constantly flubbing the cues and causing confusion. Lillian, who'd taken over the keyboard, would play the song he called, but invariably, it was not the number the girls had prepared. And while Thelma's dancing had improved, she was still no singer, which meant her stage time was limited.

If all that weren't bad enough, the mistakes did little to quell the crowd's enthusiasm for their performances. It dawned on Thelma that perhaps they weren't as talented as she'd been allowing herself to believe.

A flash of movement caught her attention—Lillian was rushing toward them, eyes wide and lips pursed in mock shock. "Lloyd won't be coming to California after all. Trouble in the conjugal bed?"

"I guess I won't have to worry about the next weigh-in," Peggy said. "There goes my appetite."

Thelma and Helen burst out laughing.

Doris looked aghast. "You don't think they still..." She couldn't even bring herself to say the words.

"Have sex, you mean? Darling, of course!" Lillian smiled, raising her shoulders and looking from side to side as if she'd just heard the most delightful news. "But I'm sensing trouble in paradise."

Thelma cocked her head, wondering what game Lillian was playing.

"Really?" asked Hattie May. "What've you heard?"

Lillian hooked Thelma's elbow, causing a burst of expensive perfume to brush gently toward her nose. "If I had to guess, I'd say Lloyd's in a tizzy at how popular this tour has been. He wants wifey home."

"Mmm," Thelma said, reassured her friend was just making small talk. Lloyd was the type of man who lived for success.

The swell and stink of the Crossley's engine announced Mrs. Young

"Girls, come along!" Mrs. Young called out, stepping off the bus. "It's a long drive from Albuquerque to Hollywood, and if we have to book another motel, I'm taking the fees out of your pay."

Thelma's hand flew to her stomach, and Lillian caught her eye.

"Motion sickness? I get it too. But I brought this!" Lillian lifted her hand to show a small white packet she held then flicked it with her fingers. "Knocks you right out. Want one?"

Thelma was sorely tempted but shook her head. Her nervous stomach had less to do with the motion than the destination. The last thing she needed was to start taking drugs now.

A short while later, as the bus bumped and lurched west across a neglected highway, Thelma watched as Bertie and the girls slept soundly. Apparently, she'd been the only one to refuse Lillian. Of course, Mrs. Young was still awake, but she couldn't imagine bantering with her boss. The woman was in a foul mood anyway. Had she and Mr. Young really fought?

The idea of a falling-out between Mr. and Mrs. Young had never occurred to Thelma. They always seemed so in tune. She realized then just how much she counted on this fact, not just for her job, but also because it had given her a sense of optimism. *What could have happened?* she wondered.

Suddenly, Thelma found herself reaching for the motion sickness bag—just in time too.

After another episode, Thelma found Lillian. "Sorry to wake you, but I give up. I'll take one of your draughts if you can spare another. I can't be awake for the next six hours."

Lillian offered a smile through sleepy eyes, handing over several packets. "You can just lick your finger and dip it in, like a Lik-M-Aid. Better living through chemistry, Dad always says."

Thelma stopped and caught her eyes, so Lillian changed the subject. "You're going to love Los Angeles. We'll go to Grauman's Chinese Theatre for a movie, then drinks at Chateau Marmont, then dinner and a show at the Trocadero."

"I think Kathleen has us pretty well booked," Thelma said but took the draughts. "Though your agenda sounds much more fun."

Lillian dug into her bag and pulled out a small vial. "I told you—better living through chemistry."

Thelma pushed Lillian's hand back into her purse. "Thank you, no."

But Lillian shooed her away. "Oh, here, just in case." She tucked the vial into Thelma's pocket. "Don't be such an old fuddy-duddy. Otherwise, you're dying before you've even had the chance to live! *Tempus fugit!*"

Thelma had no idea what *temper fewsit* was supposed to mean, but Lillian's meaning hit home. Far back as she could recollect, she'd been the responsible one. Long before the tooth infection, Vivian Miles was working constantly, which left Thelma to fend for herself. Thelma had learned to cook and clean and take care of the house by herself. When her mother did become ill, she simply took over earning the money too.

What if she let somebody else be in charge?

December 18, 1944

Dearest Thelma,

I got a little behind on my letters but not for lack of thoughts about you. They've been keeping us busy with drills, and I've barely had time to keep up with chores—forget about leisure time.

Been out on air-raid alarms the last few days, which you know as much about as I do. The radio is the only dope we get. Bastards raid without warning. They don't know what a clean fight is.

We were issued seabags yesterday, in case we have to abort over water. Our planes can't even make it past the mountain range, so I've a hunch we're shipping out soon.

Do not worry, my dearest. We have those boys on the run. I will get to you as soon as I can.

Eternally yours,

George

TWENTY-NINE

FIELD REPORT 3

EMERGENCY REPORT//EYES ONLY
SUBJECT: Tampa Port Dispatch
DATE: Feb. 21, 1945
AUTHORED BY: T. Nelson, Special
Services, ONA
TOPLINE: Launch Operation Gremlin.

BACKGROUND: No EVIDENCE OF GERMAN SPY ACTIVITY WAS detected in the Tampa port. We now believe their transport ship sank and their mission aborted. Yet as the war winds down, upticks in gang activity pose a growing threat to ordinary Americans.

Simultaneous to our surveillance efforts in the port, Sun City Emporium, the Young family business, embarked on a cross-country tour promoting postwar relocation to Florida. A discount store, their traveling troupe is made up almost entirely of social elites, including Homer Wright's daughter. Even after the death of one member, the mayor's daughter, the tour continued. Their itinerary—New York, Chicago, and Las Vegas—suggests the "Florida Girls" may be a front for widening the Giancarlo network. Meanwhile, the Youngs maintain financial ties to the Giancarlos.

RECOMMENDATION: SHIFT SURVEILLANCE TO THE YOUNGS and the Florida Girls tour.

THIRTY

BETRAYED

THEY DROVE THROUGH THE NIGHT TO GET TO CALIFORNIA, and pulled into the Hollywood Lodge motel around dawn. A note dropped into Thelma's lap as the girls filed out of the bus: "Meet me at the vending machine. L."

Lillian. So much for getting into bed.

It turned out that, for once, Helen and Peggy were too spent for chatter. Before Thelma had her hair up in rollers, they were already in bed. Thelma headed for the door. "Just need some fresh air," she said and ducked outside before anyone could ask to join.

"Took you long enough," said Lillian, emerging from the shadows.

Thelma guffawed. "Well, I actually like my roommates."

"Show-off." Lillian stuck out her tongue. "But listen. It's Hattie May."

Thelma's mind reeled. "I'm not following."

Lillian pulled a crumpled piece of paper from her robe pocket. "Here."

Thelma looked down at the thin, lined paper, recognizing the handwriting immediately.

Dear Lills,

Mum tells me you're joining the Florida Girls. Smashing! And, well, I have a favor to ask.

Tomorrow, I fly my first mission over the Hump, aka the Skyway to Hell. I won't lie. Between the ice storms and the Japanese, it's dangerous. On the flip side, it was also a grand bump in pay and benefits.

That's why this is so important. Mum has it up her bonnet that I should marry the Harper girl, Hattie May. I never should've mentioned Thelma Miles when I was home on leave. She doesn't know anything about her. You have to talk to her. Please?

Love,

G

P.S: I've nicknamed my C-56 "The Golden Hornet," and I think you know why. Don't tell Mums!

When at last she looked up from the page, Thelma regarded Lillian Wright anew. "George wanted *you* to talk to me?"

"Thelma Miles, what is that look on your face?" Lillian asked.

"Who would ask their cousin—" Thelma was fuming. Peggy had been right. George was a scoundrel. He'd been intent on marrying Hattie May and her golden ringlets all along. She was more his station. "Is he that much of a coward?"

"What? No!"

"I'll make this real easy for the both of you. I couldn't give a damn about other people's sex lives. The only thing I believe in is spirits, and that's only since my own mother died. I don't come from money. I will make my own, thank you."

"Thelma, what are you talking about?"

Not wanting her face or her words to reveal more, Thelma turned.

"What is the matter with you?" Lillian called, her voice fading as Thelma marched in the opposite direction, toward her room.

It was an effort to keep her back straight as Thelma realized how, deep down, ever since getting George's letters, she'd begun hoping that a movie deal could still happen. Then she wouldn't have to work for Sal, and she and George could be together on more equal footing. But that would be a movie. This was real life. A dark chasm opened in her chest, a feeling she recognized: betrayal. Thelma had mistaken liking Lillian with being able to trust her—as she had her own mother. But this time, she had not one but two possible outs. If the movie deal didn't happen, she had the casino.

Unsure what to do with herself after the outburst, she kept walking. She didn't want to go back to her room, so when she got to the end of the lot, she turned left and walked down the block. To her shock, she came upon Mrs. Young in a phone booth, facing out with the door open. Her boss was shouting.

"I'm telling you he volunteered! What difference does it make so long as you're getting the information you asked for on the Giancarlo operations?"

Thelma stopped and moved into the shadows beyond the streetlight. What was Mrs. Young doing out here? And why was she talking about the Giancarlos?

"Look, Agent Nelson, if anything, you put us in this position. But frankly, you know Lloyd is the better man for the job."

Agent Nelson? Was her boss talking to a federal agent about the Giancarlos? The woman seemed unaware of who they were. Was that an act? And what were the feds looking for?

Mrs. Young had stopped to listen, and Thelma, to ensure her boss didn't see her, slipped around the corner to take the long way back to the motel. She was supposed to meet with Sal in Vegas to hammer out their deal. Now she wondered if she should tell him what she'd heard. But what had she heard? She didn't need to know *what* Mrs. Young was up to, just that she was up to something. That kind of snitching would cement her position. *Or...*

What if she worked with the Youngs? Thelma could help the Youngs get information. They might take her into their fold, offer her a Sun City to run in Miami.

"Have you lost your goddamn mind?" she heard in Vivian Miles's unmistakable sharp tone.

"Ma!" Thelma responded aloud.

If her mother were still alive and coherent, Thelma knew she'd have told her not to say anything to either the Youngs or Sal. But that was her mother's way, and it had been a long while since Thelma had decided she was going to run her life differently. She would never allow herself to end up in a position where trading her daughter was the only way to survive.

The Youngs were enigmas. But the feds? If they were looking into Giancarlo, that couldn't be good either. The Florida Girls just had to win. Then she wouldn't be beholden to Sal or George or any of them.

Golden Hornet, my eye, she thought scornfully. She couldn't believe she'd been so thoroughly conned by George. Back in her room, she snuck his letters into the bathroom and opened the next one.

December 25, 1944

Dearest Thelma,

They're playing "If I Could Be with You One Hour Tonight," and I feel the overwhelming urge to confess my feelings.

I'd give anything to be with you for an hour now, but I'd rather spend my life getting to know and love you more. You are the ideal girl for me. We can make a good life together. We can even go to Miami if you want.

It's foolish to make this proposition by post, and so I won't. In the meantime, consider my proposal till we can be together in person. It may be a while. This Christmas, all I want is to live long enough to be with you and make you happy.

Last night, I taught a group of men to play ping-pong and thought of you learning to dance. Not only were they far less attractive students, none of them was nearly as good-humored as you.

All my love,

George

How had she missed the obvious? One hour? Proposition? Good-humored? Who did he take her for? Thelma had heard of soldiers keeping multiple women on the hook. She'd just never imagined playing the fool. *The cad.*

After gathering the letters in her hands, she tried ripping the stack in two, but the paper was too thick. She couldn't risk leaving them in the trash for one of the other girls to find. Patting her pocket to be sure she had her lighter, she took the stack out to the parking lot then found an unlit corner behind the dumpster and watched the pages burn. *Why does it hurt?* she wondered.

THIRTY-ONE

MRS. YOUNG BUILDS A DREAM HOUSE

The phone call with Agent Nelson left Kathleen exhausted, but there was no time to rest. While freshening up, she called instructions to Bertie.

"The site check is tonight at the Santa Monica Pier, Bertie. Mr. Smith will take you."

Her son did not reply.

"Albert?"

She walked into their room and found him already asleep on his twin bed.

"Albert!"

He started.

"Tonight. Four o'clock. Mr. Smith will take you for a run-through at the Santa Monica Pier." He nodded, but Kathleen made a mental note to stop by Peggy's room and deputize her to be sure the girls assembled on time. "I won't be there."

Kathleen was going to meet a realtor.

It was about a two-hour drive to Carlsbad from the hotel. She didn't want anyone to know she was house shopping, and she needed breakfast anyway, so she walked back toward the phone booth where she'd spied an unassuming railcar diner. She was waiting for her check when to her shock, Matteo Giancarlo sat on the barstool next to her.

"Mrs. Young." He grinned.

"Matteo?" He'd grown a mustache. "What are you doing here?"

"I'm on leave."

It was the only explanation that made sense, though he didn't look like a man on leave. "You're in your civvies," she said before she could stop herself. She had no wish to derail her day by arguing with this boy.

"Ain't against the law." Matteo shrugged. "So're you."

Was a current running between them, or was she imagining it? "If you're looking for Thelma Miles..." Kathleen wasn't entirely sure how to finish that sentence.

"That girl? Nah. Yeah, I was just helping out at your party. She wasn't gonna get you over the top, but she's an old friend of the family."

"Is that so?" Kathleen raised a playful eyebrow. Men would say anything to avoid embarrassment. It had to be awfully emasculating to have your father steal your girl. "Well, I hope you're coming to the show tomorrow."

"Show?"

"Yes, it's the Florida Girls' landmark stop. The talent-and-beauty contest at the Memphis Belle site. The winner—"

"Gets a movie contract." He smiled. "I remember."

She wanted to take the curl that had freed itself from the center of his brilliantined head and smooth it back with the rest. Had war rendered this young man charming? Considering his beastly father, he was uncommonly well-formed. *Must take after his mother.* "So, tomorrow. Are you coming?"

Matteo nodded and gave a half smirk. "I hope."

The crude innuendo snapped Kathleen out of her reverie. "Well, then."

"Well, then. What are you doing here?"

"Why, having breakfast."

"Looks to me like you're trying to get away."

Perhaps Matteo's pull owed less to his charisma than her loneliness. "I—"

"Want some company?"

Kathleen thought a moment. Matteo was far too dim to guess that she and Lloyd planned to leave St. Pete to open a health sanitorium, and she was rather enjoying feeling desired even if she suspected this boy would desire a stone were it fashioned into a fertility goddess. "I'm afraid you'll be bored stiff. I'm off to Carlsbad to look at summer homes."

"Find a house with you? Why not? I gotta find a place when I get back. Maybe I'll move to Carlsbad."

Kathleen found the idea of house hunting with Matteo odd, but if anyone failed to suspect the real plan underfoot, it was her. "I'm sure the driver won't mind."

"So, it's Peggy and Helen and Doris do most of the singing? What do the other girls do?"

The drive to Carlsbad went quickly as Kathleen nattered away about the tour, the songs, and the clothes, surprised by Matteo's attentiveness. He asked a lot of questions.

"There's the fountain," Kathleen said as they pulled up to a tap in the town square.

"What is that smell?" Matteo asked, following Kathleen toward the tap.

"Alkaline water," she said. "They're mad for it here."

"You know you got one of these in St. Pete, right? Fountain of Youth." He paused for effect. "It don't work."

Kathleen had to stop herself from mentioning the tourists it brought. After all, her hunt was supposed to be for a vacation home. "It's marvelous to bathe in," she said. "Perfect for old bones."

A mischievous grin crept over his face, but before he could speak, the realtor appeared. The thick-ankled dowager greeted the pair with suspicion. "One of the reasons I like to sell in my hometown," she said, addressing Kathleen with a sidelong glance at Matteo, "is to keep the property values up." Learning that she and Matteo were business acquaintances did little to quell her frosty airs.

The first showing was a dud, and Matteo suggested lunch. Kathleen would've been happy with a coffee and a roll, but soon, the three of them were on a beachfront patio, having wine and shrimp cocktail.

By the time the tour continued, the mood had changed dramatically. Their guide tried to ignore it, calling out points of interest. "Beyond those hills lies the mission of San Juan Capistrano. That's something you'll want to see."

"The place memorialized by Glenn Miller?" Kathleen asked.

"Ah, the lady knows her music," Matteo said.

Before Kathleen could protest the patronizing tone, Matteo belted out in song. "'When the swallows come back to Capistrano,'" he crooned, if off-key, "'that's the day you'll come back to me.'"

"Ah, the gent tries and fails to find his keys."

"Spicy," Matteo said. "Just how I like my tamales."

Kathleen burst out laughing as the realtor cast a disapproving glare into the rearview.

"There are just four more houses to see," she said. "I hope we find something suitable for the menu."

Now, Matteo and Kathleen laughed together as if the

woman had hit upon some private joke. But Kathleen couldn't stop herself. Matteo's vulgarity was oddly refreshing.

Next up was a three-bedroom bungalow with ocean views and ample additional acreage. This property was the one, but Kathleen didn't want the tour to end. They continued with the showings. In the mansion with the sunken living room, Kathleen was overcome by the urge to push Matteo into the recessed bar, but the realtor interrupted.

"Yoo-hoo! Where'd you get off to?"

They laughed even harder.

Though the broker advised that the market was "hopping hot" and Kathleen should act immediately, she hadn't entirely taken leave of her senses. "Thank you ever so much. I'll be in touch."

"Where shall we have dinner?" Matteo asked once the realtor had dropped them back at the same mineral water fountain where they'd met.

"When did you say you ship out?"

"I didn't." Matteo smiled, pointing at the hotel beyond the fountain. "Who're you looking for? Who wants a house *here*?"

"Why for Mr. Young and I," she said, wondering if Matteo's lie might have been better. "For the summer."

"Who's gonna run Bolita?"

"Oh dear, well, I haven't given that any thought."

"You better. I think it's the only reason the store's still there."

Kathleen patted her collar. "Things have changed a bit since you left."

"Not that much," Matteo said. "Anyways, first things first: we gotta eat. I'm sure they have food here."

Anyway, Kathleen thought, suppressing the urge to correct him. "We should get back."

"Your wish is my command."

When their car arrived, Matteo reached across Kathleen to open the passenger door and brushed a stray hair from her cheek. His fingertips sent shock waves through her body. Kathleen got in the car, her skin on fire.

Other than Lloyd, she'd never loved a man, emotionally or physically. But as his emphysema worsened, he'd lost the ability to perform. Finding the Pifco a tiresome substitute, Kathleen went about her days in St. Pete, keeping too busy to fret overmuch about this lack. She was thirty-six, after all. Those days were over.

"Mrs. Young?" Matteo said.

Kathleen awoke in the back seat, hot and wet, realizing her cheek was nestled against Matteo's engorged flesh. The young man was no match for Lloyd, but he had his charms. Pushing up from his thigh, she turned toward him. She'd never been this close to his face. "Please," she said, her voice hoarse, "call me Kathleen."

They kissed—gently at first then more urgently.

"I know where we can stop," Kathleen said as she noticed his long, thick eyelashes. She would kill for them.

Midway between Carlsbad and Hollywood was an exclusive resort she'd read about. The place wouldn't be their competition—in the same way the Emporium had provided necessary items at low costs, their niche in California would be to provide unnecessary items at reduced rates.

The driver had to double back, which very nearly made Kathleen change her mind. But then, as if sensing her thoughts, Matteo cast his arm over her shoulders. The sensation of his firm muscles overpowered all sense of reason.

Inside the room, Kathleen pushed Matteo onto the bed, hoisted her skirt, and straddled him, eager in a way she hadn't felt in *years*. When she was spent, her young lover—to her surprise—took charge.

Undressing her slowly, Matteo caressed every inch of her body with his mustache. "That tickles," she protested as he reached her inner thigh.

"Give me a moment," he said, taking her leg in a firm grip. "It won't."

But Kathleen was not content to merely let him take control. She knew her body, and she wanted fulfillment. It had been such a very long time. Happily, he proved adept at following instruction. When she moaned—"slower" or "harder" or "right there"—his enthusiasm did not dampen. Rather, he had a seemingly endless capacity for tumescence.

So this is what it's like with a younger man.

He was tracing the curve of her waist with his nose, his breath like a second touch, when the spell broke. "I know a marvelous spot for breakfast," he pulled back and said.

"Oh, heavens. You'll be long gone by then."

Matteo sat bolt upright. "You're kicking me out?"

"I most certainly am not," Kathleen said. "I'm just pointing out that it's time to leave." She took his face in her hands and kissed him passionately, eliciting a response that delayed his departure but only by a short while.

Later, after she watched him collect his clothes, she made him dress before kissing him goodbye again, and she didn't get out of the bed. In due time, she imagined, she'd forget this interlude. Or so she thought. Matteo Giancarlo had awakened in her passions she'd long thought covered over.

THE NEXT MORNING, KATHLEEN SAT IN THE BACK OF A CAR, furiously scribbling notes. After stepping outside their marriage for the first time, most women might lose time to guilt or at least to the fear of getting caught. But Kathleen Young was not most women. From the way she found herself appraising even the few men she'd seen that morning, up to and including her wiry-haired driver, she knew what she needed to do. Taking a lover would be far too complicated. She would redouble her efforts at work.

She studied her notepad. After sound check at the Santa Monica Pier, the girls were to stroll through the Hollywood Walk of Fame—in bathing suits, naturally. *Right.* She needed to double-check that the paper had dispatched a photographer. Then, back in the bus to head to the Oakmont Country Club, where they'd welcome the boys of the Memphis Belle and—

"Miss?" the driver asked, seeking some response to a question she hadn't heard.

"I'm sorry?"

"There's a scenic overlook just over there, ma'am. In case you'd like me to snap your picture."

Kathleen looked out the window: palm trees, sand, scrub, and ocean, of course. Just like Florida. "Very kind of you, sir. But I'm not a tourist. I've got a business appointment and can't be late."

By way of response, he hit the gas.

Kathleen smiled. This was the kind of interaction she understood. The driver wanted a tip.

What did Matteo Giancarlo want?

The question burst into her mind, unwanted and unbidden. In her day-to-day life, Kathleen was so accustomed to transactional exchanges, it was difficult to conceive of any other. What must it be like to simply take what you wanted without worrying over what you'd owe?

She sat back, nibbling on the end of her gold Cross pen. Wasn't that exactly what she'd done with Matteo? Not only had Kathleen taken what she wanted, she'd done it without a thought to the consequences. This was entirely unlike her. She began fanning herself with her pad of paper. The rocking motion of the car, she realized, was stimulating. Blood hammered between her legs. She longed to touch herself.

What is happening to me?

"Sir? If you wouldn't mind, though, is there a restroom nearby where we might stop?"

THIRTY-TWO

MEMPHIS BELLE COMPETITION

"WE SAW JOHN WAYNE," DORIS ENTHUSED, TUCKING A stray hair under the scarf covering her hair rollers. "But he wasn't with his wife!"

"That's old news," Thelma said, pushing Doris on the shoulder.

The girls were having breakfast at a diner down the block from the motel, the same diner where their boss had begun her day the previous morning, only they'd taken one of the booths.

"Don't be cross with me," Lillian said. "I can't help it if the only famous person out at eight p.m. on a Thursday night is ol' John Wayne."

"Who said anything about being mad?" Hattie May said.

"Good thing Thelma wasn't there," Helen said. "Out of all of us, you seem most likely to be disappointed."

Thelma laughed and shook her head. "Oh, I'm not reading up on them exactly." She looked at her teammates; she trusted them, even Lillian, now that she'd shown her true colors. "I'm looking for clues. How to *be* them. How to get what I want."

"Who isn't?" asked Lillian.

Before Thelma could respond, Doris, ever the peacemaker, changed the subject. "You would've loved the place, Thelms."

"Ugh, I don't think so." Peggy frowned. "Place looked like a medieval castle decorated by an old-fashioned grandma."

"You really think?" Lillian asked. "I love it. It's the latest style, Bohemian chic."

"If that's the trend, I'm destined to be left behind," Peggy said, draining her coffee cup.

"Anybody see Mrs. Young?" Thelma asked. She was keen to get the day rolling. Between their planned stops, the photo shoots, and the competition, it was going to be a long one. Though prior to this—perhaps the most important day of the tour—their boss was always lurking about their hotel lobbies, Thelma hadn't seen her for a full twenty-four hours.

"I hear she didn't come home last night," said Hattie May.

All eyes turned to her. "Where'd you hear that?" Peggy finally said.

Hattie May tugged at her Peter Pan collar. "Well, where is she?"

"Where's Bertie?" Lillian demanded.

This again, thought Thelma. *Was she trying to throw suspicion off George by turning Hattie May and Bertie into a couple?* Gathering her cigarettes and lighter, Thelma said, to no one in particular, "Who's on first?"

She rose to leave the booth. "We have a bus to catch. I haven't known either of those two to miss a stop."

"Well, Bertie did miss the show in Wichita. He was sick after that riverboat show in Iowa," Helen said.

Sick, Thelma frowned. She just needed this day to over. "You coming?"

"I can't believe we're gonna get our pictures taken on the Hollywood Walk of Fame," Doris squealed. "I'm so ready." And soon, they were all piling out.

As they walked back to the hotel, Peggy pulled Thelma aside. "What's with you and Lillian?"

Thelma pursed her lips. "You were right, Peggy. George has just been stringing me along. I'll never be part of his family. Lillian made that very clear yesterday."

Peggy looked at her, uncomprehending.

"He's still involved with Hattie May."

"Thelma!" Peggy tsked. "Are you out of your mind? That boy is crazy about you."

Looking down, Thelma spoke in a voice barely above a whisper. "Lillian showed me a letter."

"No!"

She looked up at her friend and nodded.

"I'm gonna kill him."

"No, Peggy, it's fine. I have another idea if you're game."

Peggy pursed her lips. "I can't wait to hear this."

"Good. But you're gonna have to. Come on. Mustn't be late, right?"

ON THEIR RETURN TO THE HOTEL, MRS. YOUNG materialized, skulking about in the lobby as per usual. From there, the day's events sped up. As so often happened, rather savoring these much-anticipated Hollywood moments, she watched them pass in a blur. At the Walk of Fame photo op, the stars were at Thelma's feet, but there was no time to scan the Boulevard for her favorites. If anyone on the team even glanced in the sidewalk's direction, the photographer would bark, "Money's not on the floor, girlies."

Soon enough, the troupe was shuffled off to the Oakmont Country Club, a rambling estate owned by a rancher before oil was discovered nearby. As they filed toward the door, Thelma saw that a stage had been set up in front of a decommissioned bomber. The side of the plane caught her eye, and while the rest of the girls filed into the club, Thelma stood staring at the Betty Boop–like figure painted just below the pilot's window, along with the plane's nickname, "Memphis Belle." Apparently, the competition had been named after the plane.

Peggy caught her gawking. "Hey, Thelms." She snapped her fingers by Thelma's ear. "Whatcha think George put on the side of his plane for our Little Miss Muffet? A kewpie doll?"

Thelma smiled. Eventually, she'd turn this escapade with George into a funny story, but not yet.

"Miss Miles, a word?"

Without turning to look, Thelma recognized the voice—Mrs. Young. *As if she had a choice.* Thelma spun around to see her boss, smart as ever in wide-legged slacks and a silk blouse fitted with enormous shoulder pads, marching in her direction.

Peggy took the hint. "Okay, well I—"

"No, Peggy. You may stay."

Thelma breathed a sigh of relief. Whatever she had to say couldn't be all that bad.

Mrs. Young wasted no time. "For this show, dear, I'd like you to act as emcee."

Peggy made a Rosie the Riveter fist. "Yes! That's a swell idea."

Hope, that infernal beast Thelma could not seem to quell, flickered in her chest. *Maybe there's another way forward, outside the reach of Sal or George or any man.*

"Of course, Mrs. Young. Happy to."

Satisfied, Mrs. Young took her leave, and Peggy swooped Thelma up in her arms.

"We might actually win this thing now. Come on. Let's change."

"First, I have to tell you something."

In a speedy whisper, Thelma told Peggy about Sal.

She was suitably stunned. "That makes Matteo your half brother! Ew. Does he know?" She scrambled in her purse. "Hang on. I need a ciggie before you answer."

"You know, I don't even know. I didn't get that impression when Sal told me."

"Here," Peggy said, offering her a cigarette then lighting another.

They stood a moment, smoking and thinking, until Thelma remembered the reason she needed to talk to Peggy. "Listen, Pegs, I would love nothing more than to see us win this movie deal. But I gotta say, those weeks while we cooled our heels waiting for the team to be reunited, I realized this whole thing is a fluke. Without this group? I'm just a girl from the boonies."

"You're hardly a yokel, Thelms."

"I don't have any talent for singing and dancing is what I mean."

"I don't think that's true, Thelma. You've never had any training."

Thelma crossed her arms. "What training have you had?"

"High school phys ed," Peggy said. "Girls learned basic dance. Plus, we had chorus."

"Don't cry for me, Pegs. I have a head for business. I know how to deal with people."

"You can say some pretty stupid things, Thelms."

"Flattery like that, and I'll withdraw my offer."

"There's an offer?"

"I thought you'd never ask," Thelma said, knowing she'd piqued her friend's interest. "This competition isn't our only chance at a bigger life, Peggy."

THE OAKMONT WAS ONE OF THE FLORIDA GIRLS' BEST performances to date. Lillian was a better singer and dancer than Thelma and was able to take on her parts—small as they were—without a hitch. Thelma kept the audience engaged throughout, but in the end, none of it mattered.

Their competition, California's Sunshine Girls, never even made an appearance at the Oakmont. The "tournament" consisted of an all-hands song-and-dance number that took place on the Santa Monica Pier in front of a slew of television, radio, and newspaper reporters and photographers. In less than half an hour, the California Sunshine Girls were crowned the Memphis Belles. The awards ceremony took more time to endure than the so-called contest. California's Sunshine Girls had always been meant to win.

The bus back to the motel was quiet.

Thelma watched Peggy calmly playing solitaire and felt relief knowing she'd agreed to join her in Vegas when the time came. Her friend had been less concerned than Thelma would've imagined. "Run your restaurants? Course I'm in. This upkeep"—Peggy brushed her fingers past her face and outfit, pursing her lips—"ain't gonna pay for itself."

She couldn't help but smile, remembering how—when first they'd met—Peggy had questioned Thelma's ambition to go to Miami. *Least I'm not the only one who can't resist the idea of being something other than what was prescribed.* But Pegs had been as pragmatic as Virginia Hill. "Show me a business that *isn't* dirty." It made Thelma wonder, and not for the first time, if she'd been absent the day they'd distributed life's instruction manual.

Or maybe working with Sal had been harder for Thelma to accept because, before meeting Madame St. Clair, all she'd ever seen women get out of a bargain with mafiosi was trouble. Peggy's dad died when she was an adult; Thelma had never known a life with a father, only daddies.

Hattie May's curls popped up over the seat back. "Where's Lillian?" she asked.

"Some casting director wanted to talk to her," Peggy said, like it was nothing.

Thelma stared at Peggy, and she stopped shuffling. "What? It's not like it's a surprise. Her dad owns half this town too." So much for the Wrights and their *self*-determination.

Returning to one of the bench seats, Thelma looked out the window, but the city lights and houses had been swallowed by the dark.

THIRTY-THREE

FLORIDA GIRLS

FLORIDA GIRLS LOSE TITLE, EXTEND TOUR
The Girls are winners in our book!
By Imogene Fuchs

ST. PETERSBURG, FLA., MAR. 24, 1945—
After a devastating second-place finish
in a two-man contest, the Florida Girls
announced additional show dates and an
additional fundraiser upon their return.
Of the amount raised thus far, tour
organizer and Sun City Emporium proprietor Lloyd "Doc" Young claimed, "We've
far exceeded the Million-Dollar Party."

"Fuchs!"

Dammit, thought Imogene, grabbing her notebook and pen from her desk. She'd just dropped the copy on her editor's desk. He couldn't have gotten past the first sentence. Sure enough, Briggs held her pages in one hand while he drummed his desk with the fingers of his other hand, an unlit cigar clamped in his

233

mouth. Dark half moons splotched his armpits, for though he doffed his jacket each morning from the minute he entered his office, he insisted on keeping his hat all day long. As if that could conceal his balding pate. Surely the heat build-up was no better for his head than his underarms.

"Sir?" Imogene said, pen and paper poised to capture his feedback.

"What the hell is this?"

"My story—"

"You know what I mean, Fuchs. What kind of opener is this?" He glanced back at the pages. "And there? A quote from Peggy Holmes? She's a waitress, for Chrissakes."

"'Follow the money,' you say. 'Give me some color.'"

"When have I ever said that to you, Fuchs?"

"You say it every staff meeting!"

Briggs dropped her pages, pushed back from his desk, and grabbed his cigar from his mouth. "If I wanted one of the boys covering this fluff, I'd send 'em. You want this Sunday feature or what?"

Imogene Fuchs wanted this feature more than anything. It would be her first, a bylined story. But she'd no intention of writing dreck the rest of her days.

"All right, already," she said, dropping her notetaker's stance and shrugging her shoulders. "Aren't you curious, though? Something's fishy."

Briggs looked Imogene up and down. "Fuchsy, you're smart for a man but dumb for a girl. They got a bunch of beautiful girls to pose in bathing suits, and we're gonna run those photos. Simple. Rewrite your piece as a feature. This is not news."

"But I do want to write news. I—"

"Fuchs, if you brought me a news story with that weak of a lede, I wouldn't run it either. Get out, and don't come back till you've got seven hundred words to go with these pictures." He tapped at a stack on his desk. "Now, vamoose."

"I thought it was eight hundred!"

"You want it to be six hundred?"

Imogene grunted in frustration but returned to her desk. The critique burned, but she knew her editor was right. To break news, you needed names, numbers, and sources, not innuendo. She inserted a fresh sheet of paper into her Remington. If Briggs wanted a puff piece, she would make it a gale.

FLORIDA GIRLS WIN HEARTS, EXTEND TOUR
Tour exceeds goals!
By Imogene Fuchs

ST. PETERSBURG, FLA., MAR. 24, 1945—On the heels of a dazzling cross-country tour, Sun City Emporium announced that the Florida Girls were adding new dates.

Fuchs popped her head up from her typewriter and thought a moment. *Do I even mention the competition?* Then she remembered Briggs had poolside snaps from the event. He'd want to run those.

After the team took second place in the Memphis Belle competition in Los Angeles, Lillian Wright, niece of Wright Industries President Homer Wright, snagged a movie contract.
No one wanted the tour to end.
"We have surpassed all expectations," said tour organizer and Sun City Empo-

rium proprietor, Lloyd "Doc" Young. "But there's still work to be done, money to raise for our troops, and greater public awareness of St. Pete as a destination for our boys coming home."

If anything can lure them, it's these talented beauties.

IMOGENE SAT BACK AND LOOKED AT HER COPY, WISHING suddenly that she smoked. This piece was going to be something to endure. If she knew her editor, she was going to have to switch the order of the grafs she'd written—move Sun City up before Wright Pharmacy.

Even if she proved herself on the basics, would Briggs ever give her the kind of assignment she wanted? If he wasn't going to let her work on anything bigger, she'd have to get more serious at looking into this story.

THIRTY-FOUR

SIN CITY

KATHLEEN STEPPED INTO THE WOODEN PHONE BOOTH AND pulled the accordion door shut. A light went on, and the fan whirred into action. *Clever contraption,* she thought. Then she remembered to be annoyed. Vegas was a dump in the middle of nowhere, and she wouldn't be so intimately familiar with phone booths if it weren't for Bertie and his gambling debt. And Lloyd and his weak lungs.

Her knees went wobbly, and for a moment, Kathleen felt she might cry. Kathleen did not cry. She closed her eyes. "Now is not the time," she said aloud. The moment passed.

Noting the modern handset, she felt sure this place had never even had a candlestick phone. Everything was so goddamn brand-new it made St. Petersburg, Florida, seem positively ancient. "You could find fault with the good Lord himself," she heard her father saying. She rubbed her forehead.

Anger was more convenient than remorse, but allowing either emotion would've made it impossible to keep up with the team's grueling schedule. Grabbing the telephone's shelf, Kathleen dropped onto the metal stool. Her feet didn't touch the floor. So far, this port surveillance business had done nothing but further compromise Lloyd's health.

Then there was Matteo.

Though in terms of conversation, he was about interchangeable with her Pifco, she found his services more expedient. They'd not shared a bed since Casa Laguna but nonetheless had found opportunity in supply closets, restrooms, and even once in a dark alley. Still, it had been a surprise even to herself when she suggested he travel to Las Vegas. "What's a few more days?" she'd teased. How lost in fantasy had she been because of these encounters with Matteo?

"Pepper!" Lloyd greeted her. "It's good to hear your voice."

They spoke briefly about the store, as well as a letter Bertie had sent his father.

"He's up to his old tricks," Lloyd said with more than a hint of admiration. "Listen to this: 'I met a sweet little gal. She promises to write. That makes three pen pals for me.'"

Kathleen rolled her eyes. If the Giancarlos didn't get Albert, some girl's father would. "We've got a light day today, sweetheart. Just some piano recital this evening, so if there's nothing else, I'm off to the beauty parlor."

"You don't need it." She could hear the smile in his voice, followed by a locomotive of a cough.

"Darling!"

"I'm fine, Kathleen. Really." He cleared his throat. "But there is something else."

The night before, he explained, following the usual bag delivery to the Lotus Club, Lloyd had taken his usual route along the channel behind the Club, scoping out the riverbank for any kind of suspicious activity while supposedly feeding the fish.

"A boat from Cuba arrived," he said.

Kathleen wasn't sure how this would appease Agent Nelson; travelers went to and from the island all the time.

"Only five guys get out. Cubans, all five of 'em," her husband said. "No idea what they were talking about, but it was definitely Spanish and not German they were speaking."

"And?" Kathleen admonished herself for being so short with him. "Sorry, there's no decent seat in this booth, and my dogs are barking."

"And," he rolled on, unimpressed by her half apology, "then a guy comes out from the Lotus Club and tells them to hurry."

"But you don't speak Spanish."

"No, but I get some words."

Kathleen refrained from saying it again but thought, *And?*

"Anyway, the fellow coming out of the club says Thelma Miles's name clear as day. Called her *un problema.* I couldn't make out anything after that. But, well, at least three of those boys had guns in holsters."

"Oh, Button. Are you sure? Thelma's here with me. How could she be causing trouble for them?" Kathleen looked out into the deserted reception area. "Are you sure that's what he said?"

"Sure, I'm sure. I think."

Even as he faltered, Kathleen changed her opinion. She hadn't mentioned the incident with Sal to Lloyd. Maybe Sal's wife found something. Or—and this thought only just occurred to her—what if Matteo still wanted the girl? Had they been Sal's men or Matteo's?

"Darling, I've got to run."

"Are you going to tell Thelma?"

"Tell her what? Button, I've a hunch she knew the Giancarlos long before we met her." Even as the words left her mouth, the image of Thelma Miles gawking on the street in front of Sun City in that oversized wool suit told her something was amiss. "It's like I've said all along. We don't know anything about this girl."

"Pepper, she's just a kid."

"I was her age when we met, Lloyd. Is that how you felt about me?"

"Sweetheart, I still haven't met a woman like you."

Despite herself, she smiled. "You win. And you're right. I'll say something."

After hanging up, Kathleen watched dust motes in the afternoon sun that slanted into the lobby. It was hours till she needed to call Agent Nelson.

Could her lover have been following Thelma?

But that was impossible. Matteo was only back on an extended leave, something to do with combat credits and points. Admittedly, he didn't inspire a close listen. Whatever the *problema* was, it was on Sal's end, which meant she was going to have to warn Thelma.

As she crossed the lobby, the Western Doll salon caught her eye, and she remembered her earlier plans. Now was not the time to let appearances slide. She always thought better under the hair dryer anyway.

* * *

"YOU SURE YOU DON'T WANT ME TO COME TONIGHT?" Peggy looked up from painting her nails—Revlon's Tournament of Roses, which set off her polka-dotted two-piece perfectly. Gone were the dishpan hands she'd had when they first met.

"No, absolutely not!" Thelma stopped buttoning her blouse and turned to face her roommate for emphasis. "Don't give Mrs. Young anything to wonder about. Who knows if she's even going to the show?"

For their free night, Lillian had bought all the Florida Girls

tickets to a concert with, in her words, "the dreamiest pianist."
Even if Thelma wasn't supposed to meet with Salvatore Giancarlo, she was nowhere near ready to accept the olive branch.
Outside performances, she'd avoided Lillian since California.
Between her teammate's photo shoots and meetings with Hollywood types, evasion had been simple enough. Then Peggy fixed
it so missing the evening's entertainment was a foregone
conclusion.

"Libber-whatsit? On piano? Oh, snooze. I'm hitting the
poolside casino. And Thelma's coming with me. Give our
tickets to Bertie and Kathleen."

Thelma had to hand it to her—the girl was fast on her feet.
Peggy knew darn well that Thelma was otherwise occupied.
That agility had prompted Thelma to tell her about Agent
Nelson, hoping she'd have some ready advice.

"Are you sure? How could you hear Kathleen in the phone
booth?"

"It was hot, so she had the door ajar. But she was yelling."

"Kathleen Young doesn't yell."

"She was very upset."

Peggy was unconvinced, which wasn't the same as unwor-
ried. This was new behavior to Thelma. If her mother—her best
and only friend until quite recently—believed Thelma was
blowing a situation out of proportion, she soon lost interest in
the subject. Not Peggy. If anything, it made the girl more
determined.

"I can hide in the lobby and wait for you," she offered then
blew on her nails to speed the drying.

Thelma was touched. Tucking her western-style top into
her trousers—the Sun City line was the only wardrobe Thelma
had—she grabbed Peggy's turban—also from the Emporium—
and began to tie the red-and-white fabric around her platinum
bob.

"Oh, Sal's still trying to win me over," Thelma said airily, patting her friend on her shoulders. "No point in him knowing you know about any of this."

This was true, but there was another side to her resistance. She knew Peggy was keen to leave St. Petersburg for Las Vegas, but she wanted to decide for herself whether to go into the casino business with Giancarlo. He'd said the hotel and gambling operations were part of his strategy to move the family into fully legal enterprises, but even before Madame St. Clair told her about Matteo, she didn't trust him. Women like Virginia Hill took whatever men like Giancarlo had to offer.

"Suit yourself, Miles." Now, Peggy was looking in the mirror, adding the same Revlon shade to her lips before tucking the tube into her new straw bag. "Maybe I'll hit it big, and we can retire. If nothing else, I'll let you know what I learn about the latest in men's swimming trunks." With that, she winked and was out the door.

THELMA WAS NERVOUS AS SHE WAITED IN THE LONG hallway outside Sal's room. She took a deep breath. Somehow, the man had managed to infiltrate even this environment with the smell of his cigars.

She knocked and waited. It seemed odd he wasn't waiting at the door, since the lobby had phoned his room. In New York, his behavior had verged on obsequious. She stepped back to look at the room number, stamped onto the face of a metal cactus that decorated the door: 101. This was the right place.

Presently, the door opened but just a sliver. Beyond that, Thelma made out a tall man with deep-set, hooded eyes, in a dark suit. He was pushing a five-dollar bill through the crack.

"Take it," he said. "And come back later."

"What are you talking about?" Thelma asked. "Who the hell are you?"

"Thelma Miles!" she heard Sal call out from inside the room. "What are you doing? In! In!"

Diego's eyes flashed, and in that moment, she sensed he was one of the men who'd try to kill her if he knew who she was. She needed him to think she was that girl for hire. Lifting her chin, she plucked the fiver from between his fingers and walked toward Sal.

"You met my right-hand man there, Diego Gonzalez." Giancarlo kept talking as Gonzalez followed Thelma into the living area. Naturally, Sal had a suite overlooking the pool. "Diego, this is Miss Thelma Miles. She's the one I been telling you about. Got a real head for business. Gonna set our casino up legit."

Giancarlo stood and kissed Thelma on the cheek then, with a dancelike maneuver, swirled her back to face Gonzalez.

"Charmed, I'm sure," Thelma said, sticking out her hand. Gonzalez screwed up his face but kept his arms at his sides, so Thelma grabbed his hand and shook it. He must be fairly high up in the organization for Sal to speak so openly, and it was obvious he wasn't used to having a woman at his level.

"You look beautiful. Just beautiful. Diego, isn't she beautiful?" Sal asked.

Diego Gonzalez gave Thelma a cursory onceover and grunted. "Mmhn."

Sal patted Thelma's cheek. "You're a little early. There's a few more things we've got to discuss," Sal said, gesturing toward a chair in the corner. "I got us reservations. Best steak in town. You just wait there. Relax."

"If this is about the casino, I'm all ears."

"There's my girl," Sal said, pinching her cheek with just

enough force to communicate she should shut up. "But nah, this is other business."

Cocking her head, Thelma crossed her arms. "Smart man, since I haven't agreed to work with you yet."

"What'd I tell you, Diego? She is spicy." Sal motioned her toward a chaise lounge covered in a cabbage rose print. "Two shakes."

Even if their meeting was going to have to wait a while longer, Thelma was not about to put herself in a reclining position as a precursor to negotiations. Fortunately, a small table with two upholstered wooden armchairs lined the adjacent wall, where she took a seat.

For a few moments, she took in the scene. There were two more men in the room, standing back like they weren't even there. Bodyguards, Thelma thought. It didn't bode well for legitimacy.

Gonzalez and Giancarlo were laughing about something, enjoying their conversation, ignoring her. To steady herself, she lit a cigarette. One of the security men leapt into action, taking an ashtray from the sideboard across the room and placing it before her. Thelma could get used to that.

Then she realized the two men were discussing the casino.

"You can't build a brick shithouse in this town without the unions," Gonzalez said.

"Beautiful. After last night's dinner, we've got him by the balls," she heard Giancarlo saying. "He won't be able to change a light bulb."

They laughed.

Thelma hoped they were talking about Florida but, before she could finish her own thought, knew they weren't. Diego Gonzalez was Cuban and must've come from Tampa. Even if he did live in Nevada, there was no reason for this pair to discuss Florida operations. This business was no more legitimate than Sal's southern empire.

Stabbing out her cigarette, Thelma reached for her handbag to make a hasty exit but was stopped by a knock at the door. Gonzalez gave a nod to the bouncers before heading to the door.

"Were you expecting someone?" Thelma asked Sal. "I should leave."

"Sit," he commanded, an edge in his voice she'd not heard directed her way before, that hair-trigger rage she'd detected the first time they met.

In walked Bugsy Siegel, sporting a tan check jacket with khaki-colored pants and a bold necktie with red, white, and black dice spilling down the front. Behind him was Virginia Hill in a fitted black sheath dress trimmed in pink satin, dragging a sable stole along the ground.

Sal called to his guests, introducing neither Diego nor Thelma. And though Hill offered a smirk in Thelma's direction, her presence was not otherwise acknowledged. Now in a mild state of shock, Thelma sat, spellbound. What business was this infamous gangster couple here to transact?

As their blinding glamor faded somewhat, Thelma felt as rapt as during any Broadway performance. Siegel, whom everyone knew was crazy, kept looking over his shoulder while talking to Giancarlo, as if he expected Gonzalez to pounce. Virginia positioned herself strategically between Sal, who hadn't bothered to stand, and Bugsy. It was obvious to Thelma that Diego made them both nervous.

"I gotta hand it to ya. Stealing my trick with the contract labor? I didn't see that coming," Siegel said, shifting on his feet. "We were all sewed up, but uh... Now, we're gonna need some more time. And the deal is we open first."

Sal, resting his chin on his tented fingers, sat motionless a moment before speaking. "It's a shame," he finally said, shaking his head. "Idle hands make for devil's work."

Bugsy laughed, looking from Diego to Sal and back, but neither even smiled. Sal's objective was clear to Thelma—he wanted them scared.

Hill made a move. "Sal, sweetheart," she said, stepping in front of Siegel to place a hand on the armrest of Sal's chair. Thelma couldn't be sure, but the move had to offer a fairly provocative glimpse at her décolletage. "Don't forget we have what you want too. Bugsy's name's what's making this place. And what's it matter? There's a bottomless demand for what we're selling, and you know it."

Diego spoke next. "Don't be stupid. It's not the demand we want to control—it's the supply."

Thelma was flabbergasted. Insulting a made man's woman? Bugsy Siegel had killed men for less.

Without taking his eyes off Hill, Giancarlo patted her hand. "Diego, give us a moment."

"Anything you say, boss," Gonzalez said, grabbing at his cuffs and resetting his shoulders.

Diego went for the door, but—still without turning his gaze —Sal stopped him. "Just wait in the bedroom."

That was when Thelma saw the plan—Salvatore Giancarlo planned to get the jump on his casino by opening before Bugsy Siegel. A flicker of appreciation flared, but she snuffed it out. Wasn't this exactly what she'd sworn at her dying mother's bedside to steer clear of?

But her mother never asked her to go straight, just to steer clear of mobsters. If all businesses were compromised in some way, at least with the Giancarlos, she'd be dealing with a devil she knew. And what were her options at this point?

Marrying George was not viable, but even if such a thing were possible, she'd realized she wanted to be more than someone's wife. She had no interest in children. Moving to Miami to find work in a secretarial pool, which had once sounded ideal, now struck her as hopelessly dreary. There was so much more to experience in the world. And hadn't her mother done all right for a long while? *Until I came along and ruined everything that night in Chicago.*

"I'll take care of everything for you," Sal was saying. "But I keep the Cuba traffic. Understood?"

Cuba? Thelma wondered. Now, it felt as if she'd arrived at the theater after intermission.

And then, as suddenly as they'd appeared, Hill and Siegel were leaving. On the way out, Hill leaned toward Thelma and said in a low whisper, "You musta done something right, but that outfit don't say yes." Then louder, with two raps on the table, "Bye, kiddo."

She realized just then Hill had fallen into the very trap that she'd described to Thelma less than three months earlier when they'd met at the Lotus Club. She saw Thelma as set decor, there for Giancarlo's pleasure rather than her own purpose. This pleased Thelma to no end. If she'd fooled Virginia, surely Salvatore and Diego wouldn't guess that she'd sussed out their plans. Sal didn't seem capable of running a straight business, but gambling was legal in Las Vegas. No matter how they got the casino built, she could run the joint aboveboard.

"Ready for dinner?" Sal was standing in front of Thelma, smiling as if nothing had happened.

She hooked her arm in his. "About time you took me out on the town. I'm ravenous."

A few moments later, in the lobby of the Last Frontier, Thelma's head still spinning with schemes, she and Sal came face-to-face with Mrs. Young and the Florida Girls.

THIRTY-FIVE

CASINO ROYALE

KATHLEEN MASKED THE WAVE OF NAUSEA SHE FELT AS SHE saw Salvatore Giancarlo walking toward her, a protective arm wrapped around Thelma Miles's slender waist.

What was that man doing in town? Had Matteo come to see him? The two didn't do much talking.

She looked back at the elder Giancarlo. Such an unfortunate coupling—Giancarlo towered over her, not only three times her age but seemingly three times her size. His slick pinstripe suit was in stark contrast to Thelma's Western duds, a pair of tan gabardine pants and a matching shirt with the blue yoke and white piping.

As much as she admired the look—and not just because it came from their spring Spotlight Collection—Kathleen also worried at the girl's sartorial choice. Wearing pants to a rendezvous with Sal demonstrated Thelma's ongoing protest. Unfortunately, Sal would've registered the same and would not appreciate that kind of gumption. Lloyd was right. She had to speak to Thelma.

"Ladies, why don't you go inside and get our seats? I'll be

along in a jiff," Kathleen said, shooing the girls into the auditorium. "I need to freshen up."

She turned back to face Thelma and Salvatore. Hattie May, Doris, and Helen dutifully trotted off, but Lillian stood her ground.

"Oh no ya don't," she whispered into Kathleen's ear. "This is just getting good."

Where was that goddamn Albert? He would've been useful in this situation, and he'd promised he would meet them.

Sal called out in greeting, "If it ain't the one and only head Florida Girl."

He looked Kathleen over crudely. She was turned out exquisitely in one of the Emporium's Lady Marlowe frocks; the teal brought out the gold in her hazel eyes. But this wouldn't do. She'd worn the outfit for his son.

Turning to Thelma, he tapped his nose with his forefinger. "Are you playin' hooky?"

Kathleen curled her lip but forced the twitch into a smile. "Salvatore," she said. "I see you've, ah, connected with Thelma."

Thelma had not entered the conversation. She appeared—Kathleen noted her own pun—miles away.

"Salvatore, do you know Lillian?" Never before had she teased Salvatore in this way, but her encounters with Matteo made her wild. "Salvatore Giancarlo, meet our newest Sun City Girl. Lillian *Wright. Homer Wright's* niece."

Sal's nostrils flared. Kathleen had hit the mark. Thanks to her father's friendship with President Taft, back when he was just Uncle Bill, she'd always known that industrial magnate Homer Wright was a Republican, unlike the Giancarlos. She was merely trying to insult him, having no idea that Homer had succeeded in keeping unions off his farms with the Pinkerton guards he kept on his payroll. Homer Wright had proven to be the one force Sal had been powerless to break. Kathleen, imagining a football-style rivalry between the two men, had no idea the amount of lost revenue Lillian represented.

Sal recovered quickly. Unbeknownst to Kathleen, he'd helped Doc Young buy his way out of Wright's Pharmacy. He likely assumed she thought it was a good double cross. "You be sure and tell your old man I got my eye on you, kid," he said, pointing his index and middle fingers at his eyes and then at Lillian.

The only thing Lillian noticed, unaware as she was of the behind-the-scenes machinations, was the faraway look in Thelma's golden eyes. "Are you all right, Thelma? What's the matter?" She leaned toward her friend, but Thelma was looking past her.

Kathleen feared the worst but pushed the thoughts away. She would do what she could, but the die had been cast for Thelma Miles.

Sal answered on Thelma's behalf. "We're doing great." Patting his chest, he looked around the lobby. The crowd was growing. "What are youse doing here? I thought you were staying at El Ranchero."

"We're here to see Liberace at the Persian Room," Kathleen smiled. This kind of social dance was her métier. "It's getting *jam*-packed. *Je regrette*, but I *must* have a chat with Thelma. Lillian, would you please get our seats?"

The girl narrowed her eyes, ready to object, until Thelma displayed a personality Kathleen had not seen before.

"Oh, you silly old goose! Remember? I told you I couldn't make it tonight."

The girl was positively trilling.

"Run along, Lills. And Kathleen, I'll meet up with you later so we can finalize the song and dance." She patted Salvatore Giancarlo on the back of his head, kissed his cheek, and pulled him toward the door as if she were his child.

For a moment, Lillian and Kathleen stood in the lobby as Sal and Thelma receded, engulfed by patrons swarming to see the great Liberace. Lillian whistled. "I guess Jung was right."

"Whatever do you mean?" asked Kathleen, tilting her head in Lillian's direction.

Lillian looked at her with a hint of a smirk and raised her eyebrows. "Some girls do have a daddy complex." She turned and sauntered toward the concert hall.

Kathleen felt the tips of her ears burning. She hadn't been as scandalized since her mother advised her she was free to marry Lloyd, sixteen years her senior, but it would mean severing ties with the family. The irony was that, unlike her own kin, Lloyd had never infantilized her. Much as she craved their imprimatur, she'd left her people behind gladly.

Thelma's words came back to her. What song and dance? She shook her head. Either it was a ruse, or she could expect a visit from Thelma later that night. No matter. The young lady needed a talking-to.

The mood for watching a recital had vanished. She and Matteo were supposed to meet later. Why not see if she could move their rendezvous up? With any luck, Bertie would be back in their room, and she could send him to the piano concert in her place. Then they'd have the place to themselves.

Taking a ten-dollar bill from her wallet, Kathleen walked to the concierge desk. "Say," she said, sliding the bill on the counter in front of the gorgeous attendant. "Would you send in a bottle of champagne to table ten? From Lloyd Young? See it gets there before Mr. Liberace starts. Thanks, sweetie. And keep the change."

* * *

THELMA WATCHED SALVATORE GIANCARLO SPEAR A HUNK of rare steak. He'd taken her to the Last Frontier, not for the pianist, but to see the vaudevillian, Sophie Tucker.

"I don't know about hiring that Liberace for our place. But this gal?" He nodded toward the stage. "Her, we should steal. I saw her last night. Not much of a looker, but she's got moxie."

Now is the time, thought Thelma. Her father was thinking about the business but relaxed. She cracked open her lobster claw. "Sal, if you want this business to be legit, you're gonna have to let me run it. That includes hiring decisions."

She dipped the fresh seafood into the pot of drawn butter before popping it into her mouth. She chewed slowly. The next person, she knew, to speak would be the one to give something up.

Sal put down his silverware. "Soon as we finish construction." He looked around. "Vegas is all you."

"I want Diego."

Sal snorted. "I thought you wanted to go legit."

"Look, Sal," Thelma said, putting down her fork, "I'm going to need the muscle in this town."

"Your mom did teach you some things," Sal said, adding more sour cream to his baked potato. "But no. For one, we put a halt on some of the extreme violence for the war, but that's only for men of service age. Besides, Diego don't know you're my daughter. None of 'em do. Not even Matty."

Thelma cocked her head.

"Matteo," Sal answered.

"How come?"

"Listen, sweetie, you need to get in there and prove yourself to my guys. They ain't gonna just trust you to suddenly be one of the top people in the organization. Let 'em think what they want about us for now."

"So you think if Diego was working for me, he'd know too much?"

"Diego is my Cuba guy. He don't wanna be number three forever, and now is not the time for him to find out he's number four. His younger brother Carlos is pretty itchy too."

Carlos? There were so many new people to get to know. *Best to play the daddy card,* thought Thelma, taking a forkful of Sal's spud. "Tell me about Cuba."

"Dolly, the less you know the better," Sal said.

Thelma pouted and blinked, but the act worked for only a moment.

"Aw, geez. C'mon," he said.

Sal, Thelma noticed, was a master at changing the mood around him. He motioned for the waiter. "Bring us some champagne, will ya?"

As the young man zipped away from the table, Thelma played her last card. "Sal, you asked me to run this because you need someone you can trust to build a legal enterprise. Now, you have to trust me. Or this isn't gonna work."

Smirking, Sal sat back in his chair. He nodded. "We run dice tours in and out of Cuba and clean money for the families. We do a little narco biz. But we don't run girls."

Just then, the waiter returned with their bottle. He removed the white cloth napkin from his arm, he covered the cork with a flourish, then looked from Thelma to Sal as if to say, "Watch this." With the cork satisfactorily removed—and no errant bubbles—he gingerly placed the napkin on the table, picked up a glass by the stem, tilted, poured, then repeated.

"To our deal!" Sal raised his glass.

But Thelma left hers untouched. Considering her mother's addictive personality—when she couldn't get her Nembutal, Vivian drank, even if that meant cough syrup—Thelma feared drinking. Not only that, Sal had just begun laying out the details of his operation. She wanted to stay sharp for the rest.

"I have more questions."

"I'm not big on answers."

"This one's easy. What's the story with the Youngs?" Thelma stopped herself before mentioning the agent. If she'd learned anything from the movies, it was *not* to lead the witness. "Are things... *friendly*?"

Sal put down his glass. "You know they do a lot of Bolita for us."

Thelma nodded.

"They also do a brisk business in our cigars and various other imports. We buy up the stock full price and sell it for pennies on the dollar."

The Youngs were laundering money for the mob? Thelma suppressed a smile. Were the Youngs aware they were laundering money for the mob? Was this the connection to Agent Nelson? For once, she decided to do as her mother would advise and keep a lid on it.

"So really, the thing with Bertie is my fault."

Bertie? His gambling debt? Thelma took a breath, forcing herself to keep a straight face and ask a neutral question. "How do you mean?"

"I authorized too much for him. That war's gonna end sooner rather than later, and now his debt's so big..." Sal trailed off, looking away. "Let this be your first lesson. You're in business to make money, not friends. When a customer starts costing you money, you gotta be ruthless to keep 'em in line."

Thelma disguised her gasp as a cough. Did Sal plan to kill Bertie as soon as his moratorium on murderous tactics ended with the war? Thanks to a lifetime of Vivian's dire proclamations that a mother couldn't live without her child, her first instinct was to find Kathleen and warn her. But if Sal was telling the truth, Bertie's demise was not imminent.

Sal thrust a champagne flute in her face. "Drink up. It's a sure cure."

This time, Thelma accepted the glass. Kathleen would have to wait until after the Liberace show at the very least. There was no accosting her boss with this bombshell at Sal's hotel; they would have to speak later, at their place.

"Salute!" said Sal. "To our deal. I'll have my guy draw up papers so the business is its own entity with you in charge. The Royal Casino. Fit for a king. What do you say?"

Thelma looked into Sal's eyes. Violence was the way of these gangsters. Even if there was some kind of truce because of the war, even if she'd not forgotten, she was unnerved by how thoroughly she'd thrust the concern from her mind. Yet backing out now because this truth had been made evident made no sense. After all, Sal was proposing she run the casino as a legitimate business concern. She could warn Kathleen about Bertie's debt without mentioning Sal. She allowed a smile to play at her lips. "How about the Casino Royale?"

With Sal's promise to put the business in her name on their return to St. Petersburg, they toasted, and business was done. Out came Sophie Tucker, "the last of the red-hot mamas," according to the emcee.

Tucker appeared on stage, holding what looked like a medicine bottle. She made a big show of offering a sample to men at various tables. A sandwich board draped across her shoulders read, in bold crimson letters, "Sophie's Red Hot Remedy—You've Got to be Loved to be Healthy."

Sal was a marvelous audience member, and he attentively watched Sophie perform. As the night progressed, Thelma appreciated his easy laugh. Whenever she took breaks, Sal told

Thelma stories. She discovered that, in addition to Matteo, she had a half sister.

"And you're sure that's it?" Thelma couldn't resist deadpanning.

But Sal was serious. "She's why I don't allow my girls to have kids. My girl—she's, ya know, *special*."

"Whaddya mean, *special*?" Thelma slapped her hand over her mouth almost as soon as she asked the question, but it was too late. "I'm sorry. I—"

"It's okay," Sal said with a wan smile. "She's feeble in the head. I knew it come from my side of the family, so that was it for me. No more kids."

"But I still don't get it," Thelma said.

"Dollface, I don't know if you're aware. Most of these kids end up in institutions. It is not a good life. I can't have a kid of mine end up like that, and I can't have my wife taking care of..."

Thelma bit her lip, truly unsure how to respond.

Sal's tone changed, and he was almost jovial. "When I saw you that first time, I was furious. My temper sometimes..." Sal raised his hand, palm up. "When I couldn't find Vivian, well, eventually I gave up. But I never forgot your eyes. Even when I seen you in Tampa, I didn't think it was possible, but I had my lawyer do some checking. It was you.

"Did you know your mother changed your last name?"

"Vaguely, Sal. I was ten." Thelma knew, of course—the name was a lark that had stuck after she'd asked her mother where they were going. "Miles and miles," Vivian had said, tapping Thelma's nose. "That'll be our road name."

But she didn't want to give Sal that much. "What I do know is that she lived in fear you'd find us."

"Yeah, well, don't change it now."

"You don't want another Giancarlo running around?"

Sal grabbed Thelma's upper arm, fire in his eyes. "Kid, that was never your name. Don't even joke about that."

Wriggling from Sal's grasp, Thelma made an exaggerated show of being wounded. "What's the big deal?"

"In case you didn't get it before, there's men would kill to run my business," Sal shrugged. "That's why I never did apply for an exemption for Matteo. He needed some toughening up, and after basic, he'll be at the back of the line anyways."

Thelma, still rubbing her arm, kept quiet. She wanted to ask so many questions but was afraid to interrupt. Did Queenie get it wrong, or was Sal lying now?

"You ain't so tough neither." Sal grabbed her hand and swiped his thumb across her knuckles a few times. "By the time you're running the casino, no one'll question a thing. But if they knew you and me was related? They'd think you was making a run for the business. And that wouldn't go so good for you."

Considering the men Thelma had grown up around, she'd never longed for a father, never felt the need for a man to protect her from bad influences. They *were* the bad influences. Knights in shining armor were only in the movies. But she was drawn to Sal; something about him was compelling—likable, even. Perhaps this was why her mother never got over him; her bitter complaints never fooled Thelma. It wasn't possible to hate someone like that if you didn't also love them. Keeping the hate alive was a kind of love.

"Vivian always talked about your trip to Florida like it was some kind of magic," Thelma said.

"Ah, Miami. 1924. Incredible trip. Very profitable."

Sal went on about investments, but it struck Thelma for the first time that might have been when she was conceived. There was no one to ask, but the mood had changed again as Tucker resumed her act and Sal waved her over with a fist full of cash.

With a saucy wink, she took his money and kept singing, "I'm still waiting for... the man I love!"

Sal aimed his thumb at the words "Red Hot Remedy" draped over Tucker's shoulders. "Let's tell Doc we've got Sun City's newest sales rep out west," he said then proceeded to laugh at his own joke.

"See what I mean?" Thelma heard her mother ask.

She had to concede. In less than an hour, Sal Giancarlo had gone from hoping for a passive end to Doc Young's eldest son to contriving a casual joke with the man. Salvatore Giancarlo was not to be trusted. Those warm feelings, Thelma decided, were a lapse.

* * *

THE DOOR TO THEIR ROOM WAS AJAR. *BERTIE BETTER HAVE A good explanation,* Kathleen thought. It was bad enough he failed to lock doors. He wasn't raised in a damn barn.

When she pushed, however, something blocked the entry.

"Albert?" she called.

"I'm here, Mom. Can you open the door?"

"Can *I* open the door? You're the one in the way," she complained, even as she was pushing her way in—and tripped.

Whose body was on the floor?

THIRTY-SIX

DEATH IN VEGAS

"ALBERT LLOYD YOUNG, WHAT HAVE YOU DONE NOW?" Not only was there a strange man on the floor, but he was surrounded by bloodied bath towels. Worse, now she'd opened it, Kathleen couldn't fully close the door. Was the man injured? Dead?

"Who is that?"

"Mom, I got no idea."

"*Have*, son. You *have* no idea."

"Jesus Christ."

"Language!"

"However you say it, I don't know who this fella is. Looks to me like some kind of tally wop thief."

"Albert!"

"Mom, that bastard musta had his gun drawn like this." Albert cocked his fingers toward his chin, elbow bent like a detective in a melodrama. "He was opening the door at the same time I was going out. He shot himself. A second earlier, and he'da shot *me*."

Kathleen regarded the man lying face down on the floor; he was most certainly deceased. She'd seen her share of death on

261

the family farm and even at the veteran's hospital where she'd volunteered before her debut. But she'd never seen the back of a human head blown off.

Gently hooking his hip with the toe of her satin shoe, she nudged his body on its side and leaned closer to get a better look at the man. The contents of her stomach threatened to upend. It was neither the sight nor the smell of the blood, which she assumed would've overwhelmed most women. It was the man himself, familiar. She'd seen that low forehead before. The Million-Dollar Party. Yes. This was Sal's man. This was bad.

She looked back into the halls behind her. The corridors were deserted. She checked her watch: eleven. Vegas's prime nightlife hour. And their suite was at the end of the hall.

"Help me move his legs so we can shut the door. You're sure no one heard you? When did this happen?"

"Geez, Mom. I don't know. Maybe a half hour ago. I haven't seen anyone. No one's come around."

While they shuffled the body, Kathleen had a moment to think. She wasn't buying Bertie's innocent act. An innocent person would've called the police. He'd been waiting for her to return and fix the problem. She would. If she was going to save either of them, there was no time to ponder the morals.

"Did you pay the Giancarlos before we left?"

"Mom, you and Dad drove me there yourselves. Of course I paid. What's that got to do with anything?"

"Bertie, this appears to be one of Sal's men. If you've paid—" She stopped midsentence. Sal was the one who'd added Vegas to the tour. Lloyd had mentioned additional gaming ventures, but the only time she'd seen Sal was earlier with Thelma. Had her son accrued more debt? Was taking Bertie out the whole point of their stop?

"Son, I'm only going to ask this once. Did you ever steal from those bags?"

Bertie hung his head in shame.

"Get out. Now. Join the girls at that piano concert. I'm going to take care of this."

"What? No. Then I should stay. I'm the witness—"

"Who said anything about a witness?" Kathleen regarded her son. At least he had on proper trousers, but his shirtsleeves were rolled up, and nothing looked pressed. What had he been doing? Why was he returning to their room when he was supposed to be at the piano concert? "Put on fresh clothes—with a tie—and get yourself down to that Liberace show. You are never to speak of this again. If anyone sees me? I'm just a silly woman. I was overcome and didn't know what I was doing. They'll see it was an accident. Of course, I didn't kill anyone."

"*I* didn't kill anyone."

"Albert, you covered this man in towels *and* failed to call security. This looks bad for you. Just leave and do as I say."

Bertie washed up and changed while Kathleen surveyed the hallway, glad their suite had its own corridor. The door had prevented blood from hitting her son, but the backward spray needed attending to. Dragging the vanity bench into the hall, Kathleen wiped all traces of blood and bone with a soapy hand towel and washcloth. Given that it was nearly ten p.m. on a Saturday night, not a soul was about. She needed bleach.

Bertie had been clever to surround the man with bath towels. But why had he mentioned a witness?

When Bertie high-stepped over the body past Kathleen, she hissed, "This is why I tell you to lock the door."

MATTEO DID NOT HESITATE, THOUGH RUSHING TOWARD THE action was less a matter of coming to his lover's aid than seeing whom Bertie had knocked off. He didn't buy the accident story for a second.

"I don't know why Diego woulda been coming to your room, but if my dad finds out Bertie killed him, he's a dead man."

"Bertie didn't kill him. It was an accident. Kid doesn't have the grit." Kathleen rubbed her forehead. "Why was this man coming here with a gun in the first place?"

"Hey, hey." Matteo reached for Kathleen and pulled her to his waist. "I don't think it was my dad's idea. He ain't going after men of service age." Matteo looked at the body.

Kathleen wondered if he knew about her son's debt.

"Diego's always trying to prove how great a soldier he is. Maybe Bertie fucked up a bag drop, and Diego wanted to scare him?"

Kathleen pulled away. "You don't think he was looking for me, do you?"

They could have talked all night and never figured out that Diego was looking for Matteo. Birds had spotted him with Kathleen in California; he'd brought the gun in case Matteo was with her. Plus, it usually helped get people talking.

"Why would Diego be looking for you?"

Now was not the time to mention Agent Nelson. Or ever. She deflected. "What happens when your father finds out?"

"He ain't gonna. Not exactly." Matteo smiled. "You're lucky this marble is a dark green."

It turned out that the young Giancarlo was astonishingly effective at knowing what to do. After rolling Gonzalez onto a blanket, Matteo dragged him into the bathroom. He disappeared for a few moments then returned with bleach and rags. "I seen the cleaning cart earlier," he said as he handed over the goods. "Clean this up, and leave all the towels in the tub. I gotta go get some other things."

"Then what?" Kathleen asked.

"Then nothing. You don't wanna know what happens next.

Gimme your key. I'll leave the key out front when it's safe to come back."

She looked at Matteo, so sure and sturdy in his bomber jacket and collared shirt. He was only a few years older than Albert but so much more grown.

"Matteo, when we leave here, the tour is ending." Rather than finish her thought, she embraced him. When at last they drew apart, ravaged, Kathleen was sure she was going to hell. There weren't words sufficient to cover the depravity of copulating in the presence of a dead man, but she needed Matteo to stay cooperative.

By the time Kathleen made her way to the Persian Room, the Liberace show was almost over. Still, she was surprised to see her son showed up. Was he finally grasping the seriousness of their situation? Electrifying as Liberace's performance was, Kathleen couldn't pay attention. Not that she wanted to return to the room either.

Before the applause died down, she leaned toward her son. "Bertie, I'm going to the bar at our hotel. Take this." She handed him a twenty. "Lose the girls. And don't come back to our room tonight."

He looked into her eyes, and in that moment, she saw his pain. Never as good as the old man, not as clever as his younger brother. Even as emcee, Thelma had replaced him. Gambling at least offered the possibility of coming out on top.

She touched his jaw. "We have a show tomorrow, kid."

He nodded even as she felt him disengage.

"No need to panic, Pepper," she could hear Lloyd reminding her. "That's just how boys are. They pull away from their mothers."

She'd just stood when Lillian asked, "Where's she going?"

"Mind your own beeswax," Bertie said.

Kathleen stiffened a moment but kept walking. The night's events were all too strange to contemplate.

AFTER A COUPLE OF SOLITARY BOURBONS AT THE HOTEL bar, a western-themed affair with an enormous wagon wheel chandelier and rough-hewn tables and chairs, she was ready to face her room. She checked in with the concierge and received Matteo's message: "Sleep tight. Don't let the bedbugs bite."

She felt grateful and embarrassed at once by the childish exhortation. How had she ever slept with that man? And in the presence of a corpse?

Kathleen was lost in thoughts as she walked the long corridor to her suite. She wanted to bathe and change and be absolutely certain there was no trace of Sal's man. She would switch rooms first thing in the morning. But her plan derailed before she could cross the threshold, where she found Thelma asleep in the doorway.

"Hey, you," she said, kicking Thelma in the hip. "Get up."

The girl started awake. "No! Not me," she said.

"What?" Kathleen asked. "Oh, get up, and be quiet now." She bent down and reached a hand out to Thelma. "I needed to talk to you anyway." Kathleen took a quick peek inside, thinking she'd done a terrific job, though, in fact, Matteo had given the area a final sweep.

"Let's take this conversation to the bar."

The Wagon Wheel was deserted. At a four-top over two steaming mugs of coffee, Kathleen handed her Dorothy Gray compact to Thelma. "Powder your nose, dear," she said, patting her own still perfectly coiffed head. "You're still representing the Emporium."

Thelma frowned just slightly as she accepted the compact.

"Holy smokes." She looked in the mirror, finger-fluffing her flattened waves. After a few taps of powder, she dug into her bag for her own tube of lip color. The distraction gave Kathleen a moment to clear her mind of recent events and recall her earlier conversation with Lloyd. Had the world changed in a matter of hours?

"You need to get away from Sal. He's a very dangerous man."

Thelma looked up from her work. "The same Salvatore Giancarlo you're in business with. The one you've been throwing me at—"

Holding up a hand to stop the girl from finishing her sentence, Kathleen moved on. "There's no point in looking for someone to blame."

Thelma slid the compact back across the table. "I don't know about that."

The impudence. "Thelma, dear, I'm trying to help you. I can handle myself, and I thought you could too. But we've overheard a conversation that suggested you might be in trouble."

"Whaddya mean, *I'm* in trouble?"

"Now, don't panic, dear. Mr. Young isn't sure—"

"Mr. Young?" Thelma waited a beat. "If anyone's in trouble here, it's *you.*"

Kathleen's eyes went wide. "Listen, missy," she said, wagging a finger at Thelma, trying to remember what specifically Matteo had called Thelma. A *friend* of the family? "I've been doing everything I can to keep this tour together. But I've learned some things about you, mademoiselle. You aren't quite who you pretend to be."

"Oh, that's rich. Mrs. 'I'm from the Best Family in Virginia,' I believe is how you put it?" Thelma rolled her eyes. "To think, I wanted to be just like you. But you don't have any real power. Only money."

A guffaw escaped Kathleen's mouth. Putting her fingers to her temples, she closed her eyes and spoke slowly. "I don't know what that's supposed to mean or what you think you've heard, but we are talking about *you*." Opening her eyes, she stared into Thelma's. "And we both know Sal is no stranger to you. So hush up."

Pushing her chair back, Thelma grabbed her bag to leave but instead hugged her purse to her lap. "I know about Agent Nelson," she said in a low voice.

Kathleen sat back and chortled. "Fine! What do I care?"

THIRTY-SEVEN

ENEMIES DECLARE AN ALLIANCE

Mrs. Young's response astonished Thelma. Either this woman had more influence than she'd suspected, or she was more naïve than she'd imagined. Remembering the way she'd swatted at Madame St. Clair, Thelma decided it must be the latter.

"Look, I don't know what you *think* you know about *me*, but you are above your pay grade here," Thelma said.

"Oh, *I* am?"

Thelma rubbed her eyes. "Bertie's in trouble."

The mention of her son clearly rattled Mrs. Young but only for a moment. She slammed the table with her fist. "He's serving his country!"

Her boss's response made no sense. *Unless...* "You knew about his gambling debt?"

Now, Mrs. Young grabbed the table as if she might fall out of her seat. Steadying herself, she replied in deliberate tones. "That. Is *all* under control. Because I know when Sal thinks he has a problem, he'll go to any lengths to make it go away. And I don't think it will be his wife in this situation."

This conversation was going sideways. Hanging her bag on

her chair, Thelma reached for her now-tepid coffee. "Look, I'm trying to help you. I *want* to help you." She took a sip; the brew was horrid, but she refrained from pulling a face. "You've done so much for me."

Until this moment, Thelma hadn't realized how true that statement was. To grasp now that Mrs. Young had been regarding her with judgment all along caused a spasm of pain in her chest. Tears welled in her eyes.

"I just... I don't know that I *can* get away from him."

For the first time since her mother died, Thelma wept. Great shuddering cries racked her whole body.

Mrs. Young jumped out of her chair, pulled up next to Thelma, and put a protective arm around her. "Shh. There now."

"I'm Sal's daughter," she blurted out. Had she really confessed again? Worse, she was sobbing into the arms of a woman who wasn't even her mother. What was happening to her?

Mrs. Young released Thelma. "You're...? Pardon me?"

"Nothing. Never mind," Thelma said. *Shit. Shit. Shit.*

"Oh, no, dear. I heard you. I'm just, well, *surprised* would be an understatement." Mrs. Young's brow furrowed.

Thelma was tempted to warn her about wrinkles, just as her boss might've done if the situation were reversed. Of course the woman had been judging her all along. She'd willingly put herself in a contest. Fluttering her lips, Thelma shook her head. "It surprised me too."

"Did it," Mrs. Young commented more than asked.

"Yes. I assure you. It did. Even now, no one is supposed to know."

"Well, then." Even in a sweetheart neckline and cap sleeves, Mrs. Young was a force. Despite her age—she had to be in her late thirties—she wore form-fitting clothes to her advantage.

Had that blush in her cheeks always been there? "Tell me everything."

* * *

Kathleen sat stock-still as Thelma Miles spoke. Matteo was Thelma's *half brother?* She wondered if he knew. Maybe that was why Sal had sent him off, to put Thelma in place. But had she really learned she was Sal's daughter on the day of the Flamingo Derby? The girl could keep a secret.

"Our house must've been some kind of Chicago headquarters," Thelma was saying. "He must've bought and paid for it. And the new car we used to get every two years. Till I was ten."

"Is that when you left Chicago?"

Thelma nodded.

"But why? What happened?"

"When Ma was entertaining, I'd stay at a friend's house. That night, there was an explosion at the factory where her dad worked. They went to the hospital and sent me home. I don't know what happened to him, because that's the same night we left. When I got home, I knew I was supposed to hide, but I was tired of hiding. And he saw me.

"He knew I was his, and that was his one rule. No kids." She touched the scar on her cheek. "I must look like someone in his family. I don't see it at all."

Kathleen could see it. The hair. The height. And there was something in the set of her jaw very much like Matteo's. But those amber eyes—those seemed to be hers alone. "Your mother must have loved you very much to try and protect you like that."

Thelma stared off, almost whispering. "I never thought of it that way." Then she turned toward Kathleen, resolve in her face. "In Chicago, no one worried about my father. There were plenty of orphans. But in Keokuk, I was a freak. So I spent most of my time at the library; I loved biographies.

"Then Mom got really sick... Anyway, after she died, I packed up and went to Florida. It was just a fluke, me stopping at your store."

She spoke with such guilelessness, Kathleen was convinced she was telling the truth. By the time she got to the part about fighting with Hattie May's mother, Kathleen's relief came out in a deep belly laugh. "I can't believe you missed your bus because you got into a fight with Mrs. Harper, that ol' tosspot." She pulled a handkerchief from her bosom and wiped at the sides of her eyes.

Thelma was bewildered. "I wish I found this funny."

"Oh, my dear, don't you see?" She coughed and straightened. "You're going to help get us out of this mess."

"Mrs. Young, I came to warn you. That's all. I'm not sure I can get myself out of this mess. Now he's asking me to run his casino in Vegas. I thought maybe, if we won the Memphis Belle competition, I could elude him."

"Oh, that contest was all set up in advance"—Kathleen swatted at the air—"but you see, Bertie's debt is not our biggest problem."

Thelma pursed her lips and crossed her arms. "I'm all ears."

Now, it was Kathleen's turn to confess—to a point. Her affair with Matteo was irrelevant. This girl needed to learn how to turn this situation to her advantage.

"I learned about Bertie's debt from Agent Nelson. Of all things, young Theodore showed up directly after Millicent's funeral. Can you believe the nerve?"

Kathleen did her best to describe Agent Nelson's request. "We weren't spying on the Giancarlos." She leaned forward and whispered. "We were looking for German spies."

Thelma massaged her temple. "That makes no sense, Mrs.

Young. Why would he come to you? Why not go to Sal? Sal hates the Nazis."

"Keep your voice down." Kathleen felt her neck warming. *Had* they been spying on the Giancarlos? Of course not. How could one spy without knowing what to look for? "It appears our young Theodore tried, but Sal didn't believe him. Refused to work with him."

"Why did you agree?"

Kathleen sat back. "We were strapped, and that Agent Nelson knew it," she said, taking a deep breath before revealing the store's construction debt. "The Bolita games were the only thing keeping us afloat. That's the whole reason we started this tour, to generate some revenue apart from the Giancarlos. Then Bertie's debt threatened everything. Until now."

Thelma was still staring, wide-eyed.

"You, darling. We have you."

She crinkled her nose, but Kathleen laid a reassuring hand over Thelma's. "You must trust me," she said. "Sal needs you. If he wanted Matteo running his casino, he would be. And Thelma, I need you."

Now the girl sat up straighter. *Good.*

Kathleen squeezed Thelma's hand and leaned closer. "Like I said, money isn't our biggest problem. Lloyd has the emphysema."

Sorrow spiked in Kathleen's chest as she talked about Lloyd's illness, how they wanted to leave the Emporium to the boys and move to California to heal his lungs.

"They say the waters around Carlsbad are a cure. We might even open a health sanitorium. But before we go,"—Kathleen stopped and looked over her shoulder—"we must *decouple* from the Giancarlo business. Especially considering Bertie's proclivities."

In response, Thelma sat blinking. *What was the matter with the girl?*

"Dear, these people are far worse than I imagined. While Sal was wining and dining you, he sent someone to our room to rough Bertie up. With a gun.

"But it was Sal's man ended up"—here, she leaned across the table to whisper into Thelma's ear—"dead."

Thelma yanked her head back to face her boss. "You're saying..." She mouthed, *Bertie killed someone?*

"Bertie didn't do anything." Kathleen sat back on her side of the table but lowered her voice. They were the only two customers in the place, which Kathleen had noticed was in fact called the Wagon Wheel. "The man's gun discharged accidentally."

"What? Is he still? What did you do with—"

"Bertie took care of it."

Thelma lifted an eyebrow. "Mrs. Young, I know exactly what these people are capable of. We should head up there now. Make sure that situation has actually been taken care of."

Kathleen crossed her arms and glared at Thelma. Despite her endless needling of her son, it irked her to no end when others suggested he might be deficient in any way.

"You sure Sal didn't find out you were working with the feds?" Thelma asked.

"We weren't. At least not in the way you're suggesting. And anyway, you're going to help us be free of Salvatore Giancarlo."

An unattractive snort escaped Thelma's mouth.

"What? Isn't it obvious? The man adores you. Thank heavens, for your sake, it's in a paternal way." Kathleen rubbed her brow. "Once you explain we're moving to start fresh, that Mr. Young is in fact quite ill, I'm sure—"

"Mrs. Young, if Sal finds out Diego died in your room, I don't know what he's liable to do."

"Then let's make sure he doesn't. I'll keep your secret and help you escape."

THELMA DOUBTED MRS. YOUNG COULD HELP HER ESCAPE the Giancarlos, but she needed the woman to keep that secret. By the time they arrived back at the Youngs' room, Thelma had made up her mind. Deciding she'd find their debt and erase it made her heart swell with pleasure—for a moment, anyway. She was feeling proud of a skill she'd learned at the flophouse?

Both of them held their breath as Mrs. Young opened the door to her room. The walls were a blazing white and the green marble flooring shockingly free of the violence that had occurred. Given Bertie's general reliability and precision, Thelma should've been more suspicious. But she was tired, and Mrs. Young said something about how years of cleaning the store had finally paid off. Thelma had seen a few dead bodies in her time, but she'd never witnessed a shooting. She had no idea of the skills required to clean up after such a scene.

Her boss disappeared into the bathroom and filled the tub.

She was taking a bath? "I'll do what I can, Mrs. Young," Thelma said. But she knew the only way Sal would give up on the Emporium was if the store started losing him money. Even then, he was more likely to burn the place down for the insurance payout on his debt than hand it over.

"Good girl," Kathleen said as she reappeared with two sopping wet towels. "Let's give the place a once-over, shall we?"

When the two finally parted ways, the sun was coming up.

THIRTY-EIGHT

A FOND SO LONG

"WELL, LOOK WHAT THE CAT FINALLY DRAGGED IN."

It was Lillian, looking a tad the worse for the wear herself. Not that Thelma had checked her reflection. After giving Mrs. Young's room a thorough cleaning, she couldn't wait to crawl into bed.

But Lillian Wright was waiting at her door, a bottle of RC Cola in her hand. Thelma had no choice but to pretend this was welcome. Certainly, it was less strange than cleaning up the remains of a dead body, though she hadn't seen anything to clean. Had the biggest surprise of the night been learning that Bertie had a fastidious side? She giggled.

"You okay?" Lillian asked, her furrowed brow a stark contrast to her soft blond curls. Even in a tattered bathrobe, she looked put together.

"Couldn't sleep. You?"

"Not a wink. Hattie May is snoring like a chainsaw."

"Don't you have a pill for that?"

Lillian laughed. "No pill is that strong."

Thelma nodded. "Want a smoke?"

Lillian accepted, and they stood together, leaning against

the hallway wall. She didn't want to wake Peggy and Helen. Why was her wealthy teammate in an old robe and plain cotton pajamas from Sun City? "You make those pj's look like a million bucks."

"Isn't that our job?"

"Is it? Aren't you a movie star now?"

Lillian snorted. "Not quite."

Holding her right elbow, Thelma looked at the cigarette in her hand. "Mind if I ask you something?"

"Shoot."

"Why?"

"Why what?"

"Why did you want to be a Florida Girl? You don't need the job. It's not going to open any doors—"

"That's where you're wrong."

Thelma looked askance at Lillian. "Oh, come on."

"I mean it. My father is a firm believer in self-determination. Just like that old Andrew Carnegie. And just like my uncle. Me and my sister aren't getting a dime. And I don't think George is inheriting anything either."

Thelma gasped.

"I've been trying to tell you for days now. That letter you read? I couldn't tell what you were thinking. It all happened so fast. But then I reread the note. You thought I was there to break up with you? For my cousin? As if he was going to marry that snore machine?" She was laughing now. "He wanted me to talk to his mother, you dope."

Thelma felt her fingertips burning, but there was not an ashtray in sight. "Dammit!"

"Here," Lillian offered, dropping her butt into the bottle and giving it a little shake. "Maybe we can slip this to Hattie May."

Despite herself, Thelma laughed. Relief flooded over her. Not because of George—now more than ever, she knew that had to end—but because she hadn't lost a friend. She had so few, she'd realized on this tour.

Looking back up at Lillian, she shook her head. "How are you so gay, then? It's like nothing bothers you."

Lillian looked off into the distance. "I suppose I've never thought about it."

"But don't you worry about the future?" asked Thelma.

"My mom says worry is a sin," Lillian said then looked back at Thelma with a smile. "If you ask me, it's the only one worthy of that label."

Thelma crossed her arms and thought cynically, *Because you were never forced to transgress.* "Oh, after tonight, I think we both know there's sin."

"Okay, okay, I was trying to keep it light," Lillian said, but at last her smile faded. "If you're determined to be with Sal, I mean, I won't say anything. That's up to you. But I wanted to talk to you before I headed back to California."

"You're not coming back to St. Pete?"

Lillian shook her head. "I'm staying in California. That agent convinced me I might have a shot."

Thelma looked at her friend, nodding.

"I know what you're thinking. You're not wrong. My family name didn't hurt, and I'm hoping it will keep me off the casting couch." She smirked. "Unless I want to be on the casting couch."

Thelma was shocked. So much of what she knew about the world came from books and movies, none of which presented women as the modern creatures she saw they were. There was no real difference between these women and the ones she'd worked with in Iowa. At heart, they were the same. Thelma threw her arms around Lillian. "I'm so glad we talked."

"Me too. I know your mom would be proud of you."

Thelma clung a little tighter.

THIRTY-NINE

HOMECOMING

THELMA LOOKED AT THE TIFFANY LAMP ON SAL'S DESK. So *old-fashioned.* He'd no telephone or radio, either, just a steady stream of informants. But she did love the desk, a broad polished mahogany with a writing blotter.

After mending things with Lillian, Thelma had retrieved George's letters from the depths of her suitcase. Had his *proposition* been a proposal? He'd not only said as much in his first note, he'd mentioned it again in a subsequent letter. But then he'd dropped it, and his notes had turned crisper, his sign-off downgrading from "all my love" back to "eternally yours" to simply "yours." Or was she reading too much into it?

At last, she'd decided to write back and could think of no better place to compose her thoughts than Sal's office in the early morning. Though she'd moved back into The Soreno and upgraded her room to one with a small writing table, Sal's office was a stark reminder of who she was in the world.

April 1, 1945
St. Petersburg
Dear George,

I'm sorry I've been such a slouch about writing. Even though the tour is over, there's a Grand Finale in May, and Mrs. Young is keeping us busy doing store events. You didn't hear this from me, but they're planning to host another year of Florida Girls. I won't be joining them. Peggy and I are moving to Las Vegas.

This might come as a shock, George, but I figure the best way is to tell it plain. We're very different people, you and I. We aren't meant to be sweethearts.

Take Care Always,
Thelma Miles

THELMA STARED AT THE WORDS.

"*Take care always?*" She heard in her mother's voice. "What are you, his doctor?"

But she'd written this letter three separate times already because you couldn't just cross out "love" or "XO" or even "all my best." The letter had to sound decisive—and final. Their correspondence could not continue. What would she say of her real day-to-day life?

Dear George,

Now that I'm working for Sal, I don't feel like a Florida Girl anymore. Mrs. Young is still squeezing every last photo op out of the team, but she's hands-off with me, so I keep an eye on Sal. We can't have him finding out what really happened to his man Diego. (I didn't tell Peggy about that, but she's eager enough about moving to Vegas she's happy to cover for me. It's just a few weeks till the tour ends anyway!)

Not that I'm learning much. The Casino Royale is going to be legit, but my father is anything but. He may have put a moratorium on murder, but he has a bunch of young thugs who are quite skilled at intimidation. I can't make heads or tails of how he runs this operation. Everything's in a series of discombobulated notebooks. Not exactly primers on modern business practices.

I still think fondly of you and long for a way we might be together—

It wasn't George's fault she was broken.

"Beautiful!"

Thelma snapped out of her daydream and slipped the real letter into the pocketbook at her side and stood to greet her father with a peck on the cheek.

"Sit! You look good behind a desk."

Without taking a seat himself, Sal poured a brandy and offered Thelma the glass. She shook her head.

"Ah, that's right—you don't like to drink. Considering your mother." Sal made the sign of the cross over his torso. "God rest her soul. I understand."

Just when Thelma thought she had Salvatore Giancarlo

figured, he dropped another pearl that told her otherwise. She wondered if his sentimentality was genuine. Her mother had seemed to despise him, but you couldn't hate like that without love. He sported his trademark three-piece pinstripe suit with a white pocket square, with not a hair out of place. But the man remained an enigma.

Drink in hand, Sal walked to the door to send off Petey, the burly bodyguard he'd brought on in place of Diego. Though he made it clear he was no replacement, often treating the man as if he'd been the end of Sal's beloved lieutenant. *Better he suspects his own men than Bertie,* Thelma thought. *But who would suspect Albert?*

"Bring us coffee from downstairs—sugar, cream, the works." He turned to face Thelma. "It just don't feel right signing without some kinda drink." Sal withdrew a cigar from a small humidor.

Thelma watched in fascination as he pulled a guillotine cutter from his pocket, snipped the end, held it to a lighter, and then—once the stogie was aflame—took three puffs.

"Let me try one of those," said Thelma, inhaling the fragrant aroma she loved.

"Christ, no!" Sal coughed. "Filthy habit for a girl."

Thelma was about to object when someone knocked.

Sal glanced at his Vacheron. "Right on time," he muttered. "Come in!"

A balding older gentleman in a brown tweed suit entered, his step speedy, briefcase clutched to his chest. Seeing Thelma behind Sal's desk, he squinted and jutted his head forward. On his nose sat a pair of old-fashioned pince-nez specs, which Thelma thought made him look rather like a cartoon character.

Sal, still holding his cigar, patted the fellow on the back, which caused him to flinch and look over his shoulder. Ignoring the tic, Sal blustered on. "Art, ya finally get to meet my girl Thelma. Give her your card, will ya?"

The ivory stock read, "Artemis Clauer, Esq." Thelma frowned. *E-S-Q?* Before she could ask what that meant, there was another knock.

"Come in!" Sal motioned to the table. "Leave the coffee there, Petey. And no more interruptions till I say."

Petey left without a word.

"Art?" Sal inclined his head toward the coffee service then motioned for Thelma to join them. She no longer cared what *Esq.* stood for because at last, it was time to formalize their casino deal. Once she'd perched on the sofa's edge, Sal continued.

"Thelma, Art here is like family. He knows where all the—" He stopped short. "Been the family attorney for years."

"Pleasure," Thelma purred, extending a limp hand. Eager for this deal to move forward, she was laying it on thick. Art didn't seem to notice any more than Sal.

"He's the only one in the organization knows exactly who you are. I trust him completely," Sal said. "If you have any questions, just ask."

With that, Artemis pulled a sheaf of papers from his briefcase. Half the stack went to Sal, the other to Thelma. She looked down, flummoxed by the first thing to catch her eye. "What's Why-BOR Enterprises?"

Sal chuckled. "Dollface!"

Color rose in Thelma's cheeks.

"That is Ybor," Art said, pronouncing it "ee-bore," all serious and Germanic.

It was the first he'd spoken, and Thelma started. A dark helmet against an orange sky appeared in her mind, a poster she'd seen at the post office. "Beware of spies," it read. "They're everywhere." Could this Clauer fellow have something to do with Sal's resistance to working with Agent Nelson?

Clauer was still speaking. "I was mistaken in this for many months when I first arrived."

In reply, Thelma offered the kind of smile that could be mistaken for indigestion and looked back at the pages, wanting now to stall. Maybe she should have mentioned the G-man to Sal.

She looked back at Sal, raising her eyebrows. "Gosh, there's a lot of *wherefores* and *whereases* here, and..." Another line caught her eye. *Oversight by owner.* "Could I get some water, please?"

All the while, Sal, sitting across the table, scribbled away. Initials here, signatures there. When she asked for the water, he was gathering his pages into a tidy stack. "Why doncha sign first? We can still make the floor show."

Before Thelma could think of another excuse, there was a knock at the door.

The vein on the side of Sal's temple bulged. "Not *now*, you nincompoop. What'd I tell ya?"

But Petey was walking inside before he finished his sentence. "Sir, you'll want to see this." He held up an envelope marked Western Union.

Sal snatched the telegram from the man's hand and tore it open. Reading it quickly, he dropped the page, hooked his collar with his forefinger, and unbuttoned his top button.

Thelma looked down at the telegram.

REPORT JUST RECEIVED THROUGH INTERNATIONAL RED CROSS. YOUR SON, P.F.C. MATTEO GIANCARLO, IS MISSING IN ACTION. LETTER TO FOLLOW.

—MARSHALL TO THE ADJUTANT GENERAL

HER FATHER GASPED, LOOSENING HIS TIE AS HE FELL TO the floor. A low whining sound emerged from his throat, and a dark liquid dribbled out.

Artemis threw his hands in the air and screeched.

Thelma sprang into action, snatching the telegram from the floor as she moved beside Sal. "Can you hear me?" she asked, but he just looked at her like a frightened child. She motioned toward Sal's man. "Petey, help me get him to the couch."

"No," Artemis said. "This way." He dashed past Sal's desk and pressed a panel on the wall. A portal slid open, and a second room appeared. At last, the smallish office made sense; the space had been cut in half to accommodate the hidden room.

Before they'd touched him, Sal's eyes rolled back in his head, and he started to seize on the floor. The spasms lasted only a few seconds, but when it was over, one side of his face drooped. Thelma recognized these signs.

Together, the trio hoisted Sal onto an enormous red velvet davenport, pushing aside the jewel-toned bolsters and cushions that sat atop it. Adding to the room's effect, an oblong Persian rug graced the floor, while shawls were hung on the walls. Thelma thought sarcastically that he'd either had it done up in imitation of the Chateau Marmont, or that his latest mistress must be a belly dancer. She scolded herself for the thought; Sal wasn't cheating on *her* mother.

Cradling Sal's face, she took the glass of water Petey was offering and held it to Sal's lips, but the liquid dribbled down his chin and landed with a thud on his necktie. Thelma undid the knot. "He needs a doctor. Petey, go and fetch a doctor right away."

"Dr. Pugliesi only," said Clauer, already walking the bodyguard out. "And say nothing about this. Do not let on to the men in the hall, but send them away."

Having removed Sal's tie, Thelma used the wide end to daub away the dark phlegm and water on his jaw as she unfastened his collar. He was out cold. Though she'd never seen someone fall into a spell, back at the call house, she'd seen the aftermath on several occasions. Sal had just had a stroke.

From the office, she heard the sound of papers rustling. "Hey!" she called out. "What're you doing?"

Clauer hurriedly crammed the pages into his briefcase and scuttled back to Sal's side. "I must remove these documents."

Though Thelma wore only the thin rayon crepe dress from Sun City's Socialite Collection with no jacket—even the polka-dot insert was stitched on—she started to sweat. "I was going to take those with me. To read later."

Shooting a worried look her way, Artemis continued. "But we can't risk these papers getting in the wrong hands."

Thelma stood to meet his eyes and put her fist on her hip. "How do I know they're in the right hands now?" Even as she said it, she wondered at the words coming out of her own mouth. Sal had just said he trusted this man. But could she trust Sal?

To steady herself, she reached for a cigarette from the case beside the daybed, but she had no lighter.

"May I?" Artemis reached for his pocket.

Thelma tensed, but then, he wasn't the gun-toting type.

"What's with the secrecy? Aren't they gonna find out who I am eventually? I don't—"

He held up his hand. "These papers indicate the line of

succession." He motioned toward the door with his head. "If they knew who you were, they would kill you."

Clauer reached for the cabinet beside the bed. When he straightened, Thelma saw he held a Colt revolver between his thumb and forefinger, the same gun her mother had owned. "Do not try and murder a man with this. But you can stop him from taking your life."

Returning to the office, he opened her clutch and dropped the piece inside, right next to George's letter. "Come, I'll call the car for you." Artemis held out her purse. "You should go home before—"

"No." Thelma was done being told what to do. She strode toward the desk, grabbed her bag, and pulled out the small handgun, turning it on him. "I know exactly what damage a .32 can do, and deadly or not, you don't want one of these bullets ripping through your body. Sit."

In short order, she learned the contract included a clause specifying she relinquished all rights of heritage. Should anything happen to Sal, Matteo would become the new head of the property.

"Is it a will?"

"No, it is an employment contract between partners. It is not so unusual for partners to agree on a succession plan."

Thelma thought a moment. Clauer was not cut out for espionage. Why did Sal entrust him with his secrets?

"You look confused, Miss Miles. Mr. Giancarlo directed me to share all details with you, and that is what I am doing."

"Okay. What happens in this situation?"

"Given that you haven't signed, you could walk away."

Walk away? After everything she'd given up to be here?

The door burst open; Petey was back with the doctor.

Thelma dropped her arm to hide the gun behind her back,

hoping it hadn't been seen. "Aw, gee, thanks, Petey, you're such a sweetheart. Would you mind waiting just outside? Keep the riffraff out?"

She turned to the doctor. "Dr. Pugliesi, I'm Sal's... assistant. Thelma Miles. Your patient is in the back room. I'll be with you in a moment." Keeping her right hand behind her back, she waved toward Sal's private salon with her left. "Mr. Clauer here was just leaving."

After he passed, she gently placed the gun in her hip pocket and moved toward the couch and—after scooping up Sal's signed contract and the lawyer's briefcase—thrust the bag at the attorney. "Thanks for this. I'll walk you out."

As she turned, Thelma laid the contract under her handbag and tapped her fingers at her hip, encouraging Clauer through the office's double doors. Keeping one hand in her pocket, she smiled at Petey and the boys standing guard and proceeded to cross the long hallway over the kitchen.

"Miss Miles—" Clauer began.

"Shut it till we're downstairs," Thelma said, poking his hip with the gun in her pocket.

On the short walk, Thelma made up her mind about several things. Clauer was jittery but had a big brain. On the other hand, Petey was solid if simple. Both were assets, even if Sal could never be trusted. Still, if she played this right, she just might get what she wanted after all.

"Looks to me like he's had a stroke," Thelma said in a low voice once they'd cleared the rear exit. "It might take a while, but strokes heal."

Artemis Clauer nodded slowly, considering the information.

"Look, I'm sorry about pointing the gun at you," Thelma said. "But let's face facts—with Matteo missing, if people know Sal is weak, it's going to be worse for you than me. I'm just the moll. But you? You're the missing link. People will want to talk to you."

She waited to see how he might react before floating her idea, but Artemis Clauer was doing something intoxicating. He was waiting for her to tell him what to do. Her palms tingled.

"So here's what we're gonna do. While Sal recuperates, we're gonna run things."

The slow nod stopped. "I suppose I could get word to his wife he's out of town."

Thelma hadn't considered Sal's wife or daughter.

"It would not be the first time Sal spent an extended period in his private salon with a lady friend."

WHEN THELMA FINALLY MADE THE REVERSE JOURNEY, SHE moved much more deliberately, thinking through the next steps. She needed to call Peggy. This situation was going to require more help.

The door to Sal's salon was shut. Dr. Pugliesi was sitting on the sofa, inches from the contract.

"How is he?" she asked.

While the doctor confirmed what Thelma had deduced about Sal's condition, she casually grabbed the papers and stuffed them into her purse then took a seat at Sal's desk. For a moment, the doctor looked startled. Then he continued.

"Mr. Giancarlo is resting. I've given him some phenobarbital, but I'd like to start him on some heparin as soon as possible."

Once the doctor was gone, Thelma reached again for her pocketbook and extracted the now crumpled letter she'd written to George.

There was a knock at the door—Petey.

"Miss, there's a Carlos Gonzalez here for Mr. G. Says he's Diego's brother?"

She stuffed the letter back in her bag. "Tell him to wait downstairs. And listen, Petey? Would you get a phone installed in here? Right away. Like today."

"Yes, ma'am."

Thelma could get used to this.

FORTY

SPECIAL DELIVERY

Let me call you Sweetheart.
I'm in love with you.
Let me hear you whisper
That you love me too—

THE RINGING TELEPHONE STARTLED KATHLEEN. SHE couldn't have been sleeping, could she? She'd just been listening to Bing Crosby.

But as she reached for the dial to turn the Motorola down, she realized a Sunoco ad was playing.

It was Dr. Haines's office. "Congratulations, Mrs. Charles! The rabbit died."

The nurse rolled right into scheduling future appointments, but Kathleen Young hung up the phone. Not only had she given a false name, she'd taken the ferry all the way to Sarasota to visit Dr. Haines's office even as she hoped she was wrong about what was happening to her body. She wished she had a window to jump through. Instead, she called her clothing designer and only friend, Maeve O'Reilly.

She'd not dismissed the idea that Maeve might be connected to Sal in some way, but she was integral to the tour, and so there was no dismissing her just then. She merely made a point of being more careful in their conversations. Maeve had accepted her changes to the tour itinerary without question. No mention was made of Bertie's debt or Agent Nelson. Of the California property, she said nothing of the new business, only that they were considering retiring there. Then they'd be free of the Giancarlos forever.

Or would they?

"Jesus, Mary, and Joseph!" Maeve exclaimed. "What are you, two months along?"

Kathleen looked at the floor. She had giddily confessed her dalliance to Maeve, saying it was with the California realtor. She hadn't mentioned Las Vegas. It wouldn't have made sense.

"A little less." Though it was rather more like half that time.

On the other end of the line, Maeve exhaled. "I don't suppose you could, you know, make something happen with the mister?"

Kathleen bit at her cuticles, a habit she and her mother both thought had been beaten out of her long ago. "We have tried, but..."

"Why, that's all you need to do." Maeve chuckled.

"I don't see how this is funny."

"Not laughing at you, dearie. What about..." Here, Maeve paused, searching for the right words. "Couldn't you just make the overture and then say it happened? Most men are so ill-informed."

Now, it was Kathleen's turn to laugh. "He is Doc Young. He might not be a real doctor, but he is savvy, medically speaking."

She thought back to how he'd swept her off her feet as a young girl and felt a blush rise on her neck. "Even so, you make a good point."

When she first met Lloyd, he'd had a family. This was in part why she'd never fought to get back in her family's good graces. They were scandalized enough about their differences in age and social standing. She never doubted his love, but she'd concocted a pregnancy scare to convince him to leave his wife. Could she do it again?

A high-pitched squeal emitted from the speaker. Kathleen reached to turn it off but stopped when the announcer came on.

Ladies and gentlemen, we interrupt this broadcast to deliver the tragic news that President Franklin Delano Roosevelt was pronounced dead of a massive cerebral hemorrhage today at 3:35 p.m. Central War Time. Harry S. Truman is expected to be sworn in as his successor shortly. We repeat, President Roosevelt died today.

Kathleen reached to shut off the radio. Before the war, she'd paid little attention to politics, voting Republican on her father's advice. Considering that the only Democrats she knew were the Giancarlos, she'd never felt inclined to change her registration. But with the war on, even she had voted for Roosevelt. She hoped this news wouldn't have an adverse effect on recent successes. Since the Battle of the Bulge, the Allies had turned a corner.

"Did you catch that, Maeve? President Roosevelt is dead."

"May God accept his soul."

Kathleen blanched. It was one thing to vote, quite another to be devoted. "Maeve, are you a Democrat?"

"Please, Kath." Maeve clucked her tongue. "Only fools reveal their politics."

FORTY-ONE

LADY GANGSTER

THELMA WAS SEATED AT SAL'S DESK IN THE LOTUS CLUB, looking over the ledgers she'd created. She'd written in code, of course, but the record allowed her to track income and expenses, allowing her to *systematically* inflate the numbers at their legitimate businesses.

With the additional money this pulled in, Thelma felt not one ounce of guilt over erasing the last of Bertie's debt; since joining the Florida Girls tour, he'd suddenly quit accruing more, and she didn't want to see another rogue agent of Sal's try to off him. The Youngs, however, she allowed to continue paying. Mrs. Young, though she knew Thelma was spending more time with Sal, knew nothing of this current predicament. Thelma wanted to keep it that way until word of Matteo materialized or Sal recuperated.

In the weeks since he'd read the notice that Matteo was MIA, Sal hadn't spoken a word. Though he'd regained some mobility, there was no telling if he understood more than simple commands like "open your mouth" and "lift your arm." Given that he couldn't dress or feed himself, they would inter him in his Moroccan love nest.

Sal's wife, who'd made a lifetime habit of incuriosity, had taken Clauer's story—an emergency in Vegas that required Sal's immediate, in-person attention—at face value. Had she asked, which she did not, one of the longtime managers would be running the Lotus Club in his absence. Counting on her lack of interest, they hadn't bothered to come up with a name for that person. All Carlotta Giancarlo wanted to know was that the household account would be replenished each month. Of that, Clauer told her, she could rest assured. Meanwhile, Sal needed full-time care, and it had to be kept quiet. Peggy had stepped up.

"Near the end, when Pops was real sick, we couldn't afford help. A nurse at the hospital taught me how to take care of him, and I showed my mom, my brother, and my sister. I can teach you the basics, but we're going to need more than just us two."

Sal had only been out of the hospital for two days before Thelma brought Doris and Helen in. She remembered meeting them at the door. They'd dressed for a night out—heels, hair, perfume—but she'd motioned them up the back stairs. "I have something to show you."

"What the hell, Thelma?" Helen had asked. "Since when do you have the key to Salvatore Giancarlo's private office?" She got them seated with drinks before she started in.

Having realized she could share her past without divulging every detail, Thelma offered the polite version of her story, similar to what she'd told Kathleen in Vegas about how her mother had been Sal's girl in Chicago and that Sal was her father.

Doris's body had tensed on the edge of exclamation, but Helen laid a palm on her thigh and made a faint cooing sound. Thelma went on to tell them how she and Vivian had moved so suddenly to Iowa but that she hadn't known who Sal was till the night before the tour started.

"He's no angel, my father, but he wants to open a casino in Las Vegas, and he wants me to run it. Or did. He's in the hospital. Now..." Thelma remembered the swell of emotion that overtook her. She'd never dreamed such a moment was possible.

Doris had responded first, looking directly into Thelma's eyes. "You saved my life when I couldn't even ask. What do you need?"

That was the moment everything changed. Until then, Thelma wasn't sure whether Doris was aware she knew her secret. She'd pressed the wall panel that revealed Sal's secret room, Sal's secret. Helen understood right away. "Stroke?" she'd asked.

Thelma had tried to convey Peggy's plan—hiring overnight nurses, keeping his clothes fresh, making sure he had food—but was grateful when she breezed in with a pasta marinara soup concoction she'd blended up for his supper.

"Hola, chickadees! Glad to see you're still here." She thrived in the caretaker role.

But Helen still needed some convincing.

"We have to ask." Helen was looking at Doris as she said this. Then she turned to Thelma. "How long do you think this *situation* will go on?"

Thelma heaved a sigh of relief. "Only until we hear what's become of Matteo. He has to surface somewhere."

"Or Sal could recover," Peggy interjected. "You said it yourself, Thelms. You've seen men bounce back."

"Bounce" wasn't the word Thelma would've used, and in truth, she'd seen a full recovery only once, long ago, at the first house where she and Vivian lived in Keokuk, before her mother got sick. There was a john who'd been a Sunday regular with Miss Pearl—stroked out in flagrante. They'd left him at the hospital, but within the month, he was back, only full-time.

He'd left his family and his respectable banking job to move into the house and keep their accounts. He'd shown Thelma the basics of balancing bankbooks. "You're smart enough you could run your own place like this."

She'd tried not to cringe visibly.

But now was not the time for memories. There was plenty else for Thelma to fret over. Where was Peggy?

No sooner had she wondered this than her friend was at the door. "Thank heavens you're here," said Thelma. "That Mattorini fellow is going to be here in ten minutes. Then Jake, Bumpy, and Thumbs are coming."

"I'm just peachy," Peggy said. "Thanks for asking."

"Sorry, Pegs. I've just been going over the books is all. How was the Mermaid contest at the Emporium?"

Their duties as Florida Girls hadn't ended upon their return. Mrs. Young had planned some sort of "grand finale" and kept them busy in the interim. Between the agreement they'd made and the fact that Lillian was in Hollywood, the girls were busy.

"Like you care!" She laughed. "Anyways, you need to hear what the boys are saying about Matteo."

In less time than it had taken Thelma, Peggy had learned the soldiers' names. She even spoke some Spanish. "When you bust for tips," she said, "you learn to talk to people." Maybe that was why the work had come easily to Thelma too.

"What are they saying?" asked Thelma. They'd started the rumor that Sal's silence was a protest. And until the US Army managed to locate his son, Sal would speak through Thelma exclusively.

"They think he's back."

"Matteo? Who thinks that?"

"They're *all* saying it."

That the rumor mill had churned on did not surprise Thelma, though she was disappointed it had happened so soon. "Oh, fiddlesticks, Peggy. You know as well as I do if Matteo was back, we'd have gotten a telegram."

"Not if he's gone from MIA to AWOL. They delay those letters until they're absolutely sure." Peggy lit a cigarette, punctuating her story's climax. "The boys are saying he's hiding out west."

"No. He'd have come to Sal already."

"Not if he's AWOL. Sal would never forgive him."

"He'll end up in jail."

"You think Sal isn't in jail because he's innocent?" Peggy held out her cigarette to Thelma. "Take that. You've gone pale."

Accepting the smoke, Thelma took a deep drag. Matteo could easily be a deserter. It was just a matter of time before he was back, regardless. "I'm hoping my half brother will see that this takeover was in the family's best interest."

"I thought he didn't know about you."

"Well, I'll tell him. He'll have to believe me. Especially when I turn everything over. All I want is the legal business. The casino."

"I don't know that sharing is the kid's strong suit either."

Thelma hadn't allowed herself to think beyond the day-to-day. "Then we better hope Sal keeps improving." She looked back into Sal's room, now more hospital room than lover's salon. For a moment, she feared him dead, but he started working his lips in a disturbing fashion. An improvement, she noted. She turned to Peggy. "C'mon. We're gonna have to feed him *after* the boys leave. Let's get him to the couch."

While they eased Sal toward the divan—he'd regained much

in the way of motor control, thanks to the nurse's efforts—Thelma wondered if there was anything to this gossip. To keep up the pretense that Sal was dictating Thelma's every move, they would seat him on the couch, dressed and pressed as ever for every meeting. Peggy, decked out in Florida Girls finery, would sit beside him, playing his moll while also ensuring he didn't fall over. Either no one noticed that Thelma had come around to sharing the elder Giancarlo with Peggy, or they didn't dare say a word. In any case, no one asked. Matteo would not be fooled.

Gio Mattorini was on his way to drop some laundry.

"Don Giancarlo," he said when he arrived, acknowledging Sal first as was proper.

The don—a moniker Thelma despised—listed slightly.

Leaning into Sal, Peggy tickled his chin. "He's in a good mood today." She smiled, pushing him straighter in his seat. Sal grimaced in response.

Damn, she's good, thought Thelma as she accepted the bag from Gio. "It's light," she said without even looking inside, another skill she'd learned at the flophouse. It wasn't the weight of the bag but the way Mattorini avoided looking at her as he handed it over.

Mattorini shifted on his heels. "I-I-It's the war," he stuttered.

She might've believed that, except Mattorini didn't have a stutter. Casting a look at Sal as if for approval, Thelma nodded.

"Three of my best firestarters are almost here, Gio. You don't want me sending them to your house tonight, do you?"

Back in Vegas, when Sal alluded to changes in the Giancarlos' Black Hand ops, he'd meant only that his men meted out more treatable injuries. But Thelma had changed the play altogether. The men on their way were perfect examples of why. With fewer able-bodied men available for the brutish work, she'd turned to property damage. She didn't understand why threatening property damage wasn't the standard, but then, she hadn't had to deal directly with the drunks and other shiftless types Gio collected from.

"N-No. I... I... Lemme c-come back. Later. I'll have it all."

Petey poked his head through a crack in the door. "Yes, Miss Miles?"

Thelma kept her eyes trained on Mattorini. "Later today?"

"Yes. Of c-course."

She looked back at the bodyguard. "Petey, would you kindly escort this man out? And make sure he knows how much we look forward to his imminent return."

Soon as the door was shut behind him, Peggy whistled. "Nice work," she said. "But lookie here!" Holding the base of Sal's skull, she pushed his head slightly forward in something like a nod.

"Eeerrrgggh!" screeched Sal.

"Sorry, Sal," Peggy said, righting the old man.

"I think the pointed looks are working fine, Pegs."

Just then came a light knock on the door. "Miss Miles?" It was the same tall thin boy who'd greeted her the first time she'd visited the Club. He'd grown out of his attitude but not his spots.

"Come in."

Looking around the door, he announced, "Carlos Gonzalez is here?"

"Give us a minute, will ya?"

With the boy dispatched, Thelma looked at Peggy. "What the hell?" She bolted toward the couch. "Quick, let's get Sal back in his room."

Taking Sal's right side, Thelma whispered in his ear. "Diego's brother is here, and if he wants to take over as much as his brother did, he might kill us all if he figures out you're kapooey."

Clauer had filled Thelma in on the Cuban operation. It was simple, really—another way to turn dirty money clean. Just like in Vegas, gambling was legal in Cuba. Unlike Vegas, the island was outside the reach of the US government. There were millions to be made. For now, they trafficked in illegal laborers and running gambling trips for the ultrarich. Ultimately, however, Sal wanted to close his carpet joints and invest in Cuban casinos. When she first heard the plan, a vision of herself as the head of a multinational corporation flashed in Thelma's mind, till she remembered a single casino would be more than enough. And she would see to it that the place ran aboveboard.

Thelma had barely returned to the desk and Peggy to the couch when another knock announced Carlos. Though he looked like his brother—only with a taller forehead—and exuded the same brooding energy, he wore a zip-front jacket with an extremely loud short tie.

Peggy went to the door to greet him. "*Hola, guapo! Como estas?*"

While they made small talk, Thelma moved to the bar to pour scotches all around. "Cigar? Our latest Oscuro. It may even rival your Cohiba."

"I need to speak to Mr. Giancarlo."

Taking a cigar for herself—a habit she'd come to enjoy—she cut the end with precision. "How can I help you?"

"Like I said, I need to talk to the don."

Twisting her face into a frown, Peggy sat on the desk with her scotch and looked around the room. "He's not here."

"I can wait."

Having lit the end, Thelma took a contemplative puff on her corona. "I thought I was clear. What can I help you with?"

Carlos reached into his pocket, and Thelma flinched,

though Petey would've patted him down. Still, she breathed more easily when he pulled out a notebook and pen.

"Give him this," he said, scratching something onto the page. "He'll know what it means." He tore the leaf from the book and pushed it across the desk.

But Thelma didn't look at the paper. Instead, she set her stogie in the crystal ashtray, crossed her arms, and cast her gaze back at Peggy. "We got a real live one here."

Peggy shook her head, and Thelma returned to her seat behind the desk. She motioned for Carlos to sit.

"Listen, Sal trusts you. So I trust you," Thelma said. "What I tell you now? It's not to leave this room."

Peggy inhaled sharply. Perfect.

Thelma kept her expression neutral. "Sal will never work with you on poppy trade. Especially now that Vegas is on track. We need you to keep running our cleaning business."

After a dramatic pause, Thelma continued. "No one knows what happened to your brother, but feds have been snooping around. There's an Agent Nelson who's got eyes all over this place."

Again, Peggy gasped. But this time, Thelma could tell it was more a sound of surprise than fear.

"Could've been a government job. So Sal is being extra cautious."

Carlos screwed up his face, appearing to be somewhere between anger and confusion. "Then why," Carlos began slowly, "would he put you, a woman, out front?"

Thelma downed the last of her drink and slammed the glass on the table.

Peggy started.

"Same reason you can't imagine it," Thelma said. "Get that?"

Carlos was about to speak again but seemed to think the better of it. "You give him that paper. Then we'll talk."

Pushing the note closer to Thelma, Carlos pocketed his unlit stogie. "Been a real pleasure." He turned and headed for the door.

Before he reached the handle, Thelma burst out, "We're not enemies, you know."

Carlos turned back. "Come again?"

Now, Thelma had him, but she needed to think fast, offer him something. "I can see why Sal wants you to lead on Cuba."

"Under Matteo," Carlos said.

"We all pray he returns from the front," Thelma said, making a cross like she'd seen Sal do.

Thelma looked between Carlos and Peggy, spiking her eyebrows at her friend to signal she take the lead.

"*Señor Giancarlo es un hombre inteligente. ¿Vas a interrogarlo?*"

"I'm not questioning the don."

This was Thelma's opportunity. "Nobody's questioning Sal. That's my point. But now, you know there's more than one reason he's gone dark. He trusts you to do the next right thing. Peggy?" She stood.

"But Diego was the one who knew politicians," Carlos said. "If I cannot get an audience, there will be no hotels. Nowhere to run, as you say, the laundry. That's why..." He trailed off. "Just give him that piece of paper."

A flush of excitement overcame Thelma, and she was momentarily outside her body, palms tingling. She forced the sensation away; now was not the time to ponder meaning. "You will be contacted," she finally said. "When Sal's ready. Now, get out of my sight."

When the door closed, she and Peggy locked eyes, and both counted silently to twenty before saying a word.

Peggy squealed. "You're terrifyingly good at this."

"He can't know Sal is incapacitated," Thelma said through a grin.

When she reached for the paper Carlos had left behind, Thelma's mood soured. It read, "Diego was looking for Matteo."

Matteo? In *Vegas?* And why would he look in Mrs. Young's room?

FORTY-TWO

MIRACLE ON CENTRAL AVENUE

News of Adolf Hitler's death was broadcast yesterday over Hamburg Radio. But amid the welter of conflicting rumors, considerable doubt surrounded the facts of the story. Only a short while ago, when Hitler was supposed to have gone to Berlin to lead the defense against the Russians, reports leaked out that a lookalike butcher was sent to pose as the Fuehrer while he retreated to his mountain hideout. But—

"LLOYD!" KATHLEEN YANKED AT THE DIAL, BLASTING THE RCA at full volume. "Can you believe it?"

"Shh!"

...we have confirmed proof of the German leader's death. We repeat, Adolf Hitler is dead.

"Mom!"

Archie was in the door.

"You hear that, son? God bless America! Kiss your sweet old mom! Hallelujah!"

She jumped up and embraced her son, who, for once, did not pull away.

"Now, we've got to win!"

"Son, there's still the Pacific theater. It's a long way to go till we can say that."

Kathleen ruffled her son's coppery locks. "Soon." She smiled. "Now go on and get one of the girls to cut your hair. Scoot!"

When he was gone, Lloyd made a beeline for his wife and planted an amorous kiss.

Maybe now's the time to tell him about the baby, she thought, brushing aside the pang of guilt.

"We've got to commemorate this day, Pepper. What do you say, sweetheart?"

"That's a grand idea. How about a free radio—"

"To one lucky customer?" both said at once.

"You are a genius." Lloyd gave his wife a peck, his blue-gray eyes twinkling. Taking a seat at his desk, he pulled out the public-address microphone from his drawer and plugged it into the Sears Silvertone sound system he'd recently installed. "Attention, Sun City Emporium customers..."

Following the announcement, Lloyd and Kathleen turned to business. The tour's Grand Finale event would have to change. "Instead of war bonds," Kathleen suggested, "why don't we collect for the Red Cross?"

"That'll bring our boys back home!"

As Lloyd said the words, dread registered in the pit of Kathleen's stomach. She hadn't heard from Agent Nelson in weeks, not since they'd left Las Vegas. He hadn't provided any more payouts for Bertie, but the additional shows they'd booked allowed them to make the down payment on the California property.

"No million-dollar promise this time, though, right, Button?"

"We'll see about that, Pepper."

Kathleen's smile was genuine. Perhaps the war's end would signal a truce on Bertie's debt? Since the Florida Girls' travels had ended, Bertie had resumed the weekly bag drops with one critical difference. On this side of the tour, the boy had no desire for more time with the Giancarlos.

They hadn't heard from Salvatore Giancarlo in a while, either.

Thelma had claimed that Sal lapsed into a silent protest when his son was declared missing. She said nothing, but when she let herself think about it, Kathleen knew Matteo had to have been AWOL. To think he was the father of the child she was carrying. *Disgraceful.*

Consequently, most of her waking thoughts outside running her store and home revolved around breaking the news to Lloyd. With any luck she'd never see Matteo again. She hadn't heard a word from him since Nevada.

"Darling, are you chilly?" Lloyd asked, cradling her in his arms.

She pressed against him, shocked to feel the near-forgotten sensation of him pressing back into her thigh. Kathleen looked into her husband's eyes, kissed his nose, and locked the office door.

FORTY-THREE

FIELD REPORT 4

MEMORANDUM **** EYES ONLY
SUBJECT: Recruitment Update
DATE: May 1, 1945
AUTHORED BY: T. Nelson, Special
Services, OSS
TOPLINE: Activate new recruit

IN DETAIL: BETWEEN THE DISAPPEARANCE OF DISGRACED soldier Matteo Giancarlo and the incapacitation of his father, Salvatore Giancarlo, it has become clear that the Youngs were pawns in their empire-building scheme.

These investigations have, however, revealed a potential asset in the field for our burgeoning division, a prospect who has infiltrated the Giancarlo organization while maintaining correspondence with the son of industrial magnate Homer Wright, a sworn enemy of the Giancarlos.

RECOMMENDATION: SHIFT FOCUS TO NEW RECRUIT FOR OSS, Thelma Miles.

FORTY-FOUR

THE GRAND FINALE, May 1945

Looking out into the crowd at the Vinoy's ballroom, Kathleen marveled at the changed space. In anticipation of the tourism boom to come, the hotel's owners had dropped a small fortune overhauling everything from the Honeymoon Suite to the swimming pool. The ballroom had nearly doubled in size, though accordion doors could halve the space. To her delight, they'd added a proper stage and bandstand. Surveying the sea of red, white, and blue tables, she bet that the Sun City Emporium Girls just might pull in more donations at this so-called finale than they had at the Million-Dollar Party. That was when she saw Agent Nelson.

Kathleen ducked behind the curtains before Theodore saw her; they hadn't communicated in weeks. With VE Day come and gone, Kathleen figured they were through. The Japanese couldn't possibly be aiming for Tampa Bay, and the Germans were defeated. And he'd stopped making Bertie's payments to the Giancarlos, but her son had assured her he was continuing to reduce his debt. What if young Theo knew something about what happened to Sal's bodyguard? She hadn't saved Bertie from the Giancarlos in Vegas only to have him carted off to prison now.

In the days preceding this event, the mood in town had been electric, and Kathleen and Lloyd had not been immune. Kathleen could conceivably convince her husband the child was his. If he lived to see the baby grow into someone else's features, she could invoke some family member. It wasn't like they'd meet. For the first time in months—years?—she hadn't had a care in the world. Until now.

She had to find Thelma. If anyone would have any insight into rumors about Sal's man, it was her. Kathleen made a beeline for the backstage green room, a proper dressing area now. She found her with Maeve, getting the straps adjusted on the olive-drab dress she would wear for the opening number, covering up a full-skirted fuchsia ball gown.

"Maeve," Kathleen stage-whispered.

The seamstress looked up, mouth full of pins. "Hrrgh?"

"I need to borrow Thelma."

"Hrrgh yoo yoking?"

"Ouch!" cried Thelma.

"Hrrghnn hrrill," Maeve said before giving up and removing the stick pins from her mouth. "Stand still!"

She looked at Kathleen and then her watch. "You know we're starting in... Oh, Lord!" Maeve shouted around the room. "Fifteen minutes, everyone! Fifteen minutes!

"This will only take one more," she said, clamping back down on her straight pins to return to her task.

* * *

Mrs. Young took Thelma aside the moment Maeve declared her "cooked."

"That Agent Nelson," she told Thelma. "He's been radio silent for weeks, but I've just seen him here in the ballroom."

Thelma crossed her arms and stuck her thumbnail into her mouth.

"Ach, stop that," said Mrs. Young, swatting at her hand. "My point is I assumed he'd lost interest in the port."

"You think he hasn't?"

"How could he not have? The Germans are no longer a threat."

"Maybe he's here to let you know your work is over?" she said. Though she worried she'd conjured this trouble by invoking the idea of feds on the prowl when she'd last spoken to Carlos.

Carlos. Another problem.

"You're sure Sal hasn't caught on to this business with the agent? You haven't heard anything about... anything? What about his bodyguard?"

Thelma, who knew the Vinoy far better now than she had the first time she'd had a private audience there with Mrs. Young, grabbed her boss by the elbow and pulled her into a broom closet. "What about Diego?"

Mrs. Young looked at her strangely. "His disappearance seems like the kind of thing that might merit the attention of a federal agent."

Quelling her desire to swat Mrs. Young with a mop handle, Thelma addressed what she considered the bigger problem: Bertie.

"Does your son know about Agent Nelson?" Thus far, Thelma's changes to the Giancarlo operation had been behind the scenes, and they brought in more money. She knew Mrs. Young wanted to rid Sun City of Bolita, but taking the games out of the Emporium would attract attention. She wasn't ready to let her know that her son was off the hook; the Youngs still owed some themselves.

Mrs. Young was about to protest but stopped herself. "I brought this up for your benefit. Now, the show is about to start. I don't know why I bothered." With that, she flung open the door to the broom closet and marched toward the chatter of pre-event guests.

As she followed Mrs. Young back to the makeshift green-room, Thelma wished she'd found some way to ask Sal about Agent Nelson. But the words never left her lips—too incriminating.

"Yoo-hoo! Thelma?" Peggy appeared in her periphery. "Your lipstick? Where is it?"

Thelma blinked. She'd been thinking about Sal's bodyguard. Why would Diego have been looking for Matteo when he was supposed to be on active duty?

"It's in her bag," Thelma heard Mrs. Young say.

The next moment slowed as her boss, elegant as ever in a black floor-length gown topped with an illusion bodice, dunked her hand past the toiletries on the counter and clamped down on Thelma's purse. "I just saw you put it in there." Already, she'd opened her handbag. "Honestly, I—"

"No! It's not," Thelma cried. But it was too late. Mrs. Young was riffling through the bag.

Just as suddenly, her boss snapped the clutch shut. "Nope. Not there."

Careful not to make any sudden movement lest the gun inside should discharge, Thelma pried the purse from Mrs. Young's hands. "I'll take that, thank you." She put it on the floor under the vanity then turned to Peggy. "There's a tube of

Russian Sable in my coat pocket. That'll look better with your dress."

"Okey dokey." With equal nonchalance, Peggy headed toward the coatrack.

Mrs. Young narrowed her eyes at Thelma, ready to lay into her, when Doc Young pulled back the curtain and, without sticking his head inside, yelled to the girls. "Okay, places! Places, everyone!"

* * *

"Ladies and gentlemen," Lloyd boomed from the front of the house, starting his spiel about the store and the war effort.

As the girls moved in line toward the wings, Maeve whispered into Kathleen's ear, "You'd never guess he was ill."

"That's the plan."

Looking down the row, Kathleen appreciated the designer's handiwork. Sending them out in dull outfits to then rip them off and expose bright costumes underneath was just risqué enough. With so many more fabrics available now that the war was officially over in Europe, it was the dawn of a new age in fashion design, and Maeve had outdone herself. The show was her baby; Kathleen had her own to deal with. Though she'd not yet mentioned the pregnancy to Lloyd or been to her own doctor, it was always with her, a second heartbeat refusing to quiet.

Nodding at Maeve, Kathleen edged down the hall toward the side doors leading to the dance floor. Whatever it was that this Agent Nelson wanted, she needed to find out before he mucked up their event.

"Mrs. Young?"

She turned, half expecting to see Agent Nelson, but behind her was the young man who ran the Vinoy's catering group. She couldn't remember his name, but there was no mistaking his crisp diction.

"Ever so glad to have found you," he said before launching into his request.

But Kathleen stopped listening almost immediately. She was looking over his shoulder, trying to find Theodore.

"Do we have your permission?" he asked.

To do what? To her relief, her eyes found Archie. "Archibald Young," she called. Judging by his frown, she knew she'd been heard. Both her sons detested being called by their full names. He walked toward his mother. "Please help this man. Away from the stage."

Seeing their backs in retreat, Kathleen thought the moment a precursor of things to come. She was no longer needed here.

"Mrs. Young."

She jumped. This time, it was Agent Nelson. Turning to face him, she couldn't deny his objective good looks, the even features and square jaw. Nonetheless, he had the magnetism of a tree stump.

"Theodore," Kathleen said, "your timing is as ever."

Agent Nelson looked pleased.

Moron, she thought even as she dreaded what his presence might signify for Bertie. And though the show was about to start, as she'd just realized, her presence wasn't needed. "Shall we?" she asked, nodding toward the exit.

The door swung shut behind them just as a round of applause went up. The girls must've just hit the stage. Facing Agent Nelson in the empty entry space fronting the ballroom, Kathleen wasted no time. "What can I help you with?"

Nelson furrowed his brows. "We have unfinished business."

It was the opening Kathleen hadn't dared hope for. If he'd wanted to arrest her son, he would have by now. "I knew you'd come through for Albert," she said, squeezing Agent Nelson's arm. "I must tell you, why, he's a changed boy—"

Nelson, shaking his head, finally stopped her. "This isn't about Albert."

Kathleen dropped his arm. "Oh?"

"I have questions about Thelma Miles."

"You what? Thelma?"

"Yes. We have reason—"

Now, it was Kathleen's turn to interrupt. "So that's it? You're done with my Albert? What about the rest of his debt?"

"Look, I, ahh..." Nelson trailed off.

"For months, we've been snooping around"—here, she lowered her voice—"the lowest hoodlums in town at grave personal danger. And now..." Kathleen returned to her normal, if slowed, cadence, using her index finger to tap out the syllables on his lapel. "You're not going to make good on your word?"

"I didn't say that."

Kathleen crossed her arms and looked him up and down. He didn't need her to talk to Thelma. Had he learned the girl was Giancarlo's daughter? Had it thrown suspicion about Sal's man off her son? Did he even know about the man's death? *"Better to remain silent and be thought a fool than to speak and remove all doubt,"* she could hear her mother saying.

"So, Agent Nelson, what is it you need?"

* * *

After she sang "Drinkin' Rum and Coca-Cola" with Helen and Doris, Thelma's numbers were done. She'd flubbed her lines, but the audience didn't mind. What was a "chicachi-carree" supposed to be, anyway?

Now, as she watched Doris from backstage singing Dick Haymes's "Love Letters," tears came to her eyes.

.   .   .

And, darling, then I read again right from the start
Love letters straight from your heart.

SHE TOLD HERSELF IT WAS THE EMOTION OF THE FINALE, but the fact was she'd just reread all of George's letters. She hadn't heard from him since ending things, but—thanks to letters Lillian sent—she knew George Wright was still very much alive.

Thelma shook her head, reminding herself it was over with George. She could worry about Mrs. Young and that Nelson fella later. Tonight, she had work to do.

She'd agreed to this last event, hoping to inveigle some of their casino backers into meeting in Havana. They were getting nervous. But such a gathering would show these backers the accessible paradise they could enjoy at their own casinos. As Sal's lawyer had explained, "Any vice you can think of is already there and legal."

Time to circulate.

The men were all in black tie, so Thelma relied on what she knew of the seating charts to find her marks. Approaching the first table, Thelma spotted Thomas McKaye. Her heart caught when she remembered he would've been Millie's father-in-law. Deciding against approaching him first, she turned. But he'd seen her coming.

"Say, young lady, may I have this dance?"

Smiling, she handed him her Red Cross ticket. "You know what to do with it."

Flirting, she'd realized, was her easy default, giving her time to strategize while men were flummoxed.

Despite a thick middle section, McKaye was an adept dancer. She told him so, and he blushed slightly, though it was a bit hard to tell with his ruddy complexion. McKaye had the face of a man who enjoyed a fine whiskey.

"Thank you so much for coming after everything that happened." Thelma stopped dancing, letting the very real emotion lie in the air between them.

"Blame the old ball and chain." He smiled.

She looked back up at his bulbous nose, repulsed. "I see you putting aside your emotions. No wonder you're such a successful doctor."

"Careful, you'll give an old man ideas." He smiled.

He had no idea what was coming.

"I don't know if you know this..." Thelma could see him hanging on whatever she was about to say. "But I happen to be aware there are opportunities for medical suppliers in Cuba right now. Business is very good."

He stopped and looked anew at the woman in his arms.

"Oh, let's don't stop now." Thelma smiled, and they resumed dancing. "Our very special friend, El Hombre"— Thelma hoped she was saying Batista's name correctly, since it was hard to tell what was correct over Clauer's accent—"will be here in two weeks' time. I'd be ever so thrilled if you'd be our guest at the Lotus Club to meet him and learn about a special trip."

He stiffened. "Well, I don't know if I'm inclined—"

She cut him off, whispering in his ear, pressing her breasts into his chest. "Mr. Giancarlo's invitation will not be repeated. Expect the details in your office Monday morning." Standing on her tiptoes, she gave him a peck. "I look forward to seeing you." Then she walked away.

After that, it was easy. The real estate tycoon Merrick Dixon had jumped at the chance to meet Batista in person. And wouldn't you know, former Governor Harris Ruby, whom she'd met at the christening of the new sanitation fleet, was just looking for a way to make the project happen.

ONCE SHE'D MADE HER CONTACTS, THELMA WANDERED back to the greenroom, where Doc had insisted they rendezvous at midnight. The detritus of beauty stretched before her, and she caught a glimpse of herself in the mirror. Admiring the fitted emerald-green silk dress Maeve had insisted was perfect for her, Thelma had to admit Maeve had been right about the color. The gold in her eyes shone. *"This ain't that girl from Keokuk,"* she heard her mom's voice say, feeling more than a tinge of pride. Her hand flew to her chest. She wasn't that girl. That girl would never have worked for Sal.

Peggy appeared with an open bottle of champagne and flutes for everyone. "Drinks are on me!"

As she poured, Doris and Helen joined, with Hattie May close behind. "What are we drinking to?"

"No more weigh-ins!" Peggy laughed, and they clinked glasses.

"No more bus rides," Doris said.

"No more early call times," Helen said.

Peggy started another round. "Come on, Thelms. Live a little!"

Accepting a second glass, Thelma raised her arm, "No more dinged paychecks over something I stained!"

"Or tore!" Peggy laughed.

"What's with the purse?" Hattie May asked, motioning toward Thelma's arm. "You're not meant to carry a handbag on the dance floor."

"We're not dancing now, are we?" Peggy intervened. "Why must you always be such a drag?"

"It's fine, Peggy. If you must know, Hattie May, I was unaware of that rule. And I couldn't care less about it."

Hattie May opened her mouth, but before she could speak, their boss appeared.

"There you are, Thelma. Come with me."

Relieved as she was to escape this conversation, Thelma had no patience for talking with Mrs. Young just then.

* * *

KATHLEEN DRAGGED THE GIRL TO THE LADIES' LOUNGE OFF the hotel's front lobby. "Step lively. You know we need the privacy, Thelma," she hissed.

No sooner had the door swung shut than Thelma turned to face her. "Is this about your son, the murderer?"

This girl needed some sense smacked into her. "Helping me clean up makes you an accessory, young lady. So cut the malarkey."

She was not as pleased as she thought she'd be to see that Thelma was devastated by her remark. Had she really not known?

"Thelma, I'm trying to help you. I spoke with that Agent Nelson. He's looking for you. You're in way over your head, and you know it."

Thelma looked Kathleen up and down. "Interesting."

"I mean it," Kathleen said.

"Just what makes you think he has anything on me?" Thelma asked.

"Let's not play this game now. You're the daughter of a prominent gangster who paid to insert you into my family's business and who then met with you at various locations around the country."

The girl's face hardened, and she crossed her arms. "Matteo gave you money after I was already a Florida Girl."

"Are you deaf? I run this team. I know how it came to be. It looks bad for you."

"What did you tell Agent Nelson?"

A pounding exploded at the door, and a man yelled out. "Miss Miles!"

"Carlos!" Thelma demanded as a young man wearing a windbreaker with a tie walked in. "Miss Miles, you gotta hide. Matteo's back, and he's looking for you, and—"

"He's back?" Kathleen asked, earning a strange look from Thelma.

"From the front?" she said. "That's wonderful!"

But Kathleen could tell the girl was lying. What was she playing at?

"He heard you took over the books," Carlos said. "He's gonna kill you."

Panic seized at Kathleen's gut. Had he learned Thelma was his sister? Had Matteo been spying on her?

"*Where is she?*" It was Matteo.

Carlos looked at them both. "Scram!" he said before heading for the door.

Grabbing Thelma's gown by the bodice, Kathleen dragged her into the stall just as the entry burst back open. In came Carlos, taking crablike backward steps as Matteo pushed on his chest.

"You better explain to me what you think you're doin' here, Carlos."

"Hey, Matty!"

Inside the stall, Kathleen crouched over Thelma on top of a single toilet. She peered through the crack at the side wall and saw that Matteo had grabbed Carlos by the sides of his jacket.

"Don't gimme that crap, you dumb spic. You're just as bad." Backing up, Matteo pulled the safety, aiming at Carlos' heart.

* * *

THE CLICK SNAPPED THELMA INTO ACTION. SHE COULDN'T lose Carlos, not now. And surely, once Matteo learned who she was, he wouldn't shoot his own sister. Slamming her bag into Kathleen's arms, she burst out of the privy.

"Matteo, I think there must be some misunderstanding. We're family. I'm your—"

Somewhere by her ear, a bullet whizzed past.

FORTY-FIVE

BLOOD

KATHLEEN BOLTED ONTO HER TIPTOES ON THE TOILET'S RIM as Matteo finished his sentence, and to her astonishment, Thelma left the stall. Extracting the .38 from her bag, she got the boy in her sights and extended her arm over the wall, barely a foot from Matteo's head. He'd shifted his aim from Carlos to Thelma just as Kathleen relaxed her shoulders, took a breath, and, like her daddy taught her on family hunts, applied a slow pressure to the trigger as she exhaled. It hadn't occurred to her to wonder whether the gun was loaded.

Matteo dropped instantly.

* * *

THELMA'S EARS RANG. SHE PUSHED AWAY FROM CARLOS and moved farther back into the lavatory. Her mouth was open in what she knew must be an ugly gash, but no scream came. Or maybe she couldn't hear anything. The air was tinged with gunpowder, but underneath that was another smell, intensely metallic. A red liquid pool bloomed across the floor's black-and-white checkerboard tiles—so much blood.

Suddenly, sounds rushed at Thelma. From the dance hall, the band had reached the peak of "In the Mood." High heels hit the tile floor. Mrs. Young? A thud as Carlos dropped the knife he must've drawn at some point. She made a mental note to have to talk with him about his weapon of choice.

"Shit," Carlos said to her boss, who'd appeared from the stall. "Who're you?"

Thelma came to her senses and did a quick calculation in her head. "That note you gave Sal. Carlos, did Diego know Matteo was a deserter?"

Carlos was backing away.

"Stop, Carlos. I'm not going to say anything. You have my word."

"We should call the police," Mrs. Young said.

"Shut up right now," Thelma growled at her boss. The woman looked as if she'd been struck. "Carlos, did anyone know you were coming here?"

He shook his head.

"Good, I need you to leave. Now."

"But Miss Miles, there are men, if they find out what happened here? You won't survive." He hitched a thumb toward Kathleen. "Even if she goes to jail."

"I said I'll take care of this. You know nothing. You saw nothing. You do nothing. Understood?"

As soon as the door swished shut, Mrs. Young turned to Thelma. "That was some act, Thelma, really. But what are we going to do now?"

"You need to leave too," Thelma said. "This is no act."

But Mrs. Young didn't leave. Thelma watched her take a compact from her purse, smooth her hair, and reapply her lipstick. *Unbelievable.*

"I need to make a phone call." Without waiting for a response, Thelma walked the long hallway back toward the bank of pay phones. She couldn't decipher just what she was feeling. She had no love for Matteo. In fact, she found him distasteful. Would that have changed? Mrs. Young had stolen her chance to find out.

"And you thought I was trouble?" Thelma heard her mother's voice asking. She couldn't help but smile. It was the first in a long while since she'd heard from her, and she understood —this wasn't going to be the end of their story.

Petey picked up on the first ring, and Thelma wondered momentarily who he was expecting. Did he know Matteo was back? What if he'd been to the Lotus Club already? Dammit, she *was* too mistrustful. Petey had proven he was loyal to her. Swallowing hard, Thelma told him what happened. "The bathroom's a mess, but it's far enough away from the ballroom no one will stop there on the way out, and the party's almost over. Can you help?"

"I'm on my way," he said. "You get out of there. Get back to the party. Long as you don't have any blood visible on your dress."

Thelma looked down at herself. Unbelievably, there was not a speck on her gown. It was her signature maroon, but still. *Nothing.* She flicked her wrist bracelet watch to face herself. *Nearly midnight.* Unlike her boss, Thelma wasn't used to people fixing things for her. Maybe that was how Mrs. Young could be so callous, like when Millie died. Problems seemed less real when you didn't have to fix your own.

"You always want to put people in boxes, Thelma." It was her mother again, and her palms were tingling. *"But that only cuts you off."*

"Thelma Miles."

She knew who it was without introduction. What in hell could he want? Looking up, Thelma saw a tall, oafish man in a very cheap suit. "Agent Nelson?"

The man before her looked taken aback. "Did Mrs. Young tell you about me?"

She nodded because how else could she explain it? Besides, she couldn't speak. Alarm filled her throat with the fear that she and her boss had been caught already. But Theodore Nelson, it turned out, was happy to talk.

He'd come from the bureau's New York office as part of an urgent assignment associated with the Battle of Berlin. During the course of those activities, however, Thelma Miles had come to his attention. He knew she was Sal's daughter but also that she was not part of his criminal activities.

Thelma exhaled a nervous laugh of relief at his words, eliciting a frown from Theo. Moments before, his chest puffed out with all he knew. Now, he looked deflated. She smirked and played the hard-boiled good egg he expected her to be. "Nobody's innocent."

But she read him all wrong. A shadow of concern flickered in his eyes. "I know all about your past, Miss Miles. Your mother, a runaway moll of Giancarlo's, took you to Keokuk and forced you into her business. That was not your doing."

Thelma had never felt so exposed in all her life. Nelson knew so much, and yet between her dead half brother and the fact that she'd taken on her mother's business, well, she couldn't bear the scrutiny. "I..." she began, her voice breaking, "I have to go."

"No, wait. You need to understand. We've been watching you in action. You're able to break through otherwise impenetrable lines. You have skills your country needs."

Nelson produced a business card from his pocket. "Do you have a pen?"

Thelma lifted her bag but then recalled by its heft that Kathleen had left the proverbial smoking gun inside. Instead, she clutched the handbag to her chest and stroked it. "Oh, no.

Sorry, Mr. Nelson. Just lipstick and the like." But Agent Nelson, she could see, was utterly unmoved.

"Radio seven oh two hundred," he said. "Can you remember that?"

She took his card and nodded. Was that what Kathleen thought above her pay grade? How far she'd left her boss behind.

"You can reach me there tomorrow, or you can expect me at The Soreno," he said. "You moved back there, yes?"

He waited for her to agree.

"Good. Now, go to your meeting. Oh, and congratulations. I hear the Youngs are bringing the Florida Girls back."

FORTY-SIX

THE MORNING AFTER

THE HISS OF OXYGEN MOVING FROM THE TANK TO THE TENT was giving Kathleen Young a headache. Or maybe it was the smell of betadine. As she looked at her Button through the clear panel in the canvas shelter that covered his head and chest, Kathleen's heart took a tumble. They were in a private room at Mound Park Hospital, but the way his muscles slacked back toward the pillow, they could've been in a morgue.

He'd been doing so well. Even Maeve had said so.

"Ma-a-ahm!" Bertie's voice pierced the machinery's thrum.

Kathleen's ire went up immediately. She slid the jeweled panel across her watch's face. It was nearly six. She'd been awake for twenty-four hours and was in no mood for her eldest son's self-indulgent attitude. "Albert, keep your voice down."

"But I can't find Archie."

The night before, instead of attending their Grand Finale, Bertie had been tasked with minding the store. She'd taken Archie, and now, he was here in the hospital—somewhere—needing a lift home. "Bertie, please, could you just ask a nurse?"

"Holy smokes," he said, taking in the setup around his father. "Is he gonna be okay?"

"Of course he is. You run along, and get your brother home. And Bertie?"

Bertie stopped in the doorway, shoulders slumped.

Instinctively, Kathleen's hands flew to her belly, but now was not the time to announce that a younger sibling was on the way.

"Bertie, I want to thank you for stepping up here. I know it hasn't been easy for you."

He didn't turn back, but he stretched out to his full height. "Are you still planning on going next month?"

So Bertie had heard.

Not even Kathleen had known her husband would be making that announcement to close out the party. She was in on the plan, of course, just not that he'd say it aloud. Of course, it had been she who'd encouraged getting a jump on the forthcoming economic boom. But her reasons were more personal than business. She couldn't bear the idea of the whispers that might echo around town when it became obvious she was having a child at such an advanced age, one who looked very little like a Young. If the baby had those eyes...

They'd had a plan in place. The idea was to get a second news hit by holding a press conference once the hubbub from the party dimmed. But Lloyd had gone ahead and, in true Doc Young fashion, made the ebullient declaration that he and the missus were headed for sunny California and their sons would be taking over the business.

Kathleen and Archie reacted to the bombshell on script, performing the Young family dance, all smiles and nods for the crowd the Doc had worked into a lather. "It's time for the next generation of Sun City Emporium!" he'd said, raising his fists overhead like a Barnum & Bailey ringmaster.

Rustling the notepad she'd balanced in her lap, Kathleen

moved toward her son. "Darling, you know we did it all for you." But this caused Bertie to turn away.

"Yeah, yeah, save it. I'll find Archie. Keep that sentimental goo for Dad." He waved, a dark silhouette against the still-bright hallway. "See you in the funny papers." And he was gone.

Kathleen sat back in her chair and looked back at her husband, asleep now beneath the oxygen tent. She thought about the wisdom of his timing. Public enthusiasm for the Florida Girls was at a high, ensuring turnout for the next round of auditions would be even higher. The Emporium was operating in the black. Though neither Bertie nor the store was out of debt, the tour's success had made Sun City a must-see destination for visitors. They could eliminate Bolita. They were going to have to.

She wondered if they shouldn't have spoken to Sal first. Or maybe, doing it this way, Lloyd had forced his hand. There could be no backtracking now, no backdoor machinations with the press. Maybe announcing at the Finale had been the smart move.

* * *

THELMA STUBBED HER CIGARETTE INTO THE HOTCAKES ON her plate. She'd taken maybe one bite. A waitress bustled past, and she held up her cup. "Could I get another coffee, please?"

"There's a war on, you know."

She turned from the bar to find Agent Nelson looming behind her, now in a pair of horn-rimmed glasses. Had he worn those last night? It was a blur, all except that smell, blood and gunpowder.

The waitress returned with a pot and her check. "No rush, miss."

To her dismay, Nelson sat beside her and removed his hat. The backless stools were fixed in place, leaving Thelma without the chance to scoot her chair farther away.

"You following me?" she asked.

"This place has bottomless coffee." He shrugged, but his eyes stayed fixed on Thelma, who felt very aware she'd picked her floral dress off the floor.

"Did you sleep?" he asked.

"Why wouldn't I have slept?" A teasing note in her voice. Of course, he wasn't wrong. She hadn't slept. But he knew too much about her already. How long till he found out about last night?

"You don't look like you slept. Usually, you're more... tidy."

Thelma sat back and appraised Agent Nelson; the man was immune to her charms. All pressed and proper, he exuded his schoolboy best in a white shirt, tie, and Madras-checked vest. She wondered where his jacket had gotten to then remembered it was not yet eight in the morning, and already the outside temperature was in the mid-eighties.

"I take it you're not used to seeing a woman in the morning," Thelma said.

Ignoring her remark, Nelson proceeded to make small talk. Did she know a spot for fishing? The pier. What was a good place to pick up swimming trunks? Why, Sun City Emporium, of course. What was her favorite restaurant?

That one, she couldn't answer. She wasn't about to send a federal agent to the Lotus Club.

The Lotus Club.

She had to get back.

"I'm sorry, but I have to go," she told Agent Nelson. As she put her fifty cents on the counter, she was aware he was watching her. She turned to face him. "I won't be calling you."

He raised his eyebrows and lifted the corner of his mouth. "I guess I'm not surprised."

There was no malice in his voice, but his disappointment struck her like an arrow to the heart, as if he'd expected her to be the person she thought she might be when she'd first arrived in Florida, a person who did the right thing.

"But there's something you should know. This investigation? It's not going away."

"Whatever you say, mister."

She walked two blocks farther than necessary to reach the pay phone at the Art Club. If she were to make a guess based on Nelson's expressed interests, the place would not be on Agent Nelson's radar.

She dialed the Youngs, but Archie said his parents were busy. Busy? Thelma hoped they weren't occupied with visiting the police. But that was ridiculous. Petey had confirmed he'd cleaned the area. It was too late to claim self-defense.

"Peggy, put on something devastating. We're going to the Lotus Club."

"Dolly, it's not even nine."

"That's why. We have to go now. I'll explain on the way."

Coffee in hand, Kathleen was just stepping off the elevator when she heard her husband shout, "You can't keep me here!"

There was a flurry of activity, nurses swirling in and out of his room. Kathleen set the coffee on the nurses' station and rushed down the hall as a tall, thin man in a white lab coat and black tie emerged, staring down at a clipboard.

"Doctor," she called out.

He stopped and looked up. "Yes?" He squinted. "I'm Dr. Roberts."

Kathleen stuck her hand out. "I'm Mrs. Young. You were just in my husband's room?"

A shadow passed over his face. "Please, come with me."

"If he's awake, can't we—"

"Right this way," he said, steering her back down the corridor to a small waiting room just past the deserted nurses' station.

At first, Kathleen didn't sit. Whatever he had to say, she wanted to hear it quickly so she could get to her Button. But as the doctor droned on, Kathleen Young collapsed into the unforgiving Naugahyde sofa.

"With the dilation of the alveoli and atrophy of the alveolar walls," Dr. Roberts said, "lung cancer is one of the most common comorbidities associated with pulmonary emphysema."

Had Kathleen heard his words more clearly, she'd have let the doctor have it for suggesting there was nothing unusual in this situation, that it was just a day like any other. But the words "lung cancer" sent her mind reeling. Finally, her thoughts coalesced around the only question that mattered. "How much time does he have?"

"Six months? A year? We can never—"

She heard him call after her. "Mrs. Young?"

But she wasn't stopping. Her Lloyd wanted to leave, and she was going to get him out of there, take him home, then move on to California—just like they'd planned. Maybe there was another cure. Another opinion. What did this Florida yokel think he knew?

On her way past the still-empty nurses' station, Kathleen reached for the heavy black phone on the desk.

Maeve picked up on the first ring. Soon as she heard the diagnosis, she offered to head straight over to the Youngs' place.

* * *

ONCE SHE HUNG UP WITH PEGGY, THELMA RACED TO THE Soreno, lost in a cloud of thoughts.

If Matteo had seen the books, he'd been to the Lotus Club. How much would Sal have processed? At times, he seemed aware of his surroundings. Other times, he tried to eat cigars. For all she knew, her father was asleep when Matteo arrived. The nurse they'd hired was a drill sergeant—nothing got past her. If Sal was resting, she'd have sent the queen of England packing.

Before washing up or changing, Thelma dashed a letter off to George. By the time he got it, she would be long gone. But she wanted him to hear the news from her.

After Lloyd made his announcement, he'd taken Thelma aside to ask if she'd stay on as a Florida Girl. The Youngs would be busy running their new California health sanitorium, and though Maeve was coming on full-time to head up Sun City— the boys were still children, after all—he was hoping for some continuity. But before he'd finished his public speech, Thelma was accelerating her departure strategy.

* * *

MAEVE MUST HAVE RUSHED STRAIGHT TO THE FLOR-DE-Leon. She was already there waiting by the time Kathleen and Lloyd arrived.

"Archie went back to bed," Maeve said when she greeted them at the door. "Wasn't my place to say anything, so..."

"Ah, let the boy sleep," Lloyd said, managing a smile. "G'morning, sunshine."

Once they'd shuffled her husband back to the bedroom, Kathleen noticed Maeve had already turned down the sheets and put a glass of water on the bedside table. The kindness made Kathleen's eyes sting.

"You need to get some rest too," Maeve said.

Kathleen looked at Maeve. She recognized the fabric in her shirtwaist dress from one of the Grand Finale gowns. She must've made the outfit just this week. Her unruly red curls, tucked into her signature loose bun, belied her discipline. She motioned with her head toward the kitchen.

While the coffee brewed, Kathleen thought about what she wanted to say. By the time she poured their coffees, she had a plan. "Maeve, you're like family."

"Am I?" Maeve's forehead lifted.

So much for her plan. "What do you mean?"

"I work for you," she said. "But I'm not privy to your plans."

"Maeve, I didn't know Lloyd was going to make that announcement before you heard him."

Maeve looked into Kathleen's eyes. "It's not how we discussed the announcement. I need to tell my customers, you know."

A sting in Kathleen's armpits sent a wave of heat to her face. Sweat broke out at her hairline. In an attempt to fan herself, she pulled at her sheer top, glaring across the table. "I suppose all families have secrets."

"What's that supposed to mean?"

Kathleen needed to get this conversation back under control. "Maeve, I know you work for Sal."

"Ah, Kathy, you're wrong again."

Their coffees sat untouched as Maeve revealed her allegiance to Madame St. Clair. "I know she's friends with Sal, but that's all I know. I never got involved in her business, and she sent customers my way. Queenie kept my business afloat during the Depression, and I kept her in the know. She never minded the accent that went with my wagging tongue."

Kathleen was relieved not only that she didn't need to find a way to fire Maeve but that she could finally unload her own secret.

"Maeve, I need to tell you something. A few things."

FORTY-SEVEN

ALL IN

Thelma stood on The Soreno's front porch, waiting for Peggy. All she could see beyond were the backs of other five- and six-story buildings featuring an impressive array of taupe shades. She couldn't see the bay or the masts bobbing in the water, but knowing they were there gave comfort. She bounced on a lilac metal chair, waiting for Peggy.

"This came for you yesterday."

Standing at the front door was the resident manager, Mrs. Collins, still in her rollers and peach chenille robe, barely visible behind the screen door.

"Much obliged, Mrs. Collins," she said, reaching inside. The familiar handwriting made Thelma's breath catch—George. Her first instinct was to run upstairs and read it, but a car's horn honked. She opened her purse to slip the letter inside. Dammit, she still had that gun.

Hoping Mrs. Collins hadn't noticed, she rushed toward the mint-green sedan waiting at the curb and went around to the passenger's-side door.

"What the hell, Peggy?"

"Well, hiya to you, too, toots." Peggy cracked the rear door so Thelma could slide in. "C'mon!"

But Thelma didn't budge. Doris was in the driver's seat, next to Helen, all of them dressed to the nines.

Peggy patted the seat beside her. "Get in. You were acting funny all night last night, especially after you went off with Kathleen. We all noticed."

Doris swiveled her head. "I came by your place this morning but no luck. So I called Peggy. I was there when you called."

Helen stuck her head out the front window. "With me. You sounded like a lunatic, so we figured you needed all our help."

Thelma put her hand to her chest to keep steady. Vivian Miles had loved her, but she'd never felt quite cared for. Even so, she hadn't felt alone in the world until her mother died. These women weren't family, but maybe they were something better.

"I can't let you do this," Thelma said. "Going to the Lotus Club will put you all in danger. Last night—"

"Get in."

Thelma did as she was told but didn't know where to begin. It wasn't her place to snitch on her boss, but she was done with the lies. She reached for a smoke but thought the better of exposing a murder weapon. "Does anyone have a cigarette?"

Doris looked at Thelma in the rearview. "You can't smoke in the car. Sorry. That's Mom's one rule."

Thelma looked out the window as the car made its way along Coffee Pot Bayou. This was a mistake.

"Cut that out," Peggy said, slapping Thelma's hand away from her mouth. "You'll ruin your nails."

She wanted to argue it didn't matter, since she was no longer a Florida Girl, but she needed to see the backside of this crew. No one who stayed with her would be safe.

"You've all pitched in to care for Sal, but that won't save any of us—including me—from what happened last night." She took a breath. "Matteo tried to kill me."

"Oh my God! Thelms, what happened?"

Thelma told them how Carlos had warned her about Matteo while she and Mrs. Young were talking. She didn't mention Agent Nelson.

"If I'd kept my big mouth shut, none of us would be in this mess," Thelma said. "I thought when I told Matteo I was his sister, he'd see I was trying to keep the business running. For the family.

"But we'll never know because next thing I hear is gunfire, and Matteo is face-up on the floor, his blood seeping out across the black-and-white checkered tiles." Thelma rubbed her eyes. "Mrs. Young shot him over the toilet stall."

Peggy whistled. "Who knew that lady could wield a gun?"

"Mrs. Young? As in Kathleen Young?" Helen said.

Thelma nodded. "It gets worse." Now, she couldn't stop herself, telling the girls how Sal's man Diego had died in Kathleen's room. "Supposedly in an accident with Bertie."

"You think Kathleen killed him too?" Doris asked. "But that makes no sense."

So Thelma revealed Bertie's gambling debts and how a federal agent had used that for leverage to monitor the Giancarlo port.

"What?" Helen asked.

"He was looking for German spies."

"Holy smokes," Helen said. "They copied the Russians."

Shrugs all around.

"Last year," Helen said. "When Russians infiltrated enemy lines in the catacombs around Odessa."

"Whatever you say, Helen," Peggy said. "Who knew we had tunnels?"

"What is the big deal with those tunnels?" Thelma was

exasperated. "My point is I think Diego was looking for Bertie. He owed a lot of money."

"What about that note from Carlos?" Peggy asked. "Diego was long gone before Matteo came looking for you at the party."

"What note?" Doris asked.

By the time they reached the Lotus Club, the girls had pieced together that Diego was never looking for Bertie but not why he would've been after Matteo.

"If the old man sent him to war to toughen him up, he wouldn't be happy his kid was a deserter. But how would Matteo even manage to get back? He never struck me as all that bright." Peggy made excellent points.

Helen popped her head over the car's front bench to face the back seat. "The Giancarlos know plenty of people in Italy. If that's where Matteo was stationed, someone there could've helped him get back to the States."

Peggy whacked Thelma on the shoulder. "Maybe Diego found out and was trying to force Matteo back before Sal found out?"

"But why would Diego look for Matteo in the Youngs' room?" Doris asked just as she pulled up to the Lotus Club.

"You all are thinking about this way too much. Just drop me off," Thelma said. "I'll figure it out from here."

"Not on your life." Doris cut the engine.

"No. It's too dangerous," Thelma said.

Disbelief flashed in Peggy's eyes. "Too dangerous? Sal's practically a vegetable."

Rubbing her forehead, Thelma longed for a way out of this moment. This was Kathleen's transgression, after all.

Peggy crossed her arms. "We got all gussied up for you."

Even as she admired her friend's butter-yellow strapless gown, she could see her mind was set.

"Fine. But Pegs, remind me to get that tube of Russian Sable back."

"That's my girl."

Thelma led the way through the Lotus Club's rear door. Before they made it up the narrow stairs leading to Sal's office, Thelma could hear the soldiers talking, Carlos among them. Were they too late? She'd thought Carlos's appearance at the Vinoy signaled he'd come around to her side after all. Had he turned against her? Where was Peter?

Looking back at her friends down the stairs, it struck her. There was no way all these chickadees could disappear at once. There was safety in numbers.

"Ooh, Doris," she began, speaking loudly. "Last night, when you sang 'Love Letters'... Ooh! It was just... heaven-sent!" Nodding, she gestured for them all to start talking. "And Helen, that red dress you wore! *Divine!*"

"Why, *thank* you!"

Thelma mouthed, *Louder.*

"What I wouldn't give for a rum and Coca-Cola right now!"

Thelma kept one finger revolving to keep them talking and laughing while indicating they should stay put as she crept toward the first set of double doors. Before she could slip through to eavesdrop, however, Carlos burst out.

"They heard about Matteo," he launched in without a greeting. "Jimmy, Tony, Jake, Bumpy. Even Thumbs. They're all here. They think it was the Zapates. It's war." He looked past Thelma down the hall, grabbed her arm, and hissed into her ear. "Santa Maria, why have you brought *them* here?"

Wrenching herself free, Thelma stomped her foot. "Enough, Carlos. You know who I am. I'll do what I damn well like." She looked back at her friends. "Ladies? Come with me."

In a cloud of finery and perfume, the girls wafted past Gonzalez, through the two sets of leather doors, and into the Giancarlo headquarters beyond. Smoke hung heavy in the air. Jimmy and Tony sat in the club chairs, while Bumpy and Thumbs perched on the sideboard, the liquor like a display between them. Jake was on the couch. Thelma had met with each of these soldiers individually during the past few weeks, but she hadn't been in one room with so many men in years.

"Hello, boys." Thelma knew to exude more confidence than she felt. "Glad you all made it."

Knocking on the table, she motioned for the girls to sit. Without offering to share, Thelma reached into Sal's humidor and selected a prime hand-rolled Cuban. As she went to light it, however, she noticed the door to Sal's private room was wide open. Neither Sal nor his nurse was anywhere to be seen. Thelma almost spat the cigar out of her mouth.

* * *

KATHLEEN TRIED TO STAY CALM AS MAEVE STEERED THE Cadillac over the Gandy Bridge, and she realized they were headed to Tampa. She should be by her husband's side. Lining up a second opinion. Something.

"Why on earth are we going across the bridge?"

But all Maeve offered was an enigmatic smile. After Kathleen explained last night's incident at the Vinoy, Maeve's entire demeanor had changed. "Come with me," she'd said. "But change first, and wash that hospital stink off."

The change in her designer was puzzling, and yet Kathleen was so consumed with worry for her Button she couldn't do anything but obey. After all, it was a Sunday. Much as she wanted to make moving arrangements immediately, nothing would be open. And keeping busy helped mute the sounds she could not unhear: the diagnosis, the shot, Matteo's body hitting the floor.

When Maeve pulled onto Howard Avenue, Kathleen noticed a mint-green roadster that looked familiar. They were at some place of business, but Kathleen couldn't recognize it from the back.

Stale smoke washed over Kathleen as they entered. "Why on earth have you brought me to this... *establishment?*"

Maeve regarded her longtime patron with a mixture of amusement and something Kathleen could've sworn was pity. But that was ridiculous.

"Maeve, I'm not going a step further until you tell me—"

"Kath, if I'd told you we were coming here, you wouldn't have come." Before Kathleen could speak, Maeve held up her hand. "Here's the rub. You're the one got me involved with all this business to start with. Years ago. If you hadn't encouraged me to move to New York, I never would've needed so many favors. I knew Queenie was milking me for information. You get loads more from the women. They always know more." Here, she paused, patting Kathleen on the cheek. "But I've learned a few things over the years. And now, I'm here, trying to save you."

It took a moment for her words to land. Maeve's dealings with criminals were *her* fault? How many blows was she to take? Wasn't her husband's prognosis enough?

"Maeve, these people tried to kill me last night."

"They weren't trying to kill you. They were trying to kill the girl," Maeve said.

"Are you suggesting we put the blame on Thelma?"

Maeve looked at her then with disgust. She wanted to take back the words, but it was too late.

"No. I'm taking you to Sal's office, and you're going to beg for his forgiveness," said Maeve as she pulled Kathleen up the narrow staircase.

Kathleen stopped, yanking back her arm. "Beg? What father in his right mind would listen?"

"You're going to tell him," Maeve said, fixing her eyes on Kathleen's midsection. "And he might not forgive you, but he's not the type to shoot a woman. Certainly not the mother of his grandchild."

"Maeve, I plan to raise this baby as Lloyd's."

"You should've thought about that before you pulled the trigger," Maeve said, turning to march up the steps.

If Kathleen didn't tell Sal, Maeve would. She had no choice but to follow.

* * *

Mrs. Young and Maeve burst into Sal's office just as Thelma was noticing her father's absence, so no one caught her awkward double take. From the look on Maeve's face, it was obvious this scene was not what she'd been expecting either.

If Sal wasn't in his office, where could he be? Why hadn't the nurse left word for Thelma or Peggy? Did the men know Sal had been out of commission? If Carlos knew Matteo was looking for her, surely Matteo had told others. But Thelma realized she'd been assuming Matteo had visited his father first. Perhaps he hadn't. Perhaps this situation could be salvaged after all.

"I'm glad you've joined us, Mrs. Young. Maeve." Thelma said. "Sit."

"Now you listen here. I—" Mrs. Young began, but Maeve yanked her onto the couch before she could finish her sentence, tilting her head ever so slightly toward the soldiers. Just then, Bumpy moved his hand to his hip, exposing the gun in his waistband. For once, her old boss did as she was told and shut up.

"Everyone, please." Thelma walked behind the desk and sat, calming herself with a puff of her cigar before she continued. "The last thing we can have now is fighting amongst ourselves."

"Where's Sal?" asked Jimmy, to a chorus of *yeah*s.

"Does he even know about Matteo? First, he's back. Then he's dead?" asked Thumbs. More agreement.

"Now, listen up." Thelma stood, and the room hushed even as she wondered how they'd learned of Matteo's demise. "I don't know where Sal is because he doesn't report to me. But you all know how it's been since he found out Matteo was missing. Now this?"

She shook her head, letting innuendo hang in the air. She knew better than to state that the head of their organization was overcome by grief, but the suggestion sufficed.

"If this gets out," she went on, "our entire operation is vulnerable. We are all going down if we don't stick together now. This is what we do. Why we exist. We protect each other."

"I heard Matteo's a low-down deserter," Tony said. "And when Sal heard, he put the hit out himself."

A genuine frown creased Thelma's face. *How did that rumor get started?*

"Now, why would a father kill his own son?"

All eyes went to Maeve. The network lit up in Thelma's head. Maeve had introduced her to Madame St. Clair, New York City's original queen-pin. She must be connected too.

Maeve shook her red curls. "Salvatore would not."

To Thelma's eternal gratitude, Carlos spoke next.

"Miss Miles is right," Gonzalez said. "And if the Zapate brothers don't come for us, the Antoninis will."

These were puzzle pieces Thelma was missing; she had no idea whom he was talking about. She needed to buy more time.

"The don knows more than any of us," she said. "He's likely with Mr. Clauer right now."

Thelma sent up a silent prayer that the lawyer didn't walk in next. Though she generally avoided words like "don" and "consigliere," that's what they were. And even if such designations would not help her transform operations in Vegas into a legitimate business, at the moment, she needed to invoke their power, remind these boys who they were answering to—sort of.

"Tony, Jake, Jimmy. I need all of you out on collections. Today's got to be just like any other day. Bumpy, go to the Downs. Carlos, you take Thumbs to the cigar plant in Ybor. We have to make sure nothing derails the Cuba meeting."

Thelma stopped. She needed the girls to help her find Sal. "Peggy, why don't you and the girls take lunch to Mr. Giancarlo?"

Peggy lifted her chin. Thelma's message was received.

"Carlos? You stay here. The rest of you, go."

"Wait."

To Thelma's shock, it was Mrs. Young who spoke. She'd not yet figured out what to do with her.

* * *

Watching Thelma waltz around Sal's office had surprised Kathleen, but that sensation gave way to relief once she realized Sal was not in situ. When the girl started barking commands, however, Kathleen saw opportunity.

Instead of standing, Kathleen crossed her legs and leaned on the sofa's arm, arching her back ever so slightly. She was betting that the room's testosterone level meant they were all vulnerable to feminine charms, and after Thelma's performance, she knew they'd be primed. "There's something I learned from my daddy years ago, something it seems you haven't thought of here."

All eyes turned to Kathleen.

"All due respect, Mrs. Young—"

"I'd like to hear what this lady has to say."

Dread gripped at Kathleen as she recognized the man from the night before, still in the same jacket and tie. She did not particularly want to hear what he had to say, nor did she want any of them thinking she belonged.

"Miss Miles is right—I don't know what you're dealing with here—but I do know one thing. The businessmen in this town don't support the unions."

Keeping her head still, Kathleen rolled her eyes back and forth to see what effect her words had. Thrilled as she felt to possess this gem, the revelation fell flat.

"What's that got to do with anything?" Carlos asked.

"If Homer Wright's man takes the mayor's office, it won't be good for you. The police force's allegiance will go to the highest bidder." Kathleen watched as the girl stubbed out her disgusting cigar. Finally, her words had hit home. "That's *donor*, in campaign-speak."

"Trust me, Mrs. Young." Thelma was addressing her but looking at Peggy. "That is not our most immediate problem."

That was when Kathleen understood what was off, the dynamic. She might've played this wrong. Were Salvatore in the driver's seat, she might whisper in his ear that she could help him. But Thelma was, well, female.

"If you don't know the implication here, then—"

Kathleen stopped when she noticed Maeve facing her, head cocked and eyes wide. She saw then that she was treating Thelma the same as St. Petersburg's self-aggrandizing hoi polloi had treated her, lording over her all she did not know, the connections she did not have access to. And what was the point?

She needed to get Button out of this town before the climate killed him.

"Then you should," Kathleen continued. "If you lose the mayor, you lose the unions. If you don't have that money coming in, you won't have the resources to be the highest bidder."

FORTY-EIGHT

THELMA'S CLUB

We must never forget that beyond all lurks Japan,
harassed and failing but still a people of a hundred
million, for whose warriors death has few terrors. I
cannot tell you tonight how much time or what exertions
will be required to compel them to make amends for their
odious treachery and cruelty. We have received—

A MOMENT BEFORE SHE HEARD FOOTSTEPS IN THE
vestibule, Thelma's palms tingled, and not because this inter-
minable war was not yet over. She snapped off Churchill's radio
address and wondered where Petey had gotten to. Then she
remembered she'd told everyone the day would start late.
They'd searched for Sal late into the night with no luck. If
Clauer had taken his boss to the hospital, it was under an
assumed name. Thelma had to push that thought from her
mind.

Without knocking, George opened the door, stood, and
rested his head in its frame. "I rate above Churchill?" he teased,
a curl forming at the left side of his lips in that aw-shucks look

he'd perfected, his full, toothy smile breaking out as he looked at the floor then back up at her. "Swell."

Struck by opposing urges—whether to kiss the dimple on George's chin or to hide from the warm beam of his stare—Thelma stood. "I didn't know it was you."

Still grinning, George stepped into the room. "Really?"

Their passion, though stoked over many months, had never been expressed in person. To her relief, George made the first move. He took Thelma's hand, lifted it, then twirled her around and into his arms. Gently—chastely, almost—he touched his lips to her knuckles and then her lips. He took her face in his hands and his intensified, breaking only to tease her jawline and neck —until Thelma stopped him.

"There are a few things I need to tell you first," she said, leading them both to the couch.

EARLIER THAT MORNING, WHEN AT LAST SHE'D READ George's letter, Thelma couldn't believe he was headed home, that he'd accrued the eighty-five points he needed. He almost beat the mail. When he called that morning, without thinking, Thelma had said she was at the Lotus Club.

"Where?" he'd asked.

Her first instinct was to lie, say she'd misspoken. But in the time they'd spent apart, she'd seen how right George had been when he'd told her she should be more trusting. Confiding in others the parts of herself she wanted to hide made life better. And if George wasn't a place for safekeeping her whole self, she needed to know now.

Taking a deep breath, she began, "I'm at the Lotus Club. In Tampa." She'd stopped herself, wondering if anyone was listening on the line. Maybe Sal was right not to have installed a phone or a radio. Where did that Agent Nelson get his information? Faith in others, she reckoned, shouldn't be blind.

But the words were out, and Thelma couldn't take them back. Her heart raced. She felt the color rise in her cheeks. "Can we meet up later? So we can talk?"

"I'm on my way."

ONCE SHE GOT GOING, THELMA LEFT NOTHING OUT, RIGHT up to the night that Sal laid eyes on her. Absentmindedly, she caressed the scar on her cheek.

"He did that to you?"

George's anger surprised her. "Not on purpose," she said, too quickly.

"Why would you defend him?"

She told him about Sal's fear about having other slow children. That they'd suffer. "I don't think he meant to hit me. He just lashed out when—"

The vision of her mother in a floor-length negligee, kneeling in front of Sal, flashed before her eyes. Thelma thought he was choking her mother. "Mommy!" she'd cried, rushing toward them.

"I interrupted their encounter. He knew right away I was his kid."

"It's your eyes," George said.

Thelma tilted her head.

"Those golden eyes and dark hair," George was shaking his head. "That had to come from somewhere."

"Golden?" Thelma asked.

"Twenty-four karat."

"Your plane's name—"

"You liked that?"

"George, I thought you'd named her after..." Thelma stopped, embarrassed by her misunderstanding.

"What? What could you possibly have thought I meant by Golden Hornet? The comic?"

"The what? No." Thelma dropped her forehead, confessing into George's shoulder. "Hattie May?"

"No wonder you were so sore." George tilted her chin to his face. "But that is about the most ludicrous thing I ever heard."

"Glad to provide a bright spot. This story is about to get much worse."

Vivian had rushed her out of the house that night. Thelma never saw any of her things again. At first, it seemed a grand adventure until they ran out of money in Keokuk. It was only now, as she was telling George this story, that she wondered how it must have felt to her mother to go from being a high-priced call girl to a low-rent dame in a flip joint. "It's the only place in town where I can have a kid and make money," Vivian had said on more than one occasion.

"Vivian taught me about the finer things in life, but she couldn't provide them."

"You called your mother Vivian?" George asked.

"I had to switch between the two for her customers. When I got older and I was... Well, let me tell you the rest."

At first, they had a routine. When Thelma wasn't in school, she was at the library. Though she was better at numbers than literature, math club was at school, and the other kids were vicious, taunting her endlessly about being a bastard. But she had to keep out of her mother's way, except on Sundays till early afternoon.

For those brief hours, Thelma had Vivian all to herself. They'd take long baths and pack mud and cucumbers onto their faces. Then she'd paint her mother's nails, and while they dried, she'd read to her from *Hollywood Screens*. Then they'd head out to the only movie theater in town. After the first show, her mother would slip away. Thelma would stay till closing time.

A couple years in, Vivian started having terrible pains in her mouth. By the time she got around to seeing the dentist, she needed three extractions. For the procedure, and to help manage the pain afterward, he prescribed Nembutal. That was when everything changed.

Within six months, Vivian turned yellow and sickly. Her eyes dulled, and she lost weight. Her hair turned gray, and she walked and sounded at all times as if she'd been drinking. Besides her mean temper, she lost interest in her appearance. Subsequently, clients lost interest in her. They were about to be turned out of yet another flophouse.

"So I..." Thelma held her breath. "I volunteered to take customers."

This part, she'd never admitted aloud, never said it so plainly, that all along, she'd let others think this burden had been foisted on her when in fact, she'd taken it on of her own volition.

Thelma paused to look at George. He'd been quiet, listening. She couldn't think of a time a man had ever listened to her so deeply. It was intoxicating but also terrifying.

Finally, he spoke. "I'm so sorry." If that weren't enough to shock, he went on to make his own confession. She wasn't surprised to learn that he and most of the men in his company had sought company in the arms of professionals. It was the mark it had left on him that astonished her. "They were just regular women on hard times is all—didn't know when their husbands were coming home, if ever."

Thelma's eyes widened.

"Point is you did what you had to. I might not've understood before. But during the war, we all did things we never thought we would."

George looked away from Thelma then, and she realized how, much like herself, there was a part of him that might never be touched. But they were both trying. Just what she needed for courage. He had to hear the whole story. "That's not all."

Confessing how she'd taken over Sal's business was, to Thelma's surprise, more difficult. First, she told him about the stroke. How it left her no choice.

George gave a long, low whistle. "How did you figure out what to do?"

Thelma nodded slowly. She'd learned basic accounting from that john. But when it came to seeing the bigger picture, she reckoned she owed that to him.

"Someone told me I should be less suspicious," Thelma said, gently touching George's mouth with her thumb then leaning in to plant a kiss. "I couldn't have done any of this without Peggy or Helen or Doris."

George's dimples reappeared, and Thelma felt her stomach flip.

"But why did you stay? Is it because he's your father?"

A snort escaped before Thelma could stop it. "There are a lot of moving parts here, but trust me, that isn't one of them. No, Sal offered me his casino to run. As a legit business. Can you imagine? Me. A woman. Running a major business. Where else would I get that opportunity?"

"Now that he's sick, though..." George shrugged. "What if Matteo wants to do things differently."

"It's too late." Thelma smiled. "The casino is already a separate entity."

George looked down, and Thelma felt his withdrawal like a blow to her throat. Rather than wonder, she asked, "What just happened?"

Taking a deep breath, George took Thelma by the elbows.

"I don't care about your past, Thelma Miles. But I care about your future. Sal Giancarlo hates my father."

As George described how his father had blocked Sal's unions with Pinkertons, Thelma's palms heated. Suddenly she knew without knowing, *this* was why they were together, to set right the wrongs of their fathers. She was never meant to run that casino. With that realization, the rest of her choices fell into place.

NOTHING MORE WAS SAID FOR A WHILE. THEY EMBRACED then began searching. He touched her face then her body's contours. Thelma responded to his touch. Her nipples strained against the fabric of her shirt. She arched her back. She wanted to be taken on the couch, but she stopped him.

"There's a bed," she said, struggling for words. She took him by the hand to the back wall and pressed the panel to reveal the boudoir/hospital room.

"I guess if we need to use the toilet, we're set."

Thelma burst out laughing. Could making love be joyful?

She turned to George and slid off his officer's coat before draping it carefully over an end table. Dropping her own blazer and skirt to the floor, she reached for his khaki trousers. They moved into the bedroom, and he lifted her on the daybed. What happened next was unlike anything she'd ever known. This was not some vaguely unwelcome task she was eager to finish, no. She drew him in selfishly, moving to take her own satisfaction— a feat she'd only ever heard rumors about— as perspiration broke out across her back.

George kissed her forehead, her cheeks, her neck. Her neck —never before had she known it to be so connected to her breasts, to the sensations between her legs.

During breaks over the next couple of hours, they talked about the future.

"Once Vegas is up and running, I'll take my cut and turn things over to Peggy." She reached for him again.

The shadows in the room had grown longer in the afternoon sun before they spoke again. Thelma wondered aloud if Helen and Doris might want to go to Cuba.

"At first, I was surprised at how willing they were to help out, but I think they just might be looking for an escape too."

"Because Doris is passing? Why would Helen... Oh. I get it. They're always Helen and Doris, aren't they?"

Thelma breathed a sigh of relief.

"I can see that. In Havana, they'd be more free to be themselves."

It struck Thelma how different Lillian and Kathleen and her mother were, and her heart ached. Money could be a shelter or a weapon, but the lack of it could turn anyone into a prisoner. "We'd all be freer in Havana."

"I could fly us all there. Then we could get married in Cuba."

Thelma grinned. "That's it? The romance is over already?"

"Thelma Miles, I want to romance you for the rest of your life."

He leaned forward to kiss her again. Neither heard Sal entering the office beyond.

"What in the sam hill?" His thunderous voice boomed into the bedroom moments before he did. In a flash, Thelma realized two things. First, that she'd neglected to finish closing the door to the bedroom. And second, though primary in import, she'd been a fool to think she could still run Vegas.

She hastily gathered sheets around herself and her lover. "Minute, please?" she called before realizing their clothes were in the office. She turned to George. "Stay here. I'll get our things."

Wearing only a loosely draped sheet, Thelma trod carefully into the office, where to her relief, Artemis Clauer faced her. Giancarlo was behind his desk, facing the door. "Peter!" He yelled. "Get me Diego!"

"Sal!" Thelma cried, going for joviality despite her state of undress.

Sal swiveled in his chair and scowled at her as if she were a steaming pile of garbage. "Jumpin' Jehoshaphats—who in hell're you?"

"It's me, Sal. Thelma! Your—"

"Matty's girlfriend," Artemis squeaked. "Remember? This is the girl he told you about."

Thelma's jaw dropped as Artemis, flapping his hands to get her attention, mouthed the word *Go!*

She hurried back to her task, collecting her and George's garments, feeling Sal's eyes upon her as he surveyed the changes she'd made in the office, the telephone, the radio, the accounting ledgers.

She'd just plucked one of George's trouser socks from the floor when Sal swept his arm across the top of his desk, sending the blotter, the crystal ashtray, and the telephone flying. He slammed his open palm on its surface and spoke in a slow growl. "Get. Me. Diego!"

"Give me a minute, Sal," Thelma said. "I'll get dressed and take you through everything."

Artemis, eyes wide, was shaking his head.

Sal turned to face Thelma, that murderous look in his eyes boring down on her full force. Not *everything*, of course, she thought at him. "Please. You have to take it easy. This can't be good for you."

Thelma raced back into the antechamber behind the desk before Sal could speak, whispering to George to be quick.

They weren't quick enough.

A second later, Sal followed Thelma into the bedroom.

She was just tucking in her blouse when she heard him shout, "George motherfucking Wright! What're you? Banging my son's girlfriend in my office so's you can snoop around my office!"

Out in the hall, more obscenities erupted. Sal turned back toward his office.

"We will get what we're owed!"

Carlos Gonzalez.

Thelma could tell he was on something, maybe the brown heroin that was easy enough to get around the Club, but more likely bennies, which could be found everywhere, including Sun City Emporium if you had the right prescription. On instinct, she extracted the gun from her purse.

Before George could object—and Thelma could tell that was going to be his next move—she silenced him with a stare. Surprise was the only element she had going for her now. In stocking feet, Thelma pushed into Sal's office.

The tableau she entered revealed Artemis cowering on the couch while Sal walked toward Carlos, a .38 Special leading the way. There was no time to wait; George would be next. Thelma pulled the trigger on her Colt but not before Sal got off a shot. She watched her father fall face-first onto his desk, while Artemis shrieked like a mating cat.

FORTY-NINE

IMOGENE

For a moment, Thelma regarded her father struggling on the floor, the wound to his leg unlikely to be fatal. The casino dream was over, but there was one last hope. She grabbed for her slip and blouse—where was her skirt?

George was still standing where she'd left him, trouser sock in hand. He must've killed plenty of people during the war to be home so soon; those would've been from quite a distance. "Get dressed," she said. "We have to get out of here."

"Jesus, Thelma," he said. "We have to get him to the hospital."

Clearly, George was a much better person than she had even suspected.

"He'll do it," Thelma said, nodding her head toward Clauer. Raising her voice over the peal of the now-simpering attorney, she cleared her throat. "Artemis, pull yourself together, man. You've got to take your boss to the hospital."

That did the trick. Artemis quieted down and stood.

"I'll help you get him to the car," George said with a definitive zip of his pants.

Thelma wasn't wild about that part of the plan but

supposed it was the right thing to do. Was this what it was like to be part of a couple, she wondered, to discover the depths of your own depravity?

She turned to look at her father, pale, sweating, and gasping for air. But her bullet had only grazed his hip. Whatever had happened to Sal over the last twenty-four hours, he seemed to have no recollection of her. For now. Before she and George left for Cuba, she would burn this place to the ground.

"You know what, darling? You're right. Artemis is going to need your help with Sal. And we both have to pack. Leave word for me at the Soreno when you're done."

Soon as she heard the threesome's final thud in the stairwell, Thelma scrambled for the telephone. "Operator, get me Sun City Emporium, please."

IMOGENE FUCHS CRUSHED HER PAPER IN HER LAP WHEN she heard the commotion at her door. One look at the Seth Thomas on her bedside table confirmed that the hour was ungodly. Most likely, the caller was some wayward schoolchild, looking either for Sally or a war-bond donation. Or Mormons. Though it would appall her mother, Imogene figured she'd let her silence say no by not answering the door. She deserved to savor the scoop she'd submitted mere hours earlier, her first Sunday feature, revealing that the Florida Girls were coming back the following year.

"Yoo-hoo," she heard, clear as day.

Who in the dickens?

"Mrs. Fuchs? It's Mrs. Young."

Mrs. Young as in Kathleen Young, owner of the Sun City Emporium? Christ have mercy, did that woman know no bounds? Briggs had told her all about Mrs. Young's many complaints over her coverage, but to show up at her house like this? What could she object to in this story? *Unconscionable.*

Grabbing her quilted satin robe, Imogene marched down the hallway toward the front door. Standing in her vestibule was Mrs. Young alongside one of the Florida Girls, tall and ivory-skinned, with thick black hair and striking eyes. *Thelma something?*

"There you are, dear."

Dear?

"Thank you so much for allowing us this intrusion. You remember Miss Miles?"

Almost before Imogene could collect her wits, Kathleen Young was gone.

"Mrs. Fuchs, I have information about criminal activity in this town that I believe will change your career and make St. Pete a safer place to live. But you must promise you'll keep my story a secret until after I'm dead."

Imogene Fuchs was going to need more coffee.

FIFTY

HAVANA BOUND

WHILE GEORGE CIRCLED THE TWIN-ENGINE DE HAVILLAND for his preflight check, Thelma kept an eye out for Peggy. She could scarcely believe they were less than a mile from Sun City Emporium, where they'd met, and closer still to The Soreno, the place her friend had recommended less than six months ago. It seemed a lifetime. Back then, she'd never have imagined life with friends, let alone a *fiancé*.

She heard a thwack on the side of the plane. "She looks good to go," George said. "Where's Peggy?"

Dread seized Thelma's gut. Thanks to Imogene's stories, what remained of Sal's crew had largely disbanded—they were either behind bars or absorbed into some other criminal enterprise. Not Sal, of course. Sal had skated through the system and was last seen heading to Las Vegas. There was nothing left for him here. And Fuchs was still holding information she'd given her on the Zapate brothers and the Antoninis. Soon, there'd be no one left. True to her word, the reporter had left Thelma out of the stories entirely, instead exposing how the Giancarlos leveraged businesses like Sun City through extortion and racketeering.

But Thelma knew better than to think they were spared retribution. Could Peggy have gotten caught in the crosshairs?

"I'm sure she'll be along any minute," Thelma said, looking back toward George, so dashing in his bomber jacket that, for a moment, she forgot to worry. "Though it's not like her to be late."

Thelma reminded herself that they'd just spoken that morning. *Of course she's still coming.*

But something nagged at her. Looking again toward Sun City, Thelma recalled their first conversation. "I don't get why anyone would choose Miami over St. Pete," Peggy had said. "Everything you need's here."

What if Peggy had changed her mind?

"Should we be worried about the rain?" she asked.

George walked toward Thelma and wrapped her in his arms. "Won't be more than a drizzle." Drawing back, he held her chin up so she looked directly into his sparkling periwinkle eyes. He reflected an admiration like she'd never felt. Like what Mrs. Young described when she told her why she'd married Doc. Love. Of course the woman had given up everything for it. Thelma, on the other hand, had gained everything. It was messy and complicated, choosing who to let in, which secrets to keep. But so much better than having to hide. Plus, Lillian had been wrong about his inheritance.

"It's not what I'd get if I joined the family business," George had told her, "but soon as I'm married, I'll come into a sizable fortune, money my grandfather put aside."

The possibilities were dizzying, but they'd made a solid plan, so long as Peggy showed up.

"Right now, I'm more worried about the fact we don't have night-flying equipment on board," said George. "We have five hours before the sun starts to set, more than enough time, but I'd hate to push it much longer."

"You really do know how to butter a girl up." Thelma winked. They both knew Thelma couldn't tolerate much in the way of sweet talk.

Helen and Doris were waiting for them in Havana already. From the moment Thelma brought up the idea of Cuba, they'd been more than keen.

"We'll start our own club," Doris had squealed. And soon, plans were in place. She and Helen had left on the next flight out and started prospecting for properties straightaway. Mrs. Juergen hadn't minded. "I'd never have met your father if I hadn't gone to Paris," Doris reported with a laugh. "Of course, I didn't tell her everything, but I'll take it."

Helen had left her parents a note with no forwarding address. "Better to ask forgiveness than permission," she'd said.

With the money George and Doris could bring, they would establish a nightclub in Havana. Thelma would get to run her hotel and casino after all. But without Peggy, the plan didn't work. They had no regular lounge act, and besides, the girl knew how to run a café.

"Yoo-hoo, Toots!"

Thelma broke into a run toward the cab.

"Pegs!" She pulled her friend from the car.

"All right already," Peggy said into Thelma's chest. "Give a girl some room."

Thelma's palms tingled, and she froze for a moment.

"What, did you think I wasn't coming? Geez. My dad's old cardboard suitcase finally gave up the ghost, and I had to get a new one. Treated myself to one from Rutland's Fine Goods. Wasn't even on sale."

Laughing, Thelma moved toward her friend. Life was what you made it. Why not make sensation in her hands an omen of good things to come?

"Look lively, there," Peggy motioned for Thelma to help as she struggled to pull her valise through the open door.

"Cripes, Pegs. What's in here? Gold bars?"

"You wish," she said.

Together, they grabbed the handle and walked toward George's plane.

FIFTY-ONE

CARLSBAD

KATHLEEN YOUNG HAD JUST POURED HER FIRST CUP OF coffee when she flicked open the paper and read the headline.

```
GEORGE W. WRIGHT FEARED DEAD IN CUBA
PLANE CRASH
Family Pays to Continue Search
By Imogene Fuchs
```

That little scamp, Kathleen thought, recognizing the reporter's name. She'd done fairly well for herself since Thelma insisted on an introduction. The girl must have fed the scribe information for the exposés she'd written, revealing several local gang families in Tampa, the Zapate something-or-others. And the Antoninis. Was that the name? Though she and Lloyd had transferred the business to their sons and left town mere weeks after the Grand Finale—simultaneously ridding themselves of the Giancarlos—that world seemed so distant. Now that it seemed Lloyd would live to see the baby, Kathleen would make sure it stayed that way.

She looked down into her lap, tilting her head to examine her stomach. So far, only her bustline had changed visibly. *I bet it's a girl. My boys stuck straight out. I hope so, anyway.*

Glancing back at the paper, Kathleen noted that the story of George Wright's disappearance, though front-page news all the way in California, was still below the fold. She paused to take a deep swig of her coffee before reading on.

```
June 1 — George Williams Wright, 23,
dashing scion and heir to the Wright
family fortune, is missing at sea after
apparently crashing his plane Friday
night in shoal waters off Cuba for what
was assumed to be a pleasure trip to
Havana.
The only son of Mr. and Mrs. Homer
Wright, the missing pilot was expected
to follow in his father's footsteps to
helm Wright Industries. After a massive
round-the-clock search yielded only
scattered debris of his aircraft, a
twin-engine de Havilland, the family put
its own significant resources into the
search.
Wright, a decorated army veteran, was an
experienced flier, having navigated
dangerous conditions to cross the
Himalayas and supply Allied troops,
surviving numerous attacks and crash
landings. Engine failure, rather than
```

```
pilot error, is the suspected cause of
the crash.
The plane's only stop was to be Havana's
José Marti Airport, after leaving Tampa
earlier that same day. According to the
flight's manifest, George was the only
passenger on board though several of St.
Petersburg's touring dance troupe, the
Florida Girls, are missing and presumed
to have been on board and met a similar
fate.
At this stage, the search is for
remains.
```

Returning the paper to the table—to think she'd been so offended by the idea of an eat-in kitchen she'd planned to dispense with the dining set, but the convenience was undeniable—she gazed out at the lemon tree in their courtyard. She longed to gossip about this story. Had the unnamed passenger been Thelma? Or could it have been Helen or Doris? Not long after that gathering at the Lotus Club, all three had disappeared. But there was no calling Maeve. Not that Maeve would've taken her call; Kathleen had ousted her and the Bolita games once Sal turned up at Tampa General, disoriented and with a bullet wound.

"Lloyd?" Kathleen called upstairs from the kitchen. "Have you ever been so pleased not to get your way? Imagine having the *Sun City Emporium Girls* plastered all over the papers in connection with the Wright boy."

Of course Lloyd knew about the story. It had hit the papers just after their midnight arrival in California. But she knew he wouldn't answer—couldn't. Her husband had been asleep for most of the two days since they'd returned from California Medical Hospital, where doctors had excised pieces of his diseased lung. "Button, we escaped that incestuous pit just in time."

Ever since the wheels of their plane lifted off the tarmac in Florida, Kathleen had thought less about the Emporium than she would've imagined possible. Though she spoke to the boys daily, answering their questions was a simple task. Outside that time, she was largely consumed with the health of Lloyd and their baby. Kathleen was still a young woman, at least young enough to have a child. For now, their sanitorium plans were on hold, but they were going to need to generate some kind of additional income beyond their ongoing interest in the Emporium.

The doorbell rang. "Maria?" she called, out of habit. Maria, their longtime housekeeper, had stayed behind in Florida to watch over her boys.

Tightening her silk dressing gown, Kathleen made her way to the door. Through its coke-bottom glass windows, she couldn't make out a thing. *Who could be calling at this hour?* she wondered, till she looked at her watch and saw it was almost noon.

Kathleen cracked open the door but quickly lost her advantage. "Thelma Miles? What on earth? You're not—"

"It's Thelma Wright." Thelma pressed the toe of her cork wedge shoe against the open door. "And we need to talk."

"Talk?" Kathleen pushed her bare foot against the door's opposite side to keep it from opening farther, a stalemate. "I moved halfway across the world to get away from you and your ilk. I'm not—"

"You owe me."

"You are misinformed." She crossed her arms.

"Pepper! Who is it?" Lloyd called from his bedroom.

"No one, dear," Kathleen looked back at Thelma. "A salesman." She looked into Thelma's amber eyes. "Keep your voice down. Lloyd is just out of the hospital."

"Bertie's debt." Thelma pointed at her chest. "I made it go away."

"What? No. He..." But before Kathleen could form a protest, she knew what Thelma said had to be true. After that infernal agent cut off payments, there was no way Bertie could've come up with what he still owed unless he was gambling again—and actually winning.

She looked back at Thelma, determined. "I'm pregnant!"

Thelma, though nodding, was unmoved by Kathleen's proclamation.

Before she could speak, Peggy Holmes's platinum bob appeared in the doorframe behind her. "Yeah, yeah. With Matteo's baby. We know all about that."

Kathleen made a choking sound and lost all advantage, retreating ever so slightly. "How—"

"Maeve told us," Thelma said as she urged the door open and pressed Kathleen inside and toward the breakfast nook. "Like I said. You owe me. That Nelson fella wants me in Las Vegas. Peg's going to watch Lloyd for a couple weeks, and we're going to Vegas."

"Las Vegas? Have you lost your mind?"

"Pepper?" Lloyd called, sounding alarmed.

"Sorry, darling," Kathleen called back. "You know how I get excited reading the paper sometimes."

Peggy looked at Thelma and mouthed, *Pepper?* Thelma shrugged her off but spoke quietly. "Because we're going to pose as investors and collect as much information about the Mafia's involvement in gambling as we can."

"Thelma"—Kathleen had regained herself somewhat—"it's much harder than you think, *collecting* information. The task is Sisyphean."

"Don't come at me with the foreign words, Mrs. Young," Thelma said. "We're gonna try. Or would you like me to talk to *Pepper* about your baby?"

Kathleen crossed her arms and looked between Peggy and Thelma, both resolute as a stone wall. At last, she spoke. "Fine. But no smoking. Not in the car. And Peggy Holmes, don't you dare smoke around my Lloyd."

Thelma thrust her hand forward. "Deal."

FIFTY-TWO

FIELD REPORT 5

MEMORANDUM **** EYES ONLY
SUBJECT: Operation Showgirl
DATE: June 1, 1945
AUTHORED BY: T. Nelson, Special
Services, OSS
TOPLINE: Vegas Relocation for OSS
assets.

IN DETAIL: WITH THE WAR REACHING A CLOSE, SECURING
our position as one of internal intelligence
gathering is under the greatest threat from
our own government's agencies. With the lax
measures being taken by the aforementioned,
gang activity is at an all-time high. We have
thus activated our newest recruit—an asset
with close ties to the Giancarlo gang, code
name Blackbird—in order to disrupt gang
activity in gaming. She has requested cover
for another asset, code name Hawk.

. . .

RECOMMENDATION: AS KEEPING OUR COUNTRY SECURE FROM internal threat is of utmost priority, full support, including a small satellite office, is requested.

Also By L.L. Kirchner

Florida Girls is Book 1 of The Queenpin Chronicles.

Want to see what happens next? Go to IllBehavedWomen.com to download the first chapters of Book 2, **_Vegas Girls_**. If you're not already getting my newsletter, **_Ill-Behaved Women_**, you'll be subscribed to it along with future reader bonuses, behind-the-scenes on works in progress, and commentary by, for, and about women and those who identify as such. You won't be subscribed twice.

MEMOIRS:

Blissful Thinking: A Memoir of Overcoming the Wellness Revolution, a 2023 Pushcart nominee and a Foreword Indies Humor Finalist

The raw and honest account of the search for salvation that took me from university halls in the Persian Gulf to the streets of Manhattan to a sex cult in India, all in an attempt to save my sobriety and maybe even land a second date.

American Lady Creature: My Change in the Middle East, A Qatar Memoir, re-released in 2022

Listed as one of Goodreads's funniest memoirs for women, this book delivers an unflinching look at what it took to redefine myself as a woman after a surprise divorce, the loss of my dogs, and an ungodly early menopause, all while living in one of the world's most patriarchal cultures. New edition.

Author's Note

Shortly after I moved to St. Petersburg, Florida, I learned that back in the 1920s, fictitious opinion letters were sent to newspapers across the country, expressing outrage over the town's scandalous bathing costumes. The letters were a publicity stunt, engineered to stir up enthusiasm for Florida tourism. They worked.

What a great story, I thought. But as a memoirist, there wasn't much I could do with the information.

Later, I came across a photograph of beachwear-clad women visiting California on behalf of St. Pete's own Webb City Drug, a place that billed itself as the world's most unusual emporium. Bizarrely, their junket took place during World War II.

Who sends a troupe of touring swimsuit models around the country when a war's on? I asked myself. This time, however, lockdown was underway. Why not try writing this novel?

And so, *Florida Girls* began as much historical fiction does, taking off from a kernel of historical truth. But let's face it. Most of the characters in history books are men, and so this began as the story of the fictitious Lloyd "Doc" Young. The first pages were something like the prologue. Until the characters took over. The ones who were eager for me to tell their stories were the women.

COVID was an especially terrible time for women. Our social feeds were inundated by influencers and their sourdough starters, homeschooling was foisted upon legions, and still we were expected to work full-time while watching our rights erode in real time. The moment struck me as similar to what I imagined my characters experienced with the war coming to a close. Anticipating the loss of freedoms they'd grown accustomed to, some might have taken extreme measure to preserve their liberty. For the Florida Girls it certainly did.

Like the characters, events in the book are construed—and certain timelines altered—to fit the story rather than the historic record. For example, there was a Tri-Cornered baseball game, but it took place in June of 1944. The Flamingo Derby is a conflation of the Flamingo Stakes and its precursor, the Florida Derby, races that sandwiched the timeline of this book. (The US Army took over the Tampa Bay Downs to use as a training facility for jungle warfare in 1943.) Getting a diaphragm from Margaret Sanger's clinic in 1944 would've required a doctor's prescription and even then was available only to married women. All in the realm of possibility but very expensive and not a spur-of-the-moment decision. Likewise, the Memphis Belle was a decommissioned bomber that was trotted out at bond drives, but to my knowledge, a fixed swimsuit competition was not one of them. Lucky Luciano did aid the feds from his jail cell, but it was unrelated to the Germans' attempted infiltration of US ports, nor was there a similar operation in Tampa. And finally, while the Bolita Wars were a real thing, the Giancarlos were not. While I've done my best to stay true to the mood of the era by digging into historical newspaper archives, magazines, and memoirs of the time, this is in service to the narrative. Any errors that remain are my sole responsibility.

I would be remiss if I didn't thank the legions who championed this book. Many thanks to Anne Hawley for her editorial expertise and, more so, for her tireless belief in this manuscript. I doubt I'd be here without that. To the team at Red Adept Editing for their editorial oversight. To the creative team at MAD Studios for their absolutely iconic cover. To the best cheerleaders and neighbors a writer could have, Paul Wilborn and Eugenie Bondurant. To Betsy Farber, for being the first person to read this book in its (almost) entirety (and for our regular writerly gatherings). To Sarah Dinan, for her unflagging support. And to the mighty mighty Tombolo Books in St. Petersburg, Florida.

And most of all to you, the Ill-Behaved Women who are bound and determined to make history.

About the Author

L.L. Kirchner is an award-winning screenwriter and Pushcart-nominated author whose life and work as an expat in Asia became the basis of two memoirs that combine humor with "her discerning eye" (Foreword Reviews), or, as an NPR interviewer said, her memoir is "like Eat, Pray, Love, but funny." Her writing has appeared in the *Washington Post*, *Salon*, and *The Rumpus* among numerous other outlets.

Drawing on her eclectic background as a religion editor, dating columnist, and bridal editor, her work explores feminist narratives. Read more at her blog, IllBehavedWomen.com or LLKirchner.com.

She lives in Florida with her favorite husband and their best boy, Hartley.

Florida Girls is her debut novel.

On socials everywhere @llkirchner_.

Made in the USA
Columbia, SC
02 July 2024

37852061R00236